DEFIANCE

DEFIANCE

C. J. REDWINE

BALZER + BRAY
An Imprint of HarperCollins*Publishers*

Balzer + Bray is an imprint of HarperCollins Publishers.

Defiance
For information address HarperCollins Children's Books,
a division of HarperCollins Publishers, 10 East 53rd Street,
New York, NY 10022.
www.epicreads.com

Library of Congress Cataloging-in-Publication Data
Redwine, C. J.
    Defiance / C. J. Redwine. — 1st ed.
        p.   cm.
    Summary: When Rachel's father goes missing on a mis-
sion, her attempt to escape their walled city-state and find him
brings danger, heartbreak, and a new romance with her father's
apprentice.
    ISBN 978-0-06-211718-2 (trade bdg.)
    ISBN 978-0-06-222278-7 (international edition)
    [1. Fantasy.   2. Love—Fiction.]   I. Title.
PZ7.R2456De   2012   2012008409
[Fic]—dc23   CIP
                                                      AC

Typography by Alison Klapthor
12 13 14 15 16 LP/RRDH 10 9 8 7 6 5 4 3 2 1
❖
First Edition

For Clint, who cheerfully sacrificed his free time to support my dreams. Thank you for believing in me. I love you.

CHAPTER ONE

RACHEL

The weight of their pity is like a stone tied about my neck. I feel it in the little side glances, the puckered skin between frowning brows, the hushed whispers that carry across the purple-gray dusk of twilight like tiny daggers drawing blood.

He isn't coming home.

It's hard to ignore the few citizens still milling about the gate leading out into the Wasteland, the guards who flank the opening, and Oliver's solid, reassuring bulk by my side, but I have to. I can't bear to let one sliver of doubt cut into me.

Looking past the fifty-yard perimeter of scorched ground that we keep around the wall, I search the forest for movement. The Wasteland is a tangle of trees, undergrowth, and the husks of the cities that once were, all coated in the bright, slippery green growth of early spring and the drifting piles of silvery ash that remind us of our fragility. Somewhere in its depths, bands of lawless highwaymen pillage for goods they can trade at the city-states. Somewhere beneath it, the Cursed One roams, seeking to devour what little remains of a once great civilization.

I don't care about any of that. I just want Dad to make it home in time.

"Rachel-girl," Oliver says, his brown, flour-stained fingers wrapping gently around my arm as if to prepare me for what he wants to say.

"He's coming."

"I don't think—"

"He *is*." I dig my nails into my palms and strain to see movement in the thickening twilight, as if by the force of my will I can bring him home.

Oliver squeezes my arm but says nothing. I know he thinks Dad is dead. Everyone thinks so. Everyone but me. The thought that I stand alone in my conviction sends a bright, hard shaft of pain through me, and suddenly I need Oliver to understand.

To agree.

"He's not just a courier, you know." I glance at Oliver's broad shoulders, which carve a deep shadow into the ground beneath him, and wish for the days when I was little enough to perch on his back, feeling the rumble of his voice through my skin as we walked to the gate to meet Dad after yet another successful trip. "He's also a tracker. The Commander's best. There's no way he got caught unaware in the Wasteland."

Oliver's voice is steady as he says, "He is good at his job, Rachel-girl. But something must have . . . held him up. He isn't coming home in time."

I turn away, trying to see where the perimeter ends and the Wasteland begins, but the sun is nothing but a fiery mirage below the tree line now, and the shadows have taken over.

"Last call!" one of the guards shouts, his shoulders flexing beneath the dark blue of his uniform as he reaches for the iron handle beside him and begins tugging the gate inward. I flinch as it slams shut with a harsh metallic clang. The guards weave thick, gleaming chains through the frame, securing it until the guards on the morning shift return with the key.

For a moment, we stand staring at the now-closed gate. Then Oliver wraps an arm around me and says, "It's time."

Tears sting my eyes, and I clench my jaw so hard my teeth grind together. I'm not going to cry. Not now. Later, after Dad has been officially declared dead, and my Protectorship has transferred to Oliver, I'll let myself feel the pain of being the only one left who's willing to believe that Jared Adams, Baalboden's best tracker, is still alive.

I use the wooden step box to climb into the wagon that waits for us, and reach a hand back to help Oliver hoist himself up as well.

As the wagon sways and lurches over the cobblestone streets to the Commander's compound, I wrap my fists in my cloak and try to ignore the way my stomach burns with every rotation of the wheels. Oliver reaches out and unravels my cloak from my right hand. His palm swallows mine, his skin warm, the maple-raisin scent of his baking comforting me. I lean into him, pressing my cheek against the scratchy linen of his tunic.

"I'm sorry," he says softly.

For a moment, I want to burrow in. Soak up the comfort he offers and pretend he can make it better. Instead, I sit up, spine straight, just the way Dad taught me. "He didn't come back today, but that doesn't mean he won't come home at all. If anyone knows how to survive the Wasteland, it's Dad." My voice catches on a sudden surge of grief—a dark, secret fear that my faith in Dad's skills will be proven wrong, and I'll be left alone. "It isn't fair that he has to be declared dead."

"It's probably my job to tell you life isn't fair, but I figure you already know that." His voice is steady, but his eyes look sad. "So instead, I'll tell you that hope is precious, and you're right not to give it up."

I look him in the eye, daring him to feed me a lie and tell me he still believes. "Even when it looks like everyone else already has?"

"Especially when it looks like everyone else already has." He pats my hand as the wagon grinds to a halt, its bed swaying long after the wheels have stopped.

The driver walks toward the back of the wagon, and jerks the canvas flap aside. I climb down and watch anxiously as Oliver follows. Though only faint creases mar the brown skin of his face, his hair is more gray than black, and he moves with the careful precision of age. Reaching for him, I slide my arm through his as he navigates his way off the heavy wooden step box. Together, we turn to face the compound.

Like the Wall surrounding the city of Baalboden, the compound is a massive expanse of weather-stained gray stone bolstered by ribbons of steel. Darkened windows are cut into the bulky exterior like lidless, unblinking eyes, and the roof holds several turrets manned with guards whose sole job it is to cut down any intruders before they've gone twenty paces.

Not that any citizen of Baalboden would be stupid enough to defy the man who rules us with a ferocity rivaled only by what waits for us out in the Wasteland.

Before the guard manning the spiked iron gate can open it, another wagon rumbles to a stop behind ours. I glance over my shoulder and heat stings my cheeks as Logan McEntire strides toward us, the dying sun painting his dark-blond hair gold.

I will my pale skin not to betray me and do my best to pretend I don't see him. I've spent so much time today hoping Dad would finally return from the Wasteland, I neglected to consider that any reading of his will would naturally include his apprentice.

Which is fine. As long as I don't have to speak to him.

"Oliver. Rachel," Logan says as he comes to stand beside us. His voice is its usual calm, I-bet-I-can-find-an-algorithm-to-fix-this tone, and I have a sudden desire to pick a fight with him.

Except that would make it look like I care that he's here.

And I *don't*.

His presence won't change anything. My Protectorship will be given to Oliver, Logan will take over Dad's courier duties, and I'll keep checking off the days until Dad comes home again, and life can go back to normal.

Oliver reaches out to clap his free hand on Logan's shoulder. "Good of you to come," he says. As if Logan had a choice. As if any of us have a choice.

"It feels too soon," Logan says softly as the guard opens the gate and waves us forward. "Jared's tough. We should give him more than sixty days past his scheduled return date before we're forced to declare him dead."

I glance at Logan in surprise, and find his dark blue eyes on mine, the fierce conviction in them a perfect match for what burns in me. My lips curve into a small smile before I remember I'm not going to act like I care about him.

I've had enough firsthand experience with caring about Logan McEntire to last me a lifetime.

I look away and walk into the compound without another word.

Oliver and Logan follow on my heels. A steward, dressed in black, leads us into a box of a room and quietly excuses himself, shutting the door behind him.

Straight-back wooden chairs surround a long polished table, and six torches rest in black iron brackets against stark white walls. The air feels smoky and closed off, but I don't know if the choked feeling in my throat is from lack of oxygen or from the fact that facing us at the end of the table is Commander Jason Chase, ruler of Baalboden.

The torchlight skims the gold braid on his crisp blue military jacket, scrapes over the twin furrows of the scar that twists a path from his left temple to his mouth, and dies in the unremitting darkness of his eyes.

"Sit," he says.

We obey. Our chairs drag against the stone floor, a high-pitched squeal of distress. Two men sit on either side of the Commander's chair. One worries a stack of parchment lying in front of him with nervous fingers. The other wears a studious expression on the doughy folds of his face and holds a quill poised over an inkwell, a sheet of blank parchment unfurled before him.

The Commander examines each of us in turn before sitting in his chair, his spine held at rigid attention. Without sparing a glance for the two men beside him, he says, "Oliver James Reece, Logan McEntire, and Rachel Elizabeth Adams, you have been called here today to deal with the matter of the death of Jared Nathaniel Adams."

I jerk forward at his words, leaning past Oliver on my left so I can meet the Commander's gaze, but Logan grips my right arm and pulls me back.

"Shh," he breathes against my ear.

I yank my arm from his grasp and swallow the protest begging to be unleashed. We aren't here because Dad is dead. We're here because the Commander won't allow more time for us to prove he's alive. Anger hums beneath my skin.

The Commander continues. "Upon his failure to return from his courier mission to the city-state of Carrington, I invoked the sixty-day grace period for return. Those sixty days are now over."

The round man scratches furiously on the parchment without spilling a spare drop of ink from his quill. I want to speak. To make him record my protest. Anything could have gone wrong in the Wasteland. Dad could've taken sick. Been kidnapped by highwaymen. Been driven off course by the Cursed One. None of those events are necessarily fatal. We just need to give him more time. My body vibrates, tension coiling within me until I have to clamp my jaw tight to keep from interrupting.

"Therefore, by right as ruler and upholder of law in Baalboden, I now pronounce Jared Nathaniel Adams dead."

The small, nervous-fingered man gathers the stack of papers in front of him, clears his throat, and begins to read Dad's will. I let his words slide past me, willing him to hurry up so we can leave. But when he suddenly falls silent and frowns, I start paying attention.

"Is there a problem?" the Commander asks in a tone meant to convey that there'd better not be.

"It's, ah, just a bit irregular. Highly irregular." The man's fingers clench the parchment, curling the edges until they begin to crumble.

"Continue," the Commander says to him.

A hard knot forms in the pit of my stomach.

"'In the matter of the Protectorship of my daughter, Rachel Elizabeth Adams, I do hereby appoint as her Protector . . . '" Another clearing of his throat. A swift glance in my direction.

No, not in my direction. In *Logan's*.

I grip the table's edge with clammy fingers and feel the bottom drop out of my world as the man says, "'I do hereby appoint as her Protector, until such a day as she is legally Claimed, my apprentice, Logan McEntire.'"

CHAPTER TWO

LOGAN

It takes a second for the news to sink in. For me to realize he said *my* name. Not Oliver's. Mine.

Even as I absorb the sucker punch of panic to my gut, I'm scrambling for a plan. Something we can all agree on as reasonable and just. A Protector is an older male family member or a husband. Not a nineteen-year-old orphan who carved his way out of poverty and desperation to become the apprentice to Baalboden's best tracker.

Maybe the Commander will intervene and tell us how preposterous this is. Acknowledge that I can't possibly be expected to take on a sixteen-year-old ward. Not when a man of Oliver's age and reputation is willing and able.

Instead, the Commander looks across the long expanse of table between us and smiles, a small tightening of his mouth that does nothing to mitigate the predatory challenge in his eyes.

He won't step in without seeing me beg him for it first. I press my lips closed, a thin line of defiance. I'd rather combine every element on the periodic table and take my chances with the outcome than humble myself before the Commander. Even for the worthy cause of giving both Rachel and Oliver what I know they want. I'll have to come up with another way to put Oliver in charge of Rachel. Maybe as her new Protector, it's within my rights to assign her to another?

Before I can pursue this line of thinking, Rachel leaps to her feet and says, "No!"

Oliver grabs for her, tugging her toward her chair, but she shakes him off.

"No?" The Commander draws the word out with deliberate intent, looking at her properly for the first time since we entered the room. Dread sinks into me at the way his eyes scrape over her like he'd enjoy teaching her how to keep her mouth shut.

I've seen that expression on the kind of men who frequent the back alleys of South Edge. It never bodes well for the woman they've selected as their prey.

Rachel's voice shakes. "He's not . . . I can't be. . . . This is crazy."

I snatch her arm and forcibly seat her again before she says something that gets her in the kind of trouble I can't save her from. "What she means is that this is very unexpected."

"What I *mean* is there is no way in this lifetime that I'll ever willingly answer to you." She glares at me, but her words are laced with panic.

I understand the feeling. I don't know how to be a Protector. Especially Rachel's Protector. And I don't know what words to say that would make her despise the situation less.

"You dare argue against your father's wishes?" The

Commander leans forward, placing each palm flat against the table.

"No, she doesn't."

"Yes, I—"

"You *don't*." I meet her eyes and try to convey with my expression that she should be quiet and let me handle this. Not that I've ever known Jared's headstrong daughter to be quiet about anything. But the thought of what the Commander could do to her if she angers him makes me sick with fear.

She throws me a look of absolute loathing, then pulls her arm free and turns to the Commander. "He's only nineteen. Wouldn't a man of Oliver's years and experience be a better choice?"

Her words hurt, a sudden sharp ache that takes me by surprise. The fact that I was about to suggest the same does nothing to lessen the sting.

"Your father didn't think so," the Commander says dismissively, turning his gaze from her as if she couldn't possibly have anything more to say.

"But . . . I'm nearly Claiming age. Just three months away. Surely I'm old enough not to need to stay under the roof of my official Protector—"

The Commander straightens abruptly and glares Rachel into silence. "First, you question your father's wisdom over you. Now, you question the Protectorship laws of Baalboden itself?"

"Sir, she's just a bit off balance right now. It's been a difficult day for her." The calm in Oliver's voice is strained around the edges.

The expression on the Commander's face turns the dread coursing through me into stone. Oliver can't defuse him. Rachel can't either, not that she'd try. That leaves me. Standing between the leader who's hated me for most of my life and the girl who thinks she hates me too.

"To argue against the law of Baalboden is to argue against me." The Commander chops each word into a sharp-edged weapon. "Are you absolutely sure you wish to take me on, girl?"

Stepping away from his chair, he marches toward us with slow deliberation. The torches paint grotesque shadows on his face as he passes them, and I brace myself.

Best Case Scenario: All he intends is to give Rachel a lecture, and I can wait until it's over before quietly insisting, as her Protector, that we take her home.

Worst Case Scenario: He intends to punish her physically for having the gall to argue with him, and I'll have to step in. Promise to do the job myself when I get her home. Transfer his attention from her to me. It's what a true Protector would do.

I no longer harbor false hope that I can somehow delegate the job to Oliver. The Commander won't allow it, not after this. Jared trusted *me* with the person he loved most. Not Oliver, her surrogate grandfather. Not Roderigo Angeles, her best friend's father. Me. The orphaned apprentice she once said she loved. I don't understand why Jared felt this was best for her, but I don't have to. He offered an outcast street rat a place at his table. Not just as an employee, but as a friend. I owe it to him to do my best for Rachel.

And because I understand how it feels to have the foundation you built your life on ripped away from you, I owe it to Rachel, too.

The Commander now stands behind Rachel's chair, gripping

its back with bloodless fingers. He's beginning to look close to his seventy-odd years. His skin is worn and thin, and wrinkles score the backs of his hands. Still, his frame is muscular, and he moves with the steady grace of an experienced fighter. Only a fool would underestimate him.

"If not for *me*, the survivors of the Cursed One's first attacks fifty years ago would be scattered across the ruins of their cities. Leaderless. Hopeless. Or do you forget that while the monster might lay waste to others, it never comes within Baalboden's Wall?"

The Commander leans closer, the torchlight flickering across his skin to gild Rachel's hair with flame. His words are brittle slaps against the air.

"If not for *me*, the Cursed One would have burned this city to the ground decades ago." His voice is rising, his fingers clenched against the back of her chair like he means to snap it in two.

"I will not tolerate dissension. I will not tolerate disobedience."

He grabs a handful of her hair and twists her around to face him. I clench my fists and prepare to defend her if he takes it any further. She hisses a quick gasp of pain but meets his eyes without flinching.

"And I will not tolerate a mere girl speaking to me as if she was my equal. You live because I allow it. Never forget that."

Deliberately unclenching my fists, I open my mouth to offer the Commander whatever assurances it takes to get him to calm down, but Rachel beats me to it.

"I won't forget it."

She sounds appropriately frightened and humbled, though

knowing her it's possible she's simply figured out how to show him what he expects to see. He uncurls his fingers from her hair, wipes his hand against his pant leg as if he's touched something filthy, and abruptly turns to me.

"Let that be a lesson to you in how to control your ward. It appears Jared was somewhat remiss in her education."

He has no idea just how remiss Jared's been about instilling in Rachel the docile, meek obedience expected from a woman in Baalboden. I manage a single nod, as if grateful for the tutelage.

"I should take her home now," I say, making every effort to sound as if I feel nothing about the entire proceeding.

"Indeed," Oliver says, reaching out to engulf Rachel's hand in his. His voice is just as unruffled as mine. We both know better than to show emotion to the Commander. "We'll need to pack her belongings. Or are you planning to move into Jared's house?"

It's going to be hard enough to adjust to living under the same roof as Rachel. I don't think I can bear it if I also have to adjust to leaving the solitude of my little cottage behind as well.

"She'll move to my house."

Rachel jerks as if I've slapped her. It suddenly occurs to me that maybe she can't bear the thought of leaving her home either, but it's too late to take it back. To show indecisiveness in front of the Commander is foolish in the extreme. Regret over my words mixes with anger at being forced into a position where my only choices are to give up everything or expect Rachel to instead. There's no right answer, no easy solution that will some-how make this bearable for either of us. The weight of my new responsibility feels heavy enough to crush me.

"May we leave?" Oliver asks the Commander.

His dark eyes gleaming, the Commander says, "You may." But as we push our chairs away from the table and get to our feet, he steps closer to Rachel and glances at me, malice glittering in his eyes. "Tell me, girl, why do you despise your new Protector so much? And don't bother trying to lie." His eyes slide off of me and onto her. "I'd only have to punish you." He doesn't sound sorry about this.

Rachel throws me one quick look, her blue eyes pleading. It's the same look I saw two years ago, the morning of her fifteenth birthday, when everything changed between us. I'd just won the apprenticeship to Jared, and he was out on a courier mission to Carrington, a city-state several days' journey to the east of us. Oliver was staying at the house as he always did when Jared was away, and he was busy in the kitchen baking Rachel's favorite lemon cake for her birthday treat. I'd joined Rachel on the back porch at her request. I thought she simply wanted to talk about missing Jared, or missing her mother, something we both had in common.

Instead, she sat beside me, her cheeks flushing, her eyes refusing to meet mine, and told me she was in love with me. I heard the vibrant hope in her words, heard the way her breath caught in her throat when I took too long to answer, and felt clumsy and foolish.

She looked at me as I sat, baking in the early summer sunshine, scrambling for something to say that wouldn't hurt her but wouldn't encourage the impossible. I tried to explain. To tell her I couldn't think about romance when I had so much to prove. To make her see how fast Jared would terminate my apprenticeship if he thought there was anything improper between us. To assure her she was young, and there would be others.

The words were awkward and stilted, and I couldn't figure out what to do with my hands as the hope in her eyes slowly turned to pleading and finally subsided behind a cold wall of anger. I reached out, bridging the distance between us like I could somehow erase the damage, but she jumped to her feet and left me sitting there with nothing but the echo of my promise that she'd get over me.

She's spent every second since proving me right. I haven't had a glimpse of anything beneath the fierce independence she wears like a second skin until now. Now, with the Commander demanding to be privy to details that I know humiliated her, she turns to me. I don't intend to let her down.

"I'm afraid I've behaved rather poorly toward Miss Adams in the past," I say, stepping slightly in front of Rachel so the Commander has to either deal with me or be the first to step back. "I can't blame her for hoping a good man like Oliver would be her father's choice."

He studies me with a smirk. "Either Jared didn't care about this poor behavior of yours, or he never knew about it."

I nod toward the Commander with the barest pretense of respect before turning to face Rachel. "Shall we go get your things packed?"

Her face is dead white. Even the torchlight refuses to lend her any color. Straightening her spine, she slides her shield of fierce independence back in place and says, "Fine. But only until Dad returns." Then she walks out of the room.

I move to follow her, but the Commander's hand snakes

out and digs into my shoulder. "And when is Jared planning to return?" he asks.

"I beg your pardon?"

His tone is vicious. "She said 'until Dad returns.' When do you expect his return?" His other hand rests on the hilt of his sword, and his fingers bite into my cloak like he wishes he could draw blood.

"We don't expect his return," I say calmly, though my mind is racing. If the Commander really thinks Jared simply died while traveling the Wasteland, why the sharp interest in Rachel's belief Jared will return? "Rachel only wishes things were different."

"If you know something more about Jared's recent failure to return, tell me now."

"I don't know anything."

"Don't even think about lying to me," the Commander says, malice dripping from every word.

The silence between us is thick with tension. The Commander doesn't think Jared ran into trouble on his last mission. And he certainly doesn't think Jared's dead. I'm not sure what's going on, but I know with terrible certainty that Jared is in more danger from his leader than he could ever be from the Wasteland.

"I'm not lying," I say.

The Commander leans forward, chopping off his words like he'd spit them in my face if he could. "If I find out otherwise, I'll punish the girl first. You, of all people, should understand that."

The sudden memory of my mother's broken body lying lifeless at the Commander's feet makes it nearly impossible to say, "I understand."

He releases my shoulder slowly, and I turn to leave the room, keeping my head held high. My back straight. My face schooled into an expressionless mask as if the twin fuels of panic and anger haven't been ignited deep where the Commander never thinks to look.

Jared's in trouble. I have to come up with a solution—something I can use to track him down before the Commander does. And I have to do it before the Commander decides we know more than we're telling. As I stride out of the compound, following Oliver and Rachel toward the waiting wagons, I begin to plan.

CHAPTER THREE

RACHEL

Oliver and I take a wagon to my house while Logan decides to walk the considerable distance from the compound to his little cottage in the southwest corner of town. I imagine he wants time to assess the problem of being my Protector and come up with a plan for how to handle it.

Except there is no plan that will make living under the same roof as Logan easy to bear. And there is no plan that will make me accept having Dad declared dead. This isn't one of Logan's precious piles of wire and gears. He can't fix this.

We enter my house, greeted by the lingering aroma of the sticky buns Oliver made for breakfast. I guess he'll move back to his own house now, and this little yellow rectangle with its creaking floors and generous back porch will be home to no one at all.

I stand in the front room, wishing desperately I could over-turn Logan's edict and stay right here.

"Rachel-girl, it's full-on dark. If we don't leave soon, we won't make it out to Logan's tonight."

"Then we'll stay here."

"We can't." Oliver brushes a hand against my arm and nods toward the front window. I look and find two guards standing on our front lawn, waiting at the edges of the street torch's flickering light. "I guess the Commander had some doubts about you fulfilling your father's will."

I turn away from the window—and the proof that I have no power to change my situation—and say, "Let me take a minute to say good-bye."

"I'll put your clothes into a trunk while you do."

I wander through the house, touching pieces of my childhood and letting the memories swallow me whole.

The doorway where Dad gouged out a notch and carved in the date every year on my birthday to track my growth.

The sparring room with its racks of weapons where Dad taught me how to defend myself.

The kitchen table where Dad and I joked about his terrible cooking. I run my fingers across the heavy slab of wood. This is also the table where Logan first became a part of our lives, back when he was a skinny, dirty boy with hungry eyes hiding behind Oliver's cloak. I'd watched him as the years passed. Watched him soak up knowledge and skill like a dry blanket left out in a rainstorm until eventually he turned himself into the kind of man who could command Dad's respect. And I'd foolishly thought myself in love with him.

The memory burns within me, a bed of live coals I swear I'll stop walking across. I don't want to think about Logan, about feeling soft and hopeful toward him once upon a time. Not when I'm saying good-bye because Logan couldn't be bothered to understand how hard it would be for me to lose both my dad and my home on the same night.

Grief rises, thick and hot, trying to suffocate me. My eyes sting, and I dig my nails into the tabletop as a single sob escapes me.

I will not break down.

I will *not*.

I refuse to walk into Logan's home with tear-stained eyes and trembling lips. Stifling the next sob that shakes me, I blink away the tears and clench my hands into fists. Dad would've returned by now if he could. I can't hold on to false hope any longer. He isn't coming home. Not without help.

My eyes slide toward the still-open door of the sparring room as an idea—a ridiculous, bold, almost impossible idea—takes root. Dad can't come home without help, and the Commander shows no inclination to send a search party. But Dad doesn't need a sanctioned search party. Not when he's spent years training me how to handle myself in the Wasteland, smuggling me out of Baalboden so I could go with him on his shorter missions and making sure I could defend myself against any threat.

And not when Logan knows how to track.

The memory of Logan's belief in Dad's survival skills is a tiny sliver of comfort I grab onto with desperate strength. It pains me to admit it, but Logan is better at planning than I am. If anyone can help me—if anyone in Baalboden would *want* to help me—it's Logan.

The grief subsides, sinking beneath cold, hard purpose. I walk into the sparring room, strap a leather sheath around my waist, and slide my knife into place.

I'm going to find a way over the Wall and bring Dad home. Logan can either help me or get out of my way.

CHAPTER FOUR

LOGAN

She's been under my roof for twelve hours. One hour was spent trying to cook and eat a meal without accidentally brushing up against each other and without engaging in conversation. Mostly because she looked shocked and lost, and I had no words that would make it better.

Two-point-five hours were spent listening to her move around the tiny loft above me while I worked on a design for a tracking device and told myself no one should have that much power over my ability to concentrate.

The other eight-point-five hours, we slept. Or she did. I hope she did. I lay awake for more hours than I care to recall listening for a telltale catch in her breathing that would tell me how deeply she must be hurting. She remained silent, and I remained mostly sleepless.

Now the morning light feels harsh against my eyes, and my brain feels incapable of even the most rudimentary exercise in logic. Twelve hours into my role as her Protector and I'm sure of one thing: Moving Rachel into my little brick-and-mortar cottage wasn't one of my better ideas.

The small stipend I receive as Jared's apprentice is enough to pay for a house of my own with a bit left over for tech supplies and food. I have no idea how I'm going to make it stretch to cover Rachel's needs as well. However, considering the state of our relationship, money is the least of my current difficulties.

I'm sitting on my patched leather couch when she climbs down from the loft, sunlight tangling in the red strands of her hair and shimmering like fire. Her face is pale and composed, at odds with the fierce glint in her eyes as she looks at everything but me.

I should say something.

Anything.

No, not just anything. She had a rough day yesterday. She probably needs words of comfort and compassion.

I should've invited Oliver to breakfast.

She wanders through the living room, bypassing stacks of books and running her finger along my mantel, leaving a flurry of dust in her wake.

Did I ever realize there was dust on the mantel?

The silence between us feels unwieldy. I clear my throat and try to think of the most conciliatory greeting I can compose. How are you? Did you enjoy sleeping in my tiny loft instead of the comfortable bed you've always known? It's somewhat cold outside. Did you bring your heavy cloak when you packed up all your belongings to move here because I didn't think fast enough on my feet to realize I should let you keep your home?

If those sound half as stupid coming out of my mouth as they do in my head, I can't say them. Maybe I should just offer her some breakfast.

Her shoulders are tense as she moves away from my mantel and toward the slab of pine I use as my kitchen table. Its surface is covered with papers, inkwells, wires, and bits of copper. In the center, beside a stack of carefully drawn designs, lie the beginnings of the invention I'm hoping will solve this entire situation.

Her lips are pressed tight, dipping down in the corners.

I can say I'm sorry. She'll hear the sincerity in my voice. I'll say I'm sorry and then—

She reaches her hand toward the delicately spliced wires of my new invention. I leap to my feet, scattering books across the floor, and say, "Don't touch that!"

She freezes and looks at me for the first time.

"I mean . . . it's still a work in progress and it needs . . . Did you sleep okay? Of course not. You have your cloak, right? Because the weather is . . . I'm just going to make you some breakfast."

I sound like an idiot. Being solely responsible for a girl—no, being solely responsible for *Rachel*—has apparently short-circuited my ability to form coherent speech. Partially because the only girl I've ever really talked to is Rachel, and we stopped talking two years ago. And partially because ever since she said she loved me, I've felt unbearably self-conscious around her.

She stares me down and then deliberately presses her finger against the half-finished device before her. Her expression dares me to pick a fight, and I could easily take her up on it. It might be a relief to get some of the uncomfortable, volatile emotions from yesterday out into the open.

But Rachel doesn't need to deal with my grief and anger.

She needs an outlet for her own. Any other Baalboden girl would want sympathy and the cushion of her Protector keeping all hardship from her. But while other girls were raised to be dependent and obedient, Rachel was taught to think and act for herself. I know exactly how to help her.

"Want to spar?"

She frowns and slowly pulls her hand away from the wires. "Spar?"

"Yes."

She glances around as if looking for the trap. "Why?"

"Because it's been two and a half years since you last knocked me flat on my back. I figure I'm due." Not that I'm going to make it easy for her to beat me. She'd hate me if I did.

I smile as I walk toward her and nearly trip on a stack of haphazardly organized books.

Why don't I ever put things away around here?

She lifts her chin. "I only spar with—"

Jared. She only spars with Jared, but she can't make herself finish the sentence. Her lips tremble before she presses them back into an unyielding line.

"I'm sorry." I reach a hand toward her, but she doesn't look at it, and I let it fall. "I wish I could change things. I wish I hadn't made you move in here when I should've let you stay in your home. I wish Oliver had been named your Protector, so you'd feel comfortable. And I wish Jared . . ."

I can't say I wish he wasn't dead, because I don't think he is. The Commander doesn't think he's dead either. I'm hoping to be the first to prove that theory right. If I can't finish my invention and track Jared across the Wasteland before the Commander homes in on him, I'm afraid Jared will face the kind of brutal death only our leader is capable of dispensing.

Rachel's glare softens into something bright and fervent. "You don't think Dad's dead, do you?"

I shake my head.

"I knew it. I hoped I could count on you." Her cheeks flush faintly, and she leans closer. Warmth unfurls in my chest at her faith in me. If she can learn to trust me, maybe we can start over. Rebuild our friendship and figure out how to make this impossible situation work.

She says, "I've been thinking of ways we can get out of Baalboden so we can find him. If there's a sanctioned highwayman trading day, we could . . ."

The warmth within me turns to ice as she talks, one wild escape idea after another spilling from her mouth, a collection of dangerous pitfalls guaranteed to trap her beneath the merciless foot of the Commander. The memory of his whip falling in cruel precision across my mother's back slaps at me with a swift shock of pain.

Jared is counting on me to protect Rachel. Oliver is too. And with the Commander already suspicious that we know Jared's whereabouts, the risk of getting caught in an escape attempt is high.

Too high to allow her to come along.

She'll fight me on it. Probably hate me for it. But since she already despises me, I've got nothing to lose by standing in her way.

"We aren't leaving Baalboden to go looking for Jared," I say quietly.

The sudden silence between us is fraught with tension.

"But you said you think he's alive." She sounds baffled and hurt. Regret is a bitter taste in my mouth, but I can't allow her to risk everything. Jared wouldn't want his daughter to die trying to save him.

I don't want her to die either. She may not like me now, but I haven't forgotten that of all the citizens in Baalboden, only Oliver, Jared, and Rachel ever bothered to look at me like I was worth something.

"Logan?"

I make myself meet her eyes. Make myself memorize the way they look when they aren't filled with animosity or anger. Then I shove my regret into a corner and focus on the more important task: Keep Rachel safe until I can stash her with Oliver and go out into the Wasteland to find Jared myself. I don't know what Jared could've done to gain the Commander's merciless animosity, but he's become family to me. I can't stand back and do nothing.

"I do think he's alive," I say. "But we aren't going out looking for him. It's a suicide mission, one he'd never allow you to—"

"Don't tell me what Dad would allow me to do!"

"Rachel . . . "

Her face is dead white, her eyes a blaze of misery and fury. "So, you're content to just sit here in your little house, doing whatever it is you do all day, while somewhere out there Dad needs our help?"

No, I want to tell her. I'm about ten days out from finishing an invention I made specifically because I couldn't stand to sit here doing nothing while somewhere out there Jared is missing.

But if I tell her that, it's tantamount to giving her permission to come along. And I'm not willing to do that.

I clench my jaw and say, "We aren't going."

Her lip curls, a scornful expression that seems to say I've just lived up to her lowest estimation of me, and she steps back. Her disappointment hurts, but I meet her gaze without flinching.

"I'm sorry, Rachel."

She turns and walks out of the house.

CHAPTER FIVE

RACHEL

Logan does *nothing* but spend hours hunched over his kitchen table fiddling with wires and bits of metal. I want to punch him every time I walk into the room. We barely look at each other. Barely speak. He won't change his mind, and I'm not about to beg. I don't need Logan to travel the Wasteland with me as I track Dad. All I need is a way over the Wall.

Three days after moving into Logan's house, I found his magnetic handgrips, perfect for sliding safely down the bulky steel ribs along the Wall. Three days after *that*, he unknowingly presented me with the perfect opportunity for escape.

Now I wrap my cloak around myself and push into the sparse crowds still drifting stall to stall in Lower Market, haggling over produce, rubbing linens between their fingers to check for quality, and whispering in my wake.

It's been thirteen years since a woman dared walk through Lower Market without her Protector. She paid for her actions with her life.

Flicking the hood of my cloak over my head, I make sure it hides every strand of the red hair that makes me so easily recognizable. I don't like the idea of risking my life by going through Lower Market alone, but I'm desperate for the chance to do what no one else seems willing to do—search for Dad outside the Wall.

Lower Market is laid out like a man's back. The main road forms the spine and leads toward the North Tower, while smaller roads and alleys branch off like ribs running east and west. My heart pounds a little faster as I aim for the left side of the main road and start walking.

The first stall I reach is a trestle table laden with a few remaining crates of juicy pears and thick-skinned melons. A woman and her Protector squeeze the fruit between their fingers before loading up their sack, murmuring to each other as they weigh each choice. Ignoring them, I move on. A glance at the sky tells me I have about thirty minutes until twilight and the final closing of the gate.

Puddles gouge the gritty road, courtesy of an early-afternoon rain shower. I pass the butcher, already cleaning his knives and packing away the last of his mutton, and wrinkle my nose as the rusty scent of drying sheep's blood lies heavy on the air, mingling with the smell of mud.

Two more stalls down, I reach the candle maker's and the first of the west-running roads. I tuck my head down, hiding both my hair and my face beneath my hood. No one stops me as I make the left turn, though I feel the stares burning through the heavy leather of my cloak. Probably wondering what idiot of a Protector is fine with allowing his ward to walk unescorted through Lower Market.

Of course, Logan isn't fine with this. Or he won't be, once he finds out. Right now, though, I'm pretty sure he's talking tech with vendors far away from here, but still I tighten my cloak and try to look a little less . . . Rachel. Just in case.

A man on my left is hawking a collection of hunting knives with leather sheaths. Giving his wares a cursory glance, I slide my hand beneath my cloak and run my fingers along the sheath I wear strapped to my waist. His knives are nice.

Mine is better.

Leaving my knife alone, I keep walking. I've made the journey to Oliver's tent with Dad more times than I can count, and there are never any guards on the western side of Lower Market this late in the day. Still, I move briskly and keep to the sides, hoping to avoid attracting too much attention.

I'm nearly halfway to my destination when I reach an open wagon filled with bags of dried lentils, onions, and white beans. Three men lean against the side, watching in silence as the merchant's daughter scoops beans into burlap sacks. I sidestep them but pull up short as one of the men whistles softly, a low three-note tune of warning that sends chills up my spine.

That warning whistle can only mean one thing: guards. In Lower Market at twilight.

I can't waste time wondering why guards are here, of all places, on the one day when I've decided to break the most sacred laws on the books. My heart pounds, a thunderous, uneven rhythm, and I start looking around for a way out.

I have no intention of allowing them to catch me.

CHAPTER SIX

LOGAN

"Copper tubing. Twenty-two gauge." Which I could get just about anywhere. "A spool of wire. Sixteen gauge." A little trickier to come by, especially since I'm picky about my wires, but still, not an over-the-top request. I take a second to steady my nerves before making my final request.

"That all?" the proprietor asks.

Hoping I don't sound like I'm concerned about the consequences of committing treason I say, "I'll also need a barrel of acid."

This is the moment when every other merchant I've visited today suddenly decided my money was no longer welcome. I'm scraping the bottom of Baalboden's list of possible vendors by coming here, but there aren't any others left to try unless I want to deal with the highwaymen selling their wares outside the gate.

I don't.

I'd rather not advertise to the guards patrolling the perimeter that I'm using unstable substances in my inventions.

The proprietor stares me down, his hands slowly working the tap on a large wooden barrel full of hazy golden ale. "Don't think I rightly heard you."

I keep my voice low and repeat my request as I lean against the far corner of the bar-top counter in Thom's Tankard. The wood, a dull dirt brown, is sticky with the residue of spilled drinks and fried potatoes, and I'd sooner swallow lye than eat anything on the menu, but I'm not here for food.

Thom slaps a heavy wooden mug filled with ale in front of me, though I haven't ordered a drink. "Ain't got none."

Sure he does. Or if he doesn't, he knows where to get some. There aren't any black-market vendors operating in Baalboden without Thom's knowledge.

"Where can I find it, then?"

He shrugs his massive shoulders and picks up a grimy rag to smear across the greasy countertop as if cleaning is suddenly a priority.

I'm sick of running into roadblocks. If I can't convince him to give me what I need, I won't be able to finish my current invention. If I don't finish my current invention, I can't head into the Wasteland to find Jared. And if I don't find Jared, Rachel and I are stuck together until next year's Claiming ceremony, when another hapless man can do his best to tame her strong will into something that won't get her tossed into the Commander's dungeon.

I wish him luck.

"How much for the supplies?" I ask Thom. Maybe if he sees that I refuse to go away, he'll deal with me. *Someone* has to deal with me. They can't all be afraid of the potential repercussions.

"Boy, you must be stupid."

I laugh, a short sound devoid of mirth. I'm a lot of things—Protector, orphan, inventor, outcast—but I'm not stupid.

I am, however, a little desperate.

By the look of the place, so is Thom. The grooved wooden floor is splintered and sagging. The walls are stained with soot from the torches he uses instead of lanterns. And his stock of ale behind the counter looks more than half depleted. I don't have the kind of money that will take care of the slow decline I see here.

But beneath the decline, I sense something else. In the darkened corners, in the tense, watchful eyes of the serving girl who glances repeatedly out the heavily shrouded windows, and in the huddled, quiet conversation of the six men sitting behind me—the only other patrons in the tavern—an undertone of secrecy wraps the room in deliberate seclusion.

What would Thom pay to protect those secrets from the prying eyes of the Commander and his guards? I pull a pair of small circular wooden objects from my cloak and set them on the counter. "You see these?"

He grunts and darts a look at the group in the corner. Interesting. I'm guessing he isn't their leader, or he wouldn't be looking to them for permission to continue our discussion. And they wouldn't be hiding in the corner if they were in good standing with the Commander. Which means all of us are on the same side.

I just need to make them see it.

Raising my voice only enough to reach the group's ears without sounding obvious, I say, "These are surveillance discs modified to alert you to the approach of a guard anywhere in a twenty-five-yard radius. You insert a battery in each"—I pull out a small battery from the batch I made last week and slap it on the counter—"and mount one to the outside of your building. It sends out a sonic pulse every thirty seconds and takes a reading of every citizen's wristmark in the immediate area. If any of those wristmarks carry the military code, the outside disc triggers an alarm built into the disc you keep behind the counter. A twenty-five-yard radius means you have at least a forty-second warning. More than enough time to modify any suspicious behavior before getting caught."

I sense more than hear the sudden quiet in the group behind me.

"I'm happy to give you a demonstration of their capabilities, but once I do, I expect my tubing, my wire, and my barrel of acid."

A deep voice speaks from behind me. "You're Logan McEntire, aren't you?"

Turning, I face the group. Their speaker, a man with bushy black hair, a silver-shot beard, and dark eyes, assesses me with fierce concentration.

I nod slowly, trying without success to put a name with his face. "I am."

"Guess the fine merchants of North Hub didn't have what you need. Or if they did, you aren't exactly the person they want to be seen selling it to, are you?"

"No."

The silence thickens between us, broken only by the slow steady drip of ale leaking from the barrel behind Thom and the quiet movements of the serving girl, who takes another look out the window as if searching the street for something.

"You take a risk bringing tech like that out into the open." The man gestures toward the discs lying on the counter beside me. "If you're caught, it's the dungeon or worse for you."

"The guards leave me alone as much as the rest of you do."

"And how do you feel about that?"

"Am I supposed to feel something about it?"

His stare is unwavering. "If my mother was flogged to death for breaking the law, and I was declared a social outcast when I was but six years old, I think I'd feel something about it. Especially toward the man doing the flogging."

His words rake across a long-healed scar, drawing fresh blood. He's right. My mother broke the law and paid the price. And in a perpetual example of the consequences of disobedience, the Commander declared me an outcast, fit for nothing but life on the street until I came of age at seventeen. It's impossible to separate the law and its punishments from the Commander, since in Baalboden the two are one and the same, but I've tried. It's the only way I can live here without wanting to kill him.

"She shouldn't have broken the law," I say, though it's hard to sound like I mean it.

"Or maybe the law shouldn't demand a flogging for a woman caught walking the city streets without her Protector." The man watches me closely.

This is my test. The hoop I must jump through to convince them to allow Thom to do business with me. With the memory of my mother's last moments burning into my brain, I find it easy to agree. "Maybe it shouldn't."

"Bet you're wondering what we're doing meeting here discussing things that sound like treason."

"Bet you're wondering what I'm doing standing here asking for materials banned by law."

The man smiles, a wide crack of white in his black and silver beard. "I'm Drake. I've been looking forward to meeting you for some time."

I try to match his smile, but my mind is racing. Either Drake was a friend of my mother's and has waited until now to offer his friendship, or he thinks I'm an acceptable target to be recruited into what appears to be an anti-Commander group.

Which isn't going to happen. Not that I don't share their sentiments, but my mother is a prime example of how the price of dissent isn't worth the negligible payout.

Besides, I have an invention to finish, my mentor to track across the Wasteland, and a very independent ward to keep out of trouble. My plate is full.

"Any chance I can do business with your man here?" I nod toward Thom.

"Thom, get the man his supplies. Take the discs as payment."

Thom needs an extra day to procure the acid, so I agree to come back the following evening to complete the purchase. And because I'm not a fool, I take one of the surveillance discs with me as I go. He can have it once he delivers the rest of my order.

Setting out at a brisk pace toward the prosperous North Hub section of the city, where Rachel is spending the day with her best friend, Sylph, learning how to properly host a dinner party, I try to shake off the lingering image of my mother dying beneath the bite of the Commander's whip. I've had years of practice, and the picture fades before I've gone fifteen yards. The small spark of sedition ignited within me at the dingy tavern takes much longer to dissolve.

CHAPTER SEVEN

RACHEL

There shouldn't be guards this far west in Lower Market, but I don't doubt the warning whistle in the least. My pulse kicks up, pounding relentlessly against my ears, and I clench my fists to keep my hands steady. I refuse to be caught. Stopping beside the man who gave the warning, I turn and pretend to examine a sack of pearly-white onions while I sweep the area.

Men on their own or women with their Protectors continue to drift from stall to stall, but there's a jerkiness to their movements now. A prey's instinctive awareness of a predator.

My eyes scrape over canvas tents anchored to the ground with iron pegs, linger in the shadows between the rough-hewn stalls, and finally catch sight of him.

The guard is wedged in the narrow space between Madame Illiard's display of silk Claiming dresses and the painted green stall of Parsington's Herbal Remedies.

He isn't alone—they never are—but his partners aren't as easy to spot. It takes a minute before I see them. Cloaked. Carrying sacks and baskets. Trying to look like they're just another group of citizens.

My heart is pounding so hard I worry the man beside me will hear it. I need a plan. One that keeps me out of the dungeon but still gets me to my destination in time.

The first guard raises his hand, and I spot the gleaming black oval Identidisc a split second before the green light flashes, sending a sonic pulse across a seventy-yard radius, scanning the unique wristmark every citizen has tattooed onto their left forearm at birth. My fingers want to creep to my wrist to worry the magnetic bracelet Logan insists I wear to block the disc's ability to read my wristmark, but I clench my fist and remain still.

As soon as the guard drops his gaze to the Identidisc's data, I move.

Sliding past the wagon, I duck into a tent half filled with sturdy cast-iron pots and watch for my opportunity. It doesn't take long. The citizens know better than to stand around staring at the guards. Crowds begin sluggishly moving along the street again, though conversations are muted, and most look like they want nothing more than to leave Lower Market behind.

I couldn't agree more. My heart is pounding like it wants out of my chest, and it's a struggle to force myself to think clearly, but I must. I have to plan. To find a solution that doesn't end with me trapped between two guards, trying to talk my way out of the kind of flogging that long ago cost Logan his mother.

Logan.

What would Logan do?

Logan wouldn't be in this position in the first place because he'd already have everything mapped out with the kind of meticulous precision he applies to everything—a trait that usually irritates me, but now suddenly seems more attractive. Not that I'd ever admit it to him. Still, thinking like Logan gives me an idea, and I start searching for what I need.

Before long, I see my way out. A man—single, older, stoop-shouldered—walks slowly by my hiding place. I step out, match his pace, and lower my eyes as though I've been taught to respect my betters.

The man doesn't seem to notice my presence, which saves me the trouble of trying to come up with a plausible explanation for pretending he's my Protector. When he stops to browse for new boots, I seamlessly transfer to the next single man walking west.

This one casts a quick glance in my direction, frowns, and whispers, "What are you doing? Where is your Protector?"

I widen my eyes and do my best to look surprised. "I'm sorry. From the back, you look so similar. I thought . . ." I gesture, a tiny fluttering of my hands that conveys both helplessness and distress. "He said to wait while he went to Oliver's, but there are guards, and I got scared." My voice trembles just a bit.

His frown deepens, and he steps closer. "He should know better than to leave you alone at all." He glances around the street. "There's something going on today."

I wring my hands together and consider producing a few tears. That seems to bring most men to their knees. Except for Logan, curse his stubborn soul. Not that I *wanted* Logan on his knees. Not anymore.

The man nods once, as if resolving some internal debate. "I'll take you to Oliver's. Stick close and keep your eyes down as is proper."

I nearly bite my tongue in half to keep from telling him, in great detail, where he can put his ideas of what's *proper*. Instead, I look carefully at my feet and follow my borrowed Protector as he slices through the rapidly dwindling crowds on his way to Oliver's.

Two left turns later, we're at the western edge of the market. I sidestep a woman wrestling a plucked turkey into the woven basket strapped to her back, and approach Oliver's stall. The yeasty aroma of braided raisin loaves pierced by the sharp sweetness of orange buns wraps around me, and my stomach reminds me I haven't bothered to eat since early morning. Oliver stands alone amid wooden tables draped in crumb-coated white cotton and covered with trays holding the last of his baked goods.

Turning to me, my escort asks, "Where is your Protector, young lady?"

Oliver shakes his head, sending his chins swinging, and plucks a sticky bun from the stash he always keeps for the children who visit. He knows they're my favorite. "It's a bad day for you to be at the market, Rachel-girl."

"Rachel?" the man asks.

I shrug, and my hood slips a bit. The man catches a glimpse of my red hair and swears with admirable proficiency.

"Jared Adams's daughter?"

I nod, and snatch the sticky bun Oliver tosses in my direction.

"You lied to me." He doesn't make it sound like a compliment.

I tear off a chunk of bread. "I'm sorry about that. I needed to reach Oliver's without getting hassled by a guard."

"Hassled by a guard? *Hassled?*" The man's face turns red.

"Didn't you see their uniforms? Double gold bars on the left shoulder with a talon patch directly below."

The warm, gooey sweetness of the sticky bun turns to sawdust in my mouth. Not just guards. Commander Chase's personal Brute Squad. A flogging would've been the least of my worries if I'd been caught.

Which I *wasn't*. Because I can think on my feet.

Turning away, I ignore Oliver's quiet thanks to him as the man takes his leave. I don't meet Oliver's soft brown eyes as I slip my bracelet from my wristmark and lean forward to slide the mark across his scanner.

He grabs my arm, the rich mahogany of his skin a startling contrast against the paleness of mine, and says softly, "Not today, Rachel-girl."

"How else can I pay you for the bun?"

"Put the bracelet on and leave it there. You're practically my own granddaughter. The bun was a gift."

I slide the bracelet back in place and lean into Oliver's massive chest as he opens his arms to me. The warm scent of his baking clings to him and fills me with memories of happier times when I could crawl into his lap, listen to his deep voice tell me a fairy tale, and feel my world settle back into near-perfect lines again.

"Why did you come here today?"

I shrug and wrap my arms around him. I want one last moment with him before I face the dangers of the Wasteland alone.

He hugs me back and says, "Is this about you and Logan? I'm sure it must be an . . . adjustment."

My laugh sounds more like a sob, and I choke it back. Two years ago, I would've jumped at the chance to have more time with Logan. My chest still burns whenever I let myself remember inviting him over for birthday cake, and then making sure I got him alone on the back porch so I could tell him I thought he was different. Special. A man like my father.

The kind of man I wanted to marry.

My humiliation at his exquisitely logical rejection is now coated with anger at his refusal to help me look for Dad, and every time I see him, I want to hurt him.

I give Oliver a tiny smile as I pull away. "It's fine. *I'm* fine, but thank you."

"If you're fine, why take the risk of coming here?" His smile is gentle, but beneath it is the unyielding expectation that I will tell him the truth.

And because he's the closest thing to family I have left, I give him as much of the truth as I can without making him an accomplice.

"I need to say good-bye."

"To Jared?" He glances in the direction of the Wall, and I let him assume I've come to the edge of Baalboden to feel close to Dad one last time.

"Your dad wouldn't want you taking such risks." He raises a hand to my cheek, and love glows in his eyes, filling me with bittersweet warmth.

"My dad is the one who taught me how." I stand on tiptoes and press a kiss against his weathered cheek. I already ache with missing him, but I ache with missing Dad more. Moving away from Oliver, I circle behind a table and head toward the back tent flap, fumbling with my cloak fastenings so I won't have to look at him.

"Where do you think you're going?" Oliver asks. There's a bite of apprehension in his voice now.

"I'm going to the Wall."

"I can't allow this." He starts toward me.

"I'm going." I edge to the back of the tent.

"What am I supposed to tell Logan if I let you put yourself in danger?" Oliver asks, still moving toward me, though we both know he can't catch up.

That I'm sorry? That I no longer meant any of the things I'd said two years ago? That he brought this on us both by not listening to me and helping me search for Dad? I square my shoulders, flick my hood over my hair again, and pat the sheath strapped to my waist.

"Tell him he's too late," I say, stepping out of Oliver's tent and into the shadow of the Wall.

CHAPTER EIGHT

LOGAN

"I'm here to pick up Rachel," I say when Maria Angeles opens her front door. "I hope the girls enjoyed learning how to host a dinner party."

Actually, I'm hoping Rachel didn't shock the Angeles family by expressing her strong distaste for setting a table with more than one fork per person unless you were expecting to use the second fork as a weapon. My lips quirk, and I suppress a grin before I have to explain to the formidable figure of Mrs. Angeles what I find so amusing.

She opens her mouth, snaps it shut, and stares at me. "Rachel?" she asks, as if uncertain. As if I might be at her doorstep to pick up someone else.

Dread pools in my stomach, and a lick of anger chases it up my spine. "I dropped her off here two hours ago. She said . . . never mind what she said. Is she here?"

Mrs. Angeles shakes her head, turns, and calls over her shoulder, "Sylphia, come to the door, please."

Sylph obeys immediately, but when she sees me, she flinches and her steps falter. Mrs. Angeles's voice cracks like a whip. "Where is Rachel?"

"I don't know." Her voice trembles. She's a terrible liar. I'm grateful.

"Sylph, please. If Rachel gets caught—" The unbidden image of my mother lying broken and bloody on the cobblestone streets while a crowd of citizens slowly back away fills my head. The air is suddenly too thick to breathe.

Sylph looks at the floor. "She just wanted to spend the afternoon at Oliver's."

"I would have taken her there." My tone is harsher than Sylph deserves. She isn't the mastermind. Fear drives the anger that pounds through me now with every heartbeat. I couldn't protect my mother from the Commander's ruthless punishments. But I can protect Rachel. I have to. I can't bear the thought of adding that failure to my list.

"She wanted to spend time there without . . ." Sylph doesn't continue, but I can fill in the blanks on my own. Rachel wanted to see Oliver without having to worry about me looking over her shoulder, listening in, telling her when to leave and what road to take on our journey home.

I can't blame her for chafing at the restrictions placed on her by Baalboden law, but the proof that she'd rather risk a public flogging than spend time with me hurts more than I want to admit. Barely pausing to say good-bye to Sylph and her mother, I hurry through North Hub.

As I rush through Lower Market, I note the unusual number of guards present. A flash of double gold bars above a talon on one of the guard's uniforms catches my eye.

Brute Squad.

Suddenly panic claws at me, threatening to fill my head with useless noise, and I beat it back. Rachel is okay. She has to be. I'm going to get to her before the Brute Squad notices a girl walking without her Protector. And then I'm going to lock her in my loft for as long as it takes to finish working out my plan to go looking for Jared.

I reach Oliver's stall in record time, burst through the tent flap, and say, "Where is she?"

Oliver waves his hand impatiently at the back flap. "There you are! Took long enough. She left me in the dust fifteen minutes ago. She knows I can't keep up with her." He gestures at his considerable bulk, and then snaps, "Why are you still standing there? Brute Squad is out there!"

"Where did she go?"

"To the Wall."

I stride forward and yank the back flap of the tent aside. I should've known that in the face of my refusal to make a plan to escape Baalboden with her, she'd leap headfirst into a plan of her own.

The alley behind Oliver's tent cuts through the remaining stalls on the western edge of Lower Market before merging with one of the last paved streets on this side of the city. I keep to the side, head down, looking like I'm doing nothing more than hurrying home.

Dark clouds cover the sky, and a chilly breeze is blowing, carrying hints of the storm to come. I calculate no more than ten minutes before a fierce round of early spring rain hits, reducing visibility to nothing.

I pick up my pace. I can track her through the rain if I have to, but that isn't what worries me. A glance around the streets shows the number of guards has increased in just the last few minutes. I don't believe in coincidences, which means somehow Rachel tipped them off to her intentions. She's smart, resourceful, and knows her way around weapons, but she's no match for the Brute Squad.

I'd rather not be a match for the Brute Squad either, but I'm not about to fail her.

I exit the alley, turn right, and stride along the street, my cloak wrapped close, my expression neutral. There's a guard in the doorway of the feed merchant, another pair outside Jocey's Mug & Ale, and I'm certain I catch the glint of a sword on the roof above me as I make the left into the alley between the armory and an abandoned warehouse. Under the pretense of adjusting my cloak, I scan the street.

No one seems to be following me. That doesn't reassure me about the guard on the roof, but I have quick reflexes.

The alley twists away from the street and ends abruptly at the edge of an expanse of waist-high yellow grass about fifty yards wide. Beyond the field of grass, the Wall looms. Immense steel ribs joined by tons of concrete as thick as twelve men standing shoulder to shoulder wrap around the city, holding the Wasteland at bay and the citizens beneath the Commander's thumb. Every one hundred twenty yards, a turret rises. Guards assigned to the Wall spend most of their shift in their assigned turrets. But three times a day—at dawn, at noon, and at sunset—they turn off the motion detectors and leave their turret to do a detailed sweep of their section of the Wall.

I reach the edge of the field just as the first drops of rain slam into the ground, the sun sinks below the Wall, and the low hum of the motion detector stutters into silence. The guards in the turret closest to me step into the steady downpour, swords in hand, NightSeer masks in place, and walk north with measured precision.

Rachel rises from the center of the field. The panic I've kept at bay flares to life as she stays low to the ground and races across the field in spurts—sprint, drop, roll into a crouch, and repeat. Beneath the curtain of rain, aided by the swiftly falling darkness, she's nothing but a shadow.

If I can see her, so can the guard above me. In seconds, I hear the soft whoosh of a body plummeting to the ground and brace myself. He lands slightly to the right of me, all of his attention on Rachel. I leap forward, slam my fist into the side of his head, and drag his unconscious body back under the lip of the roof. A quick scan of the area confirms that no other guards are pursuing Rachel. If I can get to Rachel before she's seen by the turret guards, maybe I can avert disaster completely. I take off after her at a dead run.

She reaches the Wall before the faint glow of the guards' NightSeer masks has completely disappeared in the distance. I estimate just under ten minutes before the guards return. Just under ten minutes to capture her, subdue her inevitable argument, and get her back into the relative safety of the city before she puts both of us on the Commander's execution list.

The driving sheets of rain make it hard to be certain, but I'm pretty sure she just dropped her skirt to the ground and started up the ladder in a pair of skintight pants. Fury overtakes my panic and fuels me. If a guard sees her dressed like that, he won't hesitate to take what he thinks she's freely offering, and then I'll have to kill him.

She makes it to the top before I reach the base. The rain pounds into me, but I barely feel it. The rungs are slippery, so I wrap my hands in my leather cloak, grasp the metal, and climb as quickly as I can.

Best Case Scenario: She's foolishly setting herself up for a covert trip down the side of the Wall and into the Wasteland, and I get the unenviable task of standing in her way, but she hasn't been noticed by any guards.

Worst Case Scenario 1: The turret guards return early, and I talk our way out of it.

Worst Case Scenario 2: The Brute Squad finds her, and we fight our way out.

Worst Case Scenario 3: Commander Chase discovers her act of treason, tries to punish her for it, and I draw my weapon against the man who rules all of Baalboden with an iron fist of terror.

I climb swiftly and pray I'm not too late.

CHAPTER NINE

RACHEL

I scramble over the lip of the Wall and race into the rounded stone turret a few yards to my left. Rain pounds the walkway as I grab the magnetic handgrips I'd snatched from Logan's supply of inventions before leaving with him for Sylph's house. The metal circles feel cold against my skin, and I hurriedly strap them onto my palms. I don't have long before the guards return.

I wave my hand cautiously in front of the iron torch bracket beside the doorway, and the handgrip slams my arm to the bracket. It takes most of my strength to yank myself free. These will easily adhere to the steel ribbing on the outside of the Wall and hold my weight as I descend. It pains me to admit it, but Logan is a genius.

Not that I'd ever tell him that.

I drag my cloak closer to my body. The rain is falling in opaque sheets. I'll be lucky if I can see two yards in front of me. Which means the guards won't be able to see me either.

But it also means I can't see what waits for me in the

Wasteland. I'm not too worried about highwaymen or wild animals. What I can't kill, I can elude. Dad trained me well. Facing the Cursed One, however, is another matter.

We don't know how long the beast lurked in its lair beneath the surface, but we know what set it loose. A rich businessman searching for a new source of renewable fuel bought up land all over the globe, hired crews, and on one fateful day, had every crew drill down through a layer of metamorphic rock deep beneath the earth's crust. Instead of finding a new source of fuel, the crews woke immense, fire-breathing beasts who tracked their prey by sound. Driven wild by the noise of the civilizations living above them, or perhaps driven by nothing more than a feral instinct to destroy anything that might be able to destroy them, the beasts surfaced and laid waste to miles of densely populated areas each time they broke through the ground.

In the ensuing chaos, every military branch positioned their most experienced squadrons in densely populated areas with the plan to set traps for the beasts. It was a suicide mission. No one could predict when or where the creatures would surface, and any troops not perfectly in position were immediately destroyed. Several squadrons got lucky and blew a beast or two apart before they themselves were killed, but the military was shattered before they could kill them all.

As a last-ditch effort, the government on our continent sent all they had left—a team of young, inexperienced soldiers and a handful of geologists—down into the bowels of the earth to seal our beast back into its lair. The team, led by Commander Chase, failed, and when the surviving members returned to the surface, there was no government. No law and order. Nothing but panic, fire, and one surviving monster systematically killing the survivors.

The Commander and his team took charge, organized food and relief efforts, and proved repeatedly that, for reasons they refused to share, the remaining Cursed One never attacked them or anyone around them. It didn't take long for the survivors to rally behind the protected men and proclaim them their new leaders. Within a decade, nine city-states led by the Commander and the other members of his team stretched across our continent, offering citizens shelter and protection in exchange for swearing allegiance to the leader of that city.

Leaving the protection of Baalboden behind means risking an encounter with the beast, especially since the Commander built his city-state closer to the creature's den than any of the other leaders. One wrong move, and I'll never be heard from again.

Which means I can't make a mistake. My hands shake as I rehearse my plan.

Run out the doorway. Grab the edge of the Wall. Vault over. Slam my hands against the steel ribbing as I fall. Slide down and escape into the vast, treacherous darkness of the Wasteland with nothing but my wits and my knife.

It can work. It has to work.

I take a deep breath and sprint out the door.

I haven't gone more than three yards before I slam into a hard, unyielding obstacle. Strong fingers reach out to grab my arms, and I look up.

Commander Chase.

Terror rips a white-hot path through my body, and I can barely breathe.

I'm dead.

He stares at me for an excruciating moment, then shoves me through the turret's arched doorway, two members of his Brute Squad on his heels. One of them strikes flint at the lantern resting on the room's table, and the sudden light stings. Fury burns in the Commander's dark eyes, and my knees threaten to collapse beneath me.

We take three steps into the room before he lets go of me with a shove that propels me backward toward the table. I stumble over the edge of my cloak and crumple to the floor, twisting my body in midair so I land with my back to him.

I need a second to tug Logan's magnetic handgrips off my palms and shove them into my inner cloak pocket. I might be going down, but I don't need to take Logan with me. Covering my actions by struggling to stand again, I feel a tiny rush of relief when the grips slide into my pocket without incident.

"You've been keeping secrets from me." There's no room in his tone for avoiding the inevitable. The two guards with him move to flank me, their hands already wrapped around the hilts of their swords.

I shake my head, my blood roaring in my ears.

He whips his right hand into the air, palm facing me, and the guards draw their swords.

"Tell me the truth, girl, or die. I don't care which you choose."

"I was trying to sneak over the Wall," I say in a voice that's parchment thin. "I want to find my father."

He nods once, and the guard beside me lays the edge of his sword against my neck. I raise my chin as the silver bites into my skin, but I refuse to beg for mercy. He should've sent a tracker when my father failed to return from his last mission. If he didn't have mercy for his best courier, he isn't going to find any to spare for me.

"I knew it." He spits the words at me. "On the day his will was read, I could see that you knew something about his whereabouts." The smile he gives me makes me feel sick. "It's nice to know the extra effort I've taken to have you followed since then is about to pay off. Now, where is he?"

"I don't know."

His smile stretches until it strains against the thick rope of scar tissue marring his face. "Of course you know where he is. He's probably supposed to meet you on the other side of the Wall. A girl doesn't go out into the Wasteland alone." His tone is full of contempt, his hand still raised as if at any moment he might fold it into a fist, giving the guard permission to kill me.

"Why not?" I ask, proud that my voice only shakes a little.

His smile dies slowly. "You're in desperate need of someone to teach you your proper place."

I bite my lip to keep it from trembling, and try to ignore the way the silver blade at my throat scrapes my skin raw.

"Where is he?" the Commander asks.

"I don't know."

He draws his own sword and steps close. The guard withdraws his blade from my neck but doesn't sheathe it.

I can smell the warm, wet wool of the Commander's military jacket mixed with the dank, foul scent of his breath. My knees feel like liquid, and I have to clamp my teeth together to keep them from chattering as his dark eyes devour me.

"You're lying." His lip curls around the words as they fall like stones between us. "If you don't know where he is, how did you expect to find him?"

"I was going to track him."

"Track him?" The Commander steps back and turns to the guard beside me. "She was going to *track him*." They both laugh.

Anger straightens my spine. "I can do it."

"Look at you." The Commander flicks his sword at me, and I flinch as the tip slices the air beside my face. "Nothing but a girl who thinks she can track one of my best couriers into the Wasteland with only pants and a cloak for protection. Women like you are the entire reason we need the Protectorship protocol. We save ourselves from your foolishness."

"It isn't foolish. I know what I'm doing. My father saw to that."

In the sudden silence following my announcement, I hear the heavy patter of the rain outside the room as it bounces off the stone walkway. I also hear the low sound of men's voices just beyond the turret. Before I can do more than cast my eyes toward the door, Commander Chase wheels toward me, his expression reminding me of a predator about to pounce on his prey.

"Did he, now?"

I nod and force myself to swallow past the icy lump forming at the back of my throat. I have to convince him Dad is still alive, and I'm qualified to find him. My plan to sneak over the Wall might be dashed to pieces, but there was nothing to say I couldn't head into the Wasteland on a Commander-sanctioned mission. Even Logan wouldn't be able to argue against that.

Well, he'd argue. But he wouldn't be able to stop me.

"And how did he make sure you, a girl, knew how to survive the Wasteland?"

"He took me with him on some of his courier missions."

Something vicious flashes across his face, and he smiles, a horrible parody of mirth. I take a step back and bump against the table behind me.

More guards enter the room, pushing another man in front of them. I barely spare them a glance, but freeze when I see who it is they've caught.

Logan.

My heart clenches, a sudden pain that makes it hard to hold Logan's gaze as he stands to the left of the Commander, his hair plastered to his head, and his blue eyes locked on mine. I'm responsible for this. He's only here because he's trying to be a good Protector. No matter how angry I am at him for refusing to help me track Dad, he doesn't deserve to receive the brunt of the Commander's wrath.

Maybe if I keep the Commander distracted with what I can offer in the effort to track down Dad, he'll spare Logan whatever harsh consequence a Protector receives when his ward goes horribly astray.

Commander Chase doesn't bother turning around. Instead, he takes a step toward me, crowding me against the table. "Did your father take you with him on his second to last mission?"

I open my mouth, but Logan shakes his head frantically and says, "No."

The Commander tosses a glance over his shoulder. "Ah, the arrival of your Protector." He swings his sword until the tip digs into the soft skin beneath my chin. I grip the table with clammy hands and try to remain absolutely still. "Not another word, or she dies."

Logan's hands curl into fists, but he clenches his jaw and remains silent.

The Commander's sword remains steady as he says, "The truth, please. Did you go with your father on his second to last courier mission?"

"Yes." I breathe the word, but even that slight movement scrapes my skin across his blade. The pain is sharp and quick, and a hot trickle of blood slowly snakes its way down my neck.

"Where did you go?"

"Rowansmark." More pain. More blood.

Logan makes a sound that reminds me of a starving alley dog stalking his next meal.

The Commander smiles. "And here is where you give me either your secrets or your life." His sword tip digs into my chin, and tears sting my eyes. "Did anything unusual happen on the trip to Rowansmark?"

I glance at Logan. His face is white. I can read the plea for silence in his eyes as easily as if he'd begged aloud. But I believe the Commander's promise to kill me. And this is my only way out of Baalboden to track Dad. I have to tell the truth.

I try to tilt my chin away from the sword's tip and pray I'm not making the biggest mistake of my life. "Yes."

CHAPTER TEN

LOGAN

Blood runs down Rachel's neck and her body trembles. Something ugly fills my chest, begging to be unleashed. It was foolish of her to risk so much to go searching for Jared. It was also incredibly brave. I know she thinks she's ready to pay the price for this act of courage, but I can't stand the thought of watching another woman I care about die.

I should've seen this coming. If I had, she might not be trapped at the point of the Commander's sword. Scanning my surroundings, I start cataloging my options.

We've been joined by the turret's pair of guards, back from their sunset inspection of the Wall. The room feels cramped and the smell of warm bodies and rain-damp cloaks chokes the air.

"So, to the matter at hand." The Commander removes his sword from Rachel's throat, and the tightness constricting my chest eases a fraction. We have a chance. As long as he thinks we have something to offer, we have a chance.

Lantern light flickers along the blood-red stone the

Commander wears on the ring finger of his left hand. The gold dragon talon bisecting the stone glows softly, and I look away.

He's watching Rachel. "You say something unusual happened. What was it?"

She casts me a quick look, but there's nothing I can do to stop this. Not until I see what he really wants, and how to convince him that keeping us alive is his only chance at succeeding.

"Someone gave him a package. Not an official one, but after we were almost out of Rowansmark," she says.

His dark eyes gleam. "And did he open it?"

She hesitates for a fraction of a second before saying, "Of course not."

He steps closer to her, his fist gripping his sword handle until the veins in his hands bulge. "We've had peace with Rowansmark for nearly four decades. Do you know why?"

"Because neither of us has the technology to destroy the other?" Rachel asks, holding his gaze while she repeats a line I'd heard Jared say countless times. My stomach drops. Now is not the time to call the Commander on his actions. Those in the courier trade are well aware of the animosity between Commander Chase and his former major James Rowan. Most of the missions to Rowansmark are spy assignments disguised as ordinary trade negotiations. The Commander has made it his business to know everything James Rowan might be up to.

I have to wonder if Jared disappeared because Rowan has been busy doing the exact same thing to the Commander.

"Interesting theory," he says. "Did you hear that from your father after he opened the package?"

"He never opened it. At least, not in front of me."

"Where is it?"

"He hid it on the journey back."

"Because he planned to return it to Rowansmark?" His voice cracks the air, full of fury, and Rachel jumps.

"He would never do that! He's loyal to Baalboden."

"You have one chance to prove that to me. Where did he hide it?" His sword arm flexes as he raises the blade toward Rachel's face.

"I'm not sure. But I know where we went, and I know Dad's hiding places," she says, sounding so confident that I'm sure the Commander will believe he needs her to help find the package. Now he needs to be convinced to send me with her. There's no way I'm letting Rachel travel the Wasteland alone with the Commander's Brute Squad.

"I know where it is," I say.

All eyes turn toward me. I find the Commander's dark gaze and hold it steadily.

"More secrets?" he asks softly, and pivots toward me, his sword pointing with unwavering accuracy toward my throat. The Brute Squad guards on either side of me tighten their grip on my arms, but I refuse to struggle. I'm not going to give the Commander that satisfaction.

"Rachel's right. She knows where they traveled and what safe houses they used on the journey. But Jared spoke to me about the package. Things he refused to share with Rachel."

The Commander's expression is tinged with malice, and the tension in the room coils within me like a living thing.

"Tell me what he told you," he says.

I can't. Revealing information now would cancel out my

usefulness and possibly Rachel's as well. Plus, I don't have any information to reveal. I'm betting he wants the package enough not to call my bluff. I don't want to consider the consequences if I'm wrong.

"I'm not sure I can accurately describe the locations he gave me. I believe I need to see it to know it," I say. "Rachel can guide me to the general location, and I'll take it from there."

He snarls at me. "Do you think you're that valuable to me, Logan McEntire?"

There's no right answer. If I say yes, I'll be killed to prove my words false. If I say no, any chance I have of accompanying Rachel will disappear, and I'll probably be killed for my interference.

"My value is for you to decide. Sir." I nearly choke on the *sir*.

The Commander slams the flat of his sword onto my shoulder, slicing into my skin. Rachel gasps and slides her hand beneath her cloak. I have a terrible suspicion there's a weapon hidden in there.

She's going to get herself killed defending me if I can't defuse this, but I don't know how. My stomach clenches as I frantically run scenarios and try to see a way out of this. There isn't one, unless the Commander believes we're both necessary to getting him what he wants.

Please let him believe we're necessary to getting him what he wants.

"Jared Adams has something I need," he says. "You and the girl will get it back for me."

Relief rushes through me. "I understand."

He spits his words at me. "You listen to me, inventor who

64

likes to play with words. You are replaceable. The girl is replace-able. I won't hesitate for a second to spill her blood and find another willing to take her place. Do you really think the life of any one citizen matters in comparison to what I decide Baal-boden needs?"

Before I can do more than draw in a sharp, panicked gasp of air, he spins on his heel and lunges toward Rachel, his sword raised.

CHAPTER ELEVEN

RACHEL

"Rachel!" Logan throws himself forward, struggling to get free of the Brute Squad holding him in place.

My back slams against the table as the Commander's sword plunges deep into the chest of the guard beside me. The man makes a wet gurgling noise in the back of his throat and reaches one hand up to grasp the blade embedded in his chest. Blood pools beneath his palm and slides along the silver in a single, sinuous streak as he slowly crumples to the floor. His eyes lock on the Commander's until the knowledge within them hardens into the far-seeing gaze of the dead.

I can't remember how to move.

The Commander places one booted foot on the guard's shoulder, grabs the hilt of his sword with two hands, and tugs. The blade comes free with a damp, sucking sound, flinging stray droplets of blood into the air as the ring on the Commander's finger glistens wetly beneath the torchlight.

I gag, and the Commander holds his bloody sword to my

throat. My knife feels useless in my numb fingers. It was so much easier to imagine killing a man before I realized what that looked like.

"I warned you I'd teach you your place," the Commander says softly.

I can't speak around the sickness rising up the back of my throat. The metallic tang of blood swamps my senses. I hold my breath, but that just forces me to swallow blood-tainted air until I feel like screaming.

He smiles. Reaching out, he fingers a long strand of my hair. The spit dries in my mouth, and I feel foolish clutching my knife beneath my cloak as if it could possibly save me.

The Commander looks at Logan, letting my hair slide slowly through his fingers. "I was going to threaten her life to gain your complete cooperation, but I've changed my mind. It would be a shame to extinguish such spirit before one has had the opportunity to tame it, don't you think?"

Something desperate and dark awakens within me, biting through my stomach like bile. I want to slap his hand away from me, but with the sword still at my throat and Logan restrained by guards, I can't move.

Logan looks like he's going to be sick, but beneath his pallor I see something I never knew he was capable of: rage. If the Commander notices, he doesn't react. He's too busy looking at me like I'm his next meal. I shudder at the predatory gleam in his eye. I can't decide if he wants to kill me or Claim me as his own.

"Sir—" Logan begins.

"Instead, I've decided the terms of your service to me will be thus: Give me your word you'll return what belongs to me, and I'll let you live. Otherwise, the girl will need to be assigned another Protector while she retrieves my package for me." He reaches out and brushes a stray drop of blood from my cheek, and I shiver. "I'm sure I can find a man willing to take her on."

"That won't be necessary." Logan's voice shakes.

"Your word?"

"You have it."

"You may take a few days to gather your supplies and plan your trip. Notify me when you're ready to depart. I'll be sending guards to accompany you." Abruptly, the Commander turns from me, wipes his blade on the cloak of the dead man beside us, and strides toward the doorway. "Toss that mess into the Wasteland," he says to the remaining turret guard, and then he and his Brute Squad disappear into the night.

CHAPTER TWELVE

LOGAN

I can't speak past the anger flooding me as we leave the Wall behind and walk through the deserted streets of Lower Market. The image of the Commander eyeing Rachel in her skintight pants while rubbing the back of his hand against her bloodstained cheek fills my head, and I plow my fist into the wall of the wooden stall beside me.

Rachel jumps and gives me a sidelong look. She's only seen the man I made myself into after Oliver and Jared took an interest in me. She has no idea the kind of things I'm capable of when backed into a corner.

But I know, and punching a wall is the best option available to me unless I plan to do something far more destructive with my anger. Like draw my sword against the Commander.

"Feel better?" Rachel asks, and I punch the wall again just to keep from letting my anger loose on her. Not that she doesn't deserve some of it.

I shake out my hand and take hold of her arm as we leave

Lower Market behind. I have to calm down. *Think*. The Commander now knows for certain Jared received a package he didn't deliver. And he understands he's found a useful tool in Rachel's fervent belief that she can save her father.

And none of it would've happened if she hadn't tried to sneak over the Wall.

"You're hurting me," she says as she matches my pace through the torch-lit streets.

"You're lucky," I say.

"That you're hurting my arm?" Her voice is full of its usual sass, but I hear the unsteadiness beneath it.

"You're lucky I'm not wringing your neck."

She remains quiet, and I soften my grip.

We move past the ridiculous wealth of Center Square, where multistoried homes gleam beneath the warmth of lanterns hung at their doorways, and no one inside knows what it's like to go hungry. When I was a boy, lonely and wild, I used to walk Center Square at night, imagining the perfect lives of the families who lived inside such beauty and wishing I belonged with one of them. That was before Oliver and Jared reached out to me, and I learned that true family is found in those who choose you. Wealth has nothing to do with it.

Leaving Center Square behind, we move south. The houses grow smaller. With the street torches farther apart, the alleys darken, and I scan the streets constantly, cataloging potential threats, discarding those I know we can handle with our eyes shut, and planning our escape route from those we might not be able to avoid.

"What were you thinking?" I ask her as we round the corner

into South Edge. Here the street torches disappear, and the only visible light hovers timidly behind windows boarded shut. I finally let go of her arm and reach for my sword even as she slides her knife free. Only a fool walks through South Edge unarmed.

"I was thinking Dad needs to be rescued," she says, her tone sharp.

Something moves in an alley to our left, and I pivot around her back and resume walking, putting my body and my sword between her and the yawning darkness of the alley's mouth.

"Let me get this straight." I bite off each word to keep from spitting them at her. "You want to rescue your dad, so you decide to sneak over the Wall alone? Do you have a death wish?"

"Don't be an idiot." She sounds like she's gritting her teeth. "I didn't know the Commander had his guards following us."

"Of course you didn't. Because you're so wrapped up in missing Jared, you refuse to look at anything else." I regret the words as soon as I say them. I hadn't realized we were being followed either, and as her Protector, it was my responsibility to see it.

I press my palm to the small of her back and guide her to the opposite side of the street. The heat from her skin seeps into mine and feels like comfort.

Which is proof my ability to think logically seems to be compromised. I'm beginning to worry being responsible for Rachel has somehow thrown me permanently off-kilter.

She steps away from my hand. "At least one of us is caught up in missing him."

"Who says I don't miss him?" A shadow moves out of a doorway behind us. A man. Taller than me by about two inches, but I have him by a good twenty pounds. Plus, he's limping. Still, I wrap my hand around her arm again and pull her through some-one's backyard, over a small fence, and onto the street running parallel to the one we were just on.

He doesn't follow us.

"Are you listening?" she asks, and I realize she's been talking the entire time.

"I am now."

"Typical. I was asking how you can say you miss him. All you do is sit around day after day, drawing pictures—"

"Pictures! They're intricately scaled plans for an invention—"

She waves her knife through the air as if she can slice through my words and draw blood instead. "Drawing pictures, piecing together your little toys—"

That takes it. "You didn't think so poorly of my little toys tonight when you planned to use my handgrips to sneak over the Wall, did you?" My voice is rising. My little *toys* are about to give us a way to find Jared and get off the Commander's radar.

Of course, I haven't actually shared that with her. I thought I was protecting her, but maybe if I'd trusted her in the first place, we wouldn't be in our current situation.

She raises a fist like she wants to punch me. "All the toys and plans and books in the world won't get us one step closer to rescuing Dad, and you just sit there like we aren't running out of time!" Her voice breaks, and I reach out to haul her close to me and out of the path of a mule-drawn wagon clip-clopping along the street.

"We *are* almost out of time. I can feel it. Can't you feel it?" Her voice is unsteady, and I'm shocked to see tears sliding down her face, chasing a trail of heat between the icy pellets of rain still plummeting from the heavens.

I've never seen her cry before. Not when she was a young girl training with a man's weapons, getting injured more often than not. Not when she was a budding woman facing me across her back porch and spilling her heart only to have me hand it back to her. Not even when it became clear Jared wasn't coming back. The fury in me sinks beneath a sudden, sharp ache, and I wish I knew how to have a civilized conversation with her.

We take the corner marking the line between South Edge and Country Low. I want to have the perfect words to comfort her, but I don't, so I walk in silence as the ramshackle houses become cozy little cottages, and the patches of dirty grass between them expand into gardens, farm fields, and small orchards. Though no street torches exist, the darkness is now friendly.

My house comes into view, and she pushes ahead of me to stalk up the stone walkway, reaching the iron-hinged wooden door first. Hanging her damp cloak on a hook beside the door, she enters the main part of the cottage while I light the pair of lanterns hanging in the entryway.

She's rummaging through the kitchen, her movements jerky with either anger or grief. Probably both. I make my way across the living room until I'm less than three yards from her.

"I know we're running out of time. But you have to trust me. I know what I'm doing."

She jumps at the sound of my voice so close behind her, and shoots a glare over her shoulder before moving toward the wooden box of a pantry resting in the corner. "I know what you're doing, too. You're going into the Wasteland with me. I'm sorry about that, by the way." She opens the pantry and rummages through it.

Sorry for what? Having to take me with her? Does she really despise me that much? The hurt that follows this thought is a slow, dull ache that takes me by surprise. My voice is sharp as I follow her and ask, "Are you really sorry?"

This time, she bangs her head when she jumps. Turning, she shoves a sack of mutton jerky into my arms and snaps, "Stop sneaking up on me."

I grab the sack before it falls, and frown. "Why are you removing food from my pantry?" I toss the jerky onto the table behind me as she pulls two dusty jars of fig paste, knocking over a bag of potatoes in the process.

"Packing, of course."

"Wait a minute."

She shoves the paste at me and rolls her eyes. "Fine. I'll finish apologizing. I didn't want you involved. I should've made it over the side before they caught you. Then this whole thing wouldn't be an issue."

I slam the paste onto the wooden table beside the jerky. "How can you say that?"

She fists her hands on her hips and ignores the potatoes rolling across her feet. "I would've been gone, Logan. Deep into the Wasteland. And if you'd kept quiet about your reasons for being at the Wall, nothing would have changed for you."

"Nothing . . ." My stomach drops as I realize how little she thinks of me.

"You'd be free to invent and read and make life better for the citizens here. Duty finished." She kicks a potato, sending it careening across the floor as something blazes to life within me.

I glare at her. "And what duty would that be? The one I swore to the memory of the man I consider my one true friend?" I lean toward her as my voice rises. "The one I swore to myself when I could see how lost you are without him?"

She takes a step back and bumps into the pantry. "I'm not lost."

"You're *lost*. And everyone knows it. Three months till Claiming age. Every available man in the city suddenly looking at you like you're . . ." I snap my mouth closed and turn my back before I say what I'm really thinking. What every man who stops to stare at the fiery beauty with the indomitable spirit and glorious red hair is thinking.

She's yelling now. "Like I'm what? Pathetic? A poor little girl who needs a man every time she leaves the house? I'm not like that. My father saw to that. You should've gone after him with me when I first asked you to. You should've gone!"

I whirl to face her, and step forward until the distance between us can be measured in breaths. She's trembling. I am too. She stares at me with wounded eyes, and I want to wipe all the ugliness out of our lives, but I don't know how.

"Rachel."

Her hair is drenched. Glistening drops of water slide effortlessly down her pale skin. I raise my hand slowly, but she doesn't flinch as I press my palm against her cheek, letting the water slide over us both. My fingertips are callused and ink-stained, rough against the softness of her skin. She looks fragile and fierce, and I long for something more than the animosity between us.

"You're right," I say quietly. "I should've gone after him. Does it make it better to know that I always planned to go?"

"When?" she whispers.

"When I finish building the tracking device I want to use to find him."

Her skin warms beneath my hand as her anger fades into something tentative and soft.

"I should've told you what I was doing." My thumb traces a path across her cheekbone, catching another drip of water. "I should've trusted you. I'm sorry."

"No, I'm sorry. Sorry I misjudged you. Sorry I got us caught tonight." She sways closer to me.

My gaze wanders to her lips, and I can't see anything but a thin trail of water gliding over her skin, gathering at the corner of her mouth, and then slowly drifting toward her neck. She raises one shaky hand and presses her fingers against her lips. Her breath catches, a tiny sound that makes me realize how close I'm standing to her.

Warmth rushes through me, and I dip my face toward hers.

"Logan?" Her voice is soft, but the sound of my name slaps some sense into me.

I jerk back a step and swear.

CHAPTER THIRTEEN

LOGAN

"I'm sorry," I say, and back up another step.

She looks away and crosses her arms over her chest. "For what? Swearing?"

"Yes. No. I mean, yes, but . . ." The haze of warmth sweeping my system drains away as cold reality sets in.

I almost *kissed* Rachel.

The realization isn't nearly as shocking as the fact that despite our differences, our current situation, and the impossibility of it all, I still ache to press her against the wall and taste her.

That thought does dangerous things to my self-control. I need something else to talk about—something else to *think* about—fast. Glancing around for inspiration, I spy the partially built invention on my table and say, "Do you see that?"

Of course she sees it. She isn't blind.

"Are we changing the subject?"

"Rachel . . ." Yes, we're changing the subject. I don't know what to say to explain my actions, and it's either talk about technology, or I'm going to go take a walk in the rain.

"Fine." She won't look at me. "What's so special about that"—she flicks a hand toward the table—"that simply must be discussed right this second?"

"It's going to lead us to your dad."

She raises her eyes to mine, her expression cautiously hopeful. "How?"

I'm grateful to be asked for an explanation I can readily give. "Your father's wristmark has a tracking device embedded in it. All wristmarks do. It's short range, just like all our tech. Designed to work within the Wall and nowhere else."

This isn't news to her. All tech is specific to the city-state where it's issued. Without a network of wires across the Wasteland, there's no way to send any kind of long-range signal. A tracking device is useful outside the Wall only if you can get within two hundred yards of someone. Without a fairly exact location for Jared, we could wander for years and never get a ping.

"The invention I'm working on is a tracker designed to pick up traces of your dad's signal, even if he's already moved on."

"How is that possible?" Cautious hope is edging toward enthusiasm in her voice.

"Sound navigation ranging. A courier's tracking signal uses active sonar, sending out sonic pulses that leave a unique echo in the environment. The guards can find a courier using an Identidisc to receive those echoes as they're sent."

"So why can't we just steal an Identidisc and use that to track Dad?"

I shake my head. "Because Identidiscs aren't designed to pick up a signal any older than two weeks."

"Why not?"

I grin. "Because I didn't design them. Besides, we aren't going to steal anything and risk showing the Commander what we're up to. The device I'm building uses passive sonar, which means it receives echoes without sending its own out. I'm tasking it to only receive the lingering echoes of Jared's unique signal."

"But if it's been months since he was in an area—"

"Sound never really disappears. I'm building a powerful battery for this, so if he's been in an area within the last six months, I'll catch his echo and we'll be able to find him."

She smiles, and genuine warmth fills her eyes. "You're a genius. Thank you."

Her words make me feel like I'm standing taller. "You're welcome."

She gestures at the half-finished invention. "Why did you apprentice yourself to Dad? It's clear inventing tech is what you love. Why train to be a courier?"

I meet her gaze for a moment, weighing the risks of telling her what I've held in secret all these years. We might not like each other half the time, and we might misunderstand each other regularly, but she's loyal to the core. Knowing I can trust her unlocks the words, and they rush from me as if they've been waiting for a chance to be heard.

"Because I *hate* living in Baalboden. Every time I look at the cobblestone streets, I see my mother dying. Every time I look at the Wall, I remember who killed her and branded me an outcast when I was just a child. If I have to stay here for the rest of my life, I might . . . I don't know if I can be the man I want to be while I live here."

She nods, her eyes remaining steadily on mine.

"I figured if I learned to be a courier, one day the Commander would send me out alone."

"And you could disappear?"

"Yes."

Her voice is sharp. "Did you think of what that would do to those of us who care about you?"

My throat feels tight as I say, "I didn't realize you would miss me. Besides, did you think of what your disappearing act tonight would've done to me?"

Her cheeks flush a delicate pink. "I didn't realize you would miss me, either."

I smile, and it takes a minute to realize my common sense is once again sliding into Kiss Rachel territory. This time, it's not because my body demands it, but because the affection in her voice beckons me.

Which clearly means I'm in dire need of another subject change.

"We don't have to worry about that now," I say. "We'll be leaving together. Give me one week, and the tracking device will be ready. We can leave the day after the Claiming ceremony."

I ignore the way her smile lights the room, and turn toward the table. "I should get to work."

"I should get some sleep." Her voice sounds breathless as she slips past me to head toward the loft.

I sit at the kitchen table and face the tracking device, shelving all distracting thoughts of Rachel. I hope the Commander is willing to give me a week to get ready for the trip. I need those seven days. Two days to finish Jared's tracking device. And five more to build one for Rachel.

I'm not going to be caught off guard again.

CHAPTER FOURTEEN

RACHEL

It's been three days since my disastrous escape attempt. Logan spends most of his time fiddling with circuitry and ink-stained plans. I spend most of my time sharpening weapons and practicing how to run a man through the heart while I do my best to forget the awful wet sucking sound a sword makes when it pulls free of a body. We have little to do with each other until the evenings when he sets aside his work, I put down the swords, and we sit on his tiny porch eating supper and watching the sun bleed itself out over the ramparts of the Wall.

We talk about Dad. Oliver. Sparring techniques. The fact that neither of us has a clue what's in the package and why Dad refused to deliver it. We talk about anything but the strange almost-kiss we shared the night I tried to go over the Wall. Its unspoken significance presses against my heart, making it hard to look at Logan without yearning for something I know neither of us really wants.

Logan made it plain years ago that romance wasn't an option.

And I'm a different girl from the starry-eyed fifteen-year-old who thought she was in love. The almost-kiss was nothing more than too much emotion, too much tension, and a split second of dropping my guard. It won't happen again.

Over breakfast, Logan announces that we need to go into town for supplies. Ordinarily, he wouldn't require me to come along. But with guards watching the cottage day and night, leaving me home alone is a risk he isn't willing to take.

I don't bother arguing. I'm eager to get away from the small confines of Logan's house, and I'm surprised to realize I look forward to spending the day shopping for supplies with him. We've somehow worked our way into a tentative truce, and it feels nice to walk next to him down the pressed dirt road leading into town.

Logan's cottage is nestled in between his neighbor's apple orchard and a planting field owned by one of the wealthy merchants from Center Square. Last year, the merchant planted corn, and the broken stubs of the harvested plants still poke through the ground like jagged teeth. A guard rises up out of the cornfield as we pass, and another steps out of the orchard. I mutter something under my breath.

"Don't antagonize them," Logan says, nudging me with his shoulder.

"Maybe they should worry about antagonizing us."

He laughs, and the sound makes my skin tingle. I'm suddenly aware of how his shoulders fill his cloak. How his hair glows like honey in the morning sunlight. The tingle racing along my skin becomes an almost painful need I don't know how to fill.

"You have no idea how to be diplomatic, do you?" he asks,

but there's no judgment in his voice.

"What's the use in being diplomatic? I'd rather just pull my weapon and wing it." I nudge his shoulder back, and warmth spreads through me as he winks and leaves his arm pressed against mine as we walk.

We leave the cornfield behind, the guard from the orchard trailing us by about twenty yards. I'd like to turn around and tell him exactly what I think about his stupid job and his stupid boss.

Logan seems to sense my intentions because he slides his hand onto the small of my back, presses gently, and says, "Remember, sometimes diplomacy is the better side of warfare."

The heat of his hand feels like tiny sparks racing through me. "Diplomacy is a lot easier to accomplish if you've got your foe on his knees hoping you don't lop off his head."

"Do you really have to go into every situation with nothing but your wits and your knife?" he asks.

"Do you really have to go into every situation with more caution than a grandmother crossing Market Square?"

"It's called a well-reasoned plan." His hand slides away, and I shiver.

The dirt road gives way to the mud-caked cobblestones of South Edge. The fetid, rotting smell of trash heaps lies ripe on the morning air, and the few people who are outside of their miserable dwellings scuttle along the street with their eyes on their feet. Another guard steps out from behind a weather-worn house, his hand on the hilt of his sword as he watches us pass.

Clearly, the Commander expects us to run. To somehow sneak over the Wall without his knowledge, take his precious missing property, and disappear. It's not a half bad idea. If Dad thought the package was something the Commander shouldn't have, I'm not about to bring it back to Baalboden. Keeping my voice low, I say, "Maybe we should sneak out of the city."

Logan makes a choked noise. "No."

"But I don't like the idea of traveling with the guards."

"And I don't like the idea of getting caught committing treason."

I slide my knife free and hold it beneath my cloak as we enter the main stretch of South Edge. Not that I expect danger in broad daylight, especially with the obvious presence of guards at our backs, but I'm not going to risk it. Logan's hand is on his sword hilt, his eyes constantly scraping over our surroundings, looking for threats. We both know the real threat resides in the stone-and-steel compound rising out of the northern edge of the city.

"We need to travel without guards. Dad risked everything to keep that package from the Commander. We can't bring it back," I say quietly.

"No, we can't. But we can't go over the Wall. Or through the gate. The Commander will be expecting both. And there isn't another way out."

"Then maybe you need to look at other options."

He gets the faraway look in his eye that I now associate with hours of scribbling incomprehensible sketches while muttering to himself like a crazy man. I snap my fingers in front of his face. He jerks to attention and says, "You're right. I need other options. Which means I have to extend today's trip a bit."

"No problem."

He smiles at me, and our eyes linger on each other for a moment before I look away, pleased that he trusts me as an equal.

The guards behind us melt away as we swing into Lower Market, but it isn't long before I realize a tall cloaked man is stalking us. I point him out to Logan as we take the main road running west, stepping around a woman and her children who shoo chickens into a crate held by their Protector.

"I see him," Logan says. "Looks like Melkin. I guess this close to the gate, the Commander feels he needs a tracker following us. Just in case."

I glance at Melkin's scarecrow-thin form. "He doesn't look like much."

"With your dad out in the Wasteland, Melkin is the best tracker at the Commander's disposal."

"I guess we should take that as a compliment."

He laughs and grabs my elbow as a fast-moving wagon lumbers by, forcing us to quickly step aside.

"So, what's the plan today?" I ask.

"The plan is you stay with Oliver while I evade our followers and gather supplies."

I yank my elbow free. "I don't think so."

"I'm leaving you with Oliver for the day, Rachel. We have nothing more to discuss."

"We have plenty to discuss," I say. "I don't want to be stuck inside Oliver's tent all day. I'm an equal part in this whole thing, and I want to help you find supplies."

"Well, you can't."

I feel my face settle into mutinous lines. Does he really think telling me I can't do something is going to stop me? When I remain silent, Logan glances at me and frowns.

"Listen," he says. "The things I need to find aren't at respectable establishments."

I lift my chin and stare him down. "You're acting like poor, delicate Rachel must be kept away from even a hint of danger."

He laughs, tries to choke it back when he sees my face, and then laughs some more.

"Delicate? You could wipe the cobblestones with just about anyone in Baalboden. I'd hardly call that delicate."

"What do you mean, *just about*?" I've worked far too hard on my sparring skills to take that kind of insult lying down. "I can get the best of anyone who comes at me."

"You can't get the best of me."

"Try me, and you'll be singing a different tune. If I let you keep your lungs."

His smile is a slow journey of warmth that lights up his face and lingers in his eyes. "I'm going to take you up on that."

My stupid traitorous mouth smiles back before I remember I'm mad at him. Quickly wiping all expression from my face, I tap my foot on the cobblestones.

He leans closer and says, "I don't undervalue you, Rachel."

"Then why not take me with you?"

"Because I need the kind of supplies an upstanding merchant won't sell me. And the place I'm going to is also home to some people who sound like they might be plotting against the Commander."

"Really?" I bounce on my toes as I think of what a group like that might do for us if we decide to escape early.

He whips his hand into the air and says sternly, "I'm not

getting involved with them, and neither are you. Getting caught up in that is a good way to ensure neither of us ever gets to leave Baalboden to search for your dad."

"Good point. But still—"

"I'm already on this group's radar, but you don't have to be."

"Fine. But I still think—"

"If we get caught, who goes looking for Jared?" He reaches out and takes my hand. I slide my fingers between his without thinking, press his calloused palm against my own and study the fierce purpose burning in his eyes. "If I get seen doing business with traitors, I alone will take the blame. You'll still be able to leave."

My lingering irritation dissolves, replaced by gratitude and something deeper. Something that tightens my chest and makes my heart hurt. I've misjudged him. Badly. His protectiveness toward Dad is eclipsed only by his unwavering commitment to protect me.

I don't deserve it. I don't, but he can't see that. He takes his responsibilities seriously, and now that I'm part of his burden, he'd face the dungeons rather than let me down.

The heat between our palms seems to scorch me, and staring into his eyes makes me feel like all my secrets are slowly rising to the surface, whispering my truth without my permission.

Pulling my hand free, I step back and look down. "Thank you." The words are inadequate, but if I open my mouth again, I'm afraid of what I'll say. Instead, I quietly follow him to Oliver's tent, the imprint of his palm on mine lingering long after the heat of his skin fades away.

CHAPTER FIFTEEN

RACHEL

I've been cooped up in Oliver's tent for hours helping him sell his baked goods when he finally says, "Why don't we take a walk?"

He doesn't have to ask me twice. I grab both our cloaks and hold the front tent flap open for him. He eases through and tosses his cloak across his shoulders to ward off the brisk afternoon breeze.

Sliding my arm through his, I drag in a deep breath of air layered with the scents of Lower Market—candle wax, leather cloaks, mutton, sun-warmed produce, dirt.

"Ready?" I tug his arm, and he chuckles as we set off.

We circle a small cluster of men haggling over a gray donkey with drooping ears, our steps slow enough to accommodate Oliver's measured tread.

"I'm glad you've made your peace with your dad's . . . absence," he says.

I flinch and look at my feet. I haven't made my peace with

that, but I don't want to tell Oliver our plans until just before we leave. Maybe it's selfish of me, but I can't bear to put the shadow of an imminent good-bye over our day.

He pulls me to a stop in front of a stall selling steaming hot skewers of beef and onions. "Two, please."

"It's too expensive," I whisper to him, even though I know he won't listen.

He treats me to one of his wide, gentle smiles, his dark eyes shining. "Who else am I going to spend my money on? I already know you won't let me buy you any of the pretty, frilly things girls your age like to have, and I'm not about to purchase another weapon to add to your collection."

"Because I don't like pretty, frilly things. And there's nothing wrong with having a nice collection of weapons."

His smile looks sad around the edges. "That may be my fault. Jared didn't know how to raise a girl, and when he hired me to look after you in his absences, I didn't do any better."

I frown as I take my beef skewer, the juices running down the stick to sear my fingertips. "Or maybe that's just the way I am. There's nothing wrong with me."

He wraps his arm around me. "I didn't say there was. You're a wonderful girl. I just worry I didn't do enough to make up for you not having your mama alive to raise you."

I lean my head against his shoulder, and then take a bite of the delicious beef. "You and Dad are all I ever needed."

"And now Logan."

Do I need Logan? We've fumbled our way into what feels like the beginnings of a solid friendship, but I'm still constantly looking to avoid awkward moments in our conversations. Moments when he remembers I once said I loved him, and he once said I'd get over it. The memory of his palm pressed to mine makes my heart beat a little faster, and I tug Oliver away from the food stand.

Oliver clears his throat loudly. "With your dad gone, and your mama dead, I guess it falls to me to explain the way things, um, work between a man and a woman."

"What? No." I shake my head violently. *Nothing* could be more awkward than Oliver giving me the here's-where-babies-come-from talk.

"Unless you'd rather have this conversation with Logan."

I stand corrected. "Stop right now."

We turn the corner by the alchemist's and move toward the gate, still choked with citizens coming to trade with the band of highwaymen who've set up temporary camp at the edge of Baalboden's perimeter. The sun hangs in the sky like a ripe orange, though the breeze still carries the last remnants of winter's chill.

"You're nearly of Claiming age. Soon, men will look at you in a certain way. Even Logan might look at you differently."

I remember the intensity in Logan's eyes as we leaned close to each other in his kitchen. The way his hand felt pressed against my skin. The moment I realized I'd misjudged his intentions and his courage. I don't know if Logan is looking at me differently now, but I feel like I can see him clearly for the first time in all the years I've known him. The new understanding I have of him makes my heart ache just a little for the two years of lost friendship my wounded pride demanded.

"I don't want you to accept a Claim by just any man who looks half decent and has a roof to offer. You're worth more than this entire town put together, Rachel-girl. Don't you forget it."

"You're biased."

He laughs, a warm, rich sound that vibrates through my cheek as I press against him. "Maybe I am. But when the time comes, don't settle. Make sure the man you choose sees you as you truly are and loves you for it."

"I will."

"Sure is going to be a proud day for me when I see you decked out in that finery on the Claiming stage. I just hope I live long enough to be a great-granddaddy to your children." He finishes his meat and tosses his stick aside.

"Of course you will." A sharp pain slices into me as I realize if Logan and I disappear into the Wasteland with Dad, Oliver will miss seeing me Claimed, and he'll never be a great-granddaddy to my future children. I glance at a passing guard, resplendent in his military uniform, and my steps falter as the full impact of our plan hits me. Not only will Oliver miss those important moments in my life, he'll be the only one left here to pay the price for our deception. I have no doubt the Commander will torture and kill Oliver as a lasting example of the price of disobedience and disloyalty.

I tighten my hand around Oliver's arm and make a decision. Logan will just have to figure out a way to smuggle Oliver out with us. I refuse to leave him behind.

We're nearly past the gate when the ground beneath us trembles. Little pebbles and loose grains of sand skip and slide across the cobblestones. Outside the gate, someone screams.

I lock eyes with Oliver, and he pushes me off the road as the citizens nearest the gate panic. Knocking one another down,

Protectors half-dragging their women, they race past us. I stumble off the cobblestones and onto the uneven space of grass between the gate and the market road. Oliver is right behind me.

The vibrations beneath us increase in strength, and I dig my fingers into Oliver's arm.

"It will surface outside the Wall," he says. His voice sounds like he's carrying a weight he can't bear to shoulder.

I look through the still-open gate and my stomach sinks. Baalboden citizens are out there. They left for the sanctioned highwaymen trading day, and they won't have time to get back inside the Wall before the Cursed One arrives.

Even as I finish the thought, several citizens break free of the frightened, milling pack at the edge of the Wasteland and sprint toward the safety of the gate. Others scramble to climb trees or get in the highwaymen's wagons, though I can't see how that will help. A guard leaves the gatehouse and races past us on horseback, no doubt heading toward the Commander's compound.

"Get back. Rachel, get back!" Oliver pulls at me as another wave of terrified citizens fight to get out of harm's way and back into Lower Market.

I take an elbow to the chest from a husky man in a tattered cloak, and spin out of the way before the mule rider behind him can crush me beneath his steed's hooves.

"Rachel!" Oliver yells as the same husky man gets knocked off the road by the mule and slams into Oliver, sending them both sprawling. The ground shakes so much it's hard to find my footing, but I claw my way over to them, grab the man's arm, and wrestle him off Oliver.

Behind me, the screams are eclipsed by a raw, primal roar of fury. I whip my head around to see the glistening black length of the Cursed One burst through the ground. It looks like a huge wingless dragon, nearly half the height of the Wall, and just as thick. It's my first actual sighting of the beast, and every instinct in me screams to run, but I can't look away. Besides, running means leaving Oliver behind, and I won't do that. I just have to hope the legend about the Cursed One never attacking inside Baalboden's Wall is true.

Lashing its serpentlike tail, the beast crushes two of the citizens running toward the gate, but its attention is on the horde of highwaymen and citizens in front of it. Horror trembles through me as the creature opens its mouth and strafes the closest wagons and people with fire.

"Rachel, leave!" Oliver is yelling at me, but I can barely hear him over the screams.

People are burning, throwing themselves on the ground and beating at the flames, but the beast just keeps spewing fire at anything that moves. Sickened, I turn and hang on to Oliver. I want to cry, to give voice to the rising shock and terror within me, but Dad taught me better than that. Losing your head in a crisis is a good way to *become* the crisis.

Instead, I loop my arm under Oliver's and tug. "Get up. We can't stay here."

The man with the tattered cloak still lies where I threw him, his eyes fastened on the destruction outside the gate. I punch him in the shoulder. "Hey! Help me get him up."

He rips his gaze away from the carnage and barely glances at me. "Help him yourself," he says, and shoves himself to his feet. He's gone before I can tell him what a filthy coward he is.

I swear and plant my feet so I can leverage Oliver off the ground. Behind me, the creature roars, people wail, and fire snaps viciously. I refuse to look. As I finish hauling Oliver to his feet, hoofbeats pound the cobblestones. I look up. The Commander now sits astride the guard's horse and is galloping straight for the gate, his whip flashing as he urges the terrified animal toward a certain doom.

Oliver wraps his arm around my waist as the Commander reaches the gate, which is choked with desperate citizens fleeing the attack. He never slows. Instead, he slashes with the whip, driving people into the side of the Wall. One man can't move out of his way fast enough, and the Commander rides over the top of him. The man lies crumpled and still in the Commander's wake.

He's going to die. Be disintegrated right in front of us. Fear and bitter hope twine themselves together within me until I can't tell them apart. I don't want Baalboden to be thrown into leaderless chaos, but I can't pretend I'd mourn him.

The beast lashes its tail, narrowly missing the Commander. His mount shies and refuses to move closer, despite repeated lashes of the whip. Abandoning the horse, the Commander leaps to the ground and strides toward the creature. People still stagger in through the gate, burned and limping. In the Wasteland, little remains of the highwaymen and citizens trapped in the Cursed One's fire.

Before the Commander can reach the beast, it trembles, a shudder running the length of its monstrous black body. Pointing its snout into the air, it sniffs and shudders again. Then just as suddenly as it appeared, it dives back below the ground, leaving the Commander standing alone outside the gate.

"Why?" I look at Oliver. "Why did it leave like that?"

He stares at the flames, his expression haunted. "Some say the Commander has power over it."

"That's ridiculous. The Commander never even got that close to it," I say as the Commander ignores the victims of the beast's fire and strides back toward Baalboden.

"No one else showed the courage to face down the Cursed One in defense of our citizens," Oliver says quietly, like it pains him to admit it.

The Commander reaches the gate and steps over the body lying there without a downward glance. Fury bites at me, chasing the last of my terror away.

"Was it courage to whip people out of the way? To run a man down like his life was worth nothing?"

"Shh." Oliver shakes my arm as the Commander nears us. "Don't talk like that."

"Somebody has to."

Oliver's voice is low and fierce. "The Cursed One never attacks inside Baalboden's Wall. Living under the Commander's rule is the price we pay for our protection. In here, we're safe."

"Not safe enough." I meet the Commander's dark gaze as he strides past us. His stare is penetrating, and my hands grow clammy at the way his eyes slide from me to Oliver as if he's just remembered something important.

We stand on the grass until the Commander is long out of sight. I spend the entire time thinking of ways Logan and I can take Oliver with us when we go.

CHAPTER SIXTEEN

LOGAN

I step out of Thom's Tankard, pleased with my purchases, and walk straight into chaos. Citizens race up the roads from the western reaches of Lower Market, pushing and shoving to gain a better position over one another. Some are crying. Yelling. Screaming.

I look toward Lower Market and see the black smudge of smoke on the horizon.

Rachel. Oliver.

All that still matters to me in this world is somewhere down in Lower Market.

The crush of people moves in mindless panic. Those who hesitate or turn against the mob are flung to the side or trampled beneath pounding feet.

I dive into the edges of the throng and push against the flow. At first, it's easy to let the occasional citizen bounce off me, but as I leave South Edge and enter the market proper, the crowds thicken and my progress slows.

I need another route to Oliver's. Ducking into the nearest stall, I reach into my boots and pull out my knives. Seconds later, I slip out the back and use them to climb my way to the roof. Drive the blade in, pull myself up, drive the other blade in, pull myself up, and then yank the first blade free so I can do it again.

Once I reach the rooftop, I can see that the smoke is coming from outside the Wall. Which means Oliver and Rachel should be safe inside his tent. He'd never try to move through this mob with Rachel by his side.

A deafening roar splits the air, and the truth hits me, a sickening blow. The Cursed One is out there. On a sanctioned highwayman trading day. Any citizen still outside the gate is as good as dead.

I've never known the beast to surface so close to Baalboden, and even though every citizen knows the Commander claims to be able to protect us, I don't trust him. The creature could enter the city limits at any second, and then Oliver and Rachel could die.

I don't think. I just *move.*

I'm running, gathering speed before I even realize what I'm doing. I reach the edge of the roof and leap. Nearly missing the next roof, I crash hard to my knees. The edge of one of my knives nicks my palm and blood flows warmly down my arm. I shove the blades back into their sheaths, push myself up, and start running again.

In the distance, screams mingle with the mindless roar of the beast. I tune them out and take a flying leap onto the side of a tent. The canvas sways precariously, and I snatch the metal pole that braces the corner closest to me. Swinging over the pole, I run and jump, slamming into the side of the next stall.

As I climb onto the roof, I hear hoofbeats pounding behind me and turn to see the Commander thundering down the road, heedless of the panicked people desperately trying to get out of his way. The gate is a mere thirty yards ahead. Oliver's tent is at least eighty yards to my left. I'm about to make the turn when a flash of brilliant red near the gate catches my eye. I strain to see past the running people, and for one second, I have a clear sight line.

Fear seizes my chest with icy fingers, and my feet move before my brain can finish telling me I'm looking at Rachel. Caught in the crush of panicked, screaming people at the gate. Close enough to the beast that if the Commander is wrong about his control over it, she'll be one of the first to die.

I hit the roof next to me, skid across it, and leap into the air without pausing for breath.

If Rachel is there, surely Oliver is with her. My heart pounds, a desperate rhythm driving me forward. I nearly fall on the next leap, and slide to the ground. Time to start fighting my way through the crowds.

The beast outside the Wall bellows and the ground shudders, nearly throwing me to my knees. Quiet descends, sharp and unnatural, punctuated only by the sound of sobs and the distant crackling of fire. I skirt two men who stand, cloaks still smoking, shining pink skin blistering along their arms. They've just come from outside, and now they stand frozen, looking around as if wondering where the beast will attack next.

I don't know if it will surface again, but I'm going to be

standing in front of Rachel and Oliver if it does.

I see her now. She's clinging to Oliver, and though her body trembles, she looks fierce and ready for battle. A handful of people pass between us, and when I see her again, she's staring at the gate with furious eyes. I follow her gaze, and see the Commander stepping over a man's prone body. He meets Rachel's eyes, and dread seizes me at the speculative look he gives Oliver.

He knows we love Oliver. If we don't leave on the Commander's schedule and bring the package back to him, he'll sentence Oliver to death for our crimes. My heart aches, sudden and fierce.

Oliver will just have to come with us. I have four days to figure out how. As the Commander disappears into Lower Market, I hurry across the cobblestones and gather Rachel and Oliver to me. Oliver claps me on the back, and I see the relief in his eyes that both of his surrogate grandchildren are still alive.

Rachel leans into me, but the tension vibrating through her resonates with me as well. I pull her closer, and watch the flames eat through the remains of the highwaymen's wagons and gutter into nothing.

CHAPTER SEVENTEEN

RACHEL

We don't leave the cottage for another two days while Logan tinkers with his invention and works on a plan to smuggle Oliver safely out of Baalboden, and I brush up on my knife-wielding skills. When we talk, we focus on how to leave. How to deal with the Cursed One if he attacks while we're in the Wasteland. And what might be inside the package the Commander wants so badly. We leave alone both the topic of our almost-kiss and the way we clung to each other in the wake of the beast's attack, and I'm grateful. I don't know how I feel about any of it, and I don't want to be the one to ruin things by talking about it.

In addition to a pair of guards, the tracker Melkin haunts the orchard near the house at night, and another tracker watches the cottage during the day as well. We can't do anything about the constant surveillance, so Logan works harder on his gadget, and I move on from my knife to practice with Dad's Switch.

The Switch is one of Logan's more useful inventions. It looks like a solid wooden walking staff, but one end is weighted enough to crush a man's skull, and the other conceals a spring-loaded double-edged blade. It takes hours of work before I can balance the heavier end, swing it like a mallet, and knock Bob, our practice dummy, flying. Even so, I'm still off balance enough that if I have to deal with two foes at once, I'll find myself skewered at the end of a sword before I can regain my footing, and I've yet to manage springing the blade after the initial hit without getting knocked to the ground.

Bob is about Logan's height and weighs in at an even one hundred seventy pounds. He's got me by forty pounds and five inches. Dad always said if I could take out the dummy, I could handle any man who tried to give me trouble.

I doubt he was thinking of Commander Chase when he said it.

Last year, Logan strung a heavy wire between two trees and hooked Bob to it. The dummy slides, swings, and moves with my own momentum, and while it isn't the same as fighting something with intelligence, he keeps me on my toes. I can run him through with my knife, yank the blade free, duck, and spin around to bury my weapon in his back while he slides toward me. The Switch is another story. I slam the weighted end of it into Bob, but can't spin the blade side around before my sparring partner swings back and sends me sprawling.

After my fourth disastrous attempt, I let fly with the most creative swear word I ever heard my father say and toss the Switch onto the grass beside me. I can't master it. Can't swing it around in time to deliver the crucial blow that could mean the difference between life and death. I lay back on the grass, squint against the glare of the afternoon sun, and suddenly feel like crying.

With Dad by my side, I'd always felt invincible. Now I feel like a freshly shorn lamb, stripped bare of a shield I never thought I'd lose. Whatever was in that package he refused to deliver, whatever he's keeping from the Commander's grasp, I have to help him. And to help him, I have to be prepared to face anything the Wasteland has to offer. Which means that failing at the Switch isn't an option.

I slowly push myself to my feet. Grasp the Switch. Close my eyes. Take a deep breath that smells of grass, sun-warmed dirt, and the fresh buds slowly unfurling in the orchard next door. If I keep my eyes closed, I can imagine Dad, standing behind me, his arms wrapped around me, his hands covering mine and holding me in place.

I widen my stance, crouch, and remember the last time we sparred together.

"Drop your shoulders a bit. You'll need the room to move." He tightens his grip on my hands when they start to slide together. *"No, you don't. Nice, wide grip. Keep it loose. Gives you balance and control. There's my girl."*

I drop my shoulders, widen my grip, and keep my eyes closed.

"All right, now, you've got a weapon on either end. You'll only have seconds to decide which one to use." He lets go of my hands, and places callused palms on my shoulders. *"Big man, sprinting toward you."*

"Weapon?"

"Doesn't matter, Rachel. He's twice your size and his speed will bring him in range within seconds. Which end do you use?" His

fingers curl around my shoulders as if willing me to know the answer.

"Blade. No time to swing the weighted end." I slide the blade free and crouch, the afternoon sun painting crimson swirls against my closed eyelids.

"Very good." He squeezes my shoulders and walks around to face me. "Now, if you must engage an opponent who is bigger, stronger, and faster, what do you do?"

"Take him down. Make it so he can't get up and come after me."

"Yes. He won't expect a Baalboden girl to know how to stop him. You get one chance to surprise him. Make full use of that advantage. Where do you make the first cut?" His eyes are deep gray, like a sky before the rain falls, and the fierce determination in them fills me with the same.

I'm Jared Adams's daughter. I can do this.

"Let him come in, then spin and slash the inner thigh as I turn. Cut open the artery." I draw in a deep breath, imagine a man barreling toward me, let him come almost too close for comfort, and then spin and slash, planting my left foot to keep my balance for the next move.

"Good! He's bleeding, but the pain hasn't hit yet, and he doesn't realize how badly he's hurt. He'll try to come after you. How do you stop him?"

"Cut the Achilles tendon as he passes me, then get out of range." I spin and slash again, the Switch beginning to feel like an extension of my arm as I thrust, turn, and slice in tune with my father's voice in my head.

He's clapping, pride and love written on his face. "You did it. I knew you could. I always knew you could."

"But what if I can't?" I lower the Switch. "What if one day I don't know what to do?" My throat closes, and I have to force myself to whisper, "What if you're gone, and I have no one left to teach me?"

But the scene in my mind falls silent. I never asked him those questions last time we sparred together. I never knew I should. And now, when I desperately want to fill in the blanks, to hear his voice tell me how to escape Baalboden, how to find him, and how to keep the Commander from finding what Dad so desperately wanted kept hidden, he's gone.

"I can teach you," Logan says quietly, and my eyes snap open.

He's a few yards away, his face shadowed by the branches of the tree he stands under. As he steps forward, I swear if I see pity on his expression, I won't speak to him ever again. But when the sunlight brushes against his face, there's no pity in his eyes. Instead, they're steady and filled with the same determination I always saw in Dad's.

He walks toward me and reaches out to slide his hand along the weighted end of the Switch I still hold.

"I miss him," he says. "That unmovable assurance he always carried with him. Like he could shoulder the weight of the world, and it wouldn't break him." His fingers brush mine, but neither of us pulls away.

My voice is quiet. "I miss his laugh. Remember?"

He smiles. "He filled a room when he was in it, didn't he?"

I nod, and the raw ache of feeling so alone subsides a bit.

"I know I can't take his place, and I don't want to. But I know how to use a Switch. And you'll need it in the Wasteland. Will you let me teach you?"

I smile a little. "If you don't mind getting humiliated by a girl, tech head."

"You're going to eat those words."

I toss my hair out of my face. "Make me."

CHAPTER EIGHTEEN

LOGAN

She stands in front of me, wild red hair streaming in the wind, a fierce gleam in her eyes. I want to reach out and touch her. Let some of the brilliant light she carries spill over onto me. I stretch out my hand, but rational thought kicks in at the last second. I grab Jared's Switch instead.

"This is too big for you. I'll make one your size, and we'll train."

"But the tracking device—"

It takes me a second to realize she still thinks I need time to work on the device to find Jared. I don't. I simply need another day or two to finish the one I'm making to find *her*. Just in case the Commander gets away with whatever treachery I'm sure he's planning.

"I can do both," I say. "Listen to me, Rachel." I wait until her eyes meet mine. "I want you to promise me that if the Commander ever makes you feel threatened, you'll do exactly what Jared taught you. Strike him down, and get away."

"If I do that while we're still in Baalboden, everyone I love will pay the price. I can't." Her voice is firm, but her eyes look shadowed. She knows the kind of danger she's in, but she's determined, if it comes to it, to lay down her life for Oliver. For me.

As if I could ever let her do that. Anger licks at me, chased by a cold frisson of fear. She isn't my Protector. I'm *hers*. And I'm not dropping this until I get her promise.

"Yes, you can." When she shakes her head, I snap at her. "You *can*. He's just a man. A cruel tyrant who doesn't deserve the power he's been abusing." Pain pierces me, swelling on a tide of something almost feral as I remember the heat floating off the dusty cobblestones, the heavy smell of my mother's blood, the way her breathing hissed in and out slowly until suddenly it was gone. *She* was gone.

"But—"

"Do you know what happens to girls in Baalboden who cross the Commander, Rachel? Do you?" My voice cracks. "They *die*. He kills them. He'll kill you if he finds out what we're planning."

"Logan—"

"He'll kill you. Do you understand?"

She nods.

I look away. At the distant orchard where men crouch behind trees waiting for us to run. Where the idyllic picture of early spring is nothing but a mirage covering the bloody truth of life in Baalboden. I look, but I can't quite erase the sight of my mother's lifeless eyes staring at something far beyond anything I could imagine. Missing her is a constant ache I carry with me.

"Logan?"

I turn toward her, braced for the pity I'm sure I'll find, but she has none. Instead, she watches me with steady understanding.

"I never told you how much I admire your mother."

The ache in my chest eases. "Really?"

"Really. Dad told me how she was the only woman in Baalboden who wasn't allowed to go through the Claiming ceremony again after her husband passed on. I guess he died before you were born?"

I nod. Mom never spoke of my father. Instead, she'd hold me close and say she was lucky. She had me, and who needed anything else?

"Dad also told me the Commander assigned himself as her Protector, but he wouldn't check in on her for weeks at a time. Don't you find that strange? Why break the protocol for your mom and no one else?"

"I don't know." But I wish I did. Maybe if he hadn't kept her from being Claimed again, she'd still be alive.

Rachel frowns, and says slowly, "It's almost like the Commander hated you from the very start. Dad said he, Oliver, and some of the other men would bring her food. See what she needed in between the Commander's visits."

"Until Oliver was sick. Jared was out on a mission. And no one else remembered us." The words are hard to say. The memories they evoke are worse. The bare cupboards. The desperation in Mom's eyes as days passed, and we slowly starved.

"She was a hero. It was unfair of the Commander to deny her real Protection. Unfair to treat her differently than any other woman here. It took courage to go to the market without permission. She did it for—"

"Me! She did it for me, and it cost her her life." I can't breathe past the sudden wave of guilt and grief tearing at me. "If I hadn't been hungry, she never would've risked it."

Rachel leans close until all I can see is her. "No. If you hadn't been there, she wouldn't have had anything left to live for at all. She loved you, and you were worth the risk. You still are."

We stare at each other as her words hang in the air between us. Then she steps back, looks at the ground, and says, "Are you going to make me a new Switch or not?"

Turning my attention back to the matter at hand is easy. Figuring out what to do with Rachel's words isn't. Setting them aside for now, I search for a stick heavy enough to turn into a Switch, and start working.

By late afternoon, I've finished making her Switch and have turned her loose on the dummy. The weighted end smacks into Bob with a satisfying crunch, and she spins the stick, releases the double-edged blade, and buries it into Bob's heart as he crashes back toward her.

She grins and yanks her weapon free. "For someone who spends his days hunched over boring old papers, you sure know how to create a nice killing stick."

Time to teach her who she's dealing with. "I didn't grow up in South Edge without learning a trick or two," I say as I pick up Jared's Switch. "Sheathe your blade. We'll count a solid touch from the blade end as a strike."

She sends her blade back into its hiding place, widens her stance, and rolls to the balls of her feet. I walk toward her, the resolve I feel to protect her blazing into something hard and bright in the face of her courage.

"I spend my days hunched over boring old papers, do I?" My stick whistles through the air, and she leaps back to dodge the blow. Spinning, I tap her with the sheathed blade before she can raise her arms in defense.

"My point," I say, and don't bother hiding my smirk.

She circles me. "Lucky shot."

I lash out again, but she's ready. Blocking me with the middle of her Switch, she whirls beneath my outstretched arms and slams the weighted end into my thigh.

Pride keeps me from swearing at the pain. Instead, I sweep her feet out from under her. She flips in midair and rolls forward as she lands, coming up with her stick ready.

The controlled grace of her movements would make Jared proud. I decide the warm emotion sweeping through me must be pride too.

"You're fast. That's good," I say, advancing toward her.

"You're not bad for a tech head."

We block, parry, and break apart. She's strong and quick, but I worry she doesn't know how to anticipate the unexpected. I step back, inviting an attack, and she charges forward, swinging the weighted end of her stick like a butcher slicing the head from a sheep. I wait until the last second, then drop to the ground and ram her with my shoulder. Her forward momentum carries her over the top of me and she lands face-first in the grass.

She spits dry blades of grass from her mouth, and swears, but a new respect for me is in her eyes.

I laugh, and my fear for her eases into something I can use to focus on planning. She stares at me, a tiny smile flitting across her lips, and the affection on her face makes me feel like the richest man in the world.

"I was a fighter long before I was a tech head." I offer her a hand up. "You need to be ready for an opponent who does the unexpected."

She takes my outstretched hand, closing her soft fingers over mine without breaking my gaze. The sun blazes a golden path through her fiery hair, and my eyes slide over her pale skin and come to rest on her lips. Warmth pools in my stomach and spreads lazily through me as I tug her hand and pull her closer.

I'm not going to kiss her. That would be . . . I don't know what that would be. I can't seem to think straight. All I see is *Rachel*, filling up my empty spaces and making me into more than I ever could be on my own.

Maybe this is what family does for one another. She's my family now. Which is why, even as I lean toward her, unable to tear my gaze away from the softness of her mouth, I tell myself I'm not going to kiss her.

She steps toward me, face upturned. I lean in.

Behind us, someone clears his throat.

CHAPTER NINETEEN

LOGAN

I drop her hand and whip around, my Switch ready. Oliver stands on our back porch with the sternest expression he can manage aimed straight at me.

Rachel steps back and bends to pick up her weapon. I find I'm suddenly very interested in the exact position of the sun, and I take a moment to study the sky. When I look back at Oliver, his brow is raised.

"Going to invite an old man in? Or going to stand there pretending I didn't just see—"

"We were sparring." Rachel hefts her Switch to prove it.

"That's not what we called it in my day," Oliver says, and motions for us to come inside the house with him.

I can't look at Rachel as we walk inside. The room feels charged with awkwardness, and I have absolutely no idea how to defuse it without just addressing my sudden, inexplicable attraction to her head on. Which I might do, if I could explain it. And if Oliver wasn't in the room.

He claps me on the shoulder and uses his other arm to drag Rachel to his side. "It's nice to see the two of you putting aside your differences and discovering how much you really have in common. Rachel, would you mind getting me some water?"

As Rachel hurries toward the kitchen, Oliver looks me in the eye. "You're a good man, Logan McEntire. You're the son I never had. I know I can trust you with her."

The weight of his trust lands heavily on top of the trust already placed in me by Jared. "It won't happen again," I say, though I don't know if I mean it.

He grins. "Oh, I wouldn't go making promises you might not be able to keep. Just see that if you do decide she's the one for you, you handle it properly."

The one for me? I stare at Rachel as Oliver leaves my side and enters the kitchen, settling his bulk at my cluttered table. It was just an impulse. She's beautiful and strong in a way I appreciate. Of course I find her attractive. It doesn't mean I'm ready to Claim her. Or anyone else, for that matter.

Feeling unaccountably irritated by Oliver's assumption, I follow him into the kitchen. Rachel settles on the floor, leaning against Oliver's legs as he takes out a towel-wrapped bundle of sticky buns and hands it to her. I take the other chair. Time to set aside the baffling subject of my feelings for Rachel and concentrate on something far more straightforward: my plan to get Oliver out of Baalboden with us.

Before I can speak, though, Oliver says, "You two may be right. I think Jared's still alive."

"What?" I lean forward as Rachel's eyes meet mine, full of

shock and eager anticipation.

"Why do you think that?" she asks, setting the sticky buns on the table.

"I talked with some folks who were out trading with that band of highwaymen that got themselves killed by the Cursed One the other day. Word among the city-states is that your father is the most wanted man in the Wasteland."

"Wanted for *what*?" I ask.

"For thievery and treason against the ruler of Rowansmark."

Rachel sits up straight. "That's a dirty lie! He never stole anything, and he wouldn't commit treason, either."

Oliver gives her shoulder a gentle squeeze. "I know that. Everyone who knows him knows that."

"He didn't steal that package from Rowansmark. Someone gave it to him," she says.

"I'm guessing whoever gave him that package is the one who committed treason," I say. "It's possible the Commander managed to bribe or coerce a citizen of Rowansmark into stealing it for him, intending to use Jared as the delivery person."

"Except Dad got suspicious, figured out what was inside—"

"And had the integrity and courage to keep it from the Commander," I say.

"But why not return it to Rowansmark if it belongs to them?" she asks.

Oliver shakes his head. "I don't know, but James Rowan is doing everything in his power to get it back. There's a reward posted. A year's supply of wheat, a head of cattle, and a lifetime appointment to Rowansmark's Military Council for whoever brings in your father. Alive."

Rachel and I are silent as the absurd generosity of the reward sinks in.

"No one's claimed the reward yet, so unless he got caught by the Cursed One, he's alive." Oliver gives Rachel's shoulder one more squeeze and heaves himself to his feet. "Thought I'd make a trip out here to tell you that." He picks up the water set before him and downs it in five long gulps. "Best be on my way. Don't want to get caught out after dark."

Rachel launches herself at his chest, clinging to him. "Not yet. We have something to tell you."

He looks at me.

"We're leaving the day after Claiming." I stand, wrapping my arm around his shoulders and hoping he understands that though I don't know how to show it, I realize I owe him my life. If he hadn't quietly defied the Commander's decree and befriended a dirty little street rat, I wouldn't be a man worthy of calling people like Jared, Rachel, and Oliver family. "We're traveling the Wasteland to find Jared. And we're bringing you with us."

"I'm too old for journeys across the Wasteland." Oliver wraps one arm around my middle as well. "I'm proud of you both. Jared would be too. Remember that, and stay alive."

"But you have to come with us!" Rachel's eyes are damp.

"We aren't coming back," I say. "We trust that Jared's reasons for not delivering the package to Baalboden are sound, so we won't be giving the Commander what he wants. When we don't come back, he'll take our treason out on you."

"How am I supposed to hike across all that wilderness looking for Jared? I'll just slow you down."

"There's another group of highwaymen scheduled to trade tomorrow. You'll go out to trade as usual, but you won't come back."

"The guards sweep the area with Identidiscs," he says.

"I have tech that can block those. You usually bring a donkey out with you to carry supplies to and from the trading area, don't you?" I ask.

He nods.

"This time, beneath your baked goods, pack clothing, food, a torch, and a weapon. Trade only for items you can use in the Wasteland. At the guards' shift change, mingle with the high-waymen's wagons, hand out baked goods to deflect suspicion if you have to, and then just walk right into the Wasteland. We'll join you the next day."

"That's downright brazen." Oliver's smile is full of pride.

"It will work. It has to." I clamp my hand on his shoulder. "You'll be invisible on the Identidisc. You can ride the donkey across the Wasteland to make the journey easier. We'll leave you at one of the safe houses until we find Jared. Then we can all build a new life together somewhere else."

His dark eyes meet mine, calm and assessing. "Seems a lot of risk for you two to take just for one old man."

"You're family. We aren't leaving without you."

"If you stay, he'll kill you." Rachel's voice breaks, and Oliver hauls her close.

"Don't cry, Rachel-girl. I aim to be a great-granddaddy. If that takes riding an ass across a godforsaken wilderness, I guess that's what I'll do."

"Thank you." I slip a magnetic wrist cuff into his hand.

"Wear that over your wristmark on trading day and the Identi-disc won't be able to find you."

Oliver holds on to us both a moment longer, and then he's gone. The cottage feels empty without him.

CHAPTER TWENTY

LOGAN

The Claiming ceremony is tomorrow. By this point, Oliver should be mingling with the traders, getting close to disappearing into the Wasteland to wait for us. I finish the last piece of equipment I need to cover every conceivable contingency for our mission. Need to evade another tracker? Not a problem. Guards refuse to be left behind? I can handle that. Rachel and I get separated? I can find her anywhere. The Commander double-crosses us?

I almost hope he tries.

I have every avenue covered, every plan fleshed out, every piece of technology working as it should. The sense of triumph I feel at having an edge on the Commander and any other tracker he employs to go after Jared is a vicious light burning within me.

Rachel feels it too. I can tell by the brightness in her eyes as she double-checks our weapons while I make sure the list of last-minute provisions I want to purchase at the market today is in my inner cloak pocket.

We've avoided touching each other since our sparring match. I don't know her reasons, but mine are clear: I'm attracted to her. I've always found her beautiful, but now I see beneath that to the courageous, passionate girl who would go against any foe to fight for those she loves. She's . . . admirable.

But I'm not sure the craving I feel to run my hands through her hair and pull her to me can be accurately labeled admiration. Until I can get it under control, I keep my distance. I have to. I'm standing in Jared's place. He trusts me. *She* trusts me, a fragile development at once terrifying and immensely gratifying.

I'm not ready to discuss my irrational inner thoughts, but still I want to reach out to her with something more than battle plans and Worst Case Scenarios. With that in mind, I look up from my market list and say quietly, "We leave day after tomorrow, and we won't be spending a lot of time together before then, so—"

"Why not?" She looks up from the weapons she's packing.

"I have some last-minute supplies and information to gather, and this is your last chance to see Sylph. I thought you'd like to spend the day with her."

Pain flashes across her face and she resumes packing the weapons.

"Anyway, I wanted to give you a compliment."

Her eyes widen, flash to mine, and then look down again. "Why?"

"Because I realize, even though it doesn't make logical sense given what I know of you, that you need softer words from me sometimes."

Now she's looking at me like I've suddenly sprouted two

heads, and I feel like an idiot.

"You're telling me you're going to give me a compliment even though I shouldn't logically need one?" Her voice doesn't sound pleased.

I pick back through my words, but don't see anything that could cause offense, so I nod. "Common sense would dictate a woman like you shouldn't be dependent upon—"

"What is that supposed to mean?" She throws the bow and arrow set she's holding onto the floor and stands, pink spots of color in her cheeks. "Why shouldn't I need a few compliments?"

I have no idea how this conversation went awry so quickly. I just want to tell her something nice. Does it have to be a ten-minute discussion about motives and semantics?

Maybe if I enunciate clearly, she'll understand. I lean toward her and say with exquisite clarity, "Because of the kind of woman you are."

Speaking slowly solved absolutely nothing. She looks like she might pick up one of the weapons and throw it at my head. I feel more than a little irritated myself.

She speaks around gritted teeth. "And what kind of woman do you think I am, Logan McEntire?"

I snap right back at her. "Confident. Strong. Capable. Stunning. An equal partner in this endeavor in every sense of the word."

The pink in her cheeks darkens, but instead of sparks, her eyes look soft and warm. I have no idea how a compliment delivered in anger can work that kind of magic with her, but I'm grateful.

"You think I'm stunning?" she asks, and suddenly I feel like the tunic laced at my throat is choking me.

"I didn't say that."

"Yes, you did," she says softly, a tiny smile on her lips even as she refuses to meet my gaze.

Did I? I scroll back through the words I threw at her and realize she's right. I did say *stunning*. Which, incidentally, isn't a crime. Anyone looking at her would think the same.

I shrug and make sure I sound casual when I say, "I guess I did. Ready?" I pull my cloak over my shoulders and wait for her to call me on my words. To demand an explanation I'm not ready to give.

Instead, she says, "Let's go." Her voice sounds stilted and unnatural, but I let it go. I have no idea what else to say.

The tension between us lingers as we walk the dusty road into town with nothing but the early-morning sounds of farm animals and birds to keep us company in our silence.

The torch boys have already extinguished the streetlights in Center Square, and we pass the stage as workers scrub the wood and set up booths in preparation for tomorrow's Claiming ceremony.

I'm grateful we'll be leaving Baalboden before Rachel reaches Claiming age. The thought of standing behind her on the stage while a group of eager townsmen try to convince me to give her over to them forever makes me want to knock their heads together. Not because I can't give Rachel to the right man for her. But I know every available bachelor in Baalboden, and while I've never really considered it before this moment, I'm quite confident none of them measure up to her.

We enter North Hub and arrive at Sylph's house. Rachel

barely says good-bye before heading inside. I plant myself on the road and wait until I see her enter the house before continuing on toward Lower Market.

Halfway there, I duck down a side street, take a short-cut through an alley, and slide into the back entrance of the butcher's, where the first of my black-market contacts waits to give me the most current information on Rowansmark and the search for Jared.

I'm going into the Wasteland armed to the teeth with knowledge, technology, and the kind of fierce tenacity the Commander always assumes no one owns but him.

I can't wait to prove him wrong.

CHAPTER TWENTY-ONE

RACHEL

Sylph, her mother, and her oldest brother are waiting for me in their main room. Sylph shoots me a quick grin as she puts on her cloak. "We're going to get my final fitting at Madame Illiard's North Hub shop. Mama won't let me buy anything from Madame's market stall. She says her only daughter will have a custom-made dress. Can you believe the Claiming ceremony is tomorrow?"

She lingers over the word *tomorrow* as if her dreams are pinned to it. Maybe they are. I try to smile as she bounces next to me, chattering about her dress and the weather predictions for tomorrow's ceremony, but it's hard to pretend. Knowing I'm leaving day after tomorrow twists me up inside until I don't know how to feel.

I want to stop wasting time. Stop lingering while somewhere out there, Dad is alone in the Wasteland. I also want to savor every precious moment I have with Sylph in case I never get the chance to see her again.

Sylph doesn't notice my lack of response. We've fallen into step behind her mother and brother, and she's whispering about her secret hope that Smithson West will Claim her. I listen with half an ear, nod at the appropriate times, and try to memorize everything I love about her while grief swells within me and makes it hard to breathe.

We've been friends since we shared a table at Life Skills, the few years of schooling deemed appropriate for a girl in Baalboden. We learned things like cooking, bargaining, sewing, and proper etiquette when out in public with our Protectors.

The boys received six more years of schooling and learned things like math, reading, the history of the Wasteland, the differing laws and protocols of the other eight city-states, and Commander Chase's pivotal role in saving the citizens of Baalboden from the Cursed One.

I never thought it was fair that anatomy decided what my brain was fit for. Dad agreed, and I'd soaked up everything he could teach me. Once, I'd tried to teach Sylph the wonders of being able to open a book and understand the words inside, but she'd shrugged it off. She didn't need to read. She'd have a Protector for that.

Now I study her dark green eyes, lit with pleasure at the prospect of our day, her black curls that constantly mock her mother's attempts to conjure a ladylike style, and the excitement quivering through her softly rounded frame, and lean forward to give her a hug.

She hugs me back. We enter Madame Illiard's shop, where fancy Claiming dresses hang near the front window and bolts of fabric line the walls in a feast of color. Two tables are set up on either side of the shop. One has baskets of useless things like beads, buttons, and rolls of ribbon. The other is empty of anything but a measuring tape and two pairs of scissors.

I don't know how anyone can spend more than five minutes inside this place without going stark-raving mad. Sylph, however, bounces on her toes and hugs her mother as they examine the almost completed Claiming dress designed just for her. Seeing them pressed close to each other as they finger the fabric and admire a piece of lace sends an unwelcome shaft of longing through me.

I don't usually miss my mother. How can I? She died right after I was born, and I never knew her. But at moments like these, I miss what we might have had together. I imagine our hair would've been the same shade of red. Our eyes the same shade of blue. Maybe we would've both loved lemon cake and hated spinach. Or maybe we would've both thought the only truly useful items in Madame Illiard's shop were the scissors, because pointy things make excellent weapons.

I'll never know, and thinking about it won't help me escape Baalboden and find Dad, so I shove the longing away and follow Sylph into the windowless back room for her fitting.

Nearly two hours pass before Madame pronounces Sylph's dress perfect. The dark green velvet hugs her upper body and falls in graceful lines to her ankles. Black lace panels shimmer between the skirt's folds, and black ribbon laces up the back. When Madame Illiard and Sylph's mother leave the room to haggle over the final cost, Sylph twirls in front of me and asks, "Don't you love it?"

"It's beautiful."

"Do you think Smithson will like it?"

"I'm sure he will."

She grabs my arm, and looks at me properly for the first time. "What's wrong? You don't think Smithson is right for me?"

"I think he's a nice man," I say, because Sylph's heart is set on him, and because it's true. He's quiet, sturdy, and seems to want nothing more than a wife, a home, and a decent crop from his patch of farmland. "He's perfect for you."

She glows for a moment, but then her expression falls. "I wish you were in this year's ceremony with me."

"I'm not yet seventeen." I try to sound as if I'm disappointed too, though I'm not. I can't even think about wanting to parade across the stage in Center Square while one of the eligible townsmen decides I'd make a perfect bride. Besides, what do I know about being an obedient wife? There are much more important qualities to have than a docile disposition.

Logan seems to agree.

Warmth spreads through me at the thought of Logan's fumbling attempt at giving me a compliment today.

Stunning.

His words feel like a gift I want to keep reopening when no one else is looking. What would Sylph say if she knew I'd almost kissed Logan? If she knew I sometimes watch him while he's bent over his inventions and want to trace my fingers over the muscles in his shoulders for no apparent reason at all?

The secret trembles at the edge of my lips, but there are other secrets right behind it. Secrets about the Commander. Oliver. Treachery. Sylph can't know anything about that. It's the only protection I can offer her after I'm gone.

Sylph is still talking, rambling on about ways to get me into the Claiming ceremony with her. None of her ideas are plausible. Finally, she slumps her shoulders and says, "You're so close to seventeen! If only your dad was still here, he could've petitioned for a special sanction . . ." Her eyes widen and fill with tears.

"Sylph—"

She runs to me and envelopes me in a cloud of velvet and lace. "I'm so sorry! I wasn't thinking."

I push her away gently. "I'm not mad. I know you didn't mean anything by it."

Her eyes brighten. "Maybe Logan could Claim you!"

My heart speeds up, but I shake my head. "Don't be silly."

She grabs my hands and dances in place. "Wouldn't that be romantic? I'd be Mrs. Smithson West. And you'd be Mrs. Logan McEntire. We could host dinner parties together, and go to Lower Market together, and—"

I laugh a little desperately and link my fingers with hers. She twirls us around, and I let her spin me, let myself ignore the Wasteland, the bounty on my father's head, and the complications lying between Logan and me. She doesn't know it, but this will be our last time together. I want to leave her with nothing but happy memories.

We stumble and fall to the floor, doubled over in breathless laughter. I wrap my arms around her and squeeze. She hugs me back, but then her laughter chokes into the kind of silence she's rarely capable of. I turn my head to see the cause and feel my stomach lurch.

Commander Chase stands in the back doorway, his sword drawn and his dark eyes cold.

CHAPTER TWENTY-TWO

RACHEL

Sylph's arms tighten around me, and I squeeze her back before slowly disengaging. My knees are shaking as I force myself to my feet, moving to stand between the Commander and my best friend.

"You're coming with me." He gestures toward the door behind him. The polished silver buttons on his crisp blue uniform catch the morning sunlight and wink like little diamonds. I look away.

It doesn't occur to me to argue, despite my promise that I would strike him down and get away if he threatened me when Logan wasn't around to help. Sylph is here. She'll pay the price for my actions just as surely as I will, and I'm not about to risk it. Besides, he still needs me.

I hope.

"Rachel!" Sylph whispers as I head toward the door. I toss one look at her and try to smile, though my lips are trembling. I step into the morning light, a breeze playing with my hair as I face the trio of Brute Squad guards waiting for me on the cobblestone street.

Their swords are drawn too.

The Commander presses his palm against my back. Without my cloak, the heat from his body scorches mine.

"Get in," he says, and the Brute Squad steps aside to reveal a large mule-drawn covered wagon.

I glance around the street, but if anyone notices what's happening, they aren't stopping to stare. I can't blame them. Shrugging off the Commander's hand, I refuse the assistance of the guard closest to me and climb into the back of the wagon. The Commander and one of the three guards follow on my heels. In a moment, the wagon lurches forward and rumbles over the cobblestone street.

The heavy canvas covering dilutes the morning sun into something dim and gray, and my eyes struggle to adjust. It takes a few seconds to notice the cloth-covered lump leaning against the far wall of the wagon. Foreboding fills me, an oily poison that makes me queasy.

I don't know what's under the cloth, but it can't be good.

"Have a seat." The Commander moves past me, knocking me into the wooden bench lining the wagon wall behind me, and settles on the opposite bench, right beside the lump. His sword is still drawn.

The guard braces himself against the back of the wagon and stands, sword drawn, blocking the exit. I want to scan my surroundings looking for possible escape routes, but I can't tear my eyes away from the lump. There's something horribly familiar about its shape, but I don't want to put it into words because it isn't possible.

It can't be possible.

"You and that inventor have been keeping secrets." The Commander's eyes are bright, hard orbs lighting the dim space with malice. "Did he really think I wouldn't know your every move before you do?"

I look at the cloth-covered lump and dread pools in my stomach. It's just the right size for a person.

Logan. The Commander's always hated Logan. He didn't want him to come with me. I look at the person shrouded in cloth and try to find my voice, though I have no idea what I'll say.

"Not going to tell me what you're up to?"

I open my mouth but nothing comes out.

"I see you need a bit of convincing." He smiles and drives his sword into the lump. Whoever is trapped beneath the cloth sucks in a raspy breath and moans. Blood blossoms beneath the cloth and spreads like a fast-blooming rose.

My breath leaves me as if I've been hit in the stomach. "Who is that?"

Oh please, oh please let it be a stranger. Another guard. Another object lesson. Please. Don't let it be Logan.

The Commander ignores me. "I don't trust Logan McEntire. I don't trust you, either, but you have a quality he lacks."

I can't look away from the blood, and I feel a scream clawing for freedom at the back of my throat.

"Do you know what that is?" He pulls his sword free, and the person beneath the cloth twitches. "It's loyalty."

I can't breathe. I try to stand, but my knees won't hold me, and I crumple to the splintery wagon floor.

Logan.

Ignoring the Commander, I crawl toward the person beneath the cloth. I'm nearly there when the Commander drives his sword into the wagon floor, inches from my face.

His voice is harsh as he bites each syllable into pieces. "Logan isn't loyal. He thinks he is, but if I put him to the test, he'd fail. His own agenda will always be more important to him than anyone else."

My breath catches on a shuddering sob, and I try to crawl around the sword. It nicks my shoulder as I pass, and the Commander laughs.

"You, on the other hand, are loyal to a fault. You won't scheme, manipulate, or betray. Not if it will cost you someone you love." He yanks his sword free of the floor and slides it into the blood-soaked lump again. "No, you'll go to the ends of the Wasteland, do everything that's asked of you, ignore your own ethics and instincts, as long as you get to save the one you love."

I've reached the cloth and am tearing at it with shaking hands while the person beneath it moans in agony.

"Please." I can't loosen the cloth. "Please!" I look at the Commander, and his scar twists his smile into a grotesque parody of mirth.

It will be a guard. A prisoner. Someone who means nothing to me. I can't bear to be wrong.

I can't bear to lose Logan.

"Allow me to help you," the Commander says in a voice filled with malice. Pulling his sword free again, he slices it through the cloth and splits it top to bottom.

I snatch at the pieces and yank them free. A scream builds in my chest as I stare.

Not Logan.

Not a stranger.

Oliver.

Oliver.

He's supposed to be outside the Wall now. Safe. He's supposed to be, but he isn't.

Oliver looks at me, sadness and pride mingling with the love he's always shown me, and then moans again. I come undone.

"No, no, no, no, no." There's so much blood. So much. It pours from his chest and covers my hands, and I can't stop it.

I can't stop it.

"You shouldn't have plotted behind my back," the Commander says, his voice as hard as the wagon floor beneath me. "You were disloyal, and now it's cost you."

"It's going to be okay," I tell Oliver. Tears burn my eyes, and I have to blink to see him. "It's going to be okay," I lie, because I don't know what else to do.

He tries to speak, but blood bubbles from his lips instead. I grab the cloth and press it against his chest with both hands.

"It's going to be okay," I say again, and press harder, though I don't know how to make my words true.

Oliver shakes his head slightly and tries to raise his arm. I grab his hand with mine and wrap our fingers together the way he used to when I was little and he was walking me through the market. His hand still swallows mine, though now his skin is like ice.

"Save him," I say to the Commander. "Please. Get him to a doctor. I'll do anything you want. Anything."

"Yes, you will," he says. "Because if you don't, I'll kill Logan in ways the citizens of Baalboden will remember for decades to come."

"Logan?" I look up, tears obscuring my view of the Commander's face. "I don't understand. This is Oliver. I want you to save *Oliver!*"

"Oh, it's far too late for him," he says and, with a flick of his wrist, drives his sword through Oliver's neck.

The scream inside me rips through my throat. I reach for the sword, but it's already gone. Throwing myself on Oliver, I shove the cloth against his neck and beg for him to look at me, though I know he can't.

He can't, and he never will again. Wild sobs choke me, and I can barely find the air to let them loose.

Rough hands grab my arms and pull me from Oliver. I scream and beat at the person behind me to no avail. The wagon stops, and two more guards enter, scoop Oliver's body up inside the cloth, and haul him out. The guard holding me tosses me to the floor and exits as well, leaving me huddled at the Commander's feet.

He crouches to my level, Oliver's blood still glistening on his blade.

"You will be in the Claiming ceremony tomorrow."

I stare at his sword, cross my arms over my chest, and rock back and forth.

"Are you listening?" He grabs my chin with his hand, forcing me to meet his gaze. "Pay attention. Logan McEntire's life depends on it."

My teeth are chattering, and my body shudders, but I make myself nod. Logan is all I have left. Whatever it takes to get him off the Commander's kill list, so help me, I'll do it.

"You will be in the Claiming ceremony. I've seen the way Logan looks at you. I have no doubt he'll try to Claim you." His smile flickers at the edges. "You are going to turn him down."

I'm too numb to protest. To wonder what the Commander thinks he sees when Logan looks at me. To argue that no one's ever turned down an eligible man in the history of Baalboden's Claiming ceremonies.

"When you turn him down, I will declare you a ward of the state. Logan's influence will be legally severed, and you will then travel the Wasteland without him." His voice lowers. "You will show my tracker where your father hid the package he received at Rowansmark, and you will return it to me, or Logan will be tortured and killed."

He lets go of my chin and runs his palm across my cheek, tangling his fingers in my hair. "Do I make myself clear?"

I nod, a wobbly, uncertain movement, and watch the blood slide down his blade.

"Until tomorrow," he says, and then he's gone.

CHAPTER TWENTY-THREE

RACHEL

The wagon lurches forward again, and it takes a moment to realize I'm not alone in the back. One of the guards is sitting on the bench behind me, holding a paper-wrapped package in one hand and a damp cloth in the other.

I scoot as far away from him as I can without touching the puddle of Oliver's blood seeping slowly into the floorboards. When he ignores me, I wrap my arms around my knees and try not to let the agonized wailing I hear inside my head leave my lips.

Oliver is dead.

Dead.

He'll never be a great-granddaddy. He'll never hand me another sticky bun, or call me Rachel-girl, or see me clear my father's name.

The truth is too harsh to touch, and I shy away from it before it sears itself into my brain and becomes real. Instead, I find a quiet place within myself where the Commander doesn't exist, my family is still intact, and I'm not covered in anyone's blood.

The harsh keening inside my head becomes muted—the grief of some other girl. Not mine.

I rock, holding myself as if I'll fly into a million little pieces if I let go.

The guard says something, but I can't hear him. If I listen to him, I might hear the grief-stricken wail of the girl who just lost something precious.

He slaps me, but I can't feel it. He says something else, then crouches down in front of me and scrubs my face with rough persistence. When he pulls back, the damp cloth in his hand is covered in bright red patches, like little crimson flowers decorating the fabric.

Bile rises at the back of my throat, and I tear my eyes away from the cloth.

He removes the string on the package he carries and tears off the paper. I don't look to see what he has. It might be covered in red too.

He's talking again, louder this time. His boots dig into the hard wooden floor beneath us as he stands. I catch a glimpse of crimson staining the edge of his right sole, and tuck my head toward my chest.

My chest is covered in rust-scented crimson.

Covered.

I beat at it. Tear at it with frantic fingers. I have to get it off me. I *have* to.

The guard helps. Rough hands unlace my tunic, and I claw my way free. I'm panting, harsh bursts of air that fill the wagon.

He attacks my skin with his red-flowered cloth again, and

I twist my body, trying to get away. I don't want him to touch me with that thing. I can't stand to have it touch me for another second.

He drops the cloth. In its place, he holds a new tunic that looks just like my old one used to look. Pure white. Crimson-free.

I let him slide it over my head. Let the rough linen threads scrape against my skin. Maybe if they scrape hard enough, I'll forget. About the crimson. About the awful wailing I still hear inside me.

About what I just lost.

The guard pulls me to my feet and fumbles with the laces on my skirt, but I don't help him. How can I? I'm not really there. I'm home, on our back porch, sipping lemonade while my family is close by, just out of sight.

He says something, but I don't hear him. I'm too busy listening to the deep rumble of men's voices coming from somewhere behind my back porch.

My skirt puddles around my feet, and he lifts me out of it.

The lemonade I sip is the perfect combination of tart and sweet. I want to share it with my family, but they stay just out of reach.

He pulls a new skirt over my head. Light blue, just like the one he removed.

Light blue like the summer sky I see from my porch.

I'm sitting on the wagon's bench.

No, I'm sitting on our rocker.

My shoes are gone.

It's summer. I don't need shoes.

Now, they're back again. A stranger is tying them. Which is silly, because I can tie my own shoes. If I want to. Which I don't, because the summer sun is hot, and I'm too tired.

I'm so tired.

I stop rocking on the porch. Or maybe the wagon stops.

I'm not in a wagon. I never was.

Hands lift me up and set me down on a cobblestone street. I stare at my boots. They're the same color and design as always, but the scuffs and creases are gone as if they never were.

Behind me, a wagon clip-clops away. I don't turn. I don't know where my porch is. Where the summer sun went. It's cold now. Cold and gray and the air feels damp against my skin.

Someone calls my name, and I look up to see Sylph, her dark eyes full of fear, beckoning from the doorway to my right. As I turn and walk toward her, I hear the faint wailing of the grief-stricken girl grow louder, and clamp my lips tight to hold it in.

CHAPTER TWENTY-FOUR

LOGAN

I've met with contacts at the butcher's, the blacksmith's, and a corner table at Thom's Tankard. No one knows anything more about Rowansmark or Jared than Oliver already told me.

I need to know what Jared took from Rowansmark, who gave it to him, and why. I need to understand why he hid it instead of bringing it into Baalboden. Most of all, I need a clear picture of the Commander's role in all of this.

I might not be able to gain more information on what is happening outside our Wall, but I know how to get information on the Commander's activities. Wrapping my cloak around myself, I walk through South Edge in circuitous routes, ducking through alleys and backyards, making sure I lose my followers. Approaching my destination with caution, I knock and wait to be allowed entrance.

Monty runs his business out of his kitchen at a table that leans precariously toward the floor. On one side of the room, stacks of goods rest in haphazard piles, evidence of a successful week in the information-for-hire trade. On the other, Monty leans back in a chair, a wicked-looking dagger lying across his lap, sipping a mug of ale and watching me with narrow dark eyes.

"Monty." I nod and settle into an open chair beside him.

He sets his mug on the table and lets his chair legs slam back onto the scuffed, dirty floor beneath him. "Logan McEntire. Haven't seen the likes of you in these parts for several years. Thought maybe you'd outgrown good old South Edge."

I don't take him up on his clever invitation to tell him what I've been doing and with whom. For one, he already knows I earned the apprenticeship with Jared. Everyone does. For another, in a room where information is part of the currency, I'm not about to part with mine for free.

Instead, I rest my elbows on the table, steeple my fingers, and look at him steadily over the top of my hands. "How many times in the past three years have you been forced to relocate before the guards arrested you or one of your clients? Five? Six? Help me out here, because I've lost track."

Monty's eyes harden, but his expression remains calm. "What is it you want, Logan?"

"It's what *you* want, Monty. What I can do for you."

He's silent for a moment, assessing me while he wipes beads of condensation from his mug of ale. Then he says, "What can you do for me?"

Reaching into my cloak, I pull out a copper circle about the size of a flat orange. It glows beneath the faint sunlight leaking in past the layer of filth on Monty's kitchen window.

"Shiny." Monty says, his tone noncommittal. "But I already have plenty of shiny."

I place the disc on the table. "Still have that stolen Identidisc around here somewhere?"

He lifts his eye to mine, and his expression reminds me of a snake. Cold. Calculating. And dangerous if cornered. Finally, he nods. "Let's say I do have one of those. What does that have to do with this?"

"The last thing you need is a guard wandering through with an Identidisc and seeing a list of anyone you happen to be doing business with at the moment. It compromises your reputation, inhibits your ability to do business, and could easily land you in the dungeon. This"—I rub my thumb across the glowing copper surface—"blocks every wristmark within a thirty-yard radius. Basically, if you turn this on whenever you do business, everyone in your house will be dark to the guards."

He blinks once more and when his eyes meet mine, greed peeks out behind the cold calculation.

I have him.

"I want proof it works," he says, and gets up to rummage through his cupboards, his dagger still grasped in his hand. In seconds, he returns to the table carrying a black Identidisc. It's an older model, but a glance at it shows the battery still has enough juice left to take a reading. I remain still while he powers it up and sends out a sonic pulse.

Both of our names show up on the screen.

So does the name Anthony Ruiz.

I frown at Monty. "Who's Anthony Ruiz?"

Monty shrugs. "A boy who delivers messages through South Edge. Never mind him, turn on your device."

I comply and wait while the Identidisc sends out another

pulse. This time the screen shows no list of citizens in the immediate area.

Monty sets down the Identidisc and looks at me. "How
much?"

"I'm thinking it's fairly priceless."

"I can put a price on anything. What do you want?"

"Money would be nice," I say, and Monty's lips thin. "But I'll
settle for useful information instead."

"What kind of information is worth a device like this?"

"I'd like to know what the Commander's been up to lately."

"That's a pretty vague request."

I nod. "Then I guess you'd better tell me everything you
know about him, his activities, and anything unusual happening in the compound, and let me decide what's useful for my
purposes and what isn't."

Monty shakes his head. "Too steep a price, Logan."

I shrug, scoop the copper disc off the table, and stand. "I'll be
on my way, then." I'm halfway through the door when he calls
me back.

"Fine. Sit down. Leave the disc. I'll tell you what I've heard."

I return to the table, set the disc in front of me, and listen
while Monty tells me the few things he knows for sure about
Commander Chase.

Fact 1: The Commander has a small object attached to a
chain and wears it underneath his uniform. Most sources agree
he never takes this pendant off.

I don't see how this is relevant or useful to me, but I file it
away just in case. If nothing else, I can use the chain to choke
him during hand-to-hand combat if it ever comes to that.

Fact 2: After Jared's disappearance, the Commander sent two couriers on missions, but neither of them were heading toward Rowansmark. They haven't returned yet, though the first is due any day.

This might be nothing more than the usual messages, negotiations, and trade between our city-state and another. But the fact that the Commander neglected to send any official message to Rowansmark in the wake of the accusations against his top courier is suspicious. Why not reach out to make peace? Offer to help bring Jared in? The only answer I can come up with is that the Commander needs to find Jared first.

Fact 3: This morning, every remaining tracker in the city except Melkin was sent out on a mission.

I've never heard of so many trackers being given missions at once. I can only assume they've been tasked to cover all four corners of the Wasteland in the search for Jared, even while Rachel and I look for the package. I don't like the fact that Melkin wasn't included in the mass send-off this morning. Either he's going to be part of our mission, or the Commander has a double-cross up his sleeve.

Let him try it. He isn't the only one who knows how to think three steps ahead.

I leave the house and a rail-thin boy with hungry eyes detaches from the surrounding shadows and approaches me. I'm guessing this is Anthony Ruiz, messenger boy.

"Logan McEntire?" He waits well out of sword range for my reply.

"Yes."

Someone bangs a door farther down the street, and the boy

tenses like he's ready to run. "Roderigo Angeles is looking for you. His wife needs you to return to Madame Illiard's shop in North Hub immediately."

Rachel. She snuck out again. And she's been caught. The image of my mother's body wavers and re-forms into Rachel lying broken and bloody at the Commander's feet.

The boy says something else, but I can't hear anything beyond the pulse roaring in my ears. I toss him a coin for his trouble and hurry toward the main street, fear driving my steps.

CHAPTER TWENTY-FIVE

LOGAN

She hasn't snuck out. Instead, she's huddled on the floor, pressed against the back wall of Madame Illiard's stockroom. I can't process this Rachel. I've never seen her like this.

Sylph is sitting near Rachel, watching her and crying. I ignore Mrs. Angeles and Madame Illiard in favor of heading straight for the girls. Sylph looks up and stands so I can take her place.

I crouch on the floor beside Rachel. She looks into my eyes, and there's nothing but glassy shock in hers. My heart sinks. "Rachel? What's wrong?"

She begins rocking as if she needs that simple rhythm to keep herself anchored.

"Can you tell me?" I ask, my mind racing. Maybe something happened to Jared, and my contacts hadn't heard of it. Maybe she's realized the magnitude of what it means to leave Baalboden forever, though I doubt that would cause this state of shock. Maybe a man hurt her. I don't know how, since she's been in the

Angeleses' care the entire time, but I have to acknowledge the possibility.

If that's the case, I'm going to hunt down the perpetrator and kill him. In the most inhumane method I can possibly devise. And then I'll invent something I can use to reanimate him and kill him all over again.

Her lips tremble, and she clamps both hands across her mouth.

"Rachel?" I ask, but she isn't listening.

Mrs. Angeles approaches me. "The Commander showed up while Rachel and Sylph were in the fitting room. He took Rachel."

Panic erases all rational thought from my head. "Where did he take her?" I ask, trying to keep my voice calm for Rachel's sake, though I hear the edge beneath it.

"We don't know."

"How long was she gone?"

"Over an hour. When she returned, she was like this."

Fierce anger surges through me. I can't speak or I might release it on those who don't deserve it. Instead, I turn back to Rachel. I'm in over my head here. I can't fix this. Can't understand where to begin making it right if I don't have all the information. And she can't bear to tell me. She might tell Oliver, but he's already in the Wasteland.

"It's going to be okay," I whisper so no one else can hear me. "You can talk about it with Oliver soon. He can help."

She rocks faster, banging her head against the wall behind her. I lunge for her, wrap my arms around her, and pull her against me. Pressing my mouth against her ear, I whisper promises I don't know how to keep. She quiets into an unnatural stillness that scares me more than the rocking did.

"He left this for her when he dropped her off," Mrs. Angeles says, and hands me a parcel wrapped with blue ribbon.

I accept the parcel and help Rachel to her feet.

"She hasn't spoken since she returned," Sylph says.

I meet her tear-filled eyes and make another promise I don't know if I can keep. "I'll get her to speak to me. She just needs to go home now."

Tightening my arm around Rachel, I guide her from the shop and into weak afternoon sunlight shining through a haze of mist that makes visibility sketchy after twenty yards or so.

I almost hope someone tries attacking us. The rage within me begs for a target.

The fact that the real target is the most well-protected man in the city makes no difference to me. He's mine now. I don't know how I'll do it, but before my life is over, I'll end his.

"I'm taking you home," I say to her, though I don't expect a response. "Will it be too difficult to walk?"

She doesn't respond to that, either, so I watch her gait carefully. If she's been violated, she'll have trouble walking.

If she's been violated . . . I can't bear to think of it.

She walks with wooden steps, her eyes on the ground. Despite the evidence that physically she can handle the journey, I can't bear to put her through it. Instead, I decide to use what little coin I still have on me to purchase a wagon ride home.

I guide her to a stop in Center Square. She stands still, looking at our feet, and I whistle for a driver. She jerks away from me at the sound, and trembles.

My heart hurts as I gather her to me again and say, "It's okay, Rachel."

She leans into me, closes her eyes, and breathes deeply. I press my lips to the crown of her head, and watch the driver ease his wagon to a stop in front of us.

I give my address to the driver and try to tug her toward the back of the wagon.

She digs her heels in and pulls against my arm.

"You don't need to walk. We'll take a ride home. It'll be easier on you this way," I say, and something within her breaks loose.

She twists free of my arm and takes off.

I race after her as she cuts through Center Square and flies into South Edge. I'm a fool. Of course he picked her up in a wagon. He wasn't going to hurt her on the streets where anyone could see and begin questioning why the Commander feels himself so far above the standard he sets for every other man in the city.

She turns a corner and slides into an alley. I follow just in time to see her stumble and fall toward the cobblestones. Lunging forward, I catch her, twisting my body so that I land on the street beneath her.

Her breath scrapes my ear in harsh pants, and she's shaking from head to toe. I gather her to my chest and say, "I'm sorry. I'm so sorry." My voice breaks, and I have to swallow hard to get the next words out. "I didn't know he had you in a wagon. I was trying to spare you the long walk home. I'm sorry."

She feels unbelievably fragile in my arms. I don't know how to get us home without hurting her further, but my options are limited.

A trio of men, swords drawn, block the mouth of the alley. The middle one smiles wide enough to show gaps where his teeth should be, and says, "Give us yer money and no one gets hurt."

For one brief, blazing second, I imagine honing the rage blistering through me into something I can use to obliterate the sorry excuses for human beings who dare to threaten us now. It wouldn't be hard. They're drunkards. Already shaking with withdrawal. Desperate to have just enough money for their next jug.

As tempting as the idea is, the confrontation isn't worth it. I can toss a small handful of coin away from us and walk out of the alley as they scramble across the filthy cobblestones to snatch it.

Or I could if I didn't have to worry about getting Rachel home.

Looking up, she sees the men and freezes. I'm about to coach her on my exit strategy when she sucks in a raspy breath, and her expression goes from blank to feral in a heartbeat. She pushes against my chest and leaps to her feet. I stand as well, reaching out a cautionary hand to her.

"They just want money. I'll take care of it."

She isn't listening. Shoving my hand away from her, she curls her lip into a fierce snarl. Before I can stop her, she whips her knife out of its sheath, raises it above her head, and rushes toward the men.

"Rachel, no!" I grab for my sword as the men brace themselves for her attack. I race for her, but I'm too late.

Aiming for the man in the middle, she ducks beneath his

raised sword arm and launches herself into him. They both slam into the street, but I don't have time to see if she's okay. The other two are attacking me.

I block, parry, thrust, and slice, but I can barely focus. Rachel is screaming, harsh bursts of sound that flay the air. I slam the butt of my sword into the man closest to me, whirl to block a blow from the other. Rachel rises from the inert body of the first man, her eyes desperate and wild, and races to jump on the back of the man I've just hit. She presses the tip of her knife into the soft tissue beneath his throat, and he raises his arm and drops his sword in surrender.

The man I'm fighting glances at them, and I take advantage of his distraction to lower my shoulder and body-slam him into the filthy brick wall beside us. I turn back to see the other man punch Rachel's knife hand away from his throat. The tip gouges his skin as it goes and a stream of blood arcs through the air. Rachel watches it and comes undone.

The man throws her to the ground, but she kicks his legs out from beneath him, and scrabbles across him, that terrible scream still ripping its way out of her throat as she punches, kicks, and tries to stab him with her knife.

I yell her name until my throat is hoarse, but she can't hear me, and the two of them are too tangled up for me to intervene without injuring her. I ready myself for the first available opportunity, and watch in horror. She takes his blows like they're nothing. Digging her nails into his skin as if it's a wall she has to climb, she claws her way up his body. She slams her knife hilt into his forehead, rendering him nearly senseless, and then flips her weapon around and drives the blade toward his throat.

I knock her off him from the side before the blade finds skin, and she sprawls on the cobblestones, her knife skittering across the alley.

She pushes herself up to her hands and knees and crawls toward it.

Leaping ahead of her, I reach it first. Grasping it, I turn and approach her carefully. Her eyes are that of a panicked animal cornered and fighting for her life. Her voice is nearly gone from screaming. She reaches for her knife, but I hold it away from her.

"Rachel." I breathe her name in a voice full of pain.

She looks at me, eyes still glassy from shock, and reaches for the knife again.

"They just wanted money," I say softly. "Just money. You don't need your knife."

She shakes her head and whimpers. I slowly extend the hand that doesn't hold her knife.

"I'm sorry." It's a hollow offering in the face of what she's been through, and I don't intend for it to be the best I can do. But for now, I just need to get her home. I can make a plan from there.

She doesn't respond.

"I don't know what he did to you, but killing someone else isn't going to make it better. I'm going to help you up. That's all I'm doing. Can I touch you?"

She looks down at herself and starts shaking again. I pull her to her feet, though I'm not sure she can stand on her own now. She's trembling uncontrollably, and I want to rip the Commander into tiny little pieces and light each of them on fire. I tuck her knife in my belt and scoop up the parcel Mrs. Angeles gave me.

"I'm taking you home," I say, though I no longer hope for a reply. "I'll figure out what to do once we get there."

And I will. I have to.

CHAPTER TWENTY-SIX

<u>RACHEL</u>

My throat is raw from the screaming I unleashed at the men in the alley, and I can't stop shaking. I don't know what's happened to me, and I don't want to talk about it. Not yet. Logan doesn't seem inclined to talk either, or maybe he's realized I'm not going to answer. We walk side by side through Country Low while a breeze plucks at newborn leaves and tangles in my hair, and the shadow of the Wall slowly stretches east.

When we reach his cottage, I leave him standing in the living area while I lock myself in the bathroom, ignite the pitch-coated logs beneath the water pump, and strip out of my garments.

I don't light a lantern, though there's no window in this room. The glow from the logs is enough for me to find my way around. I don't want to see.

The pump whistles softly to tell me the water is warm enough, and I release the handle to drain its contents into the carved stone tub resting in the center of the room. I slide into the bath and sink beneath its skin. It's quiet here, the outside noise muffled and distorted by the water around me. I pretend I'm in a cocoon, asleep, the world passing me by, and when I wake, all of this will have been a very bad dream.

The water is cooling when I finally decide to shampoo my hair and attack my skin with soap. I scrub until it hurts, but I'm still convinced the crimson stains me deep within where no soap will ever reach.

The memory of Oliver, holding my hand with icy fingers while his life spilled from his chest, is more than I can bear.

I comb through my water-heavy hair and it hangs down my back, sticking to my skin in damp strands. Pulling on a long yellow tunic and a pair of leggings to match, I open the door just in time to see Logan crumple up a thick piece of paper and throw it down. He slams his fist onto the kitchen table and swears viciously.

I cross my arms over my chest and move to curl up at the end of the couch. He meets my gaze with misery and fury in his eyes.

"Do you need anything?" he asks, and I know he's asking about more than food and water.

I shake my head, but he stands and brings me a cup of water and a plate of goat cheese, dried apple slices, and a hunk of oat bread as if I never responded. I take a bite of apple to please him, but I can't taste it.

He eases himself onto the couch, closer to me than to the other end, but still keeping a careful distance between us. He's moving slowly, as if afraid he'll spook me at any moment.

I want to tell him about Oliver. I want to open my mouth, let it all come gushing out, and find solace in weeping. But the words I need to rip Logan's world to pieces won't come. Instead,

I take a tiny bite of cheese and concentrate on chewing.

"I need to talk to you. It's okay if you don't want to respond, but I need to know you're listening," he says quietly, and waits.

I swallow the cheese, take a sip of water, and set it all on the floor at my feet. I owe him this.

I owed Oliver, too.

The thought draws blood, and my eyes slowly fill with tears. I'm tired. So tired. I ache, inside and out, and nothing seems simple anymore. Nothing seems right.

"The Commander put you into the Claiming ceremony tomorrow," Logan says, waving his hand toward the crumpled up paper. His voice is hard. "You don't need to worry, Rachel. I'm going to Claim you. I won't leave your side. He'll never get a chance to touch you again."

His expression is haunted, and I know he blames himself for today. I don't know how to comfort him when nothing soft and conciliatory lives inside me anymore.

Something catches my eye, and I turn to see a deep-blue silk dress encrusted with glittering diamonds hanging beside the fireplace. Logan follows my gaze.

"Along with a letter demanding your presence on the Claiming stage tomorrow, he sent a dress. They were both in the parcel Mrs. Angeles gave me." His fingers curl into a fist.

Beneath my grief, uncushioned by my shock, a hard kernel of anger takes root and burrows in. I failed Oliver today, yes. But I don't have to fail him again. A debt is owed for his life, and I intend to pay it.

I glance around the cottage and find my knife, cleaned and polished, lying on the kitchen table, inches from the paper announcing my new status as a participant in the Claiming. I want to hold the weapon, to feel like I have some way to keep the promises I've made to myself, but I don't know how Logan feels about giving it to me.

"You can't attack everyone who pulls a weapon," he says when he sees me gazing at my knife.

He's wrong. If you don't attack first, you lose everything. Everything.

"You scared me today," he says softly, and I look away from the knife. "They'd already demanded our money. The swords were just to intimidate us into giving them a way to buy their next drink. It was a situation you could've talked your way out of with your eyes shut. Instead, you tried to kill them."

I can't look away from the worry on his face, even though I want to tell him I've learned my lesson. The lesson he tried to teach me when he made me promise to strike down the Commander if he ever threatened me. It's branded deep into the fibers of my being now, and I don't plan to act like it isn't.

"How can I trust you to carry your weapons if you don't know who deserves a death sentence and who doesn't?" he asks, and slides closer to me, wrapping his arms around me and pulling me against his chest. "Rachel. I should've been with you today. I'm so sorry."

It's not his fault.

I should've killed the Commander.

I should've entered the wagon and attacked without hesitation.

I should've kept my promise to Logan. If I had, Oliver would still be alive.

A small whimper escapes me, and tears spill down my cheeks. I try to tell him. To make the words come, but sobs choke me instead. My fingers are icy, trembling, as Logan pulls me down beside him on the couch. I stare out his window, watching the sky darken as tiny stars tear holes in its velvet surface until I cry myself to sleep.

CHAPTER TWENTY-SEVEN

RACHEL

I wake lying next to Logan on the couch beneath his heavy wool blanket. His arm is still wrapped around my waist, his cheek pressed against the crown of my head. I keep still, letting the warmth and the solidness of his body imprint itself to mine. I want to memorize this moment, a tiny piece of what I once wanted, to hold with me while I face what comes next.

"Are you awake?" His voice is a low rumble against my ear.

I nod, though I don't want to.

"I've been thinking. About yesterday."

Oliver. I have to tell him. Now.

I struggle to sit up, but his arm tightens. "Please. Just listen for a minute."

I stop struggling, but tension coils within me.

"I don't know what happened. But I need to tell you, to convince you, that if he . . . if there was anything . . . if he hurt you in the way a man can hurt a woman, it wouldn't change how I see you. He can't break us, Rachel, unless we let him.

"I also want to make a promise to you. Will you look at me?"

I roll over, the leather squeaking in protest beneath me, and tilt my head back to stare into his dark blue eyes. He raises his hand and strokes the side of my face. His touch is far gentler than his words.

"I'm going to make the Commander pay for what he did, Rachel. I swear it. And if he dares lay hands on you today, I won't stop until he's dead."

This kind of response will ruin everything. All the Commander needs is one tiny excuse to take Logan from me forever. And I'm about to tell him something that will make his anger so much worse.

Suddenly I realize this is what the Commander is banking on. Logan will try to Claim me to protect me from the Commander's machinations, and I'll blindside him with the Commander's plan. The only one who benefits is the Commander.

Unless Logan *knows*.

The shadows of grief and loss can't obscure the startling clarity of this thought. I feel like I've emerged from a long slumber, awake and ready to act.

I'd be a fool to take the Commander at his word. I have to protect Logan, and the only way to do it is to trust him the way I promised I would. Logan won't lose it at the Claiming ceremony and give the Commander an excuse to hurt him if he's prepared to have me turn him down.

And he won't try to exact unthinking, furious revenge for Oliver if he has a chance to grieve and then formulate a plan.

My voice is still hoarse from the screaming I did yesterday as I look Logan in the eye and say, "I already knew about the

Claiming ceremony. He told me when he—"

My throat closes as the memories hit. Being inside the wagon. Oliver. Crimson everywhere.

Logan reaches up to cup my face with his palm, and I smell him—ink, fresh paper, and musk. "Listen to me, Rachel. You can take this one piece at a time. I'm in no hurry. Tell me about the Claiming ceremony. We'll start there."

"He says you'll try to Claim me."

"I will."

"But that's what he wants. What he expects."

Logan frowns, and I can almost hear the gears of his mind working, analyzing, and plotting.

"He wants me to turn you down."

"You don't legally have that right. Only your Protector does."

"You're my Protector."

"Which is what he's going to use against me," Logan says in his I-have-a-puzzle-to-solve voice. "He's going to say as your Protector, I can't both Claim you and speak for you. But why bother? What does he stand to gain? He doesn't want you Claimed by someone else because he's planning to send you into the Wasteland . . ."

I can see the answer written in his eyes even as I say it. "He'll publicly renounce your Protectorship so you can't legally stop him. He wants us separated because you aren't going with me."

"The hell I'm not." His face is hard and bright.

"He said . . ." Grief surges through my chest, burning a path to my throat.

"Tell me."

"He's going to kill you." Suddenly the words are there,

tumbling over themselves in a rush to be heard. "He said I'm loyal to a fault, and I'll do anything to avoid having him kill someone else I love."

The wagon bed. The cloth-covered lump. Crimson everywhere.

I can't breathe as the blood-soaked image of Oliver burns itself into my brain and *stays*. Pushing away from Logan, I rush to the back door, wrench it open, race across the porch and fall onto the grass, retching.

He's behind me in seconds, holding my hair back.

When my stomach is empty, he helps me sit on the bottom porch step, goes into the house, and returns with a glass of cold water and a sprig of mint.

I chew the mint and sip the water in grateful silence, but it's a brief reprieve. He needs the rest of the story, and I have to find a way to give it to him.

He sits beside me, his shoulder touching mine, and says quietly, "Did he claim to have killed Jared?"

I shake my head, and set the glass down before my hands drop it on their own. "He took me. In a wagon. There was a cloth-covered lump. And he said we were plotting behind his back." My voice rises as I rush to get through it all. "I thought it was you. I thought he'd taken you, and I prayed it would be a stranger. Another guard like the one in the tower. But it wasn't."

My voice trembles. "He stabbed the person beneath the cloth, and there was blood everywhere, and I tried to reach him, but I couldn't." I reach a hand out to Logan, for absolution or for comfort, I don't know. "I couldn't save him. I thought he was safe, waiting for us in the Wasteland, and I didn't save him. I'm so sorry!"

My voice breaks, and I drop my hand as terrible awareness comes into Logan's eyes. "Oliver?" he asks in a voice that begs me to lie. To make the truth something he can still fix.

I nod.

He stares at me, eyes glassy with shock, then jumps to his feet and strides across the yard. When he reaches the sparring area, he takes a vicious swing and sends Bob flying along his wire. Minutes pass as Logan pounds his fists into Bob as if by obliterating the dummy, he can obliterate the truth.

Finally, his arms fall to his sides and he drops to his knees on the grass. I go to him and lay a hand on his shoulder. Turning into me, he wraps his arms around me and drags me against him. I hold him and vow I will make the Commander hurt for what he's done to us. When Logan finally lifts his face to me, I can see he feels the same. His eyes are haunted, his expression hard.

"I'm sorry." My voice is small against the weight of our loss, but it's all I have to give.

"I can't believe he's gone." His voice chokes on the last word, and he scrubs his hands over his face. "Where is he?"

"I don't know."

"They took him away in the wagon?"

"Guards came in and took him." I can't look at him. I can't bear to see the shadows in his eyes. "They just . . . dragged him away."

"I want to see him. I want to . . ."

Say good-bye. Say the things he now wishes he'd said the last time he saw Oliver. I don't know if it would make it easier, but I know he needs it. I do too, but we aren't going to get it. We aren't going to get another word to say on the matter that doesn't involve the sharp end of a sword.

"He should have a proper burial."

"Yes. But he isn't going to get it." The words taste like ashes. We'll never lay Oliver to rest. Never say the words he deserved to hear. Never bring flowers to a sacred patch of ground set aside for Oliver alone. "He isn't going to get it. But he can have *justice*. If we work together."

I make sure Logan meets my eyes and say, "You can't Claim me today, or the Commander will turn it against you and separate us."

Logan looks fierce. "We're going to turn his plan against him instead. I'm going as your Protector. We'll hide our travel bags before we get to the Square. Someone will try to Claim you, and I'll agree to it, but it won't matter. When everyone is dancing and celebrating, you and I will sneak away, grab our bags, and be gone before he even realizes he's lost the game."

Suddenly, his arms are around me again, and I'm against the hard wall of his chest. "Rachel, I'm sorry you had to see Oliver die."

"No, I'm sorry. If I'd just stabbed the Commander like you said—"

"This wasn't your fault. It wasn't mine. It was the Commander's. And one day, I'll make him pay for it in full."

"No, one day *we'll* make him pay for it in full," I say.

"Yes," he says, holding my gaze. "We will. Starting today."

CHAPTER TWENTY-EIGHT

LOGAN

Rachel doesn't want breakfast but agrees to eat something when I point out she can't execute our plan on an empty stomach. I don't want breakfast either. The knowledge that I've lost the only father I've ever known burns within me.

My heart aches, a constant pain that makes it hard to breathe. Losing Oliver is like losing the best part of me. The part that believed I could rise above. The part that said I was worth something even before I proved him right.

I don't know how to move forward without him, but I have to. I have to put our plan in motion. Get Rachel away from here. Find the package. Find Jared before a Rowansmark or Baalboden tracker finds him first. And return to Baalboden with a foolproof plan for destroying the Commander and avenging us all.

I don't have solid plans in place for all of it, and I'm worried the grief that tears at me with bitter fingers will compromise my ability to think, but I do know how to get us through the

Claiming ceremony and into the Wasteland, so I decide to focus on that alone. There will be time for both grief and planning later.

Rachel dresses in the bathroom, and when she enters the living room, I take one look at her and feel as though all the oxygen has been suddenly sucked out of the air.

The dress *fits* her. The neckline dips down and curves over breasts I didn't realize until just this minute were so . . . substantial. I force my eyes to scrape over her trim waist, but in seconds I'm staring once more at the way the glittering line of thread along her neckline barely contains her.

Every man who sees her will be paying attention.

Me included.

I don't want to admit my attraction to her is strong enough to rise above my grief and my sense of responsibility, but they're *breasts*. And they're nearly spilling out of the top of her dress. I look around for a scarf or some other piece of cloth to cover her up, but all I have is a scrap of a kitchen towel, and I already know she'd never agree to it.

Which settles it. I'll have to stand in front of her the entire time.

The deep blue of the dress brings out the blue in her eyes, and the diamonds sewn into the bodice sparkle in the light.

Which draws the eye straight to her breasts.

She's wearing the dish towel. I don't care what she says.

"Acceptable?" she asks, and bends to look down at her full skirt. I want to tell her to straighten up and never bend down again, but my mouth has unaccountably gone dry.

Acceptable? She's breathtaking.

I nod, but when she slides her skirt up her leg to strap her knife sheath to her thigh, I turn around and begin rummaging aimlessly through the papers on the kitchen table.

"How am I going to reach this in a fight?" she asks, and I make the incredibly foolish mistake of turning around while her pale leg is still completely exposed.

I turn back around and address my comment to the table in front of me. "Make a slit in the silk and that stiff, crinkly stuff beneath it. You can hide the slit with your arm while you're on the stage, but you'll be able to reach your weapon if you need it."

I wait until I'm sure she's had enough time to cover herself again before turning. Her leg isn't showing anymore, but she's bending over her travel bag, packing a box of flint.

What kind of man looks at his ward like she's a temptation? Especially on the heels of such trauma and grief?

I instruct myself to regain my common sense and focus on getting ready for the day. Closing my eyes helps. First order of business: Make sure Rachel isn't in danger of going into a homicidal rage at the wrong person again.

"Be sure you know if the person you're drawing on deserves what you're about to give him," I tell her. I have to trust that she's found enough of her equilibrium to handle herself. There's no way I'm sending her into Center Square today without a weapon.

Second order of business: Make sure we have everything we need. "Let's do a last bag check," I say, and realize I can't do my end of it with my eyes shut.

Which isn't a problem because I can just look at my bag. I don't have to look at her and see her double-check the contents of her pack—fuel, clothing, Switch, dagger, and a bow with arrows.

I don't have to see the way the sunlight plays with the red-gold strands of hair she's left unbound.

She ought to look girlish with her hair down below her shoulders. Instead, the wild strands make her look both fierce and feminine, a combination I'm confident every single man signed up to Claim today will find irresistible.

When I realize I'm staring again, I look down at my bag and carefully go through it without once looking up. Everything is there, and I feel a sense of accomplishment for breaking whatever strange hold Rachel's had over me since the moment she came out wearing that cursed dress.

"I'm ready," she says, and I look at her, standing in the sunshine, grieving and beautiful, her boots peeking out from beneath her silk skirt, her eyes hard with something I've never seen there before.

I look, and I'm afraid.

That he's taken her innocence. That something will blow up in our faces today, and this will be our last moment of peace together.

That somehow I'll fail her. Oliver. Jared. Myself.

"I've made a new magnetic bracelet for you," I say, and scoop it off the table. It's a cuff of battered copper that covers the tracking device I've worked so hard to perfect. I've burned the outline of a Celtic knot into the center and filled it with brilliant sapphire wires, each attached to an inner gear that, unbeknownst to her, can turn this tracking device into a weapon.

I'm hoping I never have to activate it. But it's better to be prepared than dead.

She takes the cuff, runs her fingers over the wires, and then tugs it over her arm. "Why do I need a new magnetic bracelet if I'm going to be in the Wasteland?"

"I hid the tracking device inside of it."

"How will we know if it's working?"

"You'll feel a gentle buzz against your skin, and the wires will start to glow. They'll glow brighter the closer we come to him."

I don't tell her I've embedded a tracking device inside the cuff that will lead me to her as well. Just in case.

"Then we're ready," she says, and the hardness in her eyes makes me ache.

I want to give her something more valuable than just another one of my inventions. Something that will remind her of love. Family.

Me.

I reach into my front pocket and close my fist around the leather pouch I've carried since the day my mother died. "I want to give you something else," I say as I pull the pouch out into the open.

"What is it?" She glances at her bag as if wondering what else she can possibly add to the pile.

"No, not a weapon. Something more . . . feminine."

Which sounds incredibly stupid, but I don't know how to do this.

She frowns and looks down at herself. "I think I'm already feminine overkill."

"Yes," I say in fervent agreement, and she raises puzzled eyes to mine. But I have no intention of explaining myself. Instead, I say, "I have a gift for you. It would mean a lot to me if you'd accept it."

She holds out her hand, and I press the soft, time-worn bag into her palm while making sure to look at the wall behind her. She tugs open the brown drawstring and dumps the contents into her hand.

It's an intricately designed silver pendant made of a dozen interlocked circles with a glowing blue-black stone in the center of it. The necklace hangs on a glittering silver chain. It's the one thing of beauty I can call my own.

"It was my mother's. The only thing I have left of hers," I say, and hope she understands that this means she's my family now.

She clenches her fingers around it, and then slowly reaches out to hand it back to me. "I can't accept this."

I close my fingers around hers, the necklace still resting in her palm, meet her eyes, and say what Oliver once said to me.

"You're worth so much more than anything I can give you. If you can't believe that right now, believe in me."

She stares at me, and I hold her gaze. I don't know what she sees in my face, but she turns, lifts up her hair, and waits for me to fasten the chain.

When she turns back, the pendant rests against her chest, glowing like it was always meant to be hers. I can't tell what she's thinking. She still looks fierce, running on rage and grief. But one day, maybe, she'll look at the necklace and realize I see much more inside her than the tangled mess she feels now.

"It's a Celtic knot. The same design I burned into the cuff I just gave you. It symbolizes eternity. The stone is a black sapphire, which symbolizes faithfulness." I reach out and trace my finger over the pendant.

She looks at my finger, and then back at me, and a tiny tremble goes through her.

"It means"—I lean closer and will my words to take root within her—"I will always find you. I will always protect you. I won't let you down. I promise."

Something softens the fierceness of her gaze. It's a small shift, but I catch it. "Do you remember the first time we met?" I ask, closing my hand around the pendant, her skin warm against mine. "Reuben Little stole bread from Oliver, and you chased him through the market, cornered him in an alley, and were pelting him with items from the trash heap."

"Oliver sent you to find me, so he wouldn't have to tell my dad I'd run off into the market on my own again. I was eight," she says, and grief shivers through her voice at the memory.

It shivers through me, too, and I welcome it. It's my last connection to Oliver.

I lean a little closer, until the space between us can be measured in breaths. "You were this wild girl with spirit, brains, and so much beauty it almost hurt to look at you. I was this penniless orphan, spurned by our leader and scrounging in trash heaps for my dinner. I never thought I'd be in a position to offer you protection, but I am. And nothing is going to stop me."

"Nothing is going to stop me, either," she says, and I hear the warrior she's becoming coat her grief with purpose.

I lean my forehead to hers, our breath mingling for a moment, while my hand still clenches around the pendant and every rise and fall of her chest scrapes against my skin and makes me feel alive in a way I've never felt before.

Then she steps back, picks up her bag, and feels for the weight of her knife sheath beneath her skirt. I strap on my sword, heft my bag, and meet her gaze.

"Ready?"

Her smile is vicious as she holds her hand out to me. "Time to start paying our debt to the Commander."

I match her smile with one of my own, lock fingers with hers, and together we walk out the door.

CHAPTER TWENTY-NINE

LOGAN

As we walk hand in hand through Country Low, I realize it's the last time I'll see the fields stretching between the orchards and offering the space to breathe. The last time I'll come around this bend and see the city laid out before me. I should probably feel a sense of loss, but with Oliver dead, Jared somewhere in the Wasteland, and Rachel leaving with me, I find I have nothing left to tie me to this place but a burning hatred for the Commander.

We enter South Edge and Melkin steps out from behind a building. If he wonders why we're bringing travel bags to the Claiming ceremony, he doesn't show it. Instead, he follows us as we head toward Center Square. As soon as we turn north, he falls back, apparently satisfied that we're obeying the Commander's orders. I scan the street for any guards who might be following us as well, but see no one.

The Commander thinks he's broken Rachel so badly he's already won. I can't wait to prove him wrong.

The streets bustle today, full of people heading to the Square for the ceremony. Most of Baalboden's citizens will attend. Some because of the ceremony itself. Some because the Commander provides a banquet and dancing afterward.

The deserted shops work to our advantage. I pull Rachel into a side street a block from Center Square, and we hide our bags behind the bushes at the back of the mercantile. It's closed for the day, and if we duck out of the festivities early enough, we should have no problem reclaiming our belongings.

"That's good," I say as she pulls at the branches of a bush until it covers any sign of the bag hidden behind it. We slide back into the crowds heading toward the ceremony. The closer we come to the stage, the more color Rachel loses. We're nearly to Center Square when I stop and squeeze her hand gently.

"Look at me when you're on the stage," I say. "Look at me, no matter what he says. I won't let him hurt you."

She nods, but she's trembling. I don't know if it's from anger, trauma, or nerves. Most likely a combination of the three.

By the time we arrive, citizens have filled Center Square. Girls in brilliant jewel-toned dresses cluster together, whispering and giggling as they eye the group of eligible townsmen lined up near the platform, each looking tremendously uncomfortable. The wooden stage, the same one used to carry out Commander-sanctioned executions, is scrubbed clean and draped with red ribbon.

Sylph is here, glowing in her emerald and black dress, her hair somehow tamed into the intricate updo favored by most girls on Claiming day. A quick glance at those assembled shows Rachel is the only one who left her hair unbound. She's also the only one with a dress cut low enough to attract the notice of every male mingling at the edge of the stage. I see the moment they realize she's going to be part of the ceremony, and have to stop myself from reaching for my sword just to give them something else to think about.

I wonder which of them will have the nerve to stand up and Claim her. Mitch Patterson? I can't agree to that. I once saw his left eye twitch for an entire hour. That has to be a sign of mental instability. Wendall Freeman? He can't hold his liquor. And he tells terrible jokes. Peter Carmine? He's . . . I search for the fault I know is there and finally decide he's too short for her. Too short and too stupid.

I don't actually have proof that Peter Carmine is stupid, but he looks like he could be, and that's enough in my book.

Which just goes to show I'm the one who should be worried about mental instability and rampant stupidity. It doesn't matter who steps forward to Claim her. She isn't going to be here long enough for them to make good on their offer.

We stick to our plan. Foil the Commander on his own stage. And leave.

I have backup travel bags stashed where the Commander would never think to look, just in case the bags hidden behind the mercantile are inaccessible when we need them. I know where to hide in South Edge and how to block our wristmarks so the guards can't find us as we figure out a new way across the Wall.

And I have an alternate plan of my own ready for anything the Commander might pull.

We're as ready as we can be. I step in front of Rachel to block the ogling idiots at the stage, and a bell, sonorous and deep, echoes across the Square. The crowd stirs and whispers as the girls line up to the side of the stage, a bewildering display of color, jewels, and anxious smiles. Sylph sees us, eyes widening at the sight of Rachel in a Claiming dress, and gives a tiny, hesitant wave.

Rachel doesn't wave back. I'm not sure she even realizes Sylph is there. I don't think she sees anything but the stage, and the fact that she'll have to stand next to the Commander while she gives the performance of her life.

The girls begin mounting the stairs, taking dainty steps to avoid tripping over their long skirts. Their Protectors file after them. The eligible townsmen yank at their collars as if they're in danger of choking, and the bell peals three long notes.

The Commander is here.

It's time.

I pull Rachel to me, inhale the midnight citrus scent of her, and then I let go, and we move to take our place on the stage.

CHAPTER THIRTY

RACHEL

Armed guards enter the Square and fan out, stationing them-selves at three-yard intervals along the edges. Behind them, the twelve members of the Brute Squad march through the Square, two by two. The lead pair reaches the stage, halts, and pivots to face each other. Each subsequent pair also stops and faces each other until they've formed a tight, citizen-free aisle between them.

Another three long peals from the bell and every guard in the Square snaps his right forearm up to his forehead in a rigid salute. Silence, dense and absolute, falls across the Square as the Commander strides down the aisle toward the stage.

My mouth goes dry, my pulse pounds against my skin, and my vision narrows until all I see is him. I press my arm against my side and feel the outline of my knife sheath beneath my skirt as he approaches the steps.

I'm the last in the line of girls across the stage. As he walks up the steps, he meets my gaze and smiles as if only the two of us exist.

My skin crawls, and something hot and sharp seeps out of my grief and begs for his blood.

I reach for the slit in the side of my skirt, but he's already past me, greeting the Protectors who stand behind their daughters, and turning to face the assembled crowd.

"No weapons," Logan breathes against my ear. "Don't give him a reason."

He's right, but I don't take my hand away from the outline of my knife.

The Commander greets his citizens, says a few words about the honorable tradition of Claiming and how protecting the innocent among us keeps us strong, and gestures toward a girl on his left. Her Protector brings her forward, and a young man steps to the stage to Claim her.

My hands shake, but my thoughts are clear.

The girl's Protector accepts the young man's Claim and hands over his daughter.

The Commander expects Logan to defy tradition and Claim me even though he's also my Protector.

The girl places her hand into that of her new Protector and recites her vow of obedience while her mother dabs her eyes and her new Protector looks slightly stunned by his good fortune.

He expects me to turn Logan down and ask to be a ward of the state.

Another girl is called. Another man steps forward. Another vow of obedience.

Another step closer to sealing my fate.

I can't make this look like I'm defying the Commander's direct orders. Instead, I have to make it look like I'm just another girl, excited to see her dream of being Claimed come true, while Logan makes it look like he's clueless about the Commander's plan. The Commander can't alter the Claiming ceremony for me in front of all these people without raising serious questions. He'll have to accept the turn of events, at least publicly. We just need to get out of his reach before he finds an opportunity to deal with us privately.

Sylph's name is called, and she hurries to center stage, casting one anxious glance my way as she goes.

I don't know if she's anxious for me or for herself, but I can't afford to think about it. Not when I'm about to commit treason while making it look like I have no idea what I'm doing.

Smithson West steps forward to Claim her, but so does Rowan Hughes. The Commander turns the choice over to Sylph's father as is proper, and he doesn't even glance at Sylph as he chooses Smithson West. Sylph laughs and hugs her father, before remembering the requirements of decorum and subsiding into respectful silence.

She is repeating her vow when I look up to see the Commander's fierce dark eyes locked on mine.

I'm next.

The Brute Squad breaks formation and circles the stage. They expect trouble. They expect Logan to draw his sword against the Commander and give them a reason to act.

I'm grateful Logan is prepared to play his part.

I look back at the Commander, at the sly, feral smile twisting his scar as he calls my name, and wish for it to be over quickly.

The ribbons behind him glow crimson in the sunlight, and as I walk toward the Commander on legs that feel like saplings in a storm, the poisonous anger within me spreads. Logan walks behind me, his hand resting lightly on the small of my back.

"Rachel Adams, you are here without your true Protector." The Commander's voice booms across the Square.

This is the man who shattered my life.

The man who covered me in crimson.

"I am her assigned Protector," Logan says, his voice calm.

"And are you willing to give answer to any who wish to Claim her?" The Commander's tone mocks him, and I struggle to breathe.

This is the man who took my father. Oliver. And wants to take Logan, too.

"I am," Logan says, and the group of eligible townsmen murmur among themselves.

I doubt any of them will step forward to Claim me. I'd hardly make a suitable wife.

The Commander laughs, a hideous parody of mirth, and shakes his head. Turning to the group of men below him, he asks, "Who will step forward to Claim this woman?"

He expects Logan to see this as an opening. A way to negotiate my safety. Instead, Logan waits quietly like any other Protector would do. The only sign of tension he gives is the slight increase in the pressure of his hand against my back.

Peter Carmine steps forward. "I will Claim her."

Logan's fist clenches a handful of my dress.

The Commander frowns at Peter and turns to face Logan. "And do you accept this man's Claim?"

Logan doesn't hesitate. "I do."

If he pulls on the back of my dress any harder, it's going to rip.

The Commander looks from me to Logan, and the cold calculation on his face chills me. I press my arm against my side, feeling the weight of my knife bite into my hip. Behind me, I sense Logan change his stance, rolling to the balls of his feet.

The Commander pins me with his dark eyes. "In the absence of your father, I feel I should ask you, Rachel Adams, if you want to be Claimed." He wraps his hand over my arm and squeezes.

Heat sears a path through my brain, and I shake off his hand before I think better of it. This isn't the way it's supposed to go. He isn't supposed to deviate from the Claiming ceremony script in front of all these witnesses. I can't say I want to be Claimed without the Commander realizing I'm going against his orders. I can't say I don't want to be Claimed without giving him the leverage he needs to separate me from Logan since Logan has already given his permission.

I hope Logan thought of a plan for this scenario.

Logan's voice rings out across the Square. "As is proper, Rachel will not choose whether she gets Claimed. I choose for her."

There's no arguing with the protocol Logan has invoked unless the Commander wants to set an ugly precedent with the rest of the citizens. I see the moment this realization hits the Commander. He looks from me to Logan, and my stomach sinks.

He isn't going to let this happen.

"You have one last chance to speak," he says with quiet

menace and lays his hand on me again, digging his nails into the soft tissue of my forearm. "Do you want to be Claimed?"

The only choice I have is to stick with the prescribed Claiming script and hope the Commander refuses to make a scene in front of the citizens for fear more of them might rise up and demand the opportunity to choose their own destiny as well.

"I bow to the wishes of my Protector," I say, and fury explodes across the Commander's face.

He twists my arm and yanks me forward, breaking Logan's hold on my dress. "You realize what this means?" he asks me in a voice only I can hear. "I will kill him for your betrayal, Rachel. Renounce this Claiming and leave as planned, or I will leave you with nothing."

"Let go of her." Logan's voice, laced with terrible purpose, rings out across the Square.

The crowd erupts into a frenzy of hushed conversation, and the Commander twists my arm until I'm sure he means to wrench it from its socket. Pain is a living thing clawing at me, and I turn my face to look at Logan.

I need to know the plan. How to keep Logan alive and avoid being separated from him. I expect to see steady calculation in Logan's eyes. Instead, I see blind fury. His hand is already reaching for his sword as the Commander drives me to my knees.

He's going to attack the Commander. Try to kill him. And the Commander will stab a sword through him the way he stabbed a sword through Oliver and then laugh while I sit in silence, soaking up every drop of blood until my skin is flushed crimson with the shame of my impotence.

The brilliant rage surging within me coalesces into one fierce purpose.

Save Logan.

"I don't want to be Claimed," I say, and each word drops to the ground like a stone. I pray Logan will understand.

"You deny your current Protector's authority over you?" The Commander asks, his voice steeped in vicious triumph.

"I do."

Logan isn't looking at me. He's locked on the Commander, who still has my arm twisted above me, pinning me in a supplicant's position below him. His hand grips the hilt of his sword, his knuckles white.

If he loses control, the Commander wins.

And with the Brute Squad cutting off all escape routes, Logan doesn't stand a chance.

"What do you say to that, Logan McEntire?" The Commander looks at Logan, while the crowd moves uneasily, backing away from the stage.

I don't give Logan a chance to answer. With our plan in shambles, and my back against the wall, I say the only thing that could possibly keep him safe. "It doesn't matter what he says. He isn't my true Protector. I petition to be a ward of the state."

The Commander doesn't spare me a glance, so I raise my voice. "Do you accept me as a ward of the state?"

Some of my fury leaks into my tone, and I raise my chin. I don't care. Let him know I'm angry. Let him see the bloodlust on my face. Let him look into my eyes and discover the girl he thought he understood is gone and in her place stands a weapon of his own creation.

He turns his head slowly to stare at me, his scar pulling his lip into a snarl, and lets go of my arm to backhand me across the face.

I tumble to the floor and see Logan, sword raised, face ablaze, charge the Commander.

CHAPTER THIRTY-ONE

RACHEL

"**N**o!"

I'm screaming, but it's too late. The girls on the stage scatter, their fathers dragging them to safety as the Brute Squad swarms onto the platform, coming between Logan and the Commander. Logan drives his shoulder into the first guard who reaches him, sends the man flying off the stage, and whirls to block the sword thrust of another.

The Commander stands above me and laughs.

I slide my hand into the slit I cut in the side of my skirt, find my sheath, and pull my knife free.

Someone calls my name, and I see Sylph break away from Smithson's hold and rush toward the stage.

"Go back!" I yell and struggle to my feet, my knife ready.

Smithson catches her around the waist before she can reach me, and she slaps at him. I turn away, praying Logan isn't already dead.

He isn't. He fights like a man possessed—swinging, thrusting, and attacking with terrifying speed and force, disarming and disabling every opponent who comes at him. I had no idea he had this in him, and it's clear I'm not the only one.

The Commander stops laughing and draws his own sword.

Raising my knife, I calculate the angle I'll need to drive the blade through his back and into his heart. Before I can thrust the weapon forward, I'm body slammed from the side and sent sailing off the platform and into the crowd of eligible townsmen still milling at the base of the stage, unsure what their role in this unprecedented display of violence should be.

Hands reach for me, steady me, and try to hold me back. I punch, kick, and swing my knife until they back away. I can't save Logan unless I'm on the stage. Anyone standing between me and him is dead.

I race toward the steps, beating away the few that still reach for me, but before I can mount the stage, a guard jumps in front of me. I drive my knife through his stomach, twist it to the right, and yank it free while he's still in the act of telling me to halt.

Crimson splashes onto my pretty blue skirt. I look away from it and concentrate on reaching Logan. I'm on the stage driving my knife into the back of the guard blocking that exit before he even knows what hit him. Not stopping to check if he's dead, I vault over his body and try to see Logan.

He's trapped center stage. Eight Brute Squad. Another dozen guards. And in the center of it, the Commander.

I race forward, and the Commander screams for his guards to fall back. Logan is bruised, battered, and bleeding, but holds his sword steady. Not that it will help him now. There are too many. He can't take them all.

I can't either.

I look to the crowd, hoping for swords and friendly faces, but there's nothing but mass confusion and panic. Logan is a dead man walking, and so am I.

Except I'm not. Because I alone know where to find the Commander's precious package. Maybe he forgot that in the heat of the moment. Maybe he figured there would be others he could hurt to make me bend to his will. Maybe he's arrogant enough to think I'll be too frightened of him to disobey, even without the threat of Logan's death hanging over my head. Maybe the lives of others mean so little to him that he can't imagine a single death that could significantly alter his plans.

He's wrong.

Logan and the Commander circle each other as the guards fall back.

I creep behind the guards, looking for an opening.

The Commander thrusts. Logan blocks, but it's clear he's been injured and lacks the strength to keep up the fight for long.

He won't have to. I know how to change the game. How to take away the one advantage the Commander is banking on.

Logan whirls and swings, flinging drops of blood. His sword goes wide, and the Commander steps into the gap, using Logan's momentum against him. In seconds, he has his sword against Logan's neck, and his vicious smile twists his scar into an ugly, knotted ball of prickled flesh. The guards behind Logan grab his arms, fling his sword to the floor, and pin him in place for the Commander.

"You drew a weapon against your leader. Killed multiple guards." The Commander's voice shakes the Square as he chops each syllable into jagged shards.

I see my opportunity and slide into the circle. Logan meets my eyes, and his expression begs me to leave. Run. Escape this hell of a city and never look back.

"The penalty for this is death." The Commander turns to Logan.

"And what is the penalty for killing innocent citizens? For terrorizing a young woman? Who holds *you* accountable?" Logan is shouting, the same brilliant rage that burns through me spilling out of him.

The Commander's smile dies slowly, extinguished by the look of pure hatred he gives Logan. "*I* am the law. *I* am justice." He's spitting the words in Logan's face. "*I* am the one thing that keeps this city safe. You dare question me?"

"You aren't justice. You're a misbegotten monster too drunk on his own power to be trusted with it anymore."

Purple flushes the Commander's face, and he raises his sword arm.

"I, Commander Jason Chase, for the crime of treason and murder, do hereby sentence you to death," he says, and aims his blade at Logan's throat.

"Wait!" My voice carries across the Square and freezes everyone in place for the split second it takes me to fall to my knees where the Commander can see me, but no guard can reach me in time.

The Commander laughs. "Come to beg me to save him?"

My smile feels just as vicious as his. "He isn't the one who needs saving."

"Rachel, no," Logan breathes.

I ignore him.

"What are you going to do, girl? Kill me?" The Commander's voice is full of malice.

"No," I say. Raising my knife, I aim it at the soft spot just below my sternum and take a deep breath.

The Commander's sword, still pointed at Logan's throat, wavers. "What are you doing?"

"Taking away the one thing you really want." I say and dig the tip of the knife into my flesh, feeling a flash of pain and then the warmth of blood running down my skin.

Guards surge forward, and I scream, "Stop, or I'll do it!"

The Commander sweeps his hand up, palm out, and the guards stop.

"Rachel, please," Logan says softly. "Not this."

I don't look away from the Commander. "You want what only I know how to get. If you or anyone else in this city lays another hand on Logan, I'll kill myself and you'll never find the package."

His jaw is clenched, pulling his scar taut. "Yesterday, I wouldn't have said you had this in you."

"The girl you dealt with yesterday is gone." My voice is cold, my words rising from the terrible grief he carved into me with Oliver's death. "Give me your word before all these citizens that Logan will remain unharmed for the duration of my journey, or the knowledge of where to find the package dies with me."

His eyes are fierce pits of hatred as he slowly lowers his sword. "He will be unharmed as long as you return with what I need." He makes a gesture to the guards holding Logan, and they begin dragging him from the stage.

"Wait!" I leap to my feet. "Where are you taking him?"

"You didn't honestly think I would let my insurance policy wander around freely while you were gone, did you?" The Commander smiles. "He'll be in the dungeon until you return."

Locking eyes with Logan as the guards pull him past me, I reach up to wrap my hand around his mother's necklace.

He says softly, "Remember my promise, Rachel."

I reach a hand toward him, but he's already off the stage, being pulled through the crowd, which parts like water around him.

"You leave at dawn. Melkin goes with you." The Commander is next to me, his sword still grasped in his hand. "I suggest you hurry. I doubt even a young man like Logan can withstand the hospitality of my dungeon for long."

For one brief, glorious moment, I imagine turning, thrusting my knife through the Commander's crisp blue military uniform, and watching with pleasure as he learns just how vulnerable a flesh-and-bone man really is.

But I'd never get to Logan before the guards deliver the death sentence I would've caused. I let the moment pass and turn to stare straight into the Commander's dark eyes as I silently promise myself I'll retrieve the package, secure Logan's freedom, and deliver justice before the Commander realizes the girl whose loyalty he purchased in blood will be his final undoing.

CHAPTER THIRTY-TWO

LOGAN

Rachel is alone. I've failed her. Bitter regret swamps me, a twin to my awful grief over Oliver, but I can't give in to it. I have to pay attention and figure out how to get out of this.

The dungeon is a dank, smelly pit carved out of the foundation of the Commander's compound. Individual cells are simply hollowed-out husks within the stone. The walls are slimy with moisture, iron bars block the doorways, and a few half-hearted torches burn along the aisle between cells.

I'm dragged past five cells before the guards reach the one set aside for me. Two of the cells I pass are empty. One holds a gaunt man in filthy clothing huddled on a thin straw pallet. One holds a younger man shackled to the back wall. The cell across from mine holds a young pregnant woman wrapped in a coarse brown blanket. She doesn't look at me.

I wonder which of them is the spy planted here to gain my trust.

After pulling me into my cell, the guards fasten heavy iron

cuffs around my wrists, and take my sword, the dagger in my left boot, and my scabbard. While one guard pats me down, looking for additional blades, the other yanks on the heavy, rusted chains attached to the cuffs at my wrists, testing them for weakness. The chains loop through iron circles welded onto the back wall of the cell and restrict my ability to go more than halfway toward the doorway. I ignore them in favor of scanning the ceiling for surveillance devices. I can't find any, but decide the smartest move is to act like I'm being watched at all times.

If I'm going to escape, I can't afford a single misstep.

Satisfied I'm weaponless, the guards take my cloak and toss it just out of my reach, leaving me to the mercy of the dungeon's chill. They laugh as they slam my cage door shut and leave.

Lucky for me, they're too shortsighted to understand a man's true weapon isn't something that slides into a scabbard.

A few strong pulls assure me my chains aren't coming out of the wall without help. Which means I can't reach my cloak. Which limits my options.

Fear for Rachel is a constant hum in the background of my thoughts, but I can't give in to it. The only way I can be useful to her now is to keep a clear head and apply logic to my current circumstances.

I have my boots. My belt buckle. My empty knife sheath. Not enough to stage an escape attempt. I need my cloak, but I refuse to reach for it. I refuse to even glance at it. If I'm being watched, the fastest way to ensure I never see my cloak again is to look like I want it.

My cell has a thin, water-stained pallet lying on the stone floor, and a half-rotted wooden bucket shoved into the corner closest to me. Neither seems particularly useful in an escape effort, but you never know what might come in handy.

The shackles bite into my wrists as I stand and slowly pace the back wall, counting the measurements and feeling for drafts so I can calculate how close I am to the outside wall of the dungeon.

Heavy footsteps sound at the main entrance, and I look up to see two guards, blazing torches in hand, precede the Commander into the miserable space.

I move closer to the bucket, putting enough space between me and the door of my cell that he'll have to come all the way inside if he wants to hurt me.

He doesn't come to my cell, though. He stops in front of the cell containing the pregnant woman huddled in a blanket.

"Warm enough, Eloise?" he asks without a hint of concern in his voice.

She doesn't respond.

"I thought you should know your husband has agreed to the terms I set before him." He looks across at me. "Once he understood your life and the life of his unborn child were at stake, Melkin was quite willing to do everything I asked."

I keep my expression neutral as a tight band wraps around my chest. Melkin is the only tracker still in the city. Rachel is leaving to hunt down the missing package. It isn't hard to reach the conclusion that Melkin will be Rachel's escort in my place.

Why would the Commander need to threaten the lives of Melkin's family to get him to do his job?

I put the fact that Melkin is being asked to do something he was originally unwilling to do together with the fact that the

Commander wants me to know about it, and the band around my chest tightens further.

Rachel. It has something to do with Rachel. Nothing else makes sense. I don't need the specifics of his plan to know she's in danger.

Melkin's wife doesn't look up at the Commander as she pulls her thin blanket closer to her body, but it doesn't matter. He never expected a response. This show was for me alone.

His laugh is an ugly thing filling up the space between us as he crosses the aisle and gestures for the guards to open the door to my cell.

I back up until I have several lengths of loose chain at my disposal.

The Commander steps into my cell. The flickering torchlight illuminates his scar, throwing the rest of his face into shadow.

"You thought you could outsmart me, didn't you?" He flexes his right hand into a fist. The light slides along the golden circle of his ring, glowing within the olive-sized red stone and highlighting the wicked ridge of the raised talon through its center.

I brace myself and gather up a length of chain as quietly as I can, ignoring how bruised and battered I feel from the swordfight on the Claiming stage.

"You were always so sure of yourself. So convinced no one could outwit the great Logan McEntire." His lip curls as he spits my name at me.

Maybe I shouldn't engage him. Maybe I should keep my silence and let him talk, hoping to pick up nuggets of information along the way.

Or maybe pushing him to his limits is the best way to peel

back the mask and see what I'm truly dealing with.

"How would you know?" I ask. "You've never bothered to have a proper conversation with me."

His fist plows into my gut, slamming me back against the wall. I double over and take the opportunity to gather more lengths of chain while catching my breath.

"I don't have proper conversations with the sons of those who've been disloyal." He kicks my feet out from under me.

I hit the floor hard, and nearly lose my grip on the chain I'm holding like a rope. Pushing myself back to my feet, I say, "My mother wasn't disloyal."

His fist slams into my shoulder, spinning me to the side. I narrowly keep from hitting the wall with my face.

"I wasn't speaking of your mother." His breath is a harsh pant against my ear.

I take a deliberate step away from him. He's playing games with me. He knows I have no idea who my father was, and he's using it against me. Still, part of me wants to ask, just to finally have that gap in my past filled in.

"You knew my father."

He laughs. "You're just like him. Two men cut from the same cloth."

"And what cloth would that be?"

His face, bathed in shadow and firelight, is lit with malice. "Unworthy. Disloyal. Without honor."

I straighten and brace my feet. "You wouldn't understand honor if it was branded into your skin."

He lunges for me, but I duck back. Swinging the chains up, I wrap them around his arm. One swift jerk and I fling him onto the filthy floor of the cell. He lands hard, and I drive my knee into his back, but the guards outside the cell are already on me.

They pull me from him, toss me to the ground, and attack. I swing the chains, brutally slashing one guard's face and knocking out another's tooth. One draws his sword, but I duck out of the way. Looping the chains around the sword's hilt as I go, I yank back hard. The sword goes skidding across the cell.

Two more guards arrive, and I'm fighting for my life. Dodging blades, absorbing blows, and doing as much lethal damage as I can with the lengths of chains in my hands.

It's four on one, and I know I can't keep it up much longer. I'm hoping I won't have to.

The Commander rises from the floor and screams at his guards to stop. They back away, bleeding and cursing.

I'm bleeding and cursing too, but I hold my head high as he approaches me. I have to make his next actions seem like his idea.

"Go ahead and kill me, if you can," I say, rattling the chains in my hands as if I'm ready to go another round with the guards. "You've given me all the weapon I need."

He spews venom at me. "The second I no longer need you to ensure the girl's cooperation, you're dead." He closes the distance between us, stopping just out of range of the chains. "She'll die thinking she saved you. Melkin will see to that. But *you*, you get to live long enough to know you haven't saved anyone."

I've got the answer I needed about Melkin's arrangement with the Commander. Ignoring my anger at the thought of Rachel traveling the Wasteland in the company of a man tasked to assassinate her once her usefulness is finished, I focus on getting the second thing I need.

I rattle the chains as if I still have the energy to use them. The Commander gestures at the closest guard. "Get those things off him and remove them from his cell."

I put up a fight, make it look like I mean it, and it takes three of them to get the shackles off me. The instant I'm free, I back into a corner like I know I've been beaten at my own game.

The Commander laughs and waves at his least-injured guards. "Teach him a lesson. Just make sure you leave him alive."

Two guards advance, fists raised. I parry the first punch and absorb the second as it plows into my shoulder, but see stars as one guard's booted foot slams into my rib cage and sends me sprawling. Pain flares to life within me, and it's all I can do to curl up in a ball and endure as the guards use me as their punching bag.

I've lost track of time when the Commander calls them off. I'm bleeding from my nose and mouth, my body feels like I've been run over by a wagon, and a rib on my right side feels like someone is skewering me with a lit torch every time I breathe.

The Commander strides over to me, grabs a handful of my hair, and wrenches my face around to his. "You've lost your little game. And everyone you love will die because of it." He gestures to a guard, and I hear something sizzle and spit in the flames of the nearest torch. I can't crane my head to look because the Commander holds my hair in a vicious grip.

A guard steps closer, a long pole in his hands. At the end of the pole, the metal insignia of the Brute Squad—a curved talon beneath two slash marks—glows red-hot.

I twist away from the Commander, but he settles his knee

on my side, turning my aching rib into a breath-stealing howl of agony, and holds my face steady with both his hands.

"I beat you," the Commander says, "and every time I look at you, I'll know it."

The guard presses the blazing-hot metal into the side of my neck, and I scream.

The smell of scorched skin fills the air, and I retch as brilliant spots dance in front of my eyes. I drag in a deep breath and try to ride out the worst of the agony, but it refuses to abate.

Letting go of me, the Commander rises and says to the dungeon guard, "Water only. Don't bother offering this one any food. We won't need to keep him alive long enough to warrant it."

Leaving me huddled on the floor, burned and bleeding, the Commander and his guards leave, slamming the cell bars closed in their wake.

I wait until I hear their footsteps fade. Until the door at the entrance closes. Until I've silently recounted everything I know about the Pythagorean theorem. The conductive properties of copper. The relationship between negative mass and negative energy.

Only when I'm certain I've spent enough time looking defeated and broken that anyone watching me wouldn't question my need for warmth, do I slowly crawl across the floor.

Every inch is torture. I clench my teeth and tell myself pain is just a state of mind. I can rise above it. My body doesn't agree with my theory, so I force myself to recite the periodic table to give myself something productive to focus on.

I'm shaking by the time I reach my destination, but furious

triumph warms me from the inside as I lay hands on the one thing I wanted all along. The thing that will make inciting the Commander to remove my chains and beat me nearly senseless worth it. The thing that will make escape possible.

My cloak.

CHAPTER THIRTY-THREE

RACHEL

Dawn is a whisper in the cold morning air as I tighten the leather fastenings on my cloak, wrap it around the tunic and pants I wear, adjust my travel pack until it fits smoothly against my spine, and face the gate leading out into the Wasteland.

I'm taking my own bag with me. The Commander instructed two of his guards to accompany me home so I could pack, and neither of them batted an eye when I headed into a side street off Center Square. If they wondered why I kept a bag hidden in the bushes near a mercantile, they never asked. Instead, they kept one hand on me and one on their weapons at all times. I'm betting they thought I might try to escape.

I would have, if I didn't have to reclaim the missing package so I can ransom Logan's life. Not that the Commander is the kind of man who'll keep his word to me once he holds the package in his hands.

Which is fine. I'm no longer the kind of girl who'll keep my word to him, either.

Shelving the need to plan a way to free Logan without giving the Commander what he wants, I study my travel companion while pretending to watch the guards unchain the gate.

Melkin is tall, about Logan's height, though he doesn't have Logan's muscle. Instead, his frame is all bones and angles, his skin stretched painfully thin. With deep-set dark eyes, a nose resembling a cloak hook, and a sparse coating of mud-brown hair hanging down his back, he resembles a starving hawk.

He clutches his cloak with long, skinny fingers and darts a glance at me. "Hope you know what you're doing. I don't figure on having to rescue you every time I turn around."

I simply stare at him. I don't know him. Dad kept me, and the fact that he'd trained me, separate from the others who ran courier or tracking missions for Baalboden. I don't know Melkin, but that doesn't stop the rage inside of me from begging to lash out at him. He works for the Commander. That's justification enough.

Whatever he sees on my face causes him to blink twice, tighten his hold on his cloak, and look away as the massive stone gate swings open with a high-pitched groan.

Four guards line up on either side, ready to let us out and remain behind to stand watch throughout the day in case there are those who want in. Melkin places a hand on my shoulder and presses me forward.

I snatch his hand, crush his fingers in mine, and spin until his arm is pinned behind his back.

"Don't. Touch. Me."

He doesn't respond. When I release his hand, he watches me closely and follows me down the gritty cobblestone road past the guards and beneath the steel arch with the Commander's talon-and-double-slash insignia burned into the center of its smooth surface.

The road leads away from the Wall through the scorched ground that makes up Baalboden's perimeter and ends at the charred remains of the highwaymen's wagons. We walk it in silence until we reach the point where the road ends and the wild tangle of the Wasteland begins. Stopping, we open our packs and pull out our weapons.

Melkin straps a double-bladed leather glove to his right hand, and the six-inch blades of silver protruding from both his index and ring knuckles sparkle beneath the hesitant touch of the early morning sun. I recognize the glove as one of Logan's inventions, and it tells me plenty about Melkin.

He likes his prey close and thinks the abnormally long range of his arms will be advantage enough to keep him safe. When he straps a sword around his waist, I acknowledge that he must be proficient with his left hand as well. He takes out a thick walking stick and extends it to its full length. The black metallic surface swallows stray rays of sunlight whole.

He sees me staring and mutters, "It was a gift."

"I've never seen anything like it at any of the weapons vendors in the city."

"Because it isn't from this city. Now, you got any weapons, or am I going to be responsible for keeping the both of us alive on this trip?"

I unclasp my own bag. Minutes later, the bow and arrows are strapped across the outside of my pack, where I can easily reach back and grasp them; my knife rests against my hip; and my Switch is in my hand.

"Where are we heading?" he asks.

"Somewhere in the vicinity of Rowansmark."

"Care to be more specific?"

"No."

He shrugs, and we pause for a moment, listening, but the Wasteland offers nothing beyond the sound of birds chirping over their morning meals. Which doesn't mean there aren't highwaymen lying in wait, but at least we don't have to worry about fending off the Cursed One at the moment.

Melkin steps off the cobblestones and slides into the dark tangle of trees, vines, and undergrowth waiting for us. I follow on his heels, my Switch ready in case of trouble.

The smell hits me first. Wet moss, crisp leaves, and the soft, musky scent of tree bark. If I close my eyes, I can imagine I'm standing next to Dad, listening to the deep, reassuring rumble of his voice quietly instruct me how to listen. How to walk without leaving an obvious trail. And how to survive anything the world throws my way.

I ache for him, a sharp, sudden longing that reminds me that missing him is how I started this entire nightmare. I draw in another breath, savor it against my tongue, and let myself feel a tiny sliver of raw hope. Maybe Dad is with the package. Maybe, by searching for it, I'll find him too. Maybe if I find him, he'll know how to make everything right again.

"You coming? Or you planning on sniffing trees all day?"

I ignore Melkin and start walking. The Wasteland is a strange mix of overgrown forests, bogs, and fields and the ruins of the sky-climbing cities destroyed or abandoned over five decades ago when the Cursed One was first released.

"Mind the thorns," Melkin says quietly, swinging his walking stick in the direction of a patch of pretty green undergrowth adorned with needle-sharp thorns.

I skirt the plants and use my Switch to swipe hanging vines out of my way as I walk. Melkin stops to listen, and I halt as well, though my ears don't pick up anything beyond the usual whisper of bug wings and breeze that mark the forested area of the Wasteland closest to Baalboden.

"Hear that?" he asks in a voice designed to carry no more than a few feet.

I listen harder and finally catch it—a faint *shush* of sound that could be an animal foraging for food, or could be the slide of a boot against the branch of a tree. I release the Switch's blade with a muted snick, and catch Melkin's slight frown as my walking stick becomes a weapon.

I don't hear the sound again, but I don't make the mistake of assuming a threat doesn't exist. Clutching the Switch closer, I rest my other hand on my knife sheath.

We walk as silently as possible but don't hear sounds of pursuit again. I see the moment Melkin decides it was nothing but an animal. His shoulders drop, and the hand curled inside his bladed glove relaxes.

I don't sheathe the Switch's blade, though. Better to be ready to deal violently with others than to be caught off guard.

Rowansmark is a fifteen-day journey southwest. Eighteen if the weather is foul or we have to go around a gang of highwaymen. I pace our progress by the familiar markers we pass—the lightning-struck oak, the creek with the stepping-stone bridge, and the swaying once-white cottage almost completely covered by kudzu. We're making good time, in part due to Melkin's pace. His long legs eat up the terrain, but I have no trouble keeping up. Fear for Logan's life demands nothing less. And the anger I feel toward the Commander refuses to let me rest.

I'm going to retrace Dad's route to his Rowansmark safe house and find the package. Once I find it, I'll figure out a way to secure Logan's safety while making the Commander pay for what he's done.

A tiny inner voice whispers that if I find Dad with the package, I won't have to figure it out alone. I tamp down the buoyant sense of hope that wants to blossom within me. The tracking device on my arm is silent, the wires cold. I have no reason yet to hope for anything.

The sun melts lazily across the sky, turning the forest we walk through into a damp, humid jungle. It's too early in the spring for mosquitoes, but beetles and gnats swarm the trees, and I keep my cloak on despite the warmth.

Twice more, we hear a rustle of sound behind us, but when Melkin circles back, he finds nothing. As we're sharing the Wasteland with a host of wild animals, hearing noises isn't unusual. Still, the lessons I learned about the Commander's lack of honor are carved into me with deep, crimson letters, and I'm not reassured.

When the sun reaches the middle of the sky, Melkin drops to a crouch against the thick trunk of an ancient oak, opens his pack, and offers me a flask of water and a hunk of oat bread. I take them and find my own trunk to rest against, keeping him well within my sights while I listen closely for sounds of human pursuit.

We eat in silence until Melkin looks up, wipes his mouth with the sleeve of his faded blue tunic, and says, "Your daddy taught you well."

I stare at him. "How do you know he's the one who taught me?"

"The Commander told me. I didn't fancy on taking a helpless little girl across the Wasteland with me, but you know how to move quietly. You keep your head up, eyes open. Looks like you know what to do with that stick you carry too."

I look away.

"Sure are a quiet one, aren't you?" he asks, and caps his flask of water. "Always thought of you as a girl with spunk and guts. Never realized you were afraid to open your mouth."

The bitterness festering in me bubbles up.

"How much spunk and guts does it take to chatter nonstop about nothing of importance?" I stand and stow my flask in my bag. "I have bigger things on my mind than discussing my skills. If you want conversation, choose a better topic."

He stands as well, irritation on his face, and drives the bottom quarter of his ebony walking stick into the forest floor. I imagine I can feel the ground beneath me tremble with the force of it.

"Nobody appreciates a woman with vinegar in her soul."

I slide my pack into place and stalk toward him, a distant roaring filling my ears as the anger inside me locks on to a handy target.

"Vinegar in my soul?" I'm closing in on him, and his hand tightens within the bladed glove he wears. "Is that what they call betrayal these days?"

My voice is louder than it should be, but I can't seem to find the air I need to calm down. "You stand there and pass judgment on me like you've earned the right. What have you lost?" I'm yelling, my fist raised as if I'll hit him. "What have you lost, Melkin?"

I need to hurt him. To lash out and hope that if he bleeds, it will somehow erase the specter of Oliver's blood washing me with crimson.

"Almost everything," he says, and pulls his walking stick free of the ground, raising both hands as if to show me he means me no harm. "I've lost almost everything."

I don't know what to say to this. I can't tell if he's lying. Before I can study his eyes to see if he understands the sense of overwhelming loss howling within me, the ground beneath us rumbles slightly, and something that sounds like thunder, muted and distant, comes closer.

I meet Melkin's eyes and we leap into motion. Shoving my Switch into the strap sewn on the side of my pack for this purpose, I grab the nearest low-hanging tree branch and start climbing. Melkin lunges for the tree as well, wrapping his long arms and legs around the trunk and shimmying up its length until he finds a branch thick enough to support him.

The rumble becomes a roar, and the ground below us begins to crack.

I'm one quarter of the way up the tree. The crack runs directly below me.

"Jump!" Melkin yells.

Frantically, I scan the branches around me until I find one that reaches into the heart of the tree beside it and is thick enough to support my weight. I scramble along its length and leap for the next tree. My feet skid along the branch as I land, and I start running, grabbing branches for balance, swinging my body into the upper reaches of the tree, and then leaping for the next. Melkin is tree-leaping as well, though I'm too focused on my own survival to worry about him now.

I've put seven trees between me and my starting point when the roar becomes a deafening bellow, the ground we stood upon just a moment ago dissolves into nothing, and the Cursed One explodes out of the ground.

CHAPTER THIRTY-FOUR

RACHEL

I freeze. I'm about seventeen yards from the monstrous beast slithering its way into the open. I don't think it's enough. At the very least, I need to move higher, but I can't without alerting it to my exact location.

The Cursed One coils its body along the ground and pulls itself from the hole it created. Up close, it looks like a giant wingless dragon covered in thick interlocking black scales with a tail the length of two grown men lying end to end and a ridge of webbed spikes running along its back. Thick yellow claws protrude from its muscled limbs.

Our weapons are useless. Swords break against its scales, arrows glance off, and the only area of weakness seems to be its sightless milky yellow eyes, but to get close enough to stab the eye is to court a fiery death from its mouth.

Besides, stabbing it in the eye is pointless. Nothing dies from losing an eye.

The only escape is to stay off its radar. It tracks by sound and smell, and when it stops and swings its head slowly side to side, huffing smoky little breaths, I don't dare move a muscle. I'm grateful I don't have the food in my pack. It would only add to my human scent and make me a bigger target.

Melkin isn't as fortunate. I slant my eyes to the side and see him clinging to the upper branches of the tree beside mine, but his pack is nowhere to be seen. I guess he had the presence of mind to drop it.

The Cursed One puffs its breath out, and small flames jet through its nostrils, scorching the earth in front of it. The burned dirt seems to infuriate it, and it shakes its head, puffing increasingly large flames from its snout.

If we're quiet, absolutely silent, it will leave. I focus on breathing in and out with slow precision, though my lungs scream at me to drag air in as quickly as possible so I can flee or fight.

I won't have to do either, though. I just have to be still.

Suddenly, it jerks its head up and points its sightless eyes straight at me.

My stomach lurches, and as I glance around for a way out, I catch sight of Melkin's pack hanging on a branch several feet below me. I didn't realize he'd climbed up behind me before switching trees, dropping his pack along the way. I'm about to pay the price.

Abandoning my efforts at controlled, silent breathing, I give in to my body's demands, dragging in a huge gulp of air while I tense my muscles for action.

The beast sniffs again, its body coiling like a snake about to strike.

If I don't move, I'm dead.

I have to time it just right. Leap as it attacks and hope the noise of the fireball it spews covers the sound of me landing in another tree. Glancing at Melkin's position, I judge the distance between my tree and his. He catches my eye and jerks his chin toward the branch below him.

I brace myself and watch for my moment.

I don't have to wait long. In seconds, the beast's agitation reaches a boiling point and it rears up, takes aim, and roars a giant ball of fire straight at my tree.

I run along the branch and leap for Melkin's tree as the trunk behind me explodes into flame. I land hard, slip, and nearly fall, but Melkin's unnaturally long arm snakes down and catches me.

I dangle against the tree, my feet struggling to find purchase on the branch below me, while the Cursed One roars its fury and swings its head from side to side, obliterating everything in its path.

Panic blazes through me, sharp and absolute. I'm not going to die. Not like this. I have too many promises to keep.

My feet find the branch, and I steady myself by holding on to the trunk below Melkin. He keeps his hand on my pack, and we freeze as the Cursed One slithers around the trees, sniffing and listening.

I don't know what called it here. Maybe it was close enough to hear me yelling. Maybe we were just in the wrong place at the wrong time, though I've never been a big believer in coincidence. Whatever caught the Cursed One's attention, we're in its sights now.

Any gratitude I feel at being high enough to avoid letting it sniff out our location disappears when it bellows, a throaty roar of fury, and strafes the trees in front of it with fire. The trunk below us bursts into flame, and heat licks at my toes.

Smoke billows up, choking me, and the flames crawl steadily toward us. My lungs scream for air, my muscles shake with the need to run, and my skin feels dry and parched, but switching trees now would be my death sentence. I hold my breath to keep from coughing, and focus on remaining still.

It works. The Cursed One swings its head back and forth for another interminable minute, then curls back around, black scales glistening in the flickering light of the flames it created, and slithers its way into the gaping hole it made in the ground.

We remain still until the last trace of it disappears. Then we explode into motion. Scrambling up the trunk, we run along the length of the thickest branch we can find and tree-leap only to do the whole thing all over again.

Fire spreads quickly in the packed density of the Wasteland, but I know there's a river less than one hundred fifty yards to the west. Melkin knows it too, and we head for it in unspoken agreement.

Behind us, a wall of fire chews through the forest, spitting sparks and embers toward the sky and gushing a cloud of black smoke in our wake. We leap, climb, run, leap, and at some point, Melkin's hand reaches out and takes my heavy pack off my shoulders so I can keep up.

In the distance, I see the deep blue-black surface of the river glittering beneath the afternoon sun. My lungs burn, and my hands are raw from snatching at rough bark for balance, but I increase my pace as the wall of heat behind me whispers along my skin.

Melkin reaches the river first but doesn't jump. Instead, he waits, reaching a skinny hand back for me as I make my final leap and skid along the branch toward him. He catches me, grabs my hand, and together we dive out of the trees and into the crisp, cold water.

CHAPTER THIRTY-FIVE

LOGAN

I no longer know what time it is. I've been lying on the damp, gritty floor of this cell for hours. Maybe a day. Maybe more. Without a way to track the sun, I can't be sure.

Pain is my constant companion—stabbing me with every breath and making a mockery of my attempts at sleep. At least one rib is broken, my arms and legs ache fiercely with bone-deep bruises, and my eyes are nearly swollen shut.

But worse than all of that is the burn on my neck. Every throb of agony from my seared flesh is a reminder of the Commander's power over me. I want to use the pain to focus on a plan to remove that power from him permanently, but my thoughts are fuzzy and vague, and the pain seems so much more important.

A chill seeps into me from the stone floor I lay on, and even with my cloak, I'm shivering. I should force myself to stand up and walk. Loosen the muscles. Promote faster healing.

I inhale slowly, trying to keep from pressing my lungs against my rib cage with too much force, and place my palms flat on the floor in front of me.

My body shakes as I slowly push myself to my hands and knees, inch by torturous inch. Gray dots swirl in front of my limited vision, and my empty stomach rebels against the waves of dizziness swamping me.

I may have gained my cloak, but I'm in no shape to gain my freedom.

It's a devastating thought, but I can't hang on to it for long. Heat is eating away at my brain, blurring the edges of reality until I can't tell if the contents of my head are memories, dreams, or wisps of things not worth the effort it takes to force them into something that makes sense.

I can't stand without help. Crawling toward the wall is a slow, agonizing process, and I stop frequently to rest, laying my face against the filthy stone floor and shivering both from external cold and the internal heat that blazes through my head but refuses to warm my body.

How does one cure a fever? I can't remember. My body shakes as I force myself to keep crawling. Keep moving. Keep pushing my muscles to work through the bruises because *he'll* come back. And I refuse to let him kill me.

I reach the wall sometime later and discover my nose is bleeding. I don't know how long that's been going on, and I decide I don't care.

From a distance, I hear the main dungeon door open, and I know I should be afraid, but that takes too much effort. Instead, I dig my fingers into the rugged texture of the wall beside me, and pull myself to my feet.

The room spins in slow, sickening circles. I try to breathe through the nausea this creates, but dragging air into my lungs ignites the terrible pain in my side.

Someone is walking along the row between cells. I don't know who it is. I can't seem to turn my head to look. Instead, I lean my forehead against the cold stone of the wall and shake uncontrollably.

Rachel is out there. Somewhere. I know I should remember something important about her situation, but with fire eating at my brain, all I can think about is her hair in the sunlight. Like flames. Like the flames pounding at the inside of my skull.

I bang my head against the wall to put out the flames, but they just multiply.

Move.

I have to move.

If I don't, he'll kill me before I can escape.

I slide one foot in front of me, but it wobbles, and I have to hang on to the wall to keep from falling over.

Someone opens the door to my cell. The noise explodes inside my head, sending brutal hammers of pain into my temples. I let go of the wall to cover my ears, and pitch forward onto the unforgiving stone floor.

Footsteps hurry my way, and I reach for my sword. It isn't there, and the motion triggers the pain in my side until I'm gasping air in quick, shallow breaths.

The owner of the footsteps reaches me and crouches down. I can't see who it is, but the soft scent of lavender seeps through the stench of my cell and makes me want to close my eyes and pretend I'm in a field. Safe. Free. Lying on a bed of crushed lavender while the pain in my body subsides into nothing but memory, and those I love are still alive and well.

"Oh," a girl's voice exclaims in a whisper. A cool hand presses against my forehead.

I'm dreaming. I must be. There aren't any girls walking freely through the dungeon. My brain has cooked up a fantasy, and if I don't snap out of it, whoever is truly inside my cell with me will kill me before I can keep my promise to Rachel.

Rachel.

Rachel doesn't smell like lavender. She smells like citrus and midnight jasmine, and I wish the lavender would disappear and become Rachel's scent instead.

It doesn't.

Instead, the same cool hands that were pressed to my forehead are busy pushing something into the pocket of my cloak.

"Food," she whispers against my ear. "I'm putting medicine for your fever in the water. When the fever goes down, eat."

A cup tips against my lips and a trickle of bitter-tasting water dribbles into my mouth. I swallow reflexively, though part of me is screaming that this is a trick. A trap. Another wicked ploy of the Commander's to torture me. Maybe it's poison. Maybe it's something that will scrape me raw inside, doubling the pain until I want to kill myself just to make it end.

I turn my face and let another mouthful of water leak out onto the floor.

A girl lays her face next to mine, her outline blurry through the swollen slits of my eyelids. "Swallow," she says softly. "We're trying to help you."

I want to ask her who she means. No one helps you once

you're in the dungeon. No one has ever helped me outside the dungeon either, except for Oliver, Jared, and Rachel.

The hard, brisk steps of a guard echo down the row, coming swiftly toward my cell.

"Hurry!" she whispers and presses the cup to my lips.

The water feels good, even if it tastes vile, and I swallow. It might be a trick. It might make things worse, but the heat beating at my brain won't allow me the luxury of thinking through my options, and I'm desperately thirsty.

"What are you doing, girl?" the guard demands.

"Watering the prisoner as you asked," she says, her tone low and respectful.

"He's had enough. Get out of there."

She stands immediately and exits the cell, her steps hurried. The guard laughs as he looks at me lying on the floor, shivering while blood slowly seeps out of my nose.

I close my eyes and wish for a world where Rachel and Jared are safe and Oliver is alive.

CHAPTER THIRTY-SIX

RACHEL

The water snatches me with icy arms as I plunge beneath its surface. The sound of the fire becomes muted, a distant roaring that can't compete with the swift rush of the river's current. I lose my grip on Melkin's hand as I'm flung downstream. I can't stop spinning. Can't break free of the current. Can't get to the surface.

My lungs burn, and my brain screams at me to take a breath, but I've spun so many times in the dark embrace of the river, I no longer know which way is up. I kick out, lash with my arms, and fight against the water.

It's useless.

My ears roar, and a strange hum grows louder within my brain as my chest convulses and I cough, sucking in a mouthful of water in exchange.

The water burns my lungs, and I cough again.

More water. More coughing. More pain.

And then it's gone. The pain recedes. My chest relaxes. My

lungs stop demanding air. I'm at peace.

I let the current spin me as the world darkens into nothing, but something wraps around me, hauls me through the water, and I break the surface.

I cough feebly, but my lungs are used to water now. They don't know what to do with air. And I don't care. I want to close my eyes and let the water take me. Let the tiny sliver of peace I felt swallow me whole.

But I can't. Because whatever is holding me won't let me slide under the surface again. By the time we reach the shore, my lungs are burning for air, and the peace I felt is gone.

I'm tossed onto the shore, flipped over on my back, and Melkin looms over me like a giant wet twig. He puts his hands together, one over the other, and slams them into my chest.

Water gushes up my throat, burning and suffocating, and fills my mouth and nose. He reaches forward and turns my head to the side as I spew the water onto the sand. Twice more, he hits my chest and I have to spit out mouthfuls of water. When he raises his hands a fourth time, my lungs contract, and I start coughing on my own. He lowers his hands, turns me to my side so any water I cough up can dribble onto the ground, and collapses next to me, his breathing harsh.

I don't know how much time passes before he turns over on his side to face me.

"You gonna live?" he asks, and I see my pack is still strapped to his back.

My throat burns as I answer. "I'm fine."

I should thank him. Between this and catching me before I fell from the branch below him during the Cursed One's attack, he's saved my life twice today. I should, but I don't. Because even though he's saved me, even though he claims to have lost almost everything, he works for the Commander. I don't need anything else to justify the slow burn of anger I feel every time I look at him.

It should be Logan who caught me. Logan who saved me from drowning. Logan who asks if I'm okay.

"I'm sorry for what I said back there," Melkin says.

I frown. I don't know what he means.

"I know your daddy's been missing for months. I saw what happened during the Claiming ceremony. If anyone has a right to bitterness, I guess it's you." His dark eyes wander away from mine, and he heaves himself into a sitting position, my pack dripping water, creating tiny streams on the riverbank. The double-bladed glove he wore on his right hand is gone.

I wish he wouldn't apologize. Wouldn't sit there like he understands and ask for nothing in return. It makes it hard to aim my anger at him.

I sit up as well, digging my fingers into the wet sand beneath me as my head spins slowly, and look around us. Nothing is familiar. We've traveled so far down the river, I've lost any place markers to show me where we are. The distant horizon is free of smoke, a clear indication we traveled for miles in the swift embrace of the water.

"Where are we?" I ask, and wish for the hot, syrupy drink Oliver always gave me to cure a sore throat.

The memory of Oliver stabs into me, and I force myself to breathe through it.

"About past the King's City," Melkin says, raising one bony

arm to point to the bank above us to the left.

I turn to see a huge metal rectangle, its legs long ago turned into twisted wreckage, leaning against the top of the bank, one corner deeply entrenched in the ground. A man with jet-black hair and a smirk on his lips peers at us from the middle of the rectangle, his image sun-worn, the paint falling away in long strips. Vines twine around the top, obscuring the upper left corner, and tall grasses hide the base, but the word KING stretches across the center in faded, peeling red letters.

"How many days between this and Rowansmark?" I need familiar markers. A road I can remember. Something to help me find Dad's safe house. Every courier establishes his own off-the-main-path places to stock with essentials and use on their journeys. To share the location with others is to invite robbery and maybe even torture by those who would lie in wait hoping to extract any secrets they know.

"Maybe fifteen. We've been pushed off course by about five or six days," Melkin says, and stands, adjusting the weight of the pack on his back.

My pack. With my weapons.

I stand too, and though my knees wobble and my legs shake, I have no trouble remaining upright. A glance at the sky tells me we still have four hours until sunset. More than enough time to get past the King's City and find a safe place to camp. I unfasten my cloak, my fingers fumbling with the soggy leather bindings, and take it off. The damp garment is a dead weight against my shoulders, and I need the sun to dry my tunic and leggings as we walk. The copper cuff Logan gave me stands out in sharp relief beneath the wet material of my tunic. I hope Logan had the good sense to make the tracking device waterproof.

Melkin reaches a hand out for my cloak, and I jerk it toward my chest.

He frowns. "It's heavy. I'll carry it until you're feeling a bit stronger."

"It's mine. So is the pack." I reach for it.

He backs away. "You're in no shape to carry it."

My hands curl into fists. He has my Switch. My bow and arrows. Does he think if he takes most of my weapons, he'll have me at a disadvantage? I reach for the knife sheath strapped to my waist.

He holds his hands up, and I can't read the expression on his face. "You're a stubborn, suspicious one, aren't you?"

"With good reason." The knife slides free and I palm the hilt. "I want my weapons. You can carry the pack if you insist, but I carry my own weapons."

Never again will I be caught unaware. Unable to act.

He shrugs but watches me closely as he slides my Switch free of its sleeve and hands it to me. The bow and arrows follow, and I see I'm down to three arrows from the original twelve. The rest must be swirling along the bottom of the river.

I strap the bow and arrows to my back, return the knife to its sheath, and hold the Switch with my right hand.

"Better?" Melkin asks softly.

"I don't need your pity." I snatch up my cloak with my left hand.

"What do you need, then?" he asks, and it sounds like he really wants to know.

Oliver, alive and unharmed. Logan, by my side. Dad, waiting

for me with the package, able to help me figure out what to do next. The Commander, dead at my feet.

That's what I need, but I can't tell Melkin that. He works for the Commander, and he's only interested in the package.

"Rachel? What do you need?"

I remember Melkin saying he'd lost almost everything, the weight of unspoken grief hanging over his words, and wonder if giving him one piece of the truth might work in my favor. Especially if what I need is something he might secretly want as well. Looking him in the eye, I say, "Revenge. I need revenge."

His eyes darken and slide away from mine as he hefts the pack against his back. "Try not to harshly judge those of us with more than that left to live for," he says, and starts up the bank without looking to see if I'll follow.

Does he think I have so little left to live for? I have Logan. I have Dad. And I have a score to settle. None of those can be taken lightly. I clench my teeth around the words that want to burst free and scorch the air around me. Arguing would only give him more information than he needs to know. Instead, I dig my Switch into the soft sand beneath me for balance, and start the climb toward the King's City.

CHAPTER THIRTY-SEVEN

RACHEL

We stop for the night in the shelter of a concrete box of a building with only two sides still standing against the ravages of time and weather. We left the King's City behind two hours ago, and I'm grateful. The twisted metal remains of buildings that once housed a vibrant civilization are now blackened husks coated in ash and wrapped with kudzu. Walking among them makes me nervous. A harsh reminder of what the Cursed One is capable of doing to us if we don't remain with those who've proven their ability to protect us.

Since I have no intention of remaining beneath anyone's authority again, I turn my back on the ruins of the city and refuse to consider the idea that I may have just glimpsed my future.

Melkin hasn't spoken to me since our words on the riverbank, and that's fine with me. I have nothing left to say. I just want this leg of the journey over with.

Thankfully, I have flint and fuel in my pack, so we don't have to worry about keeping ourselves warm or keeping wild animals at bay. I work with Melkin to gather firewood and stack it in the center of the makeshift shelter. I also still have my flask of fresh water, and I offer it to him.

He raises a brow at me, but accepts it and swallows three times before handing it back. I lay my pack against one of the still-standing walls of our shelter and grab my bow and arrows.

"Where are you going?" he asks as I stride out of the shelter.

"To catch dinner."

"I'll come with you."

I toss a glance over my shoulder. "I can handle this. You get the fire going, and stop worrying that I need a babysitter."

Which might not be fair, considering I needed his help twice today. But I can handle hunting, and I need some time alone without his watchful eyes tracking my every move. Without the strain of trying to appear like I don't want to scream in frustration when we've traveled for hours, and I still don't know where we are.

He doesn't follow me, though he moves to the edge of the ruined building and watches me as I go.

Our shelter is settled against a soft swell of land covered in tall grass already gone to seed. Beyond the hill, the broken remains of an old road wind through the grass and disappear for yards at a time. On the other side of the road, a copse of trees stretches as far as I can see.

The sun is drowning beneath the weight of a purple twilight as I enter the trees, walk twenty yards into the middle of them, their skinny trunks and thin, graceful branches reaching for the heavens as if hoping to scrape against the stars, and find what I'm looking for.

A bush hugs the base of a tree, its branches curving like a bell, its leaves brushing the ground. Beneath it, a small, hollow space rests, and I crawl inside, string an arrow, and wait.

Night has nearly reclaimed the sky when I finally catch a glimpse of movement. I tense, hardly daring to breathe. My patience is rewarded as a creature about the size of a small sheep wanders close, nose to ground, snuffling. I draw in a slow, deep breath, rehearse each step in my mind, and then whip the bow up, close one eye to sight down the center, and release the arrow.

It flies true, striking the side of the animal, and I leap from cover as my quarry jerks around and starts to run with faltering steps. Crossing the distance between us in seconds, I yank my knife free, leap on the animal's back, and swing my arm beneath its neck to slice open its throat.

It dies instantly, and I wipe my knife clean on the ground beside it. Retrieving my arrow, I clean it as well and pack my weapons away. Flipping the animal over, I see I've caught a boar. A young one, by the size of its tusks.

I can't easily lift it, plus I refuse to get its blood all over me. The thought makes bile surge up my throat, and I cough, gag, and spit on the forest floor. I solve the problem by grabbing its hind legs and dragging it to the edge of the trees. I don't want to drag it across the grass and broken pieces of road to our shelter because the trail of blood could lead a wild animal straight to us while we sleep.

I don't have to.

Melkin is standing on the road, watching the tree line, his sword in his hands.

He doesn't see me at first, and I'm struck by the harsh,

predatory silhouette he makes, caught in the moment before the sun's final death and the moon's rise. Before I can continue this line of thinking, he notices me and approaches, his long stride eating the distance like it's nothing.

"Nice," he says as he sees the boar.

I shrug, though his continued attitude of tolerant courtesy toward me is starting to make me feel uncomfortable in my own skin.

He lifts the boar with a grunt and turns back toward our camp. I follow and list the reasons I have for keeping my distance from him. For being angry with him.

It all boils down to the fact that he's in the Commander's pocket.

Of course, he could think the same of me.

I mull this over as Melkin pulls a knife from a sheath strapped to his ankle and carves the boar, separating muscle from bone with swift hacking motions. He tosses choice pieces of meat onto the flames to sizzle and snap. Maybe I'm supposed to feel enmity toward him. Maybe the Commander knew anyone he used to replace Logan would be a target for my mistrust. Maybe we aren't supposed to be a team working toward the same goal, because if we begin to think for ourselves, the Commander could be in danger.

The idea warms me with something more than fury.

Something that feels like another tiny fragment of hope.

I lay my damp cloak out to dry near the flames, and take a seat beside Melkin. Far enough away that I can draw my knife before his long arms could reach me, but close enough to indicate I'm not trying to shut him out.

He glances at me, but says nothing.

I force myself to say the words I know he deserves to hear. "Thank you."

He uses a stick to nudge the meat and flip it over. The scent fills the air and makes my mouth water.

"For what?" he asks.

"For saving my life. Twice. For carrying the boar. And for"—here I choke on the words and have to push them past my lips, their inflection sounding wooden and insincere—"understanding my attitude."

He stays silent for the time it takes to skewer three large pieces of meat on a stick and hand it to me. Then he says, "Didn't think I'd hear that from you."

I shrug and bite into the meat, which burns my lips but explodes against my tongue with glorious flavor. I watch him skewer his own before answering. "You work for the Commander."

"So do you."

"Not by choice."

"And you think I do?" He looks at me, and I'm struck by the depth of misery etched into his too-thin face.

I feel my way carefully through my next words. "You're a tracker. You've worked for the Commander for years. I figured this was just another assignment to you."

He looks into the fire. "You figured wrong."

I'm not sure I have. I have only my instincts to rely on, and my instincts tell me that Melkin doesn't wish me harm, and that he carries an inner grief of his own. If I can soften him toward my cause, maybe we can be a team against the Commander.

"Maybe I'm wrong," I say. "But how am I to know for sure?"

He laughs, a small, brittle sound, and looks at me. "How can either of us know anything for sure? We've been backed into a corner, threatened with losing everything, and then set loose to circle each other like South Edge dogs afraid to lose a prize bone."

I stare at him, my mind racing. Is he really in the same situation as me? Or has he been coached to say this so I'll trust him?

He shakes his head. "One of us has to tell the truth here. I'll start. You can do with it what you will."

I say nothing, but watch him carefully for signs he might be lying.

"It's true I've worked for the Commander for eleven years now. And it's true that he assigned me to accompany you."

"Why?"

"Apparently, he thought you might need the help. You're just a girl, after all." A ghost of a smile flits across his face. "A girl who knows how to keep her head in the face of the Cursed One, who can nearly drown and still trek for four hours, and who has the skill to bring down a boar. Bet the Commander has no idea how far he's underestimated you."

I bet the Commander hasn't underestimated me at all, and Melkin's true role is to make sure I don't commit treachery. Which means Melkin could make it look like we're on the same side when all he's trying to do is buy my confidence. Calculating the odds makes me ache for Logan, who could assess the options, list the worst-case scenarios, and come up with plans to address it all in half the time it will take me to decide if I should just sneak away from Melkin in the middle of the night and do my best to survive the Wasteland alone.

"So why do you say you didn't take this assignment willingly?" I ask, and Melkin swallows hard, his Adam's apple bobbing in his throat like a cork.

He's quiet so long, I begin to think he won't answer the question. When he finally speaks, he addresses his words to the flames in a voice so low, I have to strain to hear him.

"I would have. I would've tracked the package with you and returned it, just like I've done with every other assignment he's given me. But he didn't give me a chance to prove my loyalty." He looks at me suddenly, desperate grief in his eyes. "He threw my wife in the dungeon. She's due to give birth in two months, and he threw her in the dungeon."

I don't doubt him for a second. The raw, aching pain in his voice reminds me of my own loss, and I want to stuff my fingers in my ears and pretend I can't hear him. His emotions are real, but that still doesn't mean I can trust his words.

"What do you have to do to get her out?" I ask quietly, because here is the crux of the issue. If he tells me the truth, perhaps we can work our way toward trusting each other. But if he lies . . . if I even *think* he's lying, then I'll have to think like Logan and start planning for worst-case scenarios.

He scrubs a hand over his face, breaking eye contact with me and looking at the fire again. "I have to deliver the package. Whether you agree or not." He looks at me. "I can't allow any obstacles to stand in my way."

And there it is. If I plan treachery against the Commander, he's the one tasked to stand in my way. No matter what it takes. And he will. Because his wife and unborn child are at stake.

I can't blame him for doing exactly what I would do myself.

And I can't help feeling empathy for his position. I know what it's like to have the Commander hold my loved ones over my head at the point of a sword. The difference is that I no longer believe the Commander's promises.

I don't share my conviction with Melkin, though. It wouldn't change the danger his wife is in. It would only wound him further. Or turn him against me.

Instead, I slide a little closer to him and say softly, "I have to deliver the package too. Or I lose someone I care for."

"And your chance at revenge?" he asks, and captures my gaze with his as if the fate of the world hinges on my answer.

Maybe it does. Maybe he needs to know someone is willing to take a stand against the Commander, and his current suffering won't be swept under a rug.

"Yes. I need to deliver the package so I can rescue Logan. And so I can get my revenge." The words sting the air between us.

Melkin nods once as though he's gained the answer he sought, and turns back to the fire to take first watch. I curl up on my still-drying cloak, my back to the fire, my face toward Melkin.

We might have reached a new accord between us. We might be working toward the same goal. But my knife is a comforting weight in my hand as I quietly pull it from its sheath and hold it, blade out, where I can strike anything that comes for me.

Just in case I'm wrong.

CHAPTER THIRTY-EIGHT

LOGAN

She didn't kill me. Whatever the lavender-scented girl put in my water, it soothed my feverish thinking and kept the pain somewhat at bay. I'm able to wrap myself in my cloak, lean against the wall, and sleep until the next guard makes his rounds.

By the time he reaches my cell, I've slumped to the floor and I huddle there, shivering. It isn't hard to do. The stones beneath me radiate cold. He studies me for a moment, then makes the trek back to the main door, locks it behind him, and leaves the dungeon in silence again.

I wait a few moments longer to make sure he's truly gone, and then slowly sit up, making it look like it's a struggle to do so. That isn't hard either. My muscles protest the slightest movement, the scorched skin on the side of my neck throbs, and my broken rib aches fiercely.

But my fever is gone, and I can think clearly again.

Along with the return of reason comes the knowledge that I've wasted precious time succumbing to my injuries. I don't know what day it is, or how long Rachel's been gone. My body is weak from lack of food and lack of movement. And the Commander is probably due to arrive at any moment to toy with me.

I can't fix it all at once. I have to prioritize and determine an appropriate course of action. Whatever I choose, it has to be something I can do without raising suspicion if I'm being watched by more than just the occasional guard.

Food is the first order of business. I double over as if in excruciating pain and feel within my cloak pockets until I find the wrapped lump the girl left for me. Inside the cloth is a chunk of oat bread with cheese and dried apples inside. I take small bites, rocking back and forth to simulate pain so I can hide what I'm doing. My stomach has been without food for hours, maybe days. I need to take it easy.

One third of the way through the food, I stop eating. It's enough to get my system working again, and I need to conserve what I have left. I don't know when I'll be getting more.

I settle against the wall again as exhaustion overtakes me. I'd hoped to get up and walk a bit, but my head is already spinning, and I can't risk another fall. Instead, I slowly stretch each limb and tighten my muscles for the length of time it takes to recite the periodic table. By the time I'm done, I'm shaking and slightly nauseous.

Water would be nice, but that's one problem I'm helpless to address.

Through it all, the knowledge that Oliver is gone aches within me, a constant source of pain I rub against with every thought. For just a moment, the image of my mother's smile, the feel of Oliver's arm around my shoulders, and the warmth of Rachel's trust in me bleed together into one gaping pit of loss. I'm hollowed out. Empty of everything that once gave me reasons to live.

Grief is a deep pool of darkness, and I huddle on the damp, cold floor as it sucks me under. I had something worth losing, and now that it's gone, now that *they're* gone, I'm realizing the life of solitude I always thought I wanted isn't good enough anymore.

I don't want to be alone.

I don't want to have only the cold comfort of my inventions to keep me company.

I want my family.

I want *Rachel*.

Not because she's beautiful. Not because she's my responsibility. I want her because she makes me laugh. Makes me think. Inspires me to be the kind of man I always hoped I'd be.

I want Rachel because the thought of a life without her is more than I can bear.

The grief recedes. It won't help me plan. I haven't lost Rachel. Not yet. I lean my head against the wall, careful not to rub my burned skin against the damp stone, and consider my options. Movement catches my eye, and I turn to see Melkin's wife, Eloise, staring at me.

I don't greet her. I don't need to announce to anyone that I'm capable of that. But I hold her gaze, trying to assess what I see there.

Best Case Scenario: She's an innocent caught up in all of this and means me no harm.

Worst Case Scenario 1: She means me no harm but will

unwittingly gather information she'll later deliver to the Commander under duress.

Worst Case Scenario 2: She's cunning enough to realize she might leverage her way out of here by providing the Commander with secrets about me.

Worst Case Scenario 3: She's his spy dressed up to look helpless and pregnant. Hoping I'll pity her. Hoping to play on the sense of honor the Commander swears I don't have.

The answer to every scenario is the same. Give nothing away and set in motion my plan for escape before anyone realizes I'm well enough to do so.

She's still watching me, but I close my eyes and turn away. It's easy to look exhausted and sick. I don't even have to feign it. Let her report my weakness. The fact that I can't even stand. Let her tell them the Commander has me beaten.

By the time he realizes the truth, I'll be gone.

"Stop him," someone whispers, a mere breath of sound I barely catch.

I open my eyes a fraction, and she's still watching me, her eyes pleading. Stop whom? The Commander? Melkin?

This is exactly the kind of conversation I need to avoid. I close my eyes again, and keep my silence.

"Please."

Another breathy whisper. I tamp down on the surge of irritation that wants to snap my eyes open so I can glare her into silence. Does she think I'm so easily led that I'll fall for this?

Does she really think I have the power at the moment to stop anyone?

"He isn't a killer. He isn't . . ." Her whisper chokes off into stillness as the dungeon door opens with a clang.

If "he" isn't a killer, she can only be discussing Melkin. But how she thinks I'll ever be able to reach him in time while I'm lying indisposed in a dungeon of stone is a mystery.

Not that I don't have a plan for it, of course. But she has no way of knowing that, and her misplaced faith in me rings false.

Another sign I need to be careful what I allow her to see.

The footsteps traveling the aisle are light. They stop at the first occupied cell and a door slides open with a high-pitched squeal. A girl's voice, light and calm, murmurs through the air, and my stomach tightens.

This must be my secret savior. The one who gave me hope that someone on the outside is interested in helping me. I need more information, but I have to hide the transaction from Eloise.

I slide down to the floor and curl into a ball with my back facing the cell door. The girl is talking to every prisoner she encounters. Seeing her talk to me will raise no alarms, while seeing me question her will give more away than I can afford.

She moves to the cell with the young man in chains, and her voice is clearer now. I listen to her offer him food and water and then quietly suggest he put the paste she's placed in his tin of food on his abraded wrists rather than in his mouth.

She could be arrested for that alone.

I marvel at her courage, even while I tense for the appearance of a guard. No one comes, though, and she moves on to Melkin's wife. I strain to hear their conversation and catch snippets of admonitions to eat everything in front of her and drink her water slowly. Then there's the sound of fabric hitting the floor.

"You can't give me your cloak," Melkin's wife whispers.

Because apparently she is incapable of realizing the best way to punish a good deed is to announce it to everyone else. Or because she thinks turning in the girl will somehow grant her favor with the Commander.

Her mistake could simply be one of youth and ignorance, but I have precious little sympathy for either at the moment. Rachel is young too, and she'd be far too smart to make such a stupid mistake.

The door to my cell creaks open, and I'm swamped with the delicate scent of lavender a second before she drops to the floor beside me, clutching a tin water pail and a cup.

The concern on her face doesn't falter, even as she takes in my steady, fever-free gaze. She's tall, thin in a lithe, graceful way, and the torchlight flickers beautifully against her dusky skin. The cloud of dark hair hanging down her back throws off the lavender scent every time she moves.

She seems familiar, and I try to recall where I've seen her before. One of the stalls in Lower Market? A merchant's place in North Hub? Neither of those locations fit.

She scoops a cup of water out of the pail and leans toward me.

"Day?" I mouth silently before accepting a few swallows. The water is tepid and tastes of tin. It's the most refreshing drink I've ever had.

She frowns as if I've spilled the water out of my mouth and fishes around in her skirt pocket for a scrap of cloth. Bending down, she pretends to mop my face with the cloth and keeps her face level with mine, her hair obscuring her features from anyone outside my cell.

"Tuesday," she says, and presses a small, paper-wrapped

packet into my hand. "For the pain."

Tuesday. The Claiming ceremony was Saturday. I've lost three days.

She sits up and scoops more water into her cup. I drink obediently, and watch her calm, competent movements. I've seen those movements before, but my brain still refuses to make the connection, and I let it go. I have more important things to think about. She's risked death today, not just for me, but for each of the prisoners here. I can't quite understand it.

"Why help?" I mouth to her, though I feel the answer may be too lengthy to share like this.

She dips her cloth in the remaining water and scrubs gently at my face, using her hair once more as a cloak to mask her face from any observers.

"Things must change," she says so softly, I barely catch it. "Someone needs to lead that change. We think it will be you."

I'm stunned into silence, and wait a beat too long to ask her the other questions that burn within me. She's already leaving, shutting my door behind her as if she hasn't just ignited a firestorm of speculation within me, when I remember where I've seen her.

Thom's Tankard. Wiping down tables while acting as a lookout for Drake and his men.

Drake's group has moved from trying to recruit me as a member to nominating me as a leader? I'd laugh if it wouldn't hurt my rib cage. I'm injured, locked in a dungeon, and the only people I still care about are far away from Baalboden. What part of that description makes me fit to lead a revolution here?

Not that I'm not sympathetic to their cause. The citizens of

Baalboden desperately need change. I'd been wrong to think my mother's death meant the price of dissent was too high to pay. Silent acquiescence in the face of tyranny is no better than outright agreement. My mother knew that. Now, so do I.

But revolution and change must wait their turn.

Rachel needs me.

Melkin needs to be stopped.

Jared needs to be found.

And the Commander needs to be brought to justice.

If I have to lead a revolution to accomplish that, so be it.

CHAPTER THIRTY-NINE

RACHEL

We've been traveling the Wasteland for a week now. Four days ago, we skirted a Tree People village without incident. Not that I've ever known Tree People to get involved with the affairs of those who leave them alone, but we can't take any chances. I never used to understand why people would choose to build houses in the trees in hopes of avoiding the Cursed One rather than live beneath the protection of a city-state. Now, I know that sometimes the protection of a city-state comes at too high a cost.

Two days ago, I began recognizing markers along the way and knew we were back on the path to Rowansmark. The forest has changed and thickened, easing out of pin oak trees and into silver maples interspersed with pine. The morning dew hangs just as heavy in the air as it does on the ground, and large fields of waist-high grass ripple sluggishly beneath a half-hearted breeze.

Melkin and I have fallen into a rhythm. He leads, beating back the worst of the undergrowth, and I sweep the ground behind us to cover our tracks. I hunt for our dinner each night, and he makes the fire and handles the cooking. We speak only when necessary during the day, but at night, as we eat rabbit, boar, or turkey, we talk. Though we rarely discuss anything personal, it's beginning to feel like I'm traveling with a friend.

Though I never forget that our friendship could be his way of trying to hold me to the Commander's orders, and when I catch him watching me with something dark and brooding in his eyes, I know he feels the same.

As we make camp again for the night, I can see he misses his wife. It's carved in miserable lines on his face, bracketing his mouth with tension that refuses to ease.

I miss Logan, too. More than I thought I would.

The slap of humiliation I once felt every time I thought of him is gone. In its place, I see Logan sacrificing sleep so he could finish the tracking device. Offering to teach me to use the Switch and helping me hold on to the good memories I have of Dad. Drawing his sword against the Commander, despite overwhelming odds, to protect me. Logan is the lodestone I cling to when grief over Oliver and fear for Dad threaten to rob me of what little hope I have left.

Something in me has awakened and responds only to Logan. I lie sleepless long after Melkin takes the first watch and press my fingers to my lips as I remember Logan leaning in, his breath fanning my face, his eyes locked on my mouth. A delicious ache pulses through me. I feel like a stranger waking up in my own skin—aware of every inch. Heat runs through my veins, both exhilarating and terrifying.

Exhilarating because every part of me tingles with life.

But terrifying because beneath the longing lies an inescapable truth: If he is my lodestone, it's because somehow in the last few weeks I've started to rely on him. Lean on him. Need him. My heart pounds a little faster as the realization sinks in.

I need Logan.

Not because I need saving. Not because he could plan our way out of this. But because on some basic, soul-deep level within me, he is the solid ground beneath my feet. The one who will move mountains to keep his promises. The one who looks at me and *sees*.

I can't imagine my life without him.

Everywhere I look, he's there. A constant thread binding my past, my present, and the future I want so badly to have with him. With *him*.

My eyes fly open.

I'm in love with Logan.

Not the way I thought I was two years ago, when I offered him my heart. That love was uncomplicated and innocent, designed for a simple life. The love consuming me now is fierce and absolute—forged in a crucible of loss and united by our shared strength.

I love Logan. A laugh bubbles up, even as tears sting my eyes. I reach up to clasp his mother's necklace, the symbol of his promise to me, and hold the tender, vibrant thought of him close as the stars chase one another across the sky.

Halfway through the next day's journey, we approach the clearing where Dad and I always stopped for a meal, and the ache of missing him throbs in time with the ache of missing Oliver. If I can find him now, the fierce edge of my grief will lessen. He'll know how to save Logan without giving the package to the Commander. He'll take the burden of this awful responsibility off my shoulders.

I don't realize how much I want him to be waiting for me as we move past a thin line of maples and into the small field of yellow-green grass until I see he isn't there.

He isn't here.

I know it isn't logical to feel so hopeless when I had no real reason to think he'd be camped at the edge of the clearing waiting for me, but I can't help the tears that stream down my face. Loneliness eats at me, and for the millionth time since I left Baalboden, I wish Logan was with me.

Quickly swiping my palms across my cheeks before Melkin catches me crying, I start to turn away when movement catches my eye. A slice of deep purple shimmers gently against a tree trunk on the far side of the field. Veering off course without saying a word, I move toward it, my heart suddenly knocking against my chest like it wants its freedom.

"What are you doing?" Melkin asks behind me.

I ignore him and hurry, the crisp stalks of grass parting before me and *shushing* closed in my wake. The purple is a ribbon, wind torn and water ravaged, tied around the base of the lowest branch. The initials *S. A.* are embroidered in the corner.

I know this ribbon. It's one of a handful that belonged to my mother. Dad always carried them with him when he went into the Wasteland.

I want to laugh. To dance. To open my mouth and let the fierce joy singing through me echo from the treetops.

He was here.

And he wanted me to know it.

CHAPTER FORTY

RACHEL

As if connected to my thoughts, the cuff around my left arm vibrates gently, and I glance down to see the blue wires begin to glow—a hesitant, flickering light that fills me with wild, buoyant hope.

Dad.

I can find him.

He can fix this.

I just have to hold on a little longer.

"What does this mean?"

Melkin stands to my right, watching me closely, and I scramble to find something to say. I can't tell him I think we're closing in on Dad. I don't know how he'd react, and it's best not to introduce any new elements into our precarious partnership until it's already accomplished.

"It means we're on the right track."

His skinny brows crawl toward the center of his forehead. "I thought we already knew that."

I shrug and step forward, as much to tug the ribbon free as to hide my face from his prying eyes.

"You mean this is a sign?"

When I don't answer, he shifts his weight forward, his shadow swallowing me from behind, and says in a voice I scarcely recognize as the mild, courteous Melkin I've been with for a week, "Who's working with you? Better come clean now, girl, or you'll not get a second chance."

I fold the ribbon carefully and stow it in an inner cloak pocket before turning to face him. He looms above me, all sharp angles and seething suspicion, his hand resting on his sword hilt.

"Calm down. No one's working with me, but you had to know we're following my dad's trail since he's the one who hid the package. You should be relieved I recognize his signs."

Not that he had ever once deliberately left a sign before. But he'd never left without planning to return either. I give him kudos for knowing I'd follow him, and for knowing what would show me I'm on the right track.

Melkin's hand slides off his knife and he steps back, though his eyes still look troubled. I turn from him and plunge into the trees again. I can't bear to waste time. He follows me, and in a few moments, shoulders his way past me to resume the lead, his expression once more a sea of calm.

I'm not fooled. He's afraid. Of the consequences if he fails his mission, yes. But also of me and any tricks I might pull. I want to tell him he has nothing to fear from me or my dad as long as he doesn't stand between the Commander and justice, but I don't think he'd believe me. Not completely. It's hard for him to fathom the Commander falling hard enough to lose the power to ruin lives, and Melkin has two other lives at stake beside his own.

We break for a lunch of cold rabbit leftovers, creek water, and silence thick enough to cut with a knife. Finally, I look him in the eye and say, "What's the problem?"

He chews a bite of rabbit slowly, the bones of his jaw swiveling like a set of Logan's gears. "I don't like this whole situation."

"That makes two of us."

"What if we're being led into a trap?"

I squint at him through a shaft of blinding afternoon sun. "Who do you think is leading us into a trap?"

"Someone who wants whatever is in that package."

Which could be anyone. Trackers from Rowansmark. Others working for the Commander. Highwaymen who've heard of its existence. If I wasn't absolutely sure the signal came from Dad, I'd be thinking the same thing.

I pull the ribbon from my pocket, smooth it over my knee for a moment, my fingers slowly tracing the silvery *S. A.* stitched into the corner, and then hand it to Melkin. His fingers are cold as they brush against mine.

"*S. A.*?"

"Sarabeth Adams. My mother."

Quiet falls between us, though the Wasteland is quick to fill it up with the warbling chirps of birds and the drowsy buzzing of insects. Beneath the chirping and buzzing, I catch what sounds like the faint snap of a twig.

I freeze and look at Melkin, but he's staring at the ribbon and seems oblivious. Turning, I scan the area around us, but can't see anything amiss.

I'm not reassured.

"Do you miss her?"

I snap back around to Melkin. "Not really. She died right after I was born."

I don't have time to give him more than that. Someone is behind us. I'm sure of it. I toss the rest of the rabbit meat away from me, slide my arms into my pack, and remove my knife from its sheath.

"I bet Jared does."

"I guess," I say, keeping my voice low. "Come on. We need to go."

He looks at me, the ribbon threaded through his fingers like a bedraggled set of rings. "I can't lose Eloise. She's . . ." He chokes, clears his throat, and says, "Do you think the Commander will keep his promise to set her free if I . . ."

"If you what?" I can barely focus on him. I'm standing now, my Switch in my hand, scanning the trees.

He stands as well, towering over me again, his eyes suddenly reminding me of the dark, depthless holes carved into the ground by the Cursed One. "If I do what was asked of me. Will he keep his promise if I do what he asked of me?"

His sword is out too. That's good. At least he isn't completely immune to the signals I'm sending out. My voice is little more than a breath of air as I tell him, "I think someone is tracking us. Coming for us. I heard a branch."

He hefts the sword.

"To the right. About thirty yards. Maybe more. I haven't heard anything since, but either we leave now or find a place to set up an ambush and wait." I look at him, expecting a decision, and see the endless dark of his eyes still pinned on me.

"You didn't answer my question."

I glare and consider whacking him with my Switch, except I don't want to make the noise. "We're in danger, Melkin. Get moving."

His arm snakes out and snags the front of my cloak as I try to pass him, and I stare at him in disbelief.

Does he want us to die?

"Do you think the Commander will free Eloise if I do what he asked of me?"

The idiot isn't going to move until he hears what he wants to hear. Is the Commander going to keep his word? Not unless it somehow benefits him to do so. But I'm not about to open up that can of worms while someone is bearing down on us, and Melkin's common sense has taken a flying leap to parts unknown.

"Yes," I say with as much conviction as I can manage in a whisper. "Yes, I'm sure he will. Keep your end of the bargain, and she'll be fine. Now, let's go."

He releases my cloak. Pressing his lips into a thin line, he uses his knife to gesture toward a dense line of trees to our left.

"You first."

I don't need a second invitation. Brushing past him, I slip into the trees, moving like a shadow, while Melkin slides in after me, his sword glittering beneath a stray ray of sunlight.

CHAPTER FORTY-ONE

LOGAN

I think it's Saturday now, which would mean I've been a guest in the Commander's dungeon for a week. The girl from Thom's Tankard hasn't been back since she slipped me a paper-wrapped package of medicinal powder on Tuesday. Instead, a plump, stoop-shouldered woman old enough to be my grandmother has cared for the prisoners in silence.

I decide it's a good thing I haven't seen the girl again. Thinking about revolution might distract me from the pressing issues already on my plate. The most important of those is escape, but I'm not sure I'm well enough to outrun any pursuing guards as I sprint toward the Wall. I estimate another two to three days before my broken rib will allow me to run without doubling me over in pain.

Less if I can find a cloth to bind my chest.

I suppose I could use the shirt off my back, but I'd prefer not to be so obvious. Especially when Eloise in the cell across the aisle watches me every second of the day like a desperate baby bird hoping for a worm.

The Commander hasn't visited again, and the anticipation stretches my nerves until I want something to happen just to get it over with. I'd think he'd relish the opportunity to taunt me. Hurt me. Make sure I know he's won. I decide to take his absence as a sign Melkin still hasn't succeeded in killing Rachel, and focus on readying my body for my escape. Still, waiting for the inevitable festers in the back of my mind like an infection.

I've spent the last few days sitting or lying on the dungeon floor, doing my best to look hopelessly injured while I tighten and hold my muscles until they shake from the exertion. I've also done my best to honor the grief I feel for Oliver with a solid plan of action I think would make him proud.

But mostly, I've spent my time thinking of Rachel. The way her laugh makes me want to join her before I even know why she's laughing. The light in her eyes when she stares me down and challenges my opinions. The curve of her hip in the torch-light as she climbs the ladder to my loft.

I used to feel awkward and uncomfortable with the single-minded intensity she aims at anything in front of her, and distancing myself from her gave me peace. Now, the distance between us opens a hollow space inside me that can only be filled by *her*. I don't know how to explain it, and I don't bother trying. It's enough to know I need her like I've never needed any-one else. Once I find her, I'll take the time to figure out the rest.

I promise myself it won't be much longer before I'm ready to escape this hellhole and track her down.

My food ran out this morning, but I'm not worried. I won't be locked inside this cell much longer. Still, when the dungeon door creaks open, I hope it's the girl because more food means more strength.

But instead of the girl's light tread, or the dogged shuffling of the older woman, I hear crisp, purposeful boot steps striding toward my cell.

The Commander.

The next confrontation is upon me, and I need two things from it—information and a reprieve from further injury. I flip around to put my injured rib against the wall, out of reach of the Commander's boot, and begin planning as he orders a guard to open my cell door.

He enters my cell, his scar catching and releasing the flickering torchlight like some macabre game of cat and mouse. I pretend I can barely lift my head to see him. I've been pretending this sort of weakness since I woke up cured of my fever, so if he's had me watched, this won't raise any alarms.

He laughs, a vulgar, ugly sound full of arrogance. "Look at you." In three long steps, he's at my side. "What a pathetic excuse for a man."

I let my head roll to the side a bit and peer up at him.

"I leave you alone in this dungeon for a week. The great inventor Logan McEntire. The man who always has a plan." His boot lashes out, connects with my shoulder, and sends me sprawling onto the cell floor.

It hurts, but not nearly as much as I pretend it does. He needs to feel I'm already beaten, or he'll never give me what I need.

"And here you sit. Still locked up. Still unable to make good on your promises." His smile is vicious as he plants his boot on the throbbing burned skin of my neck and leans down.

I don't have to fake the pain this time. Waves of agony roll along my jaw and send dazzling lights exploding through my brain.

"You haven't beaten her," I say, pushing the words through teeth clenched tight against the raw, unending anguish eating at me.

He leans closer, grinding his boot into my neck. "What did you say to me, you worthless cur?"

"Rachel. You haven't beaten her." I draw in a shaky breath, tasting the leather and steel of his boot on the dungeon's fetid air. "She's stronger than you think."

"She's a girl alone in the Wasteland with a man who is both stronger than her and has more motivation to do as he's told."

His voice oozes his special brand of pride—two parts power, one part blind ego.

Perfect.

"She can take him. She's smarter than you give her credit for."

He snorts, but I can almost hear the doubt slipping in.

"You won't know if you're right until it's too late to make adjustments," I say.

"You'd like me to think that. But when Melkin sends the signal, inventor, you can bet your life he'll be alone." He laughs again. "And you are betting your life, aren't you? Because the second I have what I want, you're dead."

He isn't going to tell me what I need to know. He's too smart for that. I either need to find another source of information, or wing it once I get out into the Wasteland.

He stands, his boot sliding across my burned skin like a dozen razors. I breathe heavily, trying to control the waves of pain racking me, and see Eloise staring at me with horror on her face.

Which is interesting.

She doesn't want me hurt. Because she can't stand to see another suffer? Or because she somehow thinks I can stop her husband from becoming a killer?

If I can't get the Commander to give me what I need, maybe I can force him to convince Eloise to do so instead.

"When the signal comes, I'd look long and hard at whoever sent it." I curl up on the floor in case he decides to kick any of my vital organs. "Because I'll happily bet my life that Rachel will kill Melkin when he attacks her."

"She's a girl." The Commander's voice is dismissive as he walks toward my cell door.

Time to play the big card. The one I hope will scare Eloise into spilling her guts.

"Every other girl in the city was raised with dolls and tea sets and proper etiquette. Rachel was sword fighting, clubbing our practice dummy, and learning how to eviscerate a man at close range with her knife."

Eloise worries her blanket with nervous fingers.

"Melkin won't even know what hit him. You've sent the man to his death."

The Commander shakes his head and walks out of my cell. "Do you really think I care which of them makes it back alive as long as I get what I want?"

The cell door slams shut. "Next time I see you, inventor, it will be at your execution." He leaves, taking his guards with him, and the silence in his wake is punctuated by sharp, gut-wrenching sobs from Eloise.

I wait, willing her to look at me, and finally get my wish. My voice is a thin whisper of sound as I say, "I can stop her. I can get to them in time."

She frowns but inches closer to the bars on her door. "How? I thought you could get out somehow. The girl said you could. But you haven't. You just lie there." Her voice is a faint breath of sound nearly lost beneath the sizzle of the torches lining the corridor. I have to hope the snapping flames and heavy stone walls are enough to keep the other prisoners from overhearing us.

I sit up and face her, careful not to look like I can move with ease. "Of course I haven't made it look like I'm anything but badly injured. You think they need that information?"

She chews her lower lip.

"I'm telling the truth about Rachel. She's a fierce warrior. And she went out there already angry and hoping for blood. Melkin isn't coming back unless I get out in time."

"Then *leave*."

"I will. But I need one more piece of information first. A piece I hope you have for me."

"What is it?"

There's no resistance in her tone. She believes me. Believes I can save her husband from becoming a killer, or worse, getting killed himself. I dislike the sudden weight of responsibility I feel in the face of her trust.

"I need to know the signal Melkin is supposed to give the Commander when he returns."

A frown puckers her face. "Why do you need to know that? Melkin will give the signal."

"Things happen in the Wasteland. It's a dangerous place. I give you my word I will do all I can to save both Melkin and Rachel, but if I fail, don't you want me to have the means to draw the Commander out of the city so I can deliver the justice he deserves?"

"I don't know."

"He said it himself. He doesn't care which of them comes back alive as long as he gets what he wants."

"If Melkin . . . if you're too late, why would you ever come back here?"

"Because Rachel and I aren't leaving you here. Any of you." The words roll easily off my tongue, and I wonder how long they've been breeding in the back of my mind. Probably from the moment I saw life leave my mother's eyes at the whim of our leader. I can't stomach the thought of one more innocent victim crushed beneath the bloody boot of Baalboden. "It's time for change, and we're going to deliver it."

She's silent for a moment, her hands tearing at the blanket, and then says, "He's to light a torch in the eastern oak at daybreak."

The eastern oak is a mammoth tree marking the edge between Baalboden's perimeter and the Wasteland, in direct line of sight of the far eastern turret, on the opposite side of the gate. I give the Commander credit for coming up with a signal I wouldn't have guessed on my best day, and nod to Eloise.

"I'll do my best to reach them in time, but either way, I'll come back for you."

Then I wait until snores tell me the other prisoners are all asleep before struggling to my feet for the first time in a week.

Tearing my shirt into a long strip of fabric, I wrap my chest tightly and drizzle a pinch of medicine on my tongue. I need to be able to run and fight without the interference of pain. I have the information I need, and if any guard happens to be watching, the Commander could right now be learning of my lengthy conversation with Eloise.

It's time to escape.

CHAPTER FORTY-TWO

RACHEL

While the Cursed One laid waste to every densely populated area across the land, many of the individual houses built far outside a city's limits were left standing. Some of those houses are uninhabitable due to time, weather, and neglect. But some are still safe enough to use as stopping points along our journey through the Wasteland. Every courier has found his own safe houses, stocked them with supplies, and hopes the outside still looks rundown enough to avoid catching the interest of a passing band of highwaymen.

We reach Dad's first safe house as dusk is falling. The itch on the back of my neck warning me we're being followed hasn't abated, though Melkin insists he senses nothing.

I'm not sure Melkin's mind is on the matter at hand, though, so I don't trust his instincts. He's been unapproachable since lunch, and I can't read his expression. However, he does take me seriously enough to keep his sword unsheathed for the rest of the journey.

The safe house is a two-story brick house with a wide, wrap-around porch and a line of stately columns across the front that used to be white until a century of sun faded them into something that resembles grayish clay. Ivy clings to the bricks, wraps itself around windows, and hangs down from the roof like glossy green drapes.

The front yard may have been a perfectly manicured gem once upon a time, but now the grass stretches past my thighs, wild and thick, and the trees behind the house creep closer with every passing year. Still, the house's location affords decent visibility for the entire circumference of the structure, a quality Dad insisted on in a safe house.

The wires on my arm cuff glow without flickering now, though the light is faint enough that I doubt he's still here. I don't care. It's enough to keep the wild, restless hope within me alive.

"This where he hid the package?"

"No."

"Then why're we stopping?"

I brush past him and mount the sagging front steps, making sure to skip the second from the top, where the wood is rotted to the consistency of fig pudding. "Because it's almost dark. And someone is following us. I want the protection of four walls around me."

Plus Dad might have left another sign for me inside.

Besides, Melkin looks wound tight enough to snap. He needs a break from fireside watches too.

A large padlock with a keypad on the front—another of Logan's inventions—bars the door. Dad made sure both Logan and I knew the codes to each of his safe houses. I type in the code, blocking the keypad from Melkin's view as he carefully climbs the steps behind me, and the lock opens with the barely audible snick of metal releasing metal.

The air inside is musty and heavy with mildew, and dust lies across every visible surface like a layer of gray snow. I move past the entryway and see it—footprints, faint outlines coated with less dust than the rest of the house.

He was here.

The hope inside me burns so fiercely I'm almost afraid to touch it.

Melkin shuts the door behind him, slides the bolt into place, and turns. His sword is still out.

"You can put that away now."

"What if someone's already using this place? I don't figure on surprising anyone unless I've got a weapon in my hand."

"If someone was here, they'd leave footprints in all this dust. See?" I point to the fading steps left sometime in the last few months by Dad.

Melkin grunts but keeps his knife out as he moves farther into the house, taking in the faded floral wallpaper with clusters of black mold spreading along the ceiling and the once-blue couch that has since become a muted gray. "Not if they came in through a window."

All the windows are sealed shut. Dad saw to that when he first chose this house. I don't bother telling Melkin, however. He needs to feel like he's done all he can to secure our safety, so I let him prowl the house, beating at curtains and checking under furniture until he looks every bit as grimy as the house itself.

I leave him to it and move carefully along the floor-to-ceiling windows lining the front of the house, keeping far enough back from the gauzy yellowed drapes that no one approaching the edge of the property can catch a glimpse of me.

Someone is out there. I can't see them yet, and they might be expert enough to stay just out of range, but I know we're being followed.

The question is, by whom?

Someone who knew to pick up our trail on the road to Rowansmark? It could be guards assigned to follow us, which would mean the Commander intends to break his word much earlier than I'd assumed. Highwaymen who think they've spotted easy prey? That would be the last mistake they ever made. Trackers from Rowansmark tasked to keep watch over the paths couriers take in case one of them leads straight to the package?

That's a risk I can't afford to take.

We'll either have to flush our followers out into the open or circle behind them and spring a trap. Which means Melkin is going to have to pull it together and help me.

"You're sure it isn't hidden here?" he asks directly behind me, and I whirl around, my hand reaching for my knife before sense overrides my instinctive panic.

"Sneak up behind me again, and I'll gut you like a sheep."

His eyes, black pits of something that looks like bitterness, capture mine. "Are you sure it isn't hidden here?"

"Yes. It's near the next safe house."

"He could've moved it."

"Really? With the Commander and Rowansmark already combing the Wasteland for him and for the package? He knew

when he left Baalboden for the last time that he would be followed. He's too smart to lead them right to it."

He nods, a sharp movement that severs whatever line of tension he's been teetering on since lunch, and sheathes his sword.
In his other hand, he holds a scrap of yellow.

"Found this tied around the doorknob in the kitchen."

It's another of my mother's ribbons. I take it from him, rub
my fingers over the embroidered *S. A.* at the end, and tuck it
into the same pocket that houses the purple one. I don't need
the signs to know I'm closing in—Logan's tracker sees to that—
but having this tangible connection to Dad soothes some of the
ache within me. Having Logan by my side would go a long way
toward soothing the rest.

"I saw our followers. Come up to the attic, and you can see
them too. Mind the stairs, though. Half of them are rotted
through."

I follow him, skirting spots of obvious rot and doing my best
not to rub up against too much dust. The attic is a stale, cluttered box of a room with two grimy windows, one at each end.
We head for the front window, and I scan the grass, raise my eyes
to the tree line, and find them in less than a minute.

Standing two trees in, watching the front door, and moving
restlessly beneath the fading rays of the early evening sun.

Amateurs.

Which means they're guards. Highwaymen and trackers are
far too experienced to be so obvious. I say as much to Melkin.

"I thought the same. Can't figure why the Commander
thinks we need extra protection."

"Please tell me you aren't that stupid."

He frowns at me.

"They aren't here for our protection, Melkin. If they were, they would've traveled with us from the start. They're here to pounce once we have the package."

"But we're going to bring it back. We have to. I'm not going to lose Eloise. You said you thought if I did what he asked, he'd keep his word."

I lied. But looking into the misery on his face, I can't find the cruelty to give him the truth. "Maybe they're insurance in case we decide we want whatever's in the package more than we want Eloise and Logan's safety."

"There's nothing more important than her safety."

"To *you*. But the Commander doesn't place the same value on human life as you do."

We're silent for a moment, staring at the two guards as the day subsides and the first stars of the night glitter like shards of silver in the darkening sky.

"What if they want the package for themselves?" he asks, the darkness he harbored earlier back in his voice.

"Then they'll try to kill us once we find it."

"Not if we kill them first."

Crimson. Sliding down silver blades. Covering me in guilt that won't ever wash clean.

I shake the morbid thoughts away. It's ridiculous to think I'd feel guilty shedding the blood of a guard. Especially one who is here with the express purpose of shedding mine.

But if I do this—if I deliberately ambush and kill without provocation—will I lose something I need? Something that keeps me from becoming like the Commander? Will it harden me toward violence the way repeatedly holding my knife builds calluses into the skin of my palm?

Or will it strengthen me into the kind of weapon I need to be to bring the Commander down?

"I'll go out the back and circle around. I've already checked through the window at the opposite end. There's no one watching us from behind. Give me at least an hour to work my way to them without being noticed. Then sneak out of the house as if you're going looking for the package. While they're focused on you, I'll kill them."

His voice is cold, empty, and more than a little scary. Gone is the courteous, understanding Melkin I've been traveling with for a week. In his place stands a fierce predator willing to do whatever he must to obliterate anyone who stands between him and Eloise.

I wonder if I'm catching a glimpse of who I'm becoming as well.

Banishing that unwelcome thought before it can take root, I nod my acceptance of his plan and follow him back downstairs. He leaves out the back door, and I mark time by lighting candles in the kitchen and assembling dinner from the supplies Dad keeps here. I eat my fill, leave plenty on the table for Melkin, and pack a spare travel sack with food supplies from the cupboards.

My hour is up. Checking that my knife slides easily from its sheath, I light a small torch, the better to make myself seen, and open the front door. The loamy scent of the sun-warmed ground is fading into the crisp chill of night. I creep along the length of the porch, peering beneath the boards as if I expect to find something.

My skin prickles with awareness. I'm being watched.

Which is exactly the point of this entire charade, but it doesn't make me feel any better.

When Melkin doesn't appear within the first few minutes, I leave the porch and wander to the side, still in full view of the guards at the tree line. I feel exposed with my brilliant little torch ablaze amid the overgrown grass and the distant icy stars. The tingle of awareness becomes a full-fledged, adrenaline-fueled need to draw a weapon and be ready for anything.

I don't ignore it.

Instead, I drop down, shove the lit end of the torch deep into the soft soil at my feet to extinguish it, and run as silently as I can away from the spot where I was last seen. In seconds, I hear someone crashing through the grass behind me.

I dodge to my left, drop to a crouch, and freeze. The darkness will cover me. The person following me doesn't have a NightSeer mask, or I'd see its green glow.

He also doesn't have the sense to stop moving once he no longer hears me. Soft footsteps creep toward the spot I just vacated. I slide my knife free without a sound, and ready myself.

The fear I felt earlier at the thought of shedding someone's blood without giving them fair notice is gone. In its place is cold determination.

I'm not going to die. Not until the Commander lies in a pool of his own blood at my feet.

My pursuer is close enough that I can hear him breathe now, rough, uneven pants that speak of someone without the proper training to control his breathing when it matters most. I wait until he's a mere three yards from me, and tense for my attack.

A hand snakes out from behind me and wraps around my mouth while a second hand grabs my knife hand before I can swing it back.

"Wait," Melkin breathes against my ear, and I hold still.

My follower moves forward, making enough noise to announce his presence to any but an inexperienced fool, but I trust Melkin and wait.

By the time the man moves out of range, my muscles are stiff, and I can't feel my lower legs. I turn to look at Melkin, his gaunt frame a black smudge against the starry sky.

"Who?" My voice is little more than a whisper.

"Rowansmark tracker."

That doesn't make sense. Any tracker worth his weight would've been on me before I ever knew what hit me. And if by some chance I managed to elude him, he wouldn't have chased me in such a noisy, clumsy fashion.

"Are you sure?"

"Yes. He killed the guards before I got there. Saw his handiwork. He's an expert."

"Then why act like an amateur?"

He looks at me, and the answer hits me. Because the tracker didn't want to kill me. He wanted to flush me out so he could capture me and force me to reveal the location of the package to him. The realization makes my heart pound so hard it hurts. The cruelty of Rowansmark trackers is legendary. Some say they carve off pieces of their victims and feed it to the vultures bit by bit while the person bleeds and begs. Some say they know how to kill their victims with a single, deadly touch.

On our second-to-last trip to Rowansmark, we entered the

city through an aisle of half-rotted human heads skewered on stakes. Five on one side. Six on another. An entire band of high-waymen who'd had the stupidity to try cheating Rowansmark merchants out of their coin.

What would a tracker do to me to get the location of the package stolen from his leader? My skin is icy as I turn to Melkin.

"We need to leave."

Melkin nods, and together we slowly circle back to the house. I crouch in the shadow of a tree, my knife ready, while Melkin slips inside and snatches up my pack, my Switch, and the bag of food supplies. When he returns, we melt silently into the tree line behind the house and make our way south, our weapons out, our ears straining to catch the sound of pursuit.

CHAPTER FORTY-THREE

LOGAN

I pace my cell, willing the blood to flow into my legs fast enough for me to leave before a guard decides to investigate my conversation with Eloise. The dungeon is full of the sounds of dripping water and heavy sleep. I'm chilled without my shirt, but I can't yet put on my cloak.

I need to dismantle it first.

My legs still tingle, but they'll hold me when I need to run. Approaching the far right corner of my cell, the one with the draft seeping in through the cracks, I run my fingers along the damp, craggy stone, judging distances and looking for a weakness I'm not convinced is there.

It doesn't matter. I'm about to obliterate the whole thing, weakness or not.

Turning to my cloak, I remove the five buttons lining the front flap. They come loose with a soft pop and reveal the plain steel fastenings underneath. Ignoring those, I flip the face of the buttons over and smile. The back of each holds one of my most destructive inventions to date—the gears of an ancient pocket watch attached to two tiny vials of liquid. One holds acid. The other holds glycerin. All my experiments have proven the combination to be explosive.

I hope it's enough to turn the back half of my cell into rubble.

I slide my fingers along the bottom of my coat until I feel a tiny knot of thread. Pulling on it, I rip out the extra seam I painstakingly installed just days before the Claiming ceremony and remove a length of wire already spliced into five pieces at one end. Finally, I sit down, tug my left boot free, jiggle the sole until it comes loose, and remove a tiny, copper-sheathed detonator.

The buttons attach to the wall with ease, the same gluey substance that stuck them to the plain steel fastenings on my cloak easily clinging to the wall. I carefully wrap the loose wire ends around the central gear in each button, and then back away to the cell door, taking the thin straw pallet of a bed with me.

Pulling my cloak over my shoulders, I fasten the toggles, flip the hood over my head, and crouch beneath the pallet, my back to the wall. With steady fingers, I wrap the other end of the wire around the coils on the detonator and take a deep breath.

Time to show the Commander which of us can truly outwit the other.

I press the trigger on the detonator and hear a faint clicking sound as the pocket watch gears engage and set the vials on a collision course with each other. Then the entire dungeon shakes with the force of the explosion at my back.

I don't give the debris time to stop falling. I can't. The main door at the end of the row is already opening, and a guard is shouting an alarm. Keeping the pallet over my head to protect myself from the worst of it, I stand and face the destruction of my cell.

The back corner is nothing but crumbled bits of stone and dust. A slippery pile of dirt is sliding in through the hole, but above that pile, the night sky beckons. I race forward, scramble over the debris, and dive through the hole as someone rattles a key in the door of my cell.

The straw pallet wedges against the opening as I go through it, and I push as much dirt as possible against the back side of the hole while climbing my way toward level ground.

From the main compound, an alarm bell peals, disturbing the darkness with its insistent clamor. I scan my surroundings, take in the distance between me and the iron fence around the compound, and start running.

I'm still ten yards from the fence when someone shouts behind me. I don't bother looking. It would just slow me down. Instead, I reach inside my inner cloak pocket and remove what looks like two slightly thick Baalboden coins. A quick toggle of the tiny switch embedded in the ridges of the coins releases the spring-loaded mechanism inside, and they become a smaller version of the handgrips Rachel tried to use on her disastrous escape attempt.

More shouts echo across the yard, and I catch guards with NightSeer masks running along the fence line, primed to intersect with me if it takes me longer than twenty seconds to scale the iron poles.

I lunge forward, slam my hands onto the metal, feel the magnets latch onto the iron like they're soldered to it, and start climbing.

My rib screams at me, even through the pain medicine I took, but I ignore it. I won't get a second chance at this, and I refuse to fail.

The top seems impossibly high, and my arms tremble with the effort of ignoring the weakness on my right side, but I reach it just as the guards converge below me. One grabs at my foot, but I slam my boot into his forehead, wrap my hands around the top of the fence, and vault over to the other side.

I don't wait to see who's following me.

The compound is located in the eastern quarter of the city. I turn north and run, hoping the guards take note of my direction and report it back to the Commander. Let him fortify the North Wall. Let him comb the city streets. I won't be there.

Once I'm sure I'm out of sight, I change my trajectory and head southwest, trusting the magnetic field of my handgrips to block my wristmark from any Identidiscs being used to find me.

The only way out of the city is over the Wall or through the gate. Over the past week, thanks to Rachel's prodding, I've spent an inordinate amount of time thinking of another way to escape.

Most of the ideas I came up with had one fatal flaw: They were obvious choices, and the Commander isn't a fool. I discarded them all and decided the perfect solution is the one no one would be crazy enough to try. The one that could end with me accidentally calling the Cursed One to devour me in a single, fiery gulp.

I'm going out under the Wall.

I enter North Hub, avoiding the street torches by using backyards and alleys, and circle Center Square in favor of moving west. When I've gone far enough to be sure I won't be seen by any upstanding citizens, I cut south and hurry toward Lower Market.

I'm sure the travel bag I left behind in Center Square is long gone. I'm equally sure the bag I always keep at Oliver's has been confiscated too. If the Commander thinks he's backed me into a corner where my only two choices are heading home for more supplies or hitting up merchants who've undoubtedly been warned that the penalty for doing business with me is death, he's wrong.

I have Rachel to thank for it. When I chased her to the Wall, I went through the alley between the armory and the deserted building at the base of Lower Market, and realized it was the perfect place to hide a backup escape plan. No one ever goes into the abandoned building. And as I have no ties to the place, the Commander would never suspect it as a base of operations for me.

It takes me nearly an hour to reach it. I stick to the shadows, sometimes sacrificing speed for stealth, but I never see any signs of pursuit. Either the bulk of the guards are converging on the North Wall, or the guards in the western edge of the city have the brains to keep silent about their search.

It doesn't matter which is true. All that matters is that I've reached the building. I duck inside and use the faint moonlight streaming in through a broken window to sort through my stash.

Tossing the handgrips into my pack, I don a new tunic and pants and hastily chew on some mutton jerky to replenish my flagging strength. The leather of my cloak chafes the burn on my neck, so I take a minute to snatch salve and gauze from my first-aid kit and secure a bandage in place. Then I strap on a sword, slide a sheathed dagger into my boot, wrap my cloak around myself again, and pick up my travel pack, ignoring the way my rib aches against the weight.

The distance between the building and the Wall is relatively short, but it takes me nearly twenty minutes because I'm constantly checking for guards. I aim for the curve of the Wall nearly at the halfway point between the two closest turrets. When another scan of my surroundings shows no glowing NightSeer masks, I drop to my knees at the base of the Wall and open my pack. Sliding on a mask to protect my eyes and filter the air I breathe, I tug on a pair of heavy leather gloves and remove a machine that looks like a metal crossbow with a thick spiral-shaped steel drill jutting out the front. Fastening my pack to my back securely, I slide my arms into the straps for the device, secure another strap around my waist, and flip the switch on the battery pack I built beneath the spiral drill. It comes to life with a muted whine.

Bending forward, I apply the spinning metal drill to the ground at the base of the Wall, and it chews through the dirt, flinging debris to the sides. The vibrations send sharp jabs of agony into my rib cage, and I have to constantly remind myself to breathe through the pain. When the hole is large enough to accommodate me, I slide forward and switch my goggles to NightSeer, trusting the green glow to illuminate my path even as I quickly calculate angles, trajectory, and all the possibilities for failure.

Except that failure isn't a possibility.

Not when so many depend on me.

The drill eats through the ground, and I aim deep. Deep

enough to bypass the Wall's foundations. Deep enough to avoid causing any trembles through the tons of stone and steel resting above me. Deep enough that calling the Cursed One is a real possibility.

My mask lights the dirt around me a few measly feet at a time, and the air feels damp and cloying as it brushes against my skin. Every breath ignites a fierce agony around my broken rib as if I never took any pain medicine. The need for space crushes me, whispering that I'll go crazy if I don't get back into the open *now*.

I ignore it. Mind over matter. I have plenty of other things to think about. There are math equations to solve. Minute adjustments to make. And beneath it all, a terrible grief for Oliver mixes with a desperate worry for Rachel until I can hardly tell the difference between the two.

I will not be too late.

I will *not*.

When I calculate that I've traveled well beyond the width of the Wall, I begin slowly tunneling my way back to the surface, making sure to continue my trajectory until I'm beyond the circumference of Baalboden's perimeter. I break the surface with caution, instantly shutting off the machine so I can listen for threats.

I've come up between two ancient pin oaks. Keeping my NightSeer mask on, I scan the area. I'm far enough into the Wasteland that Baalboden is a distant, looming bulk on the eastern horizon. The western Wall appears quiet.

Best Case Scenario: No one discovers my true escape point until daylight.

Worst Case Scenario: The Commander realizes my flight north was a false trail and orders a search of the entire Wall.

The answer to both is the same: Run.

I close the machine, slip off the mask because I'd rather let my eyes adjust to the dark than announce my presence to others with the mask's glow, and pack them both away. Then I slide a copper cuff from my bag, the gears on it lined with the same blue wire I used for Rachel's, and pull it over my arm.

The wires glow faintly, but they'll light up like a torch the closer I get to her. By my best guess, she should still have another week's worth of travel before she hits Jared's Rowansmark safe house. I take a moment to mentally review the map Jared once had me commit to memory for the day when the Commander would allow me to leave Baalboden on my first courier mission. If I push myself, using dangerous shortcuts Jared would never have used while on a journey with Rachel, I can cut the distance between us in half in just four days. Three if I don't sleep much.

I have to hope Melkin didn't want to risk bringing Rachel through highwaymen-infested trails either. If Rachel was spotted, she and Melkin would be viciously attacked within hours. Melkin would never make it out alive, and Rachel would wish she'd died too.

Shoving that thought aside before it takes root, I settle my pack between my shoulders and brace my arm against my aching side. Then I turn my face to the south and disappear into the Wasteland.

CHAPTER FORTY-FOUR

RACHEL

We've barely slept in the five days since we left the first safe house. The maples have turned back into oaks, and huge gnarled roots rip their way through the moss-covered ground. Traveling by day and catching naps at night while one of us remains alert for the presence of the Rowansmark tracker, we run ourselves ragged.

Melkin feels it more than I do. Lines of strain take up permanent residence on his face, digging bitter furrows across his brow. I think he worries someone will destroy his plan to return the package and ransom his wife. I can't be sure because he'll barely speak to me. The closer we come to the second safe house, the more he shuts down.

It doesn't matter. The wires on my arm cuff are glowing brighter with each passing day. Soon, it will be over. Soon, I'll find Dad, and we'll go rescue Logan.

We're less than a full day's journey from the safe house when I sense we're no longer alone. Melkin is ahead of me, using his staff to brush aside the moss that drapes across the branches around us like ribbon. I slow as if examining a mark on the ground, and whirl around, expecting to see a Rowansmark tracker.

An olive-skinned face stares at me from a branch in a tree I passed not thirty seconds ago. We lock eyes, blink, and in a flash of black hair and graceful limbs, she's gone.

It was a girl. I'm sure of it. Which means she isn't a tracker, a guard, or a member of a highwaymen gang. She must be Tree People.

I'm not threatened by her presence—it's natural for Tree People to be curious about the outsiders wandering through their area of the Wasteland—but there aren't any Tree People villages in these parts except for the one near the second safe house, and that's still hours away. It's unusual to see a Tree Girl so far from home. I file it away for further thought if necessary, and forget about her until we stop for lunch two hours later and I see her again.

This time, she doesn't pull back when I catch a glimpse of her peering out at me from the branches of a tree several yards back from where we sit. Instead, we stare at each other as I let my cloak hood drop, and she leans out of her tree enough for me to see we're about the same age. A quiver of arrows is slung over one shoulder, and she holds the bow in one hand. A long black feather dangles from an intricately swirled silver ear cuff wrapped around her left ear. Her dark eyes are full of aloof confidence.

I can't explain her, and I don't like what I can't explain. She shouldn't still be following us. I'm about to draw Melkin's attention to her when she pulls back into the tree and disappears.

I watch for her as I finish a cold lunch of turkey leftovers and the potted plums I took with us from the first safe house. Watch for her as Melkin barks at me to keep up. And watch for her as the shadows slowly lengthen into pools of darkness beneath the dying sun.

She never reappears.

Instead, the blue wires glow brightly, and I forget to be concerned about the insignificant wanderings of a Tree Girl. It will hurt to tell Dad about Oliver. It will also hurt to tell him I had to leave Logan behind, but Dad will know how to fix it.

I still haven't told Melkin we're about to find Dad. Five days ago, I would have. Five days ago, he seemed approachable, concerned only with saving his wife, and determined to protect me.

Now, he's a cold, silent ghost of the man I thought I knew. The closer we come to the package, the more he turns inward, until I catch myself shivering a little when he turns the miserable darkness of his eyes toward me.

Maybe he's finally realizing the Commander isn't a man of his word. Maybe he's beginning to understand that if we give our only leverage over to him, those we love are dead.

Maybe he's bracing himself for the worst.

We emerge from the forest, and I recognize the line of ancient oaks, their trunks as thick as one of the steel beams supporting Baalboden's Wall, their branches arching over a moss-covered path as if offering protection.

We're almost there.

I push ahead of Melkin, who offers no protest. The column of trees seems to go on forever as I hurry forward.

Almost there.

The cuff against my arm glows like the noonday sun.

Almost there.

At the end of the row of trees, a graying one-story farmhouse with once-red shutters faded to pink will be standing, and he'll be waiting. His big arms will open wide, his gray eyes will glow with pride, and I'll be home at last.

I skid on the moss as I reach the last tree, and grab on to the trunk for balance. And then I hang on to the trunk for one long desperate second, fighting vertigo as my eyes take in the impossible.

The farmhouse is gone.

Nothing remains but a pile of scorched debris and a gaping hole where the Cursed One slid back to his lair.

I look around wildly, searching. My cuff is lit up like a torch. He's here.

He's *here*.

But he isn't. I can't see him. All I see is destruction.

"Oh," Melkin says behind me as he takes in the sight.

That tiny little word makes me want to hurt him, so I leave the shelter of the trees and walk toward the debris on shaking legs.

My cuff still glows. I scan the treetops. He could be there. Waiting for me. Staying hidden from trackers.

The soil beneath me turns to ash. Cold black flakes that cling to my boots as if trying to hold me back.

Where is he?

Something moves in the trees across from me, and the Tree Girl steps out, followed by a boy who looks about Logan's age. Both of them have dusky skin and straight black hair. The girl wears hers in a long braid. The boy lets his fall loose to his shoulders. He moves, and my eyes are drawn to a white paper-wrapped package the size of a raisin loaf in his hands.

"Who are they?" Melkin whispers.

"Rachel Adams?" The boy's dark brown eyes lock onto mine, making my stomach clench. There's sympathy in his gaze. I don't want sympathy.

I just want Dad.

"Yes." My voice is nothing but a wisp. The breeze snatches it and whisks it away. I try again. "Yes."

The girl beckons me, her slim hand waving me toward her.

Maybe Dad is with them. Hiding in their village. Staying off the usual path of trackers and couriers. Maybe that's why she followed us earlier. Maybe he sent her to watch for me, knowing one day I'd come.

My boots grind the sooty embers beneath me to dust as I cross the scorched ground. The foundation of the house is still there, buried beneath the ash, a jumbled mound of broken concrete I have to climb up and over. My feet skid as I reach the top, sending me sliding down the other side. When I reach the bottom, I look up at the Tree People, but stop when I catch sight of something else.

Just beyond the edge of the destruction, where the ash bleeds gently into soil again, a soft swell in the ground is marked by a small wooden cross painted white.

I can't breathe. My ears roar, and someone says something, but I can't understand the words because I'm walking toward the grave and the wires on my cuff are glowing like brilliant blue stars.

The boy steps to the side of the grave, and holds out his hand to me. I take it without thinking, but I can't feel him. I can't even feel myself, and I don't want to. Let this be some other girl standing here, holding a stranger's hand while the rest of her world comes crumbling down.

Please.

"He died a hero, Rachel. The Cursed One would've killed my sister and me, but he led it away from us. He saved our lives." His voice catches as if he's struggling with tears. "I'm sorry."

I pull my hand free. The cross is beautifully carved and someone has painted the words *Jared Adams* in the center.

Grief is a yawning pit of darkness blooming at my core. I can hardly stand beneath its weight. The sharp edges of Oliver's death collide with the unthinkable sight before me, and something inside me shatters as I fall to my knees.

I can't bear this. I can't.

The hope that blazed within me floats like ash into the darkness.

He's here, but not here.

I want to die too. Just stop breathing and hope I find him on the other side.

He's not here.

I sink down to lie on top of the dirt.

He's nowhere.

I'm bleeding inside where no one will see. Where no one will ever know to look.

He's gone.

He's *gone*.

CHAPTER FORTY-FIVE

LOGAN

I reach the first safe house in just over three days.

I'm cutting through known highwaymen territory, running on adrenaline rather than sleep. My entire body feels battered, and my rib throbs incessantly no matter how tightly I wrap it. Every few miles, I have to stop, drag in some much needed deep breaths, and focus on getting the pain under control so I can continue. Twice, I've slept for a handful of hours, only to wake on the heels of terrifying dreams with a sense of dread churning through my system.

The pain refuses to relinquish its hold on me even during sleep, but I can't afford to give in to it. Guards will be on my trail. Maybe trackers as well, if any of them have returned to Baalboden since I left. The Commander won't sit idly by and wait for Melkin to succeed. He'll have an insurance policy in the works.

I just have to stay one step ahead.

I skirt the safe house, an ivy-covered once-white structure, and search for signs of life before leaving the cover of the trees. I don't find life, but death is waiting for me near the edge of the property. Two guards lie on the ground, the bones of their faces nearly picked clean by scavengers but the mark of Baalboden still clear on their uniforms. A small puncture wound rests over their hearts.

They were murdered efficiently, and the ramifications chill me to the core. A professional did this. Someone who knew how to kill with neat, deadly precision.

This isn't Melkin's handiwork. He's a tracker, but, as Eloise so desperately pointed out, he isn't a killer. He wouldn't know how to drop a man before he had a chance to see death approach.

It isn't Rachel's handiwork either. Rage fuels her and these kills contain less emotion than the soil on which the men fell.

Someone else is tracking the package. Closing in on Rachel and Melkin. Once he reaches his objective, their lives won't be worth more than those of the two poor souls lying at my feet.

Panic eats at me when I consider the possibility that the tracker has already found Rachel and Melkin, and their bodies wait somewhere on the forest floor for me to stumble upon as well.

Scrapping my plan to take a few hours of rest, I approach the house and type in the code for the padlock. Just inside the door, recent footsteps mar the dust. I bend to examine them. One of the boot prints is Rachel's. One is large enough to be Melkin's. And one, already coated in a thin sheen of dust, is Jared's. If Jared was here within the last few weeks, it's possible he's waiting for Rachel at the second safe house. If so, he'll protect her from Melkin until I get there.

The possibility is real, but the weight of responsibility refuses to lift from my shoulders. I can't put any hope in possibilities. I have to contend with reality, and the reality is that even if Melkin doesn't try to kill Rachel, they have an assassin on their trail, and he won't hesitate to murder them both once they have the package.

As I leave the footsteps behind and enter the kitchen to restock on fuel and food, fear wraps itself around me, whispering terrible things.

You're too late.

Rachel can't beat an assassin. He'll stab her through the heart and leave her like she's nothing. Less than nothing.

Unless Melkin kills her first.

You've lost all the family you ever had because you're too late.

Too late.

The kitchen is a mess. Supplies are ripped out of cupboards and strewn across grimy countertops. The remains of a mostly uneaten dinner lie on the kitchen table. Fear sinks into my heart and refuses to let go.

They left in a hurry. They left on the run.

I have to believe they've continued to outwit the assassin on their trail. Any other thought threatens to compromise my ability to plan ahead. Forcing the fear into a distant corner of my mind, I rewrap my rib cage and stuff additional supplies in my pack.

I need to rest, but I can't. Every second I lose is another second Rachel comes closer to death.

Instead, I quickly eat a decent meal, drink my fill of water, and swallow a small pinch of pain medicine. Locking the house behind me, I head south again, looking closely for a sign of someone following Melkin and Rachel.

It takes nearly four hours to find it, but I do. Near a small clearing where they stopped to eat, a man hunched down behind the thick cover of a flowering azalea bush. His boots dug into the dirt in a way that suggests he was leaning forward on his toes. I can't distinguish enough of the sole to judge his height and weight, but the maker's mark on the tip of his boot tells me one very important fact.

He's from Rowansmark.

Once Rachel retrieves the package, she's dead. If Melkin fails to kill her, this man will.

My body screams for rest. My head feels heavy and off-kilter. I draw in a deep breath, brace myself for the pain, and start running.

Mind over matter.

I can't afford to let my body rule me now. I have an assassin to kill.

CHAPTER FORTY-SIX

RACHEL

Voices float above me as I lie on the cold, unyielding ground. I imagine sinking below it. Letting it take me under.

Finding peace.

The piercing pain of loss is a double-edged blade I can't bear to touch. How can I grieve for him? Cry for him? Bleed for him inside when it won't change anything?

It won't change anything.

He's *gone*.

All the words I never found time to say. All the things we never found time to do. Ripped from me with merciless finality.

Gone.

But I'm not gone. I'm still here—miles from home, surrounded by scorched earth and strangers, facedown on my father's grave.

Here.

Somewhere inside me, I hear an anguished wailing—the

wordless keening of unbearable grief. I can't stand to hear it. To feel it. To let it live.

A yawning darkness within me opens wide, whispering promises to take the pain. Swallow the loss. Make it possible to draw a breath without choking on the shattered pieces no one will ever fix.

I dig my fingers into his grave and flinch as the images of Dad and Oliver sear themselves into my brain. I will choke on this grief. Lie here impotent, unable to avenge them. Loss is a gaping hole with jagged teeth, and I can't *bear* it.

I push the images away, scramble back from the edge of that gaping hole, and let the darkness within me swallow it all. The wail of grief inside me slowly subsides into a well of icy silence— deafening and absolute. The silence rips me in two, cutting me off from everything I can't stand to face. I don't try to stop it. If I feel the loss, it will break me.

And I can't break until the Commander is dead.

Because Dad's gone. And I'm still here.

And before I follow him, I have a debt to pay.

My fingers clench into fists, my nails breaking as I shove them through hard-packed dirt. Fury is a welcome companion, warming me with something that almost feels like comfort.

It's the Commander's fault Dad was ever given the package in the first place. His fault I'll never see Oliver again. His fault Logan languishes in a dungeon.

His fault Dad is dead.

I owe him for all of it.

I can't find my grief for Oliver. My fear for Logan. My agony over losing Dad forever. I can't, and I don't care.

Feeling nothing but rage and resolve makes me stronger.

One day soon the Commander will realize just how strong he's made me.

CHAPTER FORTY-SEVEN

LOGAN

When I stumble for the fourth time in ten minutes, I realize mind over matter isn't going to cut it. I need rest. If I keep going in my current state of exhaustion, I run the risk of missing a critical piece of information, blundering into highwaymen, or losing Rachel and Melkin's trail.

Plus, the pain in my side is making it difficult to think straight.

I can think of a hundred Worst Case Scenarios, but the solutions feel vague and prone to failure.

The need to reach Rachel is a constant pressure against my chest. I meant what I said to the Commander. If Melkin attacks Rachel openly, she'll drop him like a stone.

But Melkin isn't stupid. He's been traveling with her for over a week. Any misconceptions he had about her formidability as a foe must have been put to rest by now.

I find a large oak, its thick branches forming a cradle several yards off the ground, and I climb carefully, my rib screaming at me the entire way. Wrapping my cloak around me to better blend in with my surroundings, I settle my head against my knees and admit Melkin isn't Rachel's biggest problem.

The tracker will torture her before he kills her.

I shake my head and force that thought away. She won't die. I won't allow it. I'll come up with a plan. I'll find a way to reach her in time.

I will.

Closing my eyes, I give myself permission to take one hour of sleep before I move again. I conjure up the memory of Rachel's face and cling to it like a lifeline as I allow my weary eyes to close.

CHAPTER FORTY-EIGHT

RACHEL

My fingers ache with stiffness. I've been lying face-first on my father's grave for hours, clutching fistfuls of dirt as if by touching what covers him now, I can somehow touch him.

At some point, I realize the Tree Boy is sitting quietly beside me as if to let me know I'm not alone.

He's wrong.

I've never been more alone.

I turn my face to look at him and realize darkness is falling, obscuring the tree line and hiding the ugly remains of the safe house. He sits cross-legged, the package resting on his lap, his wide palms braced against his knees. His dark eyes seem to penetrate the emptiness inside me with something that looks like regret.

He can keep his regret. His sympathy. His quiet understanding.

I don't want it.

I don't need it.

All I need is the Commander's blood on my hands.

I'm still staring at him, and he slowly offers me his hand as if afraid I'll shy away at any sudden movements.

"Willow made dinner," he says as if this should make sense to me.

I ignore his hand. I'm not hungry.

"Willow's my sister." He turns to look over his shoulder. I follow his line of sight and see the Tree Girl bending over a pot on a small fire. Melkin hunches down on the opposite side of the pot, watching me. "She made stew."

Doesn't he know I don't care? I turn my face away, letting the ground scrape against my cheek. The pain feels good. Real. A tiny piece of what I should be feeling but can't now that the silence inside me has swallowed everything but rage.

"I'm Quinn."

I can't make small talk. If I open my mouth now, all the hate and fury bubbling just below the surface will spill out and consume him.

His voice is husky with something that sounds like grief. "Your father was a good man. I'm very sorry."

I look at my arm. The cuff is still glowing, confident that it's reached its intended target, and I'm suddenly, illogically angry at Logan for inventing it in the first place.

For giving me something as cruel as hope.

"You can't stay here." The boy is still speaking, though I show no indication of listening. "There are men from Rowansmark moving through the forest to the northwest searching for what's in this package. Your dad said if anything happened to him, I was to retrieve this from its hiding place and give it to you or to someone named Logan McEntire." He sounds urgent, and I'm surprised to see genuine grief and worry in his eyes.

I can't leave. What will be left to me if I walk away from this spot?

He leans forward, his eyes looking so much older than the rest of him. "I'm sorry, Rachel. I wish you had more time, but you don't. If you get caught, everything Jared did to keep this out of the wrong hands will be in vain."

His words find their mark. If I'm caught, Dad died for nothing, and I lose my leverage against the man I hold responsible. I sit up slowly, still clutching fistfuls of grave dirt. I can't bear to let it go.

He looks at my hands, a tiny frown creasing the skin between his eyes, and then digs into the front pocket of the leather vest he wears. "Here." Stretching out his hand, he offers me a small pouch.

I take it. The dirt slides into the pouch with a whisper of sound, and I pull it closed. The strings are long enough to tie behind my neck. I knot them securely and let the final piece of my father rest over my heart, just below the necklace Logan gave to me.

"Come eat. You'll need your strength."

He's right. I can't travel back to Baalboden and destroy the Commander on an empty stomach. I stand and follow him to where Willow is now using dirt to smother her cooking fire before the flames alert someone to our presence in the gathering gloom.

My body moves just like it always has. My feet follow one after the other. My nostrils capture the scent of wood smoke and meat, and my ears note the creaking of branches and the crunch of ash-coated debris beneath me. But it's all meaningless. I'm a stranger beneath my skin. I wear armor on the inside, a metal forged of fury and silence, cutting me off from myself.

I'm no longer a daughter.

No longer a granddaughter.

No longer a girl with dreams. With hope.

I'm a weapon, now.

I embrace my rage. Let it sink into my secret spaces and make me its own as I sit down beside the ruins of the fire, accept a bowl of stew, and begin to plan.

CHAPTER FORTY-NINE

LOGAN

I overslept.

It's already dark when I wake, and even while I curse my stupidity, I can tell the sleep helped. My body aches, but the overwhelming fatigue is gone. Best of all, my thoughts are clear again.

I'm two days' hard travel from the second safe house if I use shortcuts and only stop twice more for brief rests. A check of my arm cuff shows the wires glowing steadily, though the light is too dim for her to be close yet. Still, I'm reading the remnants of her signature and it's getting stronger the farther south I go. I'm on the right trail.

But someone else is too.

Taking a few minutes to eat and rewrap my rib, I think through my options.

I can continue with my current trajectory and hope to intercept Rachel near the second safe house before she finds the package and her whole world goes to hell. Or I can pick up the

Rowansmark tracker's trail and try to reach him before he acts against her.

I might be giving a slight advantage to the tracker by alerting him to my presence as I join Rachel, but his advantage is mitigated by my knowledge of his agenda.

And I can't bear to break the promise I made to Eloise. I might not be able to stop Melkin from following through on the Commander's orders, but I'm honor-bound to try.

Climbing down the tree starts a fire in my rib cage. I gently shake out my cloak, readjust my weapons, and put a tiny pinch of pain medicine beneath my tongue. Then I take a moment to assess the quality of the silence around me.

Owls hoot mournfully in the treetops. The whispery rustle of an evening breeze slides across leaves. And the occasional animal pads quietly across the moss-covered ground.

I'm reassured. If the animals feel safe, I'm safe too.

Best Case Scenario: I make good progress and don't run into anyone.

Worst Case Scenarios 1–3: I stumble onto a gang of highwaymen as I cut across their favored trails; I lose my footing in the dark and injure my rib further, making speed difficult; or I cross paths with the tracker.

The answer to each is caution, but too much caution on my part may cost Rachel her life. Hoping to strike a balance between good sense and quick progress, I pick up my pace and strain to hear any change in the cadence of the forest around me as I enter highwaymen territory, my hand on the hilt of my sword.

CHAPTER FIFTY

RACHEL

The stew tastes like ashes in my mouth, but I chew with dogged determination. It takes everything I have to force myself to swallow when I'd rather gag, but I do it.

Revenge takes energy.

Melkin doesn't eat. Instead, he sits hunched forward like a giant praying mantis, digging the tip of his knife in the sand, while he watches the rest of us in brooding silence.

The package rests beside me on the ground, a lifeless reminder of everything I've lost. What could be worth such bloodshed? Such single-minded greed from both Rowansmark and the Commander?

Setting aside my stew bowl, I reach for it.

"Don't open it."

I meet Melkin's dark stare in silence, my fingers still tugging at the bindings holding the thick paper in place.

"*Don't.*"

I unknot the bindings and rip the paper off. Beneath the

paper, a heavy black cloth is rolled up like a log. Laying it in my lap, I carefully unroll the cloth until I see what rests at its center.

A slim wand of smoke-gray metal with a hole at one end, like a flute but with only three raised finger pads along its length, gleams dully beneath the flickering light of the single torch that Melkin has allowed us.

"What is this?" I look up, first at Quinn, who shows no inclination to answer me, and then at Willow.

Her brown eyes are alive with excitement as she leans forward and says, "It's tech from Rowansmark. See the three finger pads?"

I nod, and Melkin shifts closer to me, his eyes on the wand.

"There are symbols on each pad."

I run my finger across the circles and discover a different raised design on each. "What do they mean?"

"Willow." Quinn's voice is gentle, but his sister darts a quick glance at Melkin and subsides.

I can't read the subtext of their communication, and I don't want to. I just want to understand what I'm holding so I can see the Commander's endgame and thwart it.

I need Logan. He'd know how to figure this out. How to get the information from them and make a plan.

And I need Logan because he'd understand that something inside me is broken. Something I have no idea how to mend. He'd understand, and if he didn't know how to fix it, he'd dedicate himself to learning how.

I need him, but he needs me more. He needs me calm. Focused. He needs me to get the information, make the plan, and rescue him. I'm not going to let him down.

Turning to Quinn, I speak in a voice as hard as the packed dirt beneath us. "I need to know what they mean. You told me men are looking for this. Clearly my father didn't want them to have it, or he would've just returned it. The leader of my city is looking for it too."

"Rachel, that's enough." Melkin's voice is low and furious.

I ignore him.

"If you don't tell me everything I need to know, people may die. I might die. And you said yourself, you didn't want my father's . . ." Death? Sacrifice? I can't put his loss into words. There aren't any terrible enough to convey how empty I am without him. My hand creeps up to clutch the leather pouch I wear around my neck, and Quinn's eyes are sympathetic.

I hate him for it.

"You said Dad was a hero." I throw the words at him. "You said he died saving you."

"Yes."

"I'm not asking you to die. I'm not asking you to risk anything but the truth. You can be a hero if you just tell me the truth."

"Your father didn't want you to use that." He looks at the wand.

"You have no idea what my father wanted."

He looks wounded, and the fury inside me lashes out. I grab the wand and wave it in his face. "What does this do? Tell me!"

"Stop!" Willow shoves herself between us. "Leave him alone."

"Then you tell me."

She darts a glance at her brother. "We've already done more

than we feel comfortable doing, but we owed Jared."

"And you aren't done paying your debt."

"Rachel!" Melkin's voice is harsh, but I keep staring at Quinn and Willow.

"How am I supposed to keep this safe if I don't understand it?"

Melkin makes a choked noise at the back of his throat, but I don't break eye contact with Willow. She's going to tell me. I can see it.

"Wrap it up and hide it," she says.

"Not if I don't know what it does." I lean past her to look Quinn in the face. "If you don't tell me, if I don't understand, I could trust the wrong person. Are you really okay with that?"

"Are you really planning to simply keep it safe?" he asks. I look in his eyes and realize he *knows*. He knows I'm going to use it. Knows I'm capable of it.

My chin rises. "If by keeping it safe, you mean not letting it fall into the wrong hands, then yes. I am."

"Jared didn't want you to use it. He wanted it given to Logan McEntire to be destroyed."

"Logan is in Baalboden's dungeon. To get him out, I'm supposed to give this"—I gesture toward the wand—"to our leader."

"You can't!" Willow says, and reaches as if she'll take the wand from me.

I hold the wand out of reach, and stare her down. "Then tell me what it does. I have nothing left to lose. Tell me what this does, or I'll start pushing buttons and figure it out myself."

She looks at Quinn.

"It's her decision," he says quietly. Something in the weight of his words makes me feel like he thinks the consequences will be more than I can bear.

He's wrong.

Willow slowly lowers her hands. "Fine. The finger pads create individual sound waves on a frequency humans can't hear."

"What good is that?"

"Humans can't hear it. But the Cursed One can."

I immediately slide my fingers away from the circles.

"You mean this—"

"Is a device designed to call and control the Cursed One."

A vicious sense of power blooms inside me. I cradle the device to my chest and feel unstoppable.

CHAPTER FIFTY-ONE

LOGAN

I've been on the move for at least two hours now, maybe three, and the burst of energy I felt after sleeping is long gone. So is the small dose of pain medicine I took. I can't afford to stop for rest yet, despite the pain and exhaustion, so I force myself to catalog the foliage I pass and come up with its scientific name. Mind over matter. Reason over pain.

The darkness obscures all but the smell and the most obvious of shapes, which adds an extra challenge that keeps me thinking of something other than the fire in my rib cage and my fear for Rachel.

I'm passing through a patch of pines. Sharp scent. Knobby branches. Widely spaced thin needles. Shortleaf pine. *Pinus echinata*.

What will I do if, after I find her, Melkin still tries to carry out his assignment?

The low-pitched call of a great horned owl echoes from somewhere to my left. *Bubo virginianus*.

How can I look Eloise in the eye if I have to kill her husband?

The moss beneath my boots grows in spongy clusters that spring back easily after I lift my foot. *Bryum argenteum.*

Logic could work. Melkin might listen to me. Understand the only way to rescue his wife is to take up arms against his leader.

He might not.

I have to come to terms with the idea of either killing him or finding a way to leave him behind in the Wasteland so Rachel and I can get to Baalboden before him.

Sliding silently through a few loosely spaced pines, I brush up against a wide, glossy leaf adorning a tree whose thick spread of branches blocks my view for a moment. *Magnolia grandiflora.*

The low hooting of the owl suddenly subsides as I skirt the tree and nearly run into a man standing on the other side. The fact that his back is to me saves my life.

He hears my footfalls and turns, his weapon drawn, and I drop to my knees, grab the dagger in my boot, and thrust it up as his momentum drives his abdomen onto my blade.

Before he has a chance to do more than hiss out a breath, I lunge to my feet, grab his head with both hands, and wrench it to the side. His neck grinds and pops, his body goes slack, and I lower him as quietly as possible to the forest floor.

It isn't quiet enough. If anyone else is nearby, they'll have heard something. Even if they didn't, the sudden lack of bird or animal cries around us creates an alarm just as deafening as if he'd called out to the rest of his battalion.

And it is a battalion. I can just make out the burnished

dragon scale adorning the front right pocket of his uniform. He's Rowansmark military.

I'm in deeper trouble than I thought. So are Rachel and Melkin. Being hunted by Rowansmark trackers is dangerous enough. Being hunted by an entire Rowansmark battalion turns the odds against us so completely, I feel staggered at the thought of trying to plan our way out of it. Whatever is in the package, James Rowan will clearly stop at nothing to get it back.

I pull my dagger free of the soldier, wipe it clean on his pants, and slide it back into its sheath. No highwayman would be stupid enough to attack a military encampment's night guard. I've just announced my presence to the entire battalion.

Best Case Scenario: I make good time, masking my trail by using the trees, and create a significant lead time before this man's body is discovered at watch change.

Worst Case Scenario: I bring the entire Rowansmark military down around our heads before I've even had a chance to deal with Melkin or the tracker.

I lean down and measure the dead man's foot. Slightly bigger than mine, but it will do. Tugging his boots off ignites an unending stream of agony through my chest, but I don't have time for pain medicine now. Several minutes pass while I switch our boots and wipe the ground around him so no one can see what I've just done.

It takes everything I have to walk away without limping and giving myself away to every half-decent tracker stationed with the battalion. I wander a bit, brushing away my tracks, until I find what I'm looking for: the edge of the military encampment.

Now my boot marks won't stand out. With any luck, no one will even bother to look for me so close to the heart of the battalion. And if they did, all they'd find is the curious footprint of a Rowansmark man who stretched up to his tiptoes for a moment in the middle of the forest floor.

It's going to hurt like hell. I grab a twig from the ground and wedge it in between my teeth so I can bite down against the pain without making a sound. Then I look at the low-hanging branch skimming the air a foot above me, gather myself, and leap.

CHAPTER FIFTY-TWO

RACHEL

"We're bringing that back to Baalboden."

Melkin hasn't moved from his original seat by the fire's remains, though Quinn and Willow left a while ago to weave branches, vines, and moss together into a treetop cradle they can sleep in for the night. I've been sitting by the torchlight examining the symbols on the wand, trying to figure out what they mean.

"Yes. We are." Though I'm not about to willingly hand the Commander a weapon capable of destroying everything in our world.

"I have to give it to the Commander. Alone. I have to do that, Rachel. For Eloise." His voice sounds desperate and dark, but where once I felt compassion, now I feel nothing.

"No." I lay the device in its cloth and begin carefully rolling it back up.

"For Eloise."

"Not even Eloise is worth giving the Commander the power

to destroy anyone who stands up to him."

He curses and crawls toward me. I jerk the device toward my chest and slide my knife free.

"What about Logan? What about rescuing him? He's all you have left!"

I hear the accusation beneath his words. He thought we were the same. Willing to do anything, no matter how unthinkable, if it would save us from loss. The Commander thought we were the same too.

They're both wrong.

"Eloise and Logan are dead unless we destroy the Commander."

"No." He shakes his head, fury leaping into his eyes.

I'll see his fury and double it. "Yes! Get your head out of the sand, Melkin. You work for a treacherous monster who never keeps his word. Never. The second he has what he wants from you, he'll kill you. He'll probably kill Eloise in front of you first, just because he *can*. And then you'll have done nothing with your life but hand the worst man in the world the power to rule it."

"Stop it!" he screams at me, spit flying from his mouth, his hand curled around his knife as if he needs a target.

"I won't stop. Not until he's dead. And now I have the means to do it." I push the cloth-wrapped device into the inner pocket of my cloak. "Either you go along with my plan, or you get out of my way. I don't care which you choose."

He drives his knife into the ground at his feet, and looks at me with the kind of loathing that once would have made my skin crawl. Now, his opinion of me means just as little as his foolish desire to sacrifice the rest of the world for one more moment with his doomed wife.

My father did not die in vain. I'm going to make sure of it.

God help Melkin if he tries to stop me.

CHAPTER FIFTY-THREE

LOGAN

I tree-leap as quietly as possible. Taking my time. Edging along the branches and biting on my twig hard as I use my knees to cushion each landing.

I was right. It hurts like hell. Every leap strains my rib cage. Every landing rattles it until I want to curl up, swallow enough medicine to numb the pain, and sleep for hours.

But I don't dare stop. Any second now, someone will find the dead guard and raise the alarm. I probably should've dragged his body into the woods, hidden it, and then doubled back to hide the trail, but the pain and weakness in my rib cage would've made that too time intensive. Better to flee as quickly as possible.

I'm maybe sixty yards from the encampment when I hear a shout go up. They've found him. And I can't leap quietly enough while I have Rowansmark military combing the woods for me. Quickly assessing the trees around me, I choose a tall silver maple with plenty of leafy coverage but no low-hanging branches and make the three leaps it takes to reach it.

Pain clouds my thoughts and dulls my instincts as I climb into the upper reaches of the tree. About two thirds of the way up, I find what I need and settle into a secure cradle of branches. Two of the limbs are thick enough to hold me should I need to leap, and both reach into the surrounding trees. I'm high enough that no one from the ground can look up and see me through all the foliage.

It's the best I'm going to get for the moment.

Quietly pulling my bag around, I take out the half-gone pack of medicinal powder and a Rowansmark-made cloaking device I once traded for with the highwaymen outside Baalboden.

A quick pinch of powder takes the worst edge off the pain, and I clip the cloaking device, which looks like a small oval disc, to the front of my tunic. When I flick the tiny switch on the side of the device, it vibrates once. I hope the blocking system contained within it is strong enough to withstand the technological might of Rowansmark's military.

CHAPTER FIFTY-FOUR

RACHEL

Melkin and I haven't spoken since I demanded he choose a course of action. I've decided to take his silence as compliance, though it doesn't matter to me one way or the other. My purpose is set. If he wants to give this device to the Commander, he'll have to do it over my dead body.

Quinn and Willow are sleeping in the trees close by. I suppose in the morning they'll return to wherever it is they live. That doesn't matter to me either.

All that matters is that I finally have a way to force the Commander to pay for everything he's done. The rage within me is viciously triumphant at the thought.

Leaving Melkin to keep the first watch, I unroll my travel mat over my father's grave and lie down with my face beside the carved wooden cross. Moonlight gleams on its surface, gilding his name with a beauty that should wound me. I reach out and grasp the wood with my bare hand, holding it tight as slivers gouge my palm.

It's a welcome pain, but it isn't enough to relieve the silent weight crushing me from within. Letting go, I turn my face away from the cross, away from Melkin, away from everyone, and close my eyes.

The wind sighs along the treetops and whispers over my skin like a lullaby, but I can't sleep. Soon, I'll have justice. A life for a life. It won't be enough to seal up the edges of everything that's undone within me. It won't be enough to shatter the silence and let me grieve in peace.

It won't be enough, but it's all I have, and I cling to it with desperate strength.

The wind dies down, and I hear a soft *crunch* on ash behind me. Tensing, I try to listen for it again, but I can't hear anything beyond the sudden roar of my pulse pounding inside my head.

My knife slides free of its sheath without a sound. I brace my left elbow beneath me, flip the knife blade-side out, and shove off the ground.

Melkin stands two yards from me, his knife down at his side, his eyes pits of rage and misery.

He means to take the device from me. Destroy any chance of justice. Make Dad's sacrifice worth *nothing*.

I raise my weapon. "Get back," I snarl at him in a voice I barely recognize. Cold. Empty.

"You said he'd keep his word if I just did what he asked."

His voice is cold and empty too.

"I lied."

His face contorts, his body shakes, his legs tense.

"Get. Back," I say.

He watches me, his knife hand trembling so badly that he'll

never be able to stab me with it before I disarm him, tie him up, and leave him for Quinn and Willow to deal with. Rolling to the balls of my feet, I lunge for his right arm.

His left flashes out, silver streaking through the moonlight, and I remember his ambidextrous sword work a millisecond before he can slice into me. Spinning to the side, I drop and roll forward, coming up several yards away.

He isn't trying to take the device. He's trying to kill me.

I crouch, blade out. Something feral tears through me, obliterating Eloise, his unborn child, the kind of girl I once dreamed I'd be, and every cautious word Logan ever spoke, leaving nothing but pure, scorching bloodlust in their wake.

Melkin swings his sword in dizzying circles and rushes at me. I wait until he's almost on me, and then dive forward, low to the ground, crashing into his legs and sending him flying over the top of me. His blade nicks me as it goes by, but I can't feel the pain, and he drops his sword as he lands on his side.

I'm screaming now. Raw, agonized wails that flay the air with their fury. Out of the corner of my eye I see Quinn and Willow hurrying toward us, but I have no time for them. Whirling, I lunge forward while Melkin is still reaching for his sword. He sees me and slashes out with his knife instead. The blade catches my cloak and tears into it, but I don't slow down.

I can't.

Driving my boot onto his wrist, I grind the small bones together. He yells and drops his knife.

I slam my knees onto his diaphragm and feel the air leave his lungs.

He whips his left arm up and punches me in the face, and I

land in a pile of ash on my back. He's already on his feet. Already coming for me. I can't see his weapons. I don't know which hand he'll use. And I don't have time to get up.

He's in the air, long legs dropping down, his face a mask of murderous intent.

I broke his right wrist. The weapon must be in his left hand. I roll to his right as he lands beside me, his left arm already swinging forward. Flipping my blade around, I push myself off the ground and bury my knife deep into his chest.

He sags, deflating slowly onto the ash beside me, and reaches for the knife with his empty left hand.

He isn't holding his sword. I scan the area and see it gleaming yards away from us. His knife lies beside it.

"I wanted to take it." His eyes stare into mine like a child trying to understand what he'd done wrong. "That's all."

"You were trying to kill me!"

He was. I know it. I had to have known it. I didn't just fatally wound an unarmed man who wanted nothing more than to steal from me.

His blood seeps along the knife hilt, thick and warm, and coats my hands.

"You tried to kill me." My voice shakes.

"Disarm. To take it." He coughs, a horrible wet sound that sprays me with blood.

"No. No." I pull the knife free as he slides onto the ground. "No."

My hands can't stop the bleeding, but I try. Pressing against his wound, I try to make sense of him. Of myself. Of what we've done.

What I've done.

He raises a hand, long fingers gleaming white in the moon-light. "Eloise?"

I can't look at him. I can't. But I've lied to him before, and I can lie once more. "Yes."

"Can't save you." His voice is nothing but a whisper straining against the blood filling up his throat.

"You just did." I can barely speak past the suffocating guilt choking me. I *killed* him. A desperate man. A pawn of the Com-mander's who wanted nothing more than to save his beloved wife.

He doesn't speak again, and I cover his wound with my bloodstained hands until his chest falls quiet.

CHAPTER FIFTY-FIVE

LOGAN

I hear the Rowansmark battalion before I see them. No need to use stealth when you have sheer numbers on your side, I guess. They swarm out of the trees, carrying swords and torches. Quickly, I close my eyes before the firelight costs me my night vision. I can track their movements with my ears instead.

It's immediately obvious they aren't tracking. They're hunting. Trying to flush out their prey. Walking with less than five yards between each soldier, beating at the underbrush with their swords, peering up into the trees they pass with the help of their torches.

I'll be fine. I'm up high enough that the torchlight can't reach me. I settle against the branches and wait while they spread along the Wasteland beneath me, calling to one another, swinging their swords, and making enough noise to announce their presence to anyone within two hundred yards of us.

Before long, they're gone. I wait until I can't hear them beating the bushes, until their yells fade into silence, and expect the normal noises of night in the Wasteland to resume.

They don't.

Which means I'm not as alone as someone wants me to think. Tension coils within me, and I slowly draw my knife.

It's a smart plan. Use loud, obvious hunters and hope that once the prey eludes them, he'll feel comfortable and give himself away. I'd have done the same myself.

Settling slowly against the tree, I hold myself absolutely still, ignoring the pain in my side demanding I readjust in an effort to find a more comfortable position.

It takes almost an hour, but then I hear him. A faint whisper of sound that could almost be mistaken for the breeze. Almost. But the birds are still silent, and the forest feels like it's holding its breath.

I don't try to look for him. If he's tree-leaping, I'll feel it if he lands in mine. But if I move to a position where I have better visibility, he'll catch the movement. And if he doesn't, he'll certainly catch the noise.

Instead, I wait. I don't hear him again, but eventually the birds hoot, coo, and chirp, and I hear the nocturnal ramblings of raccoons on the ground below.

He's gone.

But he and a battalion of Rowansmark military men are now between me and the safe house.

The only recourse I have is to move with extreme caution and come up with a plan as I travel. I can't single-handedly overwhelm an entire battalion. I have to hope I can outwit them.

CHAPTER FIFTY-SIX

RACHEL

I sit by Melkin's body until dawn bleeds across the sky. Quinn sits with me while Willow remains on guard somewhere in the trees.

I didn't ask him to sit with me. But somehow having him there, quietly present without offering judgment, makes the ragged edges in me settle just a bit. I haven't spoken since my final words to Melkin, but as the gloom around us lifts, I raise my eyes to Quinn's.

"I killed him."

He nods.

"I thought he was going to kill me first. He attacked me. He had his weapons out. I was sure he was going to kill me." I *was* sure, but now I'm not. Now, I'm looking back and remembering I jumped up from my travel mat with my knife already raised for battle while his was still trained at the ground. I lunged at him, blade out, before he ever raised his sword.

He was trying to disarm me and defend himself. And I killed him.

I struggle to my feet and run to the edge of the trees, where I fall to my knees and retch.

I killed him.

My stomach is empty, but I keep heaving.

I *killed* him.

I'm shaking, my teeth chattering against each other violently, when Quinn's solid arms wrap around me from behind and hold me against his warm chest.

"You thought you were defending yourself."

I did think that, but it doesn't comfort me now, and it won't comfort Eloise.

"It happened fast. Did you make the best decision you could given the information you had?"

I twist around to look at him, his warm brown eyes steady on mine, his straight black hair haloed by the early morning light. "I don't want absolution."

"I'm not offering any. Take the blame that belongs to you, and nothing else. I'm asking you to look it in the eye and face it for what it is."

But I can't face it. Not really. If I do, if I let it cut me like I deserve, everything else will spill out too. Oliver. Dad. Melkin. Logan at the Commander's mercy in a dungeon. It's all one gaping pit of loss, destruction, and grief, and if I feel it, I'll never be able to protect the device and deliver judgment.

I don't even have to ask the silence to take it from me. It's already gone. Slipping into the emptiness before I make the conscious choice to send it there, and leaving me numb.

I push away from Quinn, and he lets me. Why shouldn't he? I mean nothing to him. I'm just a broken girl who lost her father and then killed a man. And I'm about to go kill another.

Gathering my belongings, I stow them in my pack and then turn to find Quinn and Willow packed as well, standing by Melkin's body.

I can't abandon him for the forest animals to eat. Leaving my pack beside Dad's grave, I use my knife to start digging a new one a few yards away. Soon, Quinn and Willow drop down beside me and dig as well.

"I'll do it." I don't want their help. I need to do this for Melkin. Alone. A small piece of atonement in the lifetime of penance I'm going to serve for my crime.

"We can help. It will get done much faster," Willow says, but Quinn lays a hand on her arm, and they pull back.

It takes me almost an hour. I use my knife and then scoop dirt out with my bare hands, letting the dust of his grave mingle with the stains of his blood on my skin. Then the three of us lift him and lay him gently down. When Willow picks up his walking stick to lay across his chest, I hold out my hand for it.

On our first day in the Wasteland, the Cursed One incinerated everything Melkin owned except his weapons. His sword is far too long and heavy for me to carry across the Wasteland, but I can bring this back. A reminder of what I'm capable of. A faint comfort for the wife he left behind.

Together, we push the soil back into place until all that remains is a little hill of dirt. Quinn stands beside me, a solid, reassuring presence I refuse to lean on. Willow stands across from us, scanning the surrounding trees, her bow already in her hand. I should say something. A eulogy. A good-bye. But Melkin deserves to be memorialized by someone other than the girl who took his life, and I don't know how to put into words the cost of what I've done.

I turn away. I have a mission to complete. When it's over, I'll look for absolution. When it's over, I'll find what comfort is left to me.

I refuse to brush the dirt from my hands. Scooping up my pack, I arrange it against my back and slide my Switch into its slot so I can carry Melkin's ebony walking stick instead. When Quinn and Willow pick up their packs too, I frown at them.

"You don't need to come. I can find my way back on my own."

"Can you?" Quinn asks.

"I can find what I need to find."

"We'll go with you."

"Why? You don't even know me."

"I knew your father." His voice is steady, but pain runs beneath it. "And you were right when you said we still owe him a debt. I'd like to pay that debt by escorting you through the Wasteland."

There's a quiet insistence in his voice, and I'm too tired to argue. Besides, what do I care if two Tree People tag along? It isn't going to slow me down or change my plans.

"Fine. But remember how you insisted on coming with me when you find I've landed you right in the middle of a war."

CHAPTER FIFTY-SEVEN

LOGAN

I've been traveling hard for three and a half days. Tree-leaping. Sleeping in the wide crook of an oak curtained by Spanish moss. Watching the wires on my tracking cuff get brighter by the hour as I cut across the safer trails Rachel would use and shave time off my journey.

I'm closing in.

So is the Rowansmark battalion. I've seen their signs. Heard thin snatches of conversation floating back to me. I don't know how close I am to them, but they're still between Rachel, Melkin, and me.

I haven't seen any sign of the tracker, and that worries me. He could've circled behind me. Gone ahead of the battalion to find the safe house. Caught up with Rachel and Melkin.

The scenarios are endless, and they all spell disaster.

Stopping to rest in another oak tree as the sun climbs toward noon, I assess my strategy. Following the battalion isn't getting me anywhere. I need to flank them. Get ahead of them. Intersect with Rachel and Melkin before they run into them.

Moving with care, I open my pack. I'm running low on food since I haven't been able to go to ground and hunt, but I still have a few jars of preserved fruit and some sheep jerky I took from the safe-house pantry. Choosing a small ration of each, I eat quickly and then grudgingly use a small bit of pain medicine.

I'm going to have to move fast. I can't afford to feel the full effects of my journey until later.

After packing my bag and assessing the noises around me to gauge the relative safety of moving forward, I aim southeast and start tree-leaping. Within twenty minutes, all sounds of the battalion are gone, and I'm deep in the Spanish moss–draped forest of the southern Wasteland, surrounded only by birds, bugs, and the occasional rabbit or squirrel.

When I judge I've traveled far enough south to risk cutting back toward the west without running into the battalion, I take another short rest, refuel on water and some jerky, and start leaping again.

The sun is sinking toward the west, about three hours from sunset, when I glance down at the tracker cuff I wear and freeze. The wires glow at one hundred percent. My heart pounds, and I have to remind myself to breathe.

I've found her.

Somewhere in a thirty-yard radius around me, Rachel is traveling the Wasteland. I'm not too late. I'm busy scoping out my surroundings, trying to determine the best direction to take, when I hear her approach.

She's arguing with someone. Melkin, most likely. I frown

as her voice carries clearly through the thick oaks and mossy undergrowth. It's not like her to forget how to move quietly.

Her oversight works to my advantage, though, and I brace myself for the climb down when she and a boy about my age enter the small clearing at my feet. He walks close to her, his left hand hovering behind her back as if he wants to touch her but isn't sure of his welcome. I assess him quickly. About six feet. Ropy muscles on a lithe frame. Olive skin, dark eyes and hair, leather laces holding his tunic and pants in place. A Tree Person. I don't know how he came to be with Rachel, but the way his eyes watch her with interest and concern makes me want to send him back to his village.

Immediately.

Melkin isn't with her. Either he succumbed to one of the dangers in the Wasteland, or he tried to fulfill his assignment, and Rachel killed him.

I study Rachel next, and shock punches a little frisson of panic through me. Her pale skin is smudged with what looks like ash. Her cloak is torn and battered. And her *hands*. Her hands are covered in dirt and dried blood, and she clutches a long black metal walking stick like it's going to disappear if she lets go.

But worst of all is the look on her face. Cold. Fierce. Empty. Like someone snuffed out the Rachel I knew and sent out a hollow shell in her place. I hang on to the branch for another moment, trying to adjust to this new Rachel before I have to drop down and show her the shock written across my face.

"We need rest," her companion says.

"Then rest. I'm going on."

"You haven't eaten today. You've barely slept. If you keep this up, you'll collapse, and then what good will all this progress do you?" he asks, but his tone sounds genuinely curious instead of worried or upset. Like he's fine with allowing her the freedom to destroy herself as long as she's given the matter proper thought. In light of the facts he's just presented, my tone would've indicated a good shaking was in store for her if she didn't listen to common sense and take care of herself.

She doesn't respond to his invitation for self-reflection. Instead, she strides beneath my tree, her course set north, and acts like she can't hear him. He follows her. I let them both walk past me. My first meeting with this Tree Person isn't going to be me awkwardly trying to climb down a tree without hurting my rib. They're four trees up when I grasp the branch I'm on and ready myself for a painful landing.

A slight movement in the corner of my eye arrests my motion, and I hold still as a man in green and brown, a dagger in his fist, melts out of the shadows between the trees and silently follows Rachel and her companion.

The Rowansmark tracker.

Rachel must have the package. Or he thinks she does. And he's going to kill her to get it.

Except he didn't bargain on me.

He's approaching my tree. Five steps and he'll be here. I'll only have one chance to get it right.

Best Case Scenario: I kill him on my first try.

Worst Case Scenario: I miss, and never get another chance.

Best Case Scenario it is, then. Quickly assessing angles, momentum, and how much damage I can do without drawing my sword, I wait for him to walk directly below me, let go of my branch, and jump.

CHAPTER FIFTY-EIGHT

LOGAN

He senses me and turns, but he's too late. I slam into him, wrap my hands around his throat, and drive both of us onto the ground.

Pain explodes through my rib cage on impact, and I nearly lose my grip. He whips his arms up and claps them against my ears, disorienting me. I'm dizzy, unable to draw a complete breath, and losing focus fast.

Digging my thumbs into his windpipe, I will myself to hang on. He bucks beneath me and catches me in the ribs with an elbow. Agony sears through me, and my hands slip. Knocking my hands away from his throat, he throws me onto the ground beside him, pulls a knife, and looms over me.

I can't breathe. Can barely move. I'm going to die if I don't figure out a way to get the upper hand. Fast.

His knife arm goes up, and his eyes lock on mine, but before I can react, an arrow sinks into the narrow space between his eyes with a soft *thud*. He shudders, his body sags, and I scoot to the side as he crashes to the ground.

Someone whistles softly from a tree behind me, a near-perfect imitation of a blackbird, but I can't look. I can't bear to move. I can hardly bear to breathe. Soft footsteps hit the forest floor and come toward me. In seconds, a girl about Rachel's age with olive skin and a long dark braid kneels beside me, a black bow in her hands.

"Did you get him?" Rachel asks from somewhere to my left, and now I understand why she was being unnecessarily loud.

It was a trap. A trap that worked. I want to give her kudos for planning ahead, but I can't seem to get enough air to speak.

"Two of them?" the boy asks.

"This one jumped out of the tree and tried to kill the tracker. I decided not to shoot him."

I'm grateful. I hope she knows that. Pain sears my chest again, and I close my eyes, grit my teeth, and try to will it away.

"Who is he?" the boy asks.

Another set of soft footsteps approaches, and someone drops to the ground next to me. "Logan?"

I open my eyes. Rachel crouches beside me, her glorious red hair lit with fire from the sun, her bloodstained hands hovering above me as if afraid to touch me, and her blue eyes so wounded, I want to hold her until some of her pain recedes. I lift my hand and press it against her cheek. She trembles.

"This is Logan?" The girl with the bow sounds surprised. "Rachel said you were locked in a dungeon."

My voice wheezes as I say, "I escaped."

"How?"

"Blew up a wall." My eyes are still locked on Rachel's.

"Nice." The girl grins at me. "I'd like to learn that trick."

"Logan." Rachel lays a hand on my shoulder as if testing to see if I'm really there.

"I told you I'd find you."

Her fingers clench around my shoulder, and she slowly curls toward me until she's lying facedown against my chest. Her weight hurts, but I don't complain. Instead, I cradle her to me and feel the missing pieces inside of me slide firmly back into place.

CHAPTER FIFTY-NINE

RACHEL

I lie against Logan's chest listening to him breathe and shake like I've been caught out in a snowstorm in nothing but a tunic. He's here. Alive. Warm and steady beneath me. I haven't lost everything.

And yet, with Melkin's blood still on my hands, I'm not convinced. The silence inside consumes me. I want to burrow into him and feel safe. Feel the grief, the anger, and most important the hope that I know hovers somewhere just out of reach within me. Digging my fingers into Logan's shoulder, I desperately try to feel *real* again.

Beside me the body of the tracker starts beeping, a high-pitched insistent tone that has Logan pushing me to get up.

"Get back!"

He can hardly obey his own instructions. Digging one hand into the ground, he groans as he tries to lift himself off the ground. Transferring Melkin's walking stick to my other hand, I reach down to help. Quinn joins me and together we scoop our hands under his arms and drag Logan away from the body.

The beeping speeds up.

"What's going on?" I ask Logan.

"Bomb," he wheezes, his face white with strain as we drag him into the trees. "Anatomical trigger looped on a closed circuit."

"Speak English," Willow says as she falls in step beside me and bends to help carry Logan.

"When his heart stopped, the device began its countdown."

"Why would anyone—"

The blast throws us to the ground and rains bits of dirt, twigs, and a fine mist I imagine was once the Rowansmark tracker all around us. I land partially on Logan's chest, and scramble off as he moans in pain.

"What's wrong with you?"

"Broken rib."

"We need to climb. Now." Willow is already moving, grasping the nearest branch and swinging into the tree, her bow strung behind her back. "If that explosion didn't call the Cursed One, it called every highwayman within one hundred fifty yards."

"Worse." Logan sounds like he can barely get enough air to speak. "Battalion. Rowansmark. Might have heard."

Quinn jumps up and circles to Logan's other side. "Can you get into a tree if we help?"

He nods, and we each take an arm and help him sit up. He sways, and it's clear that pride is all that keeps him from crying out at the pain. He's never going to be able to climb a tree. I see the moment he realizes it and decides to sacrifice himself for the rest of us.

"I'll stall them. You go," Logan says.

Quinn frowns and looks at me.

"Ignore him. He doesn't get to play the martyr today."

"Isn't that his choice?" Quinn asks.

"Not while I'm still breathing."

Logan jerks his arm away from Quinn. "Go."

"Absolutely not," I say.

"Rachel—"

"I love how you still think if you tell me to do something, I'll just check my brain at the door and do it." I try to infuse my voice with anger, but all I feel is fear. I can't bear to lose him.

"Hey! Idiots who want to argue while disaster is heading our way! Maybe you should shut up and climb a tree." Willow pokes her head out of a bower of leaves and glares at us.

"Listen." Quinn holds up his hand for quiet. We fall silent and realize there's no rumbling. No distant roar coming closer. The Cursed One must be terrorizing people on the other side of the continent or sleeping in its lair, because it isn't coming.

"Fine. The Cursed One isn't coming. But the battalion still could be, and I'm not going to watch you die just so these two can figure out who's in charge." Willow beckons to Quinn, but he looks at Logan again, and I can tell he doesn't want to leave him behind.

"Go. I'm fine. I'll stall them. Or hide." Logan looks around, and I resist the urge to punch him only because he's already injured.

"You're coming with us."

"No, I'm not."

"Then I'm staying too."

"I didn't travel all this way just to watch you die. Please, Rachel."

He's all I have left, and he sits there like today is the day he's going to die, and I should just be fine with it.

"Stop it!" I slam Melkin's walking stick into the ground. It sinks below the surface about six inches, and the earth beneath us trembles violently.

We freeze, and everyone stares at the ground and then at me.

"What did you just do?" Quinn asks, dread in his voice for the first time since I met him.

I'm shaking my head. "I don't know. I don't—I was mad. I hit the ground with the stick, and it just went right into it and then there was—"

"A sonic pulse," Logan says. "The Cursed One will have heard that."

"Oh, now you've done it." Willow starts climbing higher. "Get in the tree, Quinn!"

"I didn't mean to. I didn't know." I pull the stick from the ground as a faint thunder rumbles beneath our feet. "It's Melkin's stick . . ."

Melkin, who shoved the stick into the ground while I was busy yelling at him, and then saved me from the Cursed One moments later. Why? Why would he call the beast and put us both in danger like that? I remembered him saying his stick was a gift. Not from Baalboden. Was it possible he hadn't known what it could do?

I don't have the answers, and I don't have time to figure them out. The rumble is growing into a distant roar. We have less than a minute to get to safety.

"Get him up." I grab one of Logan's arms while Quinn grabs the other. Ignoring Logan's gasp of pain, we heave him to his feet.

He sways, and Quinn wraps an arm around him to steady him, but when we start moving toward the nearest tree, we discover Logan's slow progress is the least of our worries.

The Rowansmark battalion surrounds us, a tight circle of soldiers standing three deep and cutting off any escape from the Cursed One.

CHAPTER SIXTY

LOGAN

We're surrounded by Rowansmark's soldiers, their swords drawn as they establish a perimeter forty yards away from us, caging us in. We'll be destroyed, while they can stay relatively safe if they keep quiet after the Cursed One bursts through the ground in front of us.

We're going to die.

Willow drops out of the tree above us, swings her bow into position, and stands next to her brother like she doesn't want him to die without her.

I don't want to die without Rachel, either. I'm a fool for not seeing it before. I didn't dream of her, worry for her, and push myself across the Wasteland for her to fulfill my responsibility to Jared. It took being thrown into a dungeon to realize I need her.

It takes facing imminent death to realize I love her.

I love her.

A fierce light consumes me from the inside out. It blazes through my body until I think there's no way I can contain it. I don't want to contain it. I want it to overtake me completely. It's illogical. Wonderful. Almost painful.

And I'm not going to die without telling her.

She moves against my side, and I turn to her, expecting her to fall into my arms and cling to me while fire consumes us. Instead, she shoves Melkin's walking stick into my fist and says, "Hold this."

She doesn't wait to see if I've complied. She's tugging a roll of black cloth from her cloak pocket, her expression fierce.

"Rachel, I—"

"You can save us," she says, and pulls a dark gray metallic flute with three finger pads down its center from the middle of the cloth. "Here."

She trades me the walking stick for the flute. Symbols decorate the top of each finger pad, but I don't know what they mean. The ground beneath us trembles violently, and the Rowansmark men step back, some of them furtively glancing up at the safety of the trees above them.

"I don't know—"

"It's a device to control the Cursed One through sound waves. Push the button to send it away."

"I don't know which button that is!"

The ground begins to crack, a jagged seam heading straight for us.

"Better figure it out, tech head, or we're dead." Willow hooks her arm through her brother's and drags them both backward, stopping about fifteen yards from the line of swords behind us.

"I can't read these symbols." Panic is beginning to claw at me.

"Experiment, then," Rachel says. "Deduce. Make connections.

Do what you do best." She grabs my face and looks at me with absolute trust. "I have faith in you."

The ground twenty yards in front of us explodes and spews the glistening black length of the Cursed One into the air. Its scales glitter beneath the sunlight, and its film-covered eyes swing in our direction as it sniffs the air, huffing puffs of smoke and rumbling in fury.

We're about to die. I don't know how to work this thing she's handed me. I can't understand the symbols on the finger pads. All the faith in the world won't change that. Still, I'm going to try. But not before I say what I need to say to her.

"I love you, Rachel."

Her eyes widen, but before she can say anything, I turn toward the beast and push a button with shaking fingers.

CHAPTER SIXTY-ONE

<u>LOGAN</u>

The beast roars and shakes its body, its scales rattling together like a thousand coins falling on a cobblestone street. Then it gathers itself, swings its muzzle toward us, and bellows. A brilliant crimson-orange fireball explodes out of its mouth.

We dive for the ground, and my rib cage screams at me as searing heat rolls over the top of us and sends the men behind us running.

Wrong button.

Panic erases every logical thought from my mind. I take a deep breath and fumble with the device I hold.

The creature coils its body and digs its claws into the ground as it drags itself toward us, its milky yellow eyes glaring at nothing while it homes in on its prey. Desperately, I stab the second button.

Nothing happens.

"It's not working. It's not working!"

"It has to." Rachel reaches over and slams her fist on the top two buttons at the same time. The beast rears back, swings its head to the left, and strafes the line of Rowansmark soldiers with fire.

The flames incinerate most of them on the spot, but a few fall to the ground wailing in agony. The surrounding trees explode into flame, a deafening thunder of dry wood hissing and cracking.

Hope battles with the panic inside me, and I clench the device tight and hit the bottom two buttons simultaneously. The creature swings to the right and sends a fireball hurtling into the ranks of men standing there.

Chaos reigns. Men are screaming, running, swinging into trees and leaping for safety. There is no perimeter of swords around us anymore. What's left of the battalion is scattered, racing for safety while their fallen comrades disintegrate into ash and the lines of trees on either side of us burn fiercely. The Cursed One roars and coils itself to strike again.

"Send it back," Rachel says, as if I know what I'm doing.

I hit the top and bottom buttons at the same time and the beast slithers away from us, spitting fire. There aren't any combinations of buttons left except to push all three, and I'm afraid that will send it straight toward us. It's the only direction left for him to go.

I don't have much time left before the beast realizes we're the last remaining prey in the area. My hands still shake as fear pounds through me, but I grasp the device with white knuckles.

Pressing the first button alone seemed to antagonize the creature. Logic would deduce that's the sound used to call it to the surface in the first place. The second button had no discernible effect unless used in conjunction with one of the other buttons.

That left the third as the most reasonable choice for driving the Cursed One back to his lair at the center of the Earth. I whisper a prayer and press it.

The beast shudders and lashes the forest with his enormous spiked tail, sending a hail of branches and corpses flying, then slides back toward the gaping hole in the ground. I hold my breath as it comes closer, my finger white with the strain of pressing against the third button. The beast never hesitates. It simply slithers back into the tunnel it created and disappears from view. I keep my death grip on the device until I can no longer feel the vibrations of its movement beneath me.

All around us, sparks hiss and spit as fire chews through the ancient oaks, and the few surviving Rowansmark soldiers moan in pain on the forest floor. They don't have long before either the flames or the smoke put them out of their misery. The fire is spreading east to west, though that could change at the mercy of the wind. We have to put distance between ourselves and this spot. Not just because of the fire, but because as soon as they realize the Cursed One is gone, the last remnant of Rowansmark's battalion will return to finish their assignment.

"Help me up."

Rachel, Quinn, and Willow reach for me. My head swims from the pain in my side, and the scorched skin beneath the bandage on my neck throbs as the heat of the fire scrapes against it. I can't possibly put enough distance between myself and this place in this condition. I hand the device back to Rachel and reach for the packet of pain medicine. There isn't much left, and I don't know what else I'll have to face between here and

Baalboden, but if I don't reduce some of the pain now, I'll never get the chance to find out. I tip the packet against my lips and let the rest of the powder slide onto my tongue. A moment later, Rachel has the device packed away in her cloak, and the worst of the pain is ebbing. I cast one more glance at the fire now burning between us and the surviving soldiers, then we disappear into the Wasteland, leaving the burning wreckage of Rowansmark's battalion in our wake.

CHAPTER SIXTY-TWO

RACHEL

We travel as fast as Logan's injury will allow us, and just before sunset set up camp in a small, sturdy log cabin we find hidden in a copse of overgrown fir trees. A steady rain falls from steel-gray clouds and slides against my skin with cool, soft fingers. The rain is an unexpected boon that will both douse the flames we left behind and wash away our tracks.

Quinn and Willow are coming to Baalboden with us. Quinn because he feels honor-bound to pay his debt to my father by helping Logan with the arduous journey. Willow because she refuses to leave her brother's side, and because the prospect of seeing us try to bring down our leader fascinates her on a level I might find disturbing if I had the energy to care.

I don't. I just want to get moving so we can lay a trap for the Commander. We have the device. We understand how to use it. He doesn't stand a chance.

The cabin provides a welcome refuge from the rain, and Logan falls asleep almost as soon as we settle inside. I eat a cold dinner, wrap my cloak around me, and sit beside him. We haven't had a chance to talk privately since fleeing the fire, but his words keep blazing to life inside me with glorious persistence.

I love you, Rachel.

Once, I would've taken those words as a romantic, sugar-coated fairy tale and built a castle of dreams on them. Now, they're a hard-won promise forged in fire and loss by a man who means every word he says. I want to brand them into my skin as proof that I still have something left to fight for.

I wish I had the courage to give those words back to him, but the ugly brokenness inside me holds me back. I'm not the same girl Logan fell in love with. I'm not the same girl he fought to reach. I'm a hollow version of myself, and I have no right to grasp for happiness when I've caused so much misery. The thought slices into me, but the silence greedily swallows the pain before I can truly feel it.

I press close to him and study his face while he sleeps. Fading purple and yellow bruises blossom just beneath the skin of his left cheekbone, cuts run across his arms and hands, and a dirty gauze bandage covers a palm-sized area on his neck. I rummage through his pack, find his small first-aid kit, and gather the supplies I'll need to clean and re-bandage whatever lies beneath the gauze.

I pull the filthy tape away from his skin, remove the gauze, and immediately feel sick. The insignia of the Brute Squad is burned into the side of Logan's neck in a welt of blistered red skin turning black at the edges.

He's been branded. Marked for life by the man everything in me longs to destroy. Every time anyone looks at Logan, they'll know the Commander once had him at his mercy and proved to be stronger.

I dab antiseptic across the wound, sloughing away dead skin and trying not to gag at the sight. I want to torture the Commander before he dies. Hear him scream for mercy and know I have the power to deny him. The thought fills me with a heady sense of power, and my lips peel back from my teeth in a snarl as I gently cut away the blackened skin at the edge of the wound.

Logan stirs restlessly but doesn't wake as I spread salve over the burn and attach a fresh patch of gauze. I lie down, press myself against him, and ignore Quinn and Willow as they huddle in a corner, speaking in low voices.

I might not be able to torture the Commander. I might not be able to make him beg. Once the Cursed One is called, destruction is swift and certain. But I'll make sure the Commander's death is so horrific, so legendary, that for the rest of Logan's life whenever anyone sees the mark on his neck, they won't see a man who was once broken before his leader. They'll see the mark of a man who helped destroy the most powerful person in our world, and they'll tread with caution.

Holding this thought close, I close my eyes and drift to sleep as Logan breathes steadily beside me, Quinn and Willow fall silent in their corner, and the rain taps lightly against the cabin's moss-draped roof.

In the morning, after a quick breakfast of dried fruit, I help Logan pack his gear, and stuff half the contents of his pack into mine when he isn't looking. He doesn't want me to notice how much pain he's in, but I see it.

He reaches up, fingers the new patch of gauze on his neck,

and looks at me. "This is fresh."

"I changed it last night while you slept."

"Is it . . . did it look bad?"

"A little."

"It's probably permanent."

"It adds character." My smile feels wobbly at the edges, so I firm my lips before he notices.

"At least it takes the attention off my face." His smile doesn't wobble at all.

"What's wrong with your face?" I peer at it closely, looking for injuries I may have missed last night in the uncertain light of dusk.

"Nothing." He laughs a little. "It was a joke. You know, people won't have to look at my ugly face because they'll be too busy admiring the Commander's handiwork on my neck."

I scowl. "Your face is just as handsome as ever. And if we do this right, no one will look at your neck without shivering a little at the thought of the leader who went down in flames."

"You think I'm handsome?" A hesitant smile tugs at his lips.

"What? I don't know." I'm suddenly very interested in the state of his boots. Peering at them closely, I pray he'll change the subject. He doesn't.

"That's what you said."

Heat blazes across my face, and I turn away. "I also said we're going to take down the Commander. That's probably the more important part of that whole conversation."

"Not necessarily. Rachel, can we talk about what happened during the Cursed One's attack?"

I love you, Rachel.

The heat in my cheeks creeps down my neck, and when Willow and Quinn slide their leather packs against their backs and walk toward us, I'm grateful for the reprieve. A weak stream of sunlight slips in through the filthy window near the front door and sparkles against the silver ear cuff Willow wears. Her bow is already clutched in her left hand.

"Ready? Or do you two still need a minute?" She looks at my flushed face with something like amusement.

I bend over, pick up our packs, and hand Logan his. His fingers brush mine, and he says quietly, "We're going to have to talk about it sooner or later."

I know we are. But I want a few more moments to hold those four precious words close before he sees the kind of girl I've become. Without looking at him, I settle my pack against my back and lead the way out the front door.

CHAPTER SIXTY-THREE

RACHEL

We walk silently through the moss-draped oaks, Willow and Quinn preferring to travel through the trees above us. I can see Logan trying not to limp as each step jars his rib cage.

"Can you carry this for me?" I shove Melkin's walking stick toward him. If he leans on the end that doesn't slide into the ground, he can use it as a cane.

"Why?"

"Because I want to bring this back for Melkin's wife."

"You're doing an admirable job of carrying it yourself."

Stubborn, prideful man.

"But it was Melkin's. And I no longer want to touch it." I realize the words are true the moment they leave my mouth. I don't want his walking stick. I don't want to remember the bitter misery in his eyes as he asked me whether the Commander would spare his wife if he did as he was asked.

And I don't want to remember the way he kept his knife pointed at the ground while I attacked him.

Logan takes the stick and points the dangerous end toward the sky. "Are we going to talk about Melkin?"

"No."

"Let me rephrase that. What I meant to say is: We're going to talk about Melkin."

"No, we aren't."

We circle the base of a wide oak, its trunk gnarled and scarred, and head into a copse of pine trees. Willow tree-leaps ahead of us until she's nothing but a distant flash of movement in the stillness of the forest. Quinn stays behind us, the occasional rustle of leaves the only reminder of his presence. The air warms gently as we walk, though the shadows still cling to their predawn chill.

"What happened to Melkin?"

"What part of 'we aren't going to talk about this' is difficult to understand?"

His voice is gentle. "How can I help you, if you won't tell me what happened?"

What happened? I felt hope. Burning, brilliant hope that turned to ash beside my father's grave. I then killed my traveling companion for the crime of wanting desperately to save his wife. And I can't feel anything but icy silence for all of it.

We leave the sharp-scented pine behind and enter a field of deep green grass spiked with wildflowers. Willow is already in the center of the field, an arrow notched, her head constantly swiveling, searching for threats. The sun is a fierce, unblinking eye above us, and I feel flushed from its heat.

"I know he was sent into the Wasteland to kill you and return the package to the Commander. His wife had the cell across from mine. She's pregnant. That's enough motivation to sway almost any man into doing the unthinkable."

I can't stand the heat prickling against my skin and reach to unfasten my cloak.

"What happened to your hands?"

The fastening sticks, and I tug at it desperately. He reaches out and captures my fingers in his.

"You have bloodstains on your hands." His touch is gentle.

I want to slap his hand away and hear him condemn me. Tell me he's changed his mind. Tell me he doesn't love me now that he knows what I've done.

But he doesn't know. Because I haven't told him.

"Please," he says.

I take a deep breath, hold on to those four beautiful words for one more moment—*I love you, Rachel*—and then I tell him.

"I killed him." My voice sounds cold and empty as it echoes across the field of wildflowers. His hand tightens on mine.

"Why?" he asks. There's no censure in his voice.

"Because I thought he was attacking me."

"Then it was self-defense."

"No." Up ahead, water glitters beneath the morning sun, a piercing beauty that hurts my eyes. "No, it wasn't."

"Rachel, he was tasked with killing you once you found the package. It was self-defense."

"He wasn't going to kill me. I thought he was, but he wasn't. He was trying to disarm me. Steal the package and leave me behind. Alive." The words make me sick. I thought I'd feel relief to have it out in the open, but I don't.

He's quiet, though his fingers are still wrapped around mine as we approach the diamond-bright surface of a lake. Willow has tossed all but her undertunic aside and is wading into the water, her bow and arrow still clutched in her hands.

"If you thought he was trying to kill you, defending yourself is understandable, Rachel. I would've done the same."

"No, you would've stopped." I whirl to face him, suddenly desperate to make him see. "You'd have kept control. I know you."

Beneath the steadiness of his gaze, pain lingers. "Like I kept control when the Commander backhanded you during the Claiming ceremony?"

"That's not the same."

"I fail to see the difference." He steps close to me. "You were afraid. You knew you couldn't let him take the device and bring it to the Commander. Instinct kicked in, and you did what you had to do."

I shake my head. "You would've seen the signs, and stopped."

"Sweetheart, you haven't been reading people right since Oliver."

My voice is a rough whisper. "And Dad."

We're at the edge of the lake. Logan stops walking and faces me. "What about your dad?"

The words won't come. Maybe they don't exist. I strain to feel it. To let it cut me so I can cry. So I can share grief with the one person who will understand the depth of what I've lost.

"Please don't." His voice is quiet. Pained. His fingers curl around mine and force them open, and I realize I've clenched my fist so tight, my broken nails have gouged four crescents of crimson into my palm. My blood mixes with Melkin's, and I can't look away.

"He's dead, isn't he? Jared's dead."

I look at him.

"I'm so sorry." He drags me against him, and I lean into his shoulder.

"Why aren't you crying?" He pulls back and cups my face in his hands. Pain is carved into his face.

"I can't."

"Why not?" He's rubbing my cheeks with his thumbs as if he can transfer his living, breathing grief into my skin, shattering the icy silence within me into something he can understand.

I can't allow that. If I grieve now, how will I ever find my way out again in time to keep my promises?

"Because there will be nothing left of me if I do." I look at my hands, bleeding and bloodstained, the dirt from my father's grave mixing with the dirt from Melkin's in the creases. "And because I don't deserve it. I deserve to bleed."

I hold my hands up to him.

"I earned this. I did this. I deserve to be marked."

"No." He takes my hands in his. "You don't."

It's useless to argue. I know what I've become inside. If he can't see it now, it won't take long before he does.

I don't protest as he takes off my cloak and insists I strip down to my undertunic. He pulls off all but his pants, and I wince at the ugly purple and black bruises spreading like decaying blossoms across his chest. Then he lifts the leather pouch containing the dirt from my father's grave over my head, sets it aside, and leads me into the lake.

I don't want to let him wash my hands, but he pulls them beneath the water and carefully scrubs away the blood, the dirt, and the evidence of all that's been.

The crimson has seeped beneath my skin, entered my veins, and become a part of what's left of me. No amount of scrubbing can erase that.

"Yesterday, when the Cursed One came out of the ground, I said I loved you."

"I'm not ready to talk about it."

"Oh."

He sounds hurt. I don't want to hurt him. I just don't know how to get past the silence consuming me and find anything that feels like hope.

He clears his throat. "I didn't mean to . . . I guess I thought—"

"It's fine." From the corner of my eye, I see Quinn dive off a rock, slicing through the water with the barest hint of a splash.

"No, it's not *fine*."

I squint against the tiny pricks of light dancing over the surface of the water.

He sounds wounded. "I thought you'd at least be a little bit receptive."

I can't look at him. "I would've been. I *was*. Before."

"Before? Before what?"

I whip my head back to face him. "Before everything! Before I saw Oliver get murdered right in front of me. Before I knew Dad was . . . gone. Before Melkin. Before I became *this*." I gesture toward myself, wondering how he can think washing the blood off my hands makes it any less real.

He steps closer, his eyes glowing with fierce conviction. "You're still the same beautiful, stubborn, strong, fascinating Rachel you were before any of that happened."

My laugh sounds more like a sob, and I clamp my lips shut.

"Listen to me. I know it's bad for you. I see that. But shutting yourself off from something good because of all the bad is unfair. To both of us." His cheeks darken, and his eyes slide away from mine. "Unless you don't feel the same, and this is your way of trying to let me down easy, and I've just made a spectacular fool of myself."

He lets go of my hands, cramming damp fingers through his dark blond hair, and doesn't look at me. "I've just made a fool of myself, haven't I?"

"No."

"Yes, I have." He steps back. "What is it about you that makes rational behavior so difficult for me? Never mind. Forget I asked that. You're right. It's fine."

Hurt and embarrassment are written all over his face, and I realize the only one being a fool is me. He's offering me the one thing of beauty I can still claim as my own. I have to cling to it if I ever want to find my way back to the girl I used to be. And it isn't fair of me to deny him the truth just because I worry it means less coming from someone as broken as me.

"No, it isn't. It isn't fine at all," I say.

"We can stop this conversation right now."

"I don't want to."

His laugh is weary. "That makes one of us. At least now I know how you felt two years ago."

"I can do it again." The words are out before I give myself time to lose my nerve. I don't know how to do this. Love is a piercing ache that refuses to slide into the silence. I'm grateful to hold on to something real, but I don't know how to make him see it.

He stops backing away and looks at me. "Do what again?"

I mean to say something heartfelt and sincere like "give you my heart." Something that will erase his fears and leave us with one perfect moment in the midst of everything.

Instead, I step toward him, catch my foot against a rock on the lake bottom, and trip. Crashing into his chest, I plunge us both beneath the surface.

The water is crisp on top and murky below, where our feet kick up eddies of sand and rock. He catches me, his hands wrapped around my arms, as we plummet toward the bottom. My hair floats out to surround him, and he stares at me while above us the sun pierces the surface with golden darts.

Maybe this is better than words. Maybe this is all I need to show him he didn't offer his heart to me in vain.

He lets go, and I reach for him. Twining my fingers through his, I feel something soft warm the silence within me a little as he tangles his legs with mine until I can't tell where one of us ends and the other begins.

But it isn't enough. The ache within me pushes against my chest, tingles down my arms, and hurts the tips of my fingers. I need more. I need to disappear into what we are together.

I need *him*.

I pull him against me as we start floating back toward the surface, and he smiles.

We break the surface together, and the air feels alive in a way it didn't before. He smoothes my hair out of my eyes, and I impatiently shove his hands out of my way so I can reach him.

"Kiss me," I say, and I don't even have time to blush at the audacity of my words before he slides a hand into the hair at the nape of my neck and tugs me toward him.

Our noses bump, and his laugh sounds breathless. "Sorry."

"Don't be sorry. Hurry up and kiss me."

He tightens his arms around me and touches his lips to mine. His kiss is rough, tastes like lake water . . . and is the best thing I've ever felt. I press against him, consuming him like I'll never get enough, and when we break apart, my pulse pounds against my ear, and his chest rises and falls like he's been running.

"Done yet?" Willow calls from somewhere behind me. I hear Quinn shush her, but I don't care.

Because Logan is looking at me like I'm precious to him. And the silence inside me cracks open, just a little. Just enough to let a small piece of hope float to the surface. I grab on to it with desperate fingers.

He keeps one hand on the small of my back and uses the other to trace the Celtic knot on the necklace he gave me the day of the Claiming ceremony.

"I promised to always find you, remember?"

"I remember."

"I promised I would always protect you. You've been wounded badly because I failed to keep that promise."

I shake my head, and the tears spill over, scalding my cheeks with heat.

"But I won't fail you in this, Rachel. No matter what has happened. No matter what you've done. No matter what you will do. I will always love you. I swear it."

His hand clenches around the pendant, and he leans down to capture my gaze with his. "I will always love you."

His arms flex, pulling me against his chest, and his lips hover just above mine, our breath mingling in the dazzling morning air.

"I love you," he whispers and then he kisses me again, his lips rough against mine, his breathing ragged as he devours my fear and makes me long to feel this way forever.

CHAPTER SIXTY-FOUR

LOGAN

We don't push ourselves on the return trip to Baalboden. I tell Rachel it's to let my rib heal, and I think she believes me. But really, I just want time with her. Time to lie next to her at night, holding her against me while I watch the rotation of the stars. Time to walk beside her during the day and try to draw her into conversation so we can get what has hurt her out into the open, where it can start to heal.

I ache to hear her tell me she loves me, but forcing her to put words to how she feels pushes her farther into the silence she seems comfortable calling home now. I tell myself to be patient and understanding, but inside there's a longing only those words will fill, and it hurts to ignore it.

I'm restless. Hungry for something she keeps just out of my reach. It doesn't help that Quinn and Willow are traveling with us. As grateful as I am for their assistance, having others within earshot cuts down significantly on the things I'd like to share with Rachel. So, at the end of another day's journey, when

Willow announces she wants meat for dinner and is going hunting, I look Quinn straight in the eye and say, "You should go with her."

"Logan." Rachel puts her hand on my arm.

"I don't need help bringing down a rabbit," Willow says.

"But there might be highwaymen out there. Or more trackers from Rowansmark. It never hurts to be cautious." I look at Quinn. "You should *go*."

They all stare at me in silence for a second before Willow says, "Why don't you just come right out and say, 'Hey, I want private time with Rachel so I can kiss her senseless like I did at the lake'?"

"Willow!" Quinn frowns at her.

"That's not what he meant," Rachel says, refusing to look at me.

Willow laughs. "Yes, it is. He's itching to get his hands on you without an audience."

"That's *not* what he meant," Rachel says again, pink flushing her cheeks.

"Actually, I meant—" I start to say, but Willow cuts me off.

"What? It's true. He looks at you like he'd like to dip you in sugar and eat you up."

"Willow Runningbrook, that's enough." Quinn's eyes flash, and I catch a glimpse of something feral beneath his smooth exterior. It's gone as soon as I see it, submerged beneath the calm he wears like a second skin.

Willow tosses her hands into the air. "Apparently, honesty is a crime in this group. Look." She points at Rachel. "You're all, 'Revenge is all I want! I'll figure out my love life later!' and he"—she points to me—"is afraid revenge will kill you before he has a chance to really touch you—"

"No, he isn't."

I step forward. "Willow has a point."

"Willow needs to learn to share only those observations that others ask her to share." Quinn steps forward as well.

Willow shrugs and shoulders her bow. "I got tired of tiptoeing around the obvious." She winks at me. "How much time do you need to kiss her senseless?"

"He's not going to—"

"At least an hour," I say, dragging Rachel into my arms and kissing her before she can say another word.

I don't hear Willow leave or Quinn follow her. I can't hear anything beyond the wild pounding of my heart and the soft catch of Rachel's breath as I fist my hands in the back of her tunic and pull her against me like I can't stand to have a single sliver of air between us.

"Logan." Her voice is as shaky as the hand she puts on my chest, and I can't bear it. I can't bear to hear her tell me to stop. To pull back. I can't bear to be apart from her when she's all I have.

"Don't," I say, and she tilts her head back to look at me. "Don't keep me at a distance."

"Who said anything about keeping you at a distance?" Her smile lingers in her eyes.

But when she leans in to kiss me, I'm the one who pulls back because suddenly just being with her isn't enough. Not nearly enough.

"Logan?"

I close my eyes and reach for the courage to ask her to give me the words I need.

Her lips brush mine, sweet and hesitant, and I open my eyes. She's all I can see. All I can taste when I breathe in. Her body molds itself to mine like she was made for me, and I want her to feel it too. To acknowledge it.

To hope for it in the middle of so much hopelessness.

"Rachel, I need . . ." The words won't come. I don't know how to say that I need everything she is without making it sound like more than she can give.

Please don't let it be more than she can give.

"What do you need?" Her face is luminous beneath the golden fingers of the waning sun.

And suddenly the words are there, falling into place like I always knew the way to reach her. "I need to know what you need. What you want. Not from the device, not from the Commander, but from me."

She stiffens, shoulders lifting toward her jaw as if to protect herself from a blow she has to know I'll never deliver.

"Please." I can barely push the word out. "Please, Rachel. Look past the loss, the grief. Look at *me*."

She closes her eyes. I feel like I've been slashed open inside where no one will ever see me bleed. But then she takes a deep breath, relaxes her shoulders, and looks at me, tears filling her eyes.

"I need *you*, Logan. Just you."

I tighten my grip on her tunic. "Why?"

"Because I still love you." Her voice catches. "I never stopped. I thought I had. I wanted to. But somehow . . . it's like part of you lives inside the most important part of me, and I don't know how to separate the two." Tears spill over, tracing a glistening path down her cheeks. "I love you, Logan."

Joy surges through me, brilliant and wild. I cup her face in my hands and wipe away her tears. "I love you too, Rachel. Always." And then I do my best to use the full hour I've been given to kiss her senseless.

CHAPTER SIXTY-FIVE

RACHEL

I can't sleep. My lips are still swollen from Logan's kisses, and the ache I feel for him wants to spill out of my fragile skin, envelop me, and tempt me to forget everything that lies ahead.

But I can't. Beneath the ache, the silence lives within me, demanding justice for Dad. For Oliver. For all of us. Willow accused me of wanting nothing but revenge. She was wrong.

I want redemption.

I just don't think I can get it without exacting revenge first.

After tossing and turning on the soft bed of moss I made for us, I give up trying to sleep. I'm careful not to wake Logan as I get up. He looks peaceful beneath the pale light of the stars. I want to trace the lines of his face and memorize the way his skin feels beneath my fingertips, but I don't. He needs to rest until it's time for him to take the night watch shift from Quinn.

I walk a few paces away and sit with my back to a thick, silver-trunked oak. A few yards to my left, Willow sleeps in her tree cradle, her bow in hand. I don't see Quinn, but it doesn't matter. I didn't get up for conversation. Besides, his calm stoicism is unnerving, and I never know what to say to him.

I sit in silence, listening to the distant hooting of an owl and the occasional whisper of a breeze as it tangles itself within the leaves above me. It's the first time in days that I haven't had someone talking to me, watching me, or expecting something from me. It doesn't take long for my thoughts to fill the void with violent images. Oliver's eyes growing distant as his blood spills onto me. Logan's mother lying at the Commander's feet, her back flayed raw, slipping away from her little boy until there's nothing left. Dad, risking everything to keep the Commander from gaining a weapon he could use to obliterate any opposition, and then giving his life to save Quinn and Willow and trusting Logan and me to finish his mission.

"Want company?" Quinn asks quietly. I have no idea how long he's been standing in front of me.

It's on the tip of my tongue to say no, but I was wrong. I do want conversation. Even with Quinn. Anything to save me from the overwhelming images in my head.

"Sure," I say, and he sits against the tree across from me, his long legs folded under him, his eyes scanning the area before coming back to rest on me.

"I hate it when people ask me how I'm doing," he says as if this conversational opener should make sense to me. And strangely, it does. Because the last thing I want to be asked right now is how I'm doing.

"I wasn't going to ask you that."

He smiles, a flash of white teeth against his dark skin. "I'll return the favor."

We sit in silence for a moment, then he says, "You're a lot like your dad, you know."

The words both hurt and heal, and I don't know how to respond.

"He always seemed so sure of himself, didn't he?" he asks.

"Because he always knew what to do."

Quinn smiles again, yet I swear I see sadness on his face. "No one always knows what to do, Rachel. We all just do the best we can with what we've got. Sometimes it works. Sometimes it ruins everything."

He looks away, and the breeze tugs at his black hair.

I say the words before I really think them through. "What did you do that ruined everything?"

"It's complicated."

I know the feeling. I'm about to back out of the conversation with the excuse of needing more sleep when he takes a deep breath and looks at me.

"I killed a man too. I thought I had to. I'm still not sure if I was right, but because of my actions, Willow and I were cast out of our village." His voice is low and steady, but sadness runs beneath it. He sits in silence for a moment, then says, "What's been done is done. I've had to learn how to live with what was left."

Shock robs me of speech for a moment. I lean closer to study his face, looking for the lie. For proof he's saying what he thinks I need to hear so he can gain my trust. The only thing I find in his expression is naked truth. I feel like an intruder. "I'm sorry. I didn't mean to pry."

He leans forward and traces patterns into the soil at his feet.

"You aren't prying. You asked because you know how it feels to think you've ruined everything. You're hoping if my story has a happy ending, there's hope for yours."

I shift uneasily against the tree trunk. I'm not sure I want to know, but I have to ask, "Does yours have a happy ending?"

His finger pauses, pressing into the dirt as he slowly raises his head to look at me. "I don't know. I haven't reached the end."

"Oh. I guess I thought . . . you seem so settled. So comfortable with yourself and others. I thought maybe you—"

"Had answers? I might." He shrugs. "But they're answers I had to find for myself. I don't think they'll work for anyone else."

I should probably feel awkward, sitting in the dirt across from a boy I barely know talking about the things that haunt us, but instead, I feel a tiny sliver of comfort. Here is someone who understands. Who knows what it feels like to have blood on his hands and not know if the guilt he feels should be his to bear alone. And he isn't broken. He's found a measure of peace, with himself and with others.

It gives me hope that someday, after I'm finished with the Commander, I might be able to shatter the silence inside me, grieve for those I've lost, and find a way to forgive myself for what I've caused. Someday, I might find my own measure of peace.

He leans back, and we sit in companionable silence while the tree branches creak and shiver in the wind and the stars slowly trek across the vast darkness of the sky above us.

CHAPTER SIXTY-SIX

LOGAN

"Absolutely not." Quinn's tone discourages any argument.

"But they might need us." Willow stands, arms crossed over her chest, staring her brother down across the fire at our final camping spot before reaching Baalboden.

I couldn't care less about their argument. Whether they come with us or move on. I'm too busy running through tomorrow's plan of action, looking for weaknesses.

"You don't want to go into Baalboden with them because they might need you," Quinn says. "You want to go because you want to see if they can take out their leader."

"That's definitely a side benefit."

"Which is why I'm saying no."

She rolls her eyes. "You're no fun anymore, you know that?"

He freezes and something dark flashes through his eyes. That's the second time I've seen hints that what goes on beneath his surface doesn't always match the calm he wears on the outside. Which won't matter if he chooses to move on.

But if he stays in Baalboden once the Commander has been defeated, I'm going to have to keep an eye on him.

Willow slowly uncurls her arms and says, "I didn't mean to say that."

"I know." He turns away and begins gathering what he'll need to make a tree-cradle bed for her.

"Quinn." She hurries to him, wraps an arm around his shoulders.

"You think I don't know you're paying the price for my actions?" he asks quietly, and the pain in his voice seems to hit Willow hard. "Every moment of every day I carry the burden for causing you to be an outcast with me."

Definitely more going on beneath his surface than he wants us to know. I wonder what he did that caused the two of them to be punished like this.

Willow's lips tremble, and she steps in front of him to make him look at her. "I chose you. Do you hear me, Quinn Running-brook? You're all the family I need."

They walk to the edge of our campsite, talking in low tones. I give up speculating about what kind of crime would cause a Tree Village to cast out two of their own, and run through Worst Case Scenarios for tomorrow instead. In a few moments, Willow disappears up a tree, and Quinn returns, his face shadowed.

"We'll go no farther. Our debt to Jared has been paid." His eyes seek out Rachel's and linger. "Be safe."

I slide my arm around her shoulders and pull her closer to me. "We will."

"Where will you go?" Rachel asks.

He shrugs. "We'll find another Tree Village to take us in.

Somewhere far from our first home."

"But the next closest Tree Village is a two-week journey east," she says, and turns to me. "They could live in Baalboden, couldn't they? Once the Commander is gone?"

I didn't realize she'd come to care for Quinn and Willow, and I wish she could let them go. I could lie and say it's because I can hardly guarantee any stability in Baalboden until after we succeed in restructuring the government, but the truth is I don't like the interest in Quinn's eyes when he looks at Rachel.

I can't tell her that, but I look at Quinn and make sure my expression doesn't match my words as I say, "Of course they can. But they might not feel comfortable living on the ground."

Quinn smiles. "We'll camp here for several days. See how it goes in Baalboden. We can decide what to do at the end of the week." His eyes are still on Rachel.

She smiles back. "Good. Once the Commander is gone, we'll see about finding you and Willow a place. There are plenty of trees in Baalboden."

My smile feels stretched thin as I say, "Thank you for helping Rachel and for assisting me. I won't forget it." I stand and shake Quinn's outstretched hand. His eyes flick toward me, and then he looks once more at Rachel, nods, and backs out of the clearing to take the first night watch.

I bank the fire and sit beside Rachel to talk through our plan one last time. I've barely started running scenarios when she interrupts.

"You're not tall enough to pass as Melkin."

It's the same argument she's been using for hours now.

"I'm tall enough. Plus, only Melkin knew the signal to give."

"Only Melkin and his *wife*. Who was next to you in the dungeon. You don't think the Commander might be expecting you to show up like this?"

She has a point, but since the only other recourse is to let her face the Commander herself, I keep arguing.

"It doesn't matter what he expects. He wants this"—I point to the device lying on a cloth between us—"too much to stay away. By the time he realizes it's me, he'll see I have the device and he'll start negotiating."

Her laugh is bitter. "He doesn't negotiate, Logan. He executes."

"Which is why I'll be the one taking the risk. Just in case."

"I can handle it."

Of course she can. But *I* can't handle it if it all goes wrong, and I have to watch her die.

"I need you to call the Cursed One for me. I need you to stay out of sight and use Melkin's staff to call the beast before the Commander takes the device from me."

"Oh, that's just perfect. We take revenge on the Commander, and all I get to do is shove a stick into the ground? No. I promised Oliver and Dad I would kill him. I'm not going back on that."

"And I promised I would always protect you. So—"

"So use Melkin's stick in time to call the Cursed One before—"

"No!"

"I have to kill him. I have to. It's the only way I'll have peace."

She's shaking. Maybe we both are. My emotions are running so high I can hardly think straight. I can't allow Rachel to take the risk, but if I don't, I'm not sure she'll ever forgive me.

Best Case Scenario: She evades any treachery on the Commander's part and remembers which combination of finger pads controls the Cursed One so she can turn the beast against him without dying herself.

Worst Case Scenario: Everything else.

Unless . . .

"I don't think the Commander knows what the device looks like."

"What makes you say that?" she asks.

"Did Melkin know exactly what he was looking for?"

She frowns and shakes her head. "I don't think so."

"I can guarantee if the Commander ever had the opportunity to see this thing in person, he'd already own it and the person who'd shown it to him would be dead."

"Agreed."

"So, at best, he only has a general idea of what it looks like."

Her smile looks more like a snarl. "So make a duplicate."

"And you can hold the real one while you hide. I'll keep Melkin's staff so my disguise looks more authentic."

"And when the Cursed One comes, I'll kill the Commander."

"Yes." I pull her to me so I won't have to see the vicious fury on her face and hope that by giving her what she so desperately wants, I haven't destroyed more of the girl I love.

We unstring Rachel's bow and use the lightweight black wood to mimic the design of the device. I still have copper wires hidden in the seams of my cloak. A few minutes later, I have a passable imitation of the Rowansmark tech.

We go over the plan, in detail, three more times until Rachel refuses to discuss it again. I don't push the issue. Pulling her against me, I wrap myself around her and listen to her breathe as the darkness hides the device, the terrible fury in her eyes, and the evidence that this may be our last night together.

Her breathing slows, an even cadence that comforts me. I brush my lips against her ear and whisper promises I'll die to keep.

CHAPTER SIXTY-SEVEN

RACHEL

Dawn is a faint, gray smudge on the horizon as we reach the ancient oak marking the line between Baalboden's eastern perimeter and the Wasteland. Logan hunches inside his cloak, his hood pulled forward to cover most of his face. The fake Rowansmark tech is in one hand and Melkin's staff is in the other.

I stay back several trees, the true device in my cloak pocket and a brilliant blaze of triumphant rage warming me from the inside out.

We've gone over the plan, the list of everything Logan worries can go wrong, and both of us are as ready as we can be. We might die. The whole thing might blow up in our faces, and we might fail. But it doesn't matter. What matters is that we're here. Standing against him. Committed to delivering justice, no matter what it costs.

Logan turns to look at me, his blue eyes lit with something I now recognize as uniquely mine. "Ready?"

"Yes."

The torch is embedded in the heart of the tree, far below the tall canopy of branches. He strikes flint at it, and fire blazes immediately, throwing shadows over his face as he waits.

I melt back into the forest a few yards, far enough that I can't be seen by anyone approaching Logan, but close enough that I can still see and hear what is going on, and climb into a tree. It takes two hours, but we finally see the Commander and the eight surviving members of his Brute Squad stride across the perimeter toward the oak.

It's too easy. Surely the Commander suspects treachery. He knows Logan escaped. He must wonder if Melkin could really carry out his assignment against me. And yet he walks toward us as if he doesn't have a care in the world.

The hair on the back of my neck rises, and seconds later, a team of guards slide out of the eastern Wasteland and converge on Logan.

No wonder it took two hours. The Commander needed time for his guards to exit the gate, enter the Wasteland, and circle around behind us. It's a trap, but we knew it would be. The Commander never meant to keep the one who delivered the package alive. We just never realized there would be *so many*. Logan thought the Brute Squad would be all the Commander deemed necessary to take down the one insignificant person delivering his precious package.

Logan turns, sweeps the ranks of guards behind him with a glance, and tightens his grip on the staff.

We'd planned for Logan to fall back during the confusion of the Cursed One's arrival, but there are too many guards behind him. He has nowhere to go. He can't call the Cursed One and survive unless he shimmies up the oak and starts tree-leaping. In our planning, that was a last resort, as there are too many ways that could end in disaster. The moment he diverts his attention to climbing the tree and avoiding the lit torch sticking out of its belly, the Commander could kill him. Any one of the guards could kill him. No, he'll need to talk his way out. Find a way to use the device for leverage. Maybe admit it's a fake and get the Commander to leave him alive because he knows where the real one is.

All of those are flimsy excuses for a plan. They won't work. Any of them. I can't think of a way out, but surely Logan can. He always can. I strain to see him past the three rows of uniform-clad backs between us.

The Commander reaches him but stays several feet back. Logan is looking at the ground, but I see the moment he comes up with a plan. His shoulders straighten. He lifts his head, throws back his hood, and looks the Commander in the eye.

Then he slams the staff into the ground.

My fury at the Commander dissolves into terror for Logan. He hasn't made a new plan. He's called the Cursed One with almost no chance of escape, and now he's going to die in front of me.

My fingers shake as I snatch the device out of my cloak pocket.

The Commander laughs, a cruel sound smearing the morning

air with malice. "Logan McEntire. I suppose you think I'm surprised to see you instead of Melkin."

First two buttons together turn the beast east. Bottom two
buttons turn it west. I wish my hands would stop trembling.

Logan holds up the fake device. "I brought what you want.
But it's going to cost you."

The Commander's smile is full of hate. "No. It's going to cost
you." He waves the guards forward. Swords gleam, an impossibly thick row of sharp silver teeth reaching for Logan. "You've
outlived your usefulness to me. To all of Baalboden. It's been
nineteen years of waiting for my investment to pay off, and I
can't wait to rid my city of the stench of you."

I forget the device for a moment as the Commander's words
sink in, and Logan goes pale. What does he mean, he's been waiting for this? No one knew when Logan was born that one day he'd
be in this position. A tremor runs through the earth. I can't think
of the Commander's words right now. I have bigger problems.

My hands are clammy as I grip the device. Top and bottom
buttons send it north. All three send it south.

The ground shakes. A distant roar surges closer. The guards
stumble to a halt and look around, fear on their faces.

"You're going to die." Logan's voice rings out clearly.

The Commander's smile snags on his scar and morphs into
a predatory mask. He lunges for Logan, snatches the fake tech
from his hands, and backs away. The guards back away as well,
their swords raised as if they can protect themselves from what's
coming, but there are still too many of them between Logan and
safety.

The soil cracks. The guards run. The Commander laughs. And Logan turns to leap into the oak tree as the Cursed One explodes out of the ground, black scales clinking together in deafening harmony, his mouth already spewing orange streams of fire.

Clumps of ground, roots, and branches fly through the air, a shower of debris that knocks a few guards flat on their backs. I check for the Commander's location, and try to breathe through the panic seizing my chest.

North. I need to send the beast north. My mind goes blank for a crucial second, and the creature roars at the oak tree, sending the entire thing up in flames.

"Logan!" I scream, racing along my branch toward where I last saw him.

He's already leaping clear. The guards behind him have abandoned their positions and are running for their lives. Logan races into the forest, sees me, and yells, "North! Send it north!"

My fingers find the top and bottom buttons before my brain can translate the thought. The beast surges toward the Commander as he flees toward the northern edge of the city's Wall. Fire leaps from the creature's mouth. Two members of the Brute Squad are incinerated and then crushed beneath the thing's monstrous length as it races forward. Now nothing stands between it and the Commander.

Reckless triumph surges through me. We've got him. There's no escape. No way to stop the Cursed One. Logan climbs onto the branch beside me and together we watch, ignoring the screams of the guards as they run into the Wasteland behind us.

Ignoring the crackling flames as they eat through the ancient oak tree. We watch and wait for justice.

The Commander stops, holds out the fake tech, and tries to manipulate the gears wired to its surface.

I laugh but choke on it when the Commander throws the fake device to the ground, rips open his uniform, and pulls out a heavy silver chain with what looks like a thick dragon talon curved around a silver ball.

The beast jerks to a stop and snorts.

"No." I press the bottom two buttons again. The Cursed One roars, but doesn't advance. "Why isn't it attacking?" I press the buttons repeatedly, and the beast coils in on itself, scales clanking. It shakes its head and blasts the ground beneath it with fire.

It will attack itself. But it won't attack the Commander.

"I can't get this to work!"

"Something about that necklace makes the beast unwilling to attack," Logan says.

The Cursed One trembles as I press more buttons, willing it to get over whatever issue it has with the Commander's necklace and destroy him with fire. It shudders, giant ripples tearing along its frame, but it refuses to attack.

"The necklace protects him. Where did he get it?" Logan mumbles beneath his breath, listing options, trying to make connections.

"Who cares where he got it? Let's go rip it off of him."

"He's had that necklace for as long as anyone can remember. In drawings of him protecting the first survivors fifty years ago, you can see the chain around his neck before the rest of it disappears beneath his coat. That was right after his team returned from the beast's den. What do you want to bet all the city-state leaders have necklaces just like this one?"

"I don't want to bet anything. I want the Commander to suffer and die. We have to kill him ourselves." I'm already reaching for my knife, but Logan stays my hand.

"Keep the Cursed One as close to him as you can to distract him." He throws off his cloak, drops to the forest floor and draws his sword. "I'm going after him."

"Wait!"

He looks at me, cold purpose on his face, his dark-blond hair turned red by the flames behind him, and says, "I know you want to be the one to kill him. But please don't ask me to send you against the Commander in the presence of the Cursed One with nothing but your knife."

I do want to be the one to kill him. But more than that, I want him *dead*. My knife is no match for the Commander. Logan has a much better chance.

"I wasn't going to argue."

"Then what were you going to do?"

The fire hisses and pops as the oak tree caves in on itself, and I jump down to the forest floor beside Logan. I regret all the things I never said to Dad and to Oliver. I'm not going to have regrets here, too.

I throw my arms around his neck. "I love you, Logan. Always."

A fierce smile lights his face for a moment, and he grabs the front of my tunic, hauls me against him, and kisses me. "I love you, too. Always." Then he's gone, and I'm pressing buttons with frantic fingers, trying to keep the Cursed One as close to the Commander as possible to give Logan a chance.

CHAPTER SIXTY-EIGHT

LOGAN

I circle through the tree line to position myself behind the Commander. No one stops me. Every guard in the area is either running for his life or already dead.

The Cursed One roars, spitting fire in every direction, blackening the dirt perimeter that encircles Baalboden.

The Commander holds his necklace in front of him and laughs.

I heft my sword in the shelter of the trees twenty yards behind the Commander. All of my anger, pain, and loss coalesce into an unyielding sense of purpose.

He's mine. For Oliver. For Jared. For Rachel. For my mother. For the citizens of Baalboden who crave change.

For me.

My sword flashes in the sunlight as I step away from the trees and gauge my approach. I can sprint forward. Bury my blade in the back of his neck before he knows I'm there. And take the talisman that keeps the Cursed One at bay so I can hold off the creature's attack until Rachel sends it back to the depths of the Earth.

Raising my sword, I lower the point to the necessary trajectory, drag in a deep breath, and start running. I'm over halfway there when the entire plan falls to pieces.

The Cursed One jerks its head up as if it hears something and suddenly lunges west.

Straight for Baalboden.

The Commander yells, drops his talisman against his chest, and runs toward the city. Rachel bursts out of the trees, her face filled with desperate terror as she presses the bottom two buttons on the device. The ones that should turn the beast away from Baalboden.

The Cursed One never deviates.

Fire bursts from its mouth as it strafes the Wall. The stone is scorched black, but the Wall is too thick for even the Cursed One to destroy. Any relief I feel disappears in an instant as the beast rears up, plunges into the ground, and explodes into the air on the other side of the Wall in a shower of cobblestone, dirt, and flame.

"No!"

Rachel is screaming. Running toward the Wall. Slamming the third button. The one that *should* send the Cursed One back into the bowels of the Earth.

I race to join her as plumes of thick black smoke billow up from the city. The turret closest to us explodes into flame and slowly topples to the ground in a hail of sparks and fiery chunks of wood.

The Commander veers north, apparently thinking to run the

entire way around the Wall to get to the gate. He's a fool. By the time he reaches it, the city will be nothing but rubble.

"It isn't working. Help me!" Rachel thrusts the device into my hands, and I drop my sword so I can push the finger pads.

We're close enough to the Wall now that we can hear the screaming from inside. There's no way over the Wall. No gate unless we take the time to run all the way around the circumference of the city like the Commander. Rachel doesn't hesitate. We reach the jagged hole left by the Cursed One, and she leaps into it.

I follow. We slide down about fifteen yards before the tunnel turns upward again.

She's clawing her way toward the surface. I'm digging for footholds right behind her. Above us, the citizens in the East Quarter are screaming in agony.

We scramble through the crater left by the Cursed One, and my stomach sinks as I take in the chaos. Everything is burning. *Everything.* Brilliant gold and crimson flames chew through homes, spew thick black smoke toward the sky, and race blindly for the next piece of dry wood. Windows explode outward, sending hundreds of diamond-bright slivers of glass through the air. And through it all, the monstrous shape of the Cursed One coils, lashing out with its tail to crush wagons, buildings, and people. Strafing entire streets with blistering fire. Bellowing a hoarse, guttural cry that shakes the ground.

The few people still on their feet are running in a blind panic. As fire leaps from building to building, street to street, intent on destroying the entire East Quarter, the Cursed One abruptly heads toward North Hub, blasting anything that moves with flames.

"Make it stop, Logan! Make it go away."

I try. I push the button, and the creature pauses, shakes its head, and slams the ground with its spiked tail, shattering the cobblestones beneath it. Then it slides north again, spreading destruction and death in its wake.

Either our device is malfunctioning, or someone else is out there with another piece of tech capable of overriding this one. It doesn't matter which is true. The end result is the same. Baalboden's protective Wall has become a death trap for anyone left inside its embrace.

"We can't stop it."

She whirls toward me, her eyes full of tears. "We have to!"

"We *can't*. All we can do is rescue as many people as possible."

She doesn't argue as I pull her toward a side street that isn't yet on fire. It takes an agonizing three minutes to find what we need. In that time, the Cursed One turns North Hub into a blazing inferno. I pray the citizens there heard the screaming of their neighbors and had enough warning to start running.

The fourth backyard I check has a wagon and a panicked horse stomping in a double-stall animal shed. I hand the device to Rachel, and hitch the horse to the wagon as fast as I can. She stands beside me, staring at the wagon and shaking, but when I offer her a hand up to join me in the driver's seat, she doesn't hesitate.

We head down the alley and turn north. The sky is a haze of thick black smoke. Entire streets are nothing but sheets of flame. I crack the reins against the horse's back, and we thunder toward the destruction.

A few people still stagger about, and we stop to haul them into the wagon bed. Most of the East Quarter is in shambles, but set apart from the rest is the Commander's compound, untouched by fire. I calculate less than five minutes before the flames bridge the distance and begin destroying it. Which means Eloise and the other prisoners face a terrible death if I can't figure out a way to free them in time.

A man rides by us on a sturdy-looking donkey. I recognize him as one of Drake's companions from Thom's Tankard. "Hey!" I call out, and he turns.

"Logan? Logan McEntire?"

"The prisoners in the dungeon. They won't be able to escape without help. Can you—"

He turns his donkey toward the compound without waiting to hear the rest of my sentence.

"There should be a hole in the wall of the corner cell," I yell at his retreating back.

The northern roads are all impassable, so I turn the wagon and head south. The ground shakes as the Cursed One turns southwest and bellows, lashing at buildings with its tail. The streets in front of us are clogged with wagons, people on donkeys or horses, or families hurrying toward the gate on foot. At our backs, a wall of impossible heat precedes the flames that race toward us.

We've failed them. All of them. We thought to destroy the leader who tormented them, and instead, we've brought destruction down on their heads. Rachel sits beside me, her finger holding down the third button continuously. Her tears are gone. In their place is the white-faced shock I first saw when I picked her up at Madame Illiard's after Oliver's murder.

We inch our way through the streets, surrounded by sobbing, screaming people and the thunderous roar of Baalboden succumbing to its fiery death in our wake. The Cursed One is a black blur in the distance—twisting, lunging, and roaring its triumph as it consumes South Edge. The crowds grow dense, nearly impassable, as we head west, and when we reach the gate, I stare at it in disbelief.

The gate is closed. Locked. And the guards are nowhere to be seen.

Suddenly, a girl runs alongside the wagon, grabs the board beside me, and swings onto the platform. I glance at her and recognize my jail visitor. Her face is alive with purpose as she looks at me.

"Can you get us out?"

Is she crazy? A ton of concrete and steel stand in our way. How am I supposed to move that?

The ground beneath us shakes as the Cursed One explodes out of South Edge and into Lower Market, spewing fire.

We're next.

"Logan!" She snaps her fingers in front of me. "Can you get us out?"

A ton of concrete and steel. No way to get so many people over it. Or under it. We'll have to go through.

"I'll have to build a bomb."

"Tell me what you need."

"The abandoned warehouse beside the armory. There are two black metal barrels full of liquid. I need those and a supply of canning jars with lids. Can you help me get them?"

She cups her hands around her mouth and whistles, an

ear-splitting note that momentarily silences those in our immediate vicinity.

"Logan can get us out. Dad"—she calls to my right, and I turn to see Drake standing there, soot stains on his patched tunic and part of his beard singed away—"get a team to the abandoned warehouse by the armory and bring back the metal barrels of liquid you find there."

He nods, grabs a hulking man wearing a tattered cloak, and they head toward the armory.

The girl looks at the crowd surrounding us. "The rest of you, go through the homes near here and bring me every jar and lid you find. Empty the contents if you must."

A few people immediately do her bidding, but most of them stare at us with nothing but confusion on their faces.

"Do you want to live?" She screams it at them, and more of them start moving. Before long, a line of people are dumping jars of every size into the back of the wagon.

North Hub and East Quarter are nothing but billowing clouds of black smoke. South Edge is a burning inferno behind us. Survivors of those three districts mingle with citizens from the western reaches of the city and jostle against the unyielding surface of the Wall like sheep penned in for a slaughter. I see Thom, his clothes still smoking, leading a donkey with Eloise perched on its back. He elbows his way toward us.

Another explosion rips through the air behind us, accompanied by a chorus of screams. The Cursed One is coming our way. I give it ten minutes before the beast reaches the gate and turns the citizens of Baalboden into nothing but a memory.

It'll be a miracle if we make it out alive.

"What's your name?" I ask the girl.

"Nola."

"Thank you, Nola." It's less than she deserves, but it's the best I can give.

Eight minutes left. Rachel is still holding down the button. I press a kiss against her head and say, "I love you."

She looks at me, tears gathering in her eyes. "I love you, too."

Six minutes. The ground beneath us trembles, violent shudders that send people to their knees. The flames are so close now, we can hear them crackling in the distance.

Five.

"Make way!" Drake and three other men stumble into the crowd, their clothing singed. Each pair holds a black barrel.

I let go of Rachel.

"Open the jars," I say to Nola, and yell to the people in front of me to clear out of my way as Drake and his helpers load the barrels onto the wagon bed.

People stumble to the side as my wagon pushes through. Rachel drops the device and climbs into the wagon bed to help open jars.

Four minutes.

Pulling the horse to a stop twenty yards from the gate, I look at Nola. "Get them away from the gate. Close enough that they can run through as soon as it's open, but far enough that they won't be injured by falling debris."

While Nola barks orders at the citizens filling the street, I leap into the wagon bed and point to Drake and one other. "Fill as many jars as you can with the liquid in your barrel. Be careful. It's acid. It'll burn your skin."

"Better than being dead," Drake says, and starts his task.

"You two fill the rest of these jars with the liquid in your barrels. It's glycerin. Don't let it come in contact with the acid, whatever you do. It would kill us all."

"What can I do?" Rachel stands beside me. "Give me something to do."

"Press the button. Just keep pressing it."

She climbs over the wagon seat and grabs the device again.

Three minutes.

Plumes of black smoke rise from the west now as the fires in North Hub eat through the city at a frightening speed. From the outside, it must look like the entire city is already up in flames.

I check the progress of the men in the back. Each team has about nine jars filled and capped now. Drake's hands are blistered raw, but he refuses to let his teammate dip for him.

Nine is good, but I don't know if it will be enough.

"Everyone who will listen to me is out of the danger zone." Nola appears beside the wagon. "Blow it up, Logan."

"Keep filling," I say to the men, and snatch the dagger from my boot so I can cut the horse free of the reins. He takes off running as soon as he's free, and I look at Rachel. "Come out of the wagon."

She scrambles down and stands beside me, still holding the device.

"We're going to flip the wagon over and use it as a shield."

Two minutes.

I call out a warning to the men, and they lift the filled jars and metal drums clear of the wagon bed. Then we flip the wagon to its side and crouch behind it. A quick count shows

I have nearly twenty jars of each liquid now. Eighteen of acid. Nineteen of glycerin.

It will have to be enough.

Grabbing a jar of acid, I lob it at the gate. It explodes against the stone in a hail of glass and sizzling liquid. I bend down and pick up two more. Two of the men grab jars of acid too, and we throw all six of them against the gate. When they reach for more, I stop them.

"Save those. We'll need them."

One minute.

I scoop up two jars of glycerin. The men do the same. "Stay down," I say to Rachel and Nola, and then we throw the jars.

The glass missiles arc through the air, slam into the damp concrete, and shatter. The gate explodes in a brutal hail of concrete slabs, steel splinters, and suffocating dust. People scream as tons of debris come raining down around us. Some are crushed, others are knocked off their feet, still more are sliced open by the lethal barrage.

It's a sea of wreckage, blood, and chaos, but there's a hole in the gate big enough to fit three wagons side by side. Beyond the ruins, the Wasteland gleams like a jewel-green beacon of safety. Behind us, the roar of the beast is closing in.

"Get as many of them out as you can," I say to Nola, Drake, and the others. They hurry to comply, and I pick up another jar of each liquid as the Cursed One incinerates the last block of buildings between it and the gate and comes for us.

CHAPTER SIXTY-NINE

RACHEL

I lean down beside Logan and pick up two jars as the beast comes closer. Grim determination anchors me to the ground as the fire eats through Lower Market and the cobblestones shake beneath the weight of the Cursed One's approach.

We did this. We brought it here. We have to do everything in our power to destroy it. It's the only chance the people outside the gate have of surviving.

"You should leave too," Logan says.

"Don't be an idiot. Whether we live or die, we'll do it together."

He doesn't argue.

We wait as the beast slithers its way over the cobblestone street toward us, its movements jerky, as if something beyond itself is driving it forward. We wait while it fills the grassy clearing between the gatehouse and the gate with fire. And we wait until we can see the milky yellow of its unseeing eyes.

I grip the jars with bloodless fingers, and ready myself.

"Now!" Logan yells.

We throw the jars and they explode against the impenetrable scales of the beast. The force knocks the creature to its back. It bellows, flips over, and comes for us.

"Again!"

The second round of explosions blows a section of its tail to pieces. Wild triumph surges through me.

We can beat it.

"It can be killed. Did you see that? It can be killed!" I reach down for two more jars, and the Cursed One jerks to a stop, shuddering as if held back by something. I lob the jars, and the beast bellows as they hit it in the side, sending a shower of ebony scales clattering to the ground and revealing a small patch of gray skin beneath.

"It's vulnerable!" I scream over the sound of flames and the roar of the beast.

Determination slides quickly into vicious purpose as I stare at the beast's exposed skin. I can't avenge Oliver. I can't stop the Commander. But I can destroy the creature that took Dad from me.

Logan would argue. Calculate angles and odds. Take a moment to plan. But if I do that, I could miss my chance. The fury inside me begs for vengeance. Promises that if I just obliterate the cause of my pain, I can find peace. I hold on to the bright, jagged edges of that idea and let it fill me up until I can't see anything else.

Then, as Logan bends down for more jars, I snatch my knife out of its sheath and charge straight for the Cursed One.

"Rachel!" Logan screams my name, but I keep running.

The beast bellows, a tortured sound full of pain and rage.

I skid on debris.

It whips its head in my direction.

I grip my knife with steady fingers.

It jerks its nose, sniffing the air.

Nine more yards. I raise my blade.

Its claws dig into the ground.

Eight yards.

"Rachel, no!" Logan screams again.

Seven.

The beast's tail slams into the ground.

Six.

It shudders and pins me with its sightless eyes.

Five.

I brace to launch myself forward. It lowers its snout and roars, blasting me with an unending stream of fire.

CHAPTER SEVENTY

LOGAN

"No!" I stumble, hit my knees against the pavement, and scream, "Rachel!"

One second she was there, running straight for the Cursed One, her knife raised above her head. The next, there was nothing but flames.

I can't breathe. Can't think beyond the swelling tidal wave of unbearable grief rising up to suffocate me.

She's gone.

Gone.

Ripped from me, just like Oliver and Jared. Just like my mother.

"Rachel!" My breath sobs in and out of my lungs as I choke on her name. I dig my fingernails into the cobblestones beneath me as everything I'd built my world on turns to ash.

I have nothing left. Nothing but the merciless creature in front of me, still spewing the wall of flame that killed her.

Nothing but the terrible need to take it with me as I die.

She'd promised we'd be together. Live or die. We'd do it together.

I'm going to make her keep her word.

And I'm going to take the Cursed One with me.

Pushing myself to my feet, I face the beast and raise the jars above my head. I'll ram them down the creature's throat and hope I find my family waiting for me after death swallows me.

Despair is nothing but cold, brittle determination driving me forward. One last plan. One last calculation. One last effort and my life will count for something as I join her.

Vaulting over a pile of broken steel, I brace myself to leap straight into the beast's mouth, but then I see the impossible.

Rachel.

She's sliding on her stomach beneath the wall of fire, her knife aiming straight for the monster's unprotected side. She's covered in soot, her clothing singed and torn.

She's the most beautiful sight I've ever seen.

The stream of fire exploding out of the beast's mouth sizzles into a puff of acrid smoke. It twists its head toward Rachel and sniffs the air.

I'm not about to let it kill her.

"Hey!" I yell and run forward. "Here! Look here!"

It ignores me.

Rachel's forward momentum slows as she hits the scales blown off the beast's side. She can't stab its side before it realizes she's there. She can't, unless I provide a distraction.

I calculate trajectories, pray I haven't misjudged the velocity needed, and hurl the jars I carry. They explode a few yards in front of the Cursed One and send me flying backward onto a pile of rubble.

The creature snaps its head toward the sound of the explosion and roars a stream of fire at the offending noise. Rachel belly-crawls over debris, pushes her left hand into the ground for balance, and raises her knife. The blade flashes crimson and gold in the light of the fire, and she buries it in the monster's side.

The Cursed One screams and spits fire as it coils in on itself. Rachel is trying to pull her knife free, but its tail knocks into her, sending her sprawling. I push off the wreckage and race to her. Grabbing her beneath her arms, I haul her backward as the beast screams again.

"Get a sword. Another knife. Let's finish it," she says.

But it's too late. The creature jerks its head up, trembling as if being held still against its will, then dives into the ground, scales and debris sliding in after it as it burrows toward its lair.

I pull Rachel to her feet and crush her to me. She wraps herself around me and holds on as if I'm all that is keeping her from drowning. My hands are shaking, and my throat feels raw from screaming, but in the midst of the wreckage around us, all I can feel is gratitude that Rachel is still alive. I want to hold her until the shaking passes, until the terrible panic I felt when I thought she was dead leaves me, but I can't. We're surrounded on three sides by fire.

"We have to get out of here," I say, and start leading her toward the shattered gate.

"I don't understand what just happened."

"I don't either. It left without trying to finish us off. It never leaves when it knows its prey is still alive."

Rachel stumbles over a slab of concrete and grabs for me. "It didn't look like it had a choice. It was behaving the same way it did when you controlled it out in the Wasteland."

"But if it wasn't obeying our device, then who was controlling it? Maybe Rowansmark has tech even stronger than the device the Commander tried to steal?"

She shakes her head. "I don't know." Looking at the carnage around us—the flames, the rubble, the bodies trapped in what would become their funeral pyre—she shudders. "It doesn't matter who was controlling it. We started this, Logan. We brought it here."

It does matter, because if the total annihilation of Baalboden was the goal, whoever was controlling the Cursed One can send it back to finish off the survivors. And it matters because I have no doubt the Commander and anyone else hungry for power will stop at nothing to get their hands on tech like that. We can't let that happen. Today is vivid proof.

But she's right. We called the Cursed One. We started this. And we'll need to live with that. I don't know how we'll do it. I'm weary, inside and out. I want to take her hand. Walk away from the destruction. Disappear into the Wasteland. We could travel for weeks. Months. Find a quiet place where there are no power-hungry leaders, no cities, no memories to reach out and slice into us when we least expect it.

We could, but then who would hunt down and destroy the tech that caused today's devastation? Who would honor the memory of Jared's sacrifice and exact justice for the Commander's actions? The weight of what must be done settles on my shoulders as I take Rachel's hand.

We climb over the debris, walk through the hole in the gate, and turn to face the city. She leans into me as I wrap my arms around her, and we watch Baalboden burn.

CHAPTER SEVENTY-ONE

RACHEL

The city burns for three days. Most of its citizens never make it out. The ones who do are divided between worshipping the ground Logan and I walk on for rescuing them, and blaming us for bringing disaster upon everyone by rebelling against the Commander's protection.

We can't find the Commander. I don't see how he could've made it back into the city when we had to blow the gate to pieces to get out, but I suppose it's possible he's one of the charred bodies lying inside what used to be Baalboden.

I think it's much more likely that when he realized his city was doomed, he ran into the Wasteland with his guards like the coward he is. The thought sparks a weak flame of fury within me, but I'm too exhausted to keep it alive.

Sylph made it out, along with her new husband. I recognize a few other faces of girls I knew in Life Skills. Melkin's wife made it out too. I'm grateful, even though the sight of her fills me with suffocating dread.

When those who hate us leave to seek asylum in another city-state, I don't try to stop them. Neither does Logan.

The rest of them elect Logan as their new leader. Some of them simply because he rescued them by blowing up the gate. But most of them want him as their leader because he publicly stood up to the Commander at the Claiming ceremony, an unprecedented act of courage he then trumped by escaping from the dungeon.

There's talk of rebuilding elsewhere. Quinn and Willow join our group, and Willow quickly finds a kindred spirit in Nola. As Drake, Logan, Willow, and Nola organize teams of survivors to search the ruins for salvageable goods, I slip away and enter what's left of Baalboden.

The city is a carcass of bones and ash. Hollowed out. Every vestige of life burned into silence.

We understand each other.

The magnitude of what I've caused is a crushing weight I refuse to lift. Let it consume me. Let it drive me to my knees. It's less than I deserve.

I leave the rubble of the gate behind and walk the charred, twisted streets until I reach the ruins of the home I shared with Dad. The home where Logan first joined us as an apprentice. Where Oliver visited regularly with sticky buns and fairy tales.

The ash clings to me as I sink down to sit where our kitchen table used to be. If I close my eyes, it can all go back to the way it used to be. If I close my eyes, I can see Dad, his gray eyes shining with pride as I find my first target with a bow and arrow. Oliver opening his arms wide for me as he walks up to the front door.

If I close my eyes, I'm still whole.

But I can't close my eyes. I don't dare. I *need* to see this. To sear it into my brain so I never forget. When seeing isn't enough, I dig my fingers into the ash and let the silky texture cling to me like a scar I'll wear for the rest of my life.

"Rachel."

Logan drops down into the ash beside me and grabs a handful too.

"This is where I signed a contract with Jared. I had to work hard to look only at the paper and not get caught staring at his beautiful daughter." He looks to the right. "And that's where I suffered my first defeat in combat at the hands of a girl two years younger than me. You knocked my feet out from under me. I never saw it coming, because it never occurred to me a girl would know how to fight."

I follow his gaze and see us. Fighting. Laughing. Living.

There's no life here now.

"Someone else wanted this to happen. Someone else pushed the controls that sent the Cursed One into the city. It wasn't your fault," he says, and the silence within me shivers like pieces of broken glass.

"I started it all. Don't you see that? I tried to climb over the Wall and got caught, and look at the result." I fling my hand to encompass the blackened ruins around us. The wind tugs gently at the ash I hold and it floats away like bits of silver.

"No." He scoots closer to me, and takes my chin in between his thumb and forefinger. "You wouldn't have tried to get over the Wall if I'd told you what I was working on. I thought I was protecting you, but I should've trusted you."

His eyes are steady, and a world of pain and resolve lives inside them.

"But beyond all that, none of this would've happened if the Commander hadn't tried to steal something that didn't belong to him. We aren't done, Rachel. He needs to be found and stopped. The other city-states need to be warned about the weapons Rowansmark has. If there is a master device out there capable of controlling the Cursed One, we need to find and destroy it. And there are people depending on us for leadership." He looks over his shoulder.

I follow his gaze and see Sylph, her face resolute, a new-found gravity carved into her by everything she's lost. Beside her, Smithson stands tall and steady, his arm curved around her shoulders. Nola, Willow, and Quinn are next to him, looking fierce and ready. Drake and Thom stand slightly behind them, their eyes trained on me, while behind them teams of survivors comb the wreckage for anything we can use to start over. I look at them and realize I see something I never thought I'd see again.

Hope.

They're broken, but they aren't beaten. They want to live. Not just breathe in and out, watching one day fade into the next. They want to *live*.

And they want us to help them do it.

I'm so tired. I want to lie down, sink beneath the ashes, let them slide gently into my lungs and carry me to Dad and Oliver. I want to, but I can't. Because Logan is right. We have to find the Commander. Warn the other leaders. And bring whoever invented the hellish device that started all of this to his knees.

My debts have yet to be paid.

Tugging at the leather pouch I wear, I let the ashes I hold trickle inside to become one with the dirt from my father's grave. Logan reaches for me, and together we stand and walk toward the group waiting for us. Linking arms with Sylph on one side and Logan on the other, I lean my head against him in the ruins of what once was as the sun sets one last time on Baalboden.

ACKNOWLEDGMENTS

I have a deep fear that I'll thank the many, *many* people who have helped make this book possible and end up forgetting someone. My hubby assures me this won't happen. But we both know I'm the girl who constantly forgets to charge her cell phone and can never remember anyone's name. So . . . if you contributed to *Defiance* and I somehow forget you in this list of thanks, I humbly beg your pardon and promise you cookies and lemon bars to make up for it.

First, I have to thank God for giving me the ability to tell stories and for being the foundation beneath my feet.

And because dedicating the book to him isn't enough, I also want to thank my husband. Clint, thank you for letting me disappear for hours to write while you changed diapers, handled dinner, and made it possible for me to meet my deadlines. This book wouldn't have happened without your commitment to supporting my dreams. I love you.

Thanks also to Zach, Jordan, and Tyler for watching the baby so I could write, eagerly asking me about my story, and proudly announcing to everyone that your mom was going to publish a book. I'm also grateful to you, Johanna. Finally bringing you home from China gave me so much incentive to write the book I thought might be too big for me. You are amazing kids, and I'm so blessed to be your mom.

Thank you, Mom and Dad, for feeding my love of reading and for raising me to believe I could do anything I set my mind to.

I also owe a huge debt of gratitude to my awesome agent, Holly Root, for always believing in me and for being fiercely in my corner. You are a rock star in my world.

This book wouldn't be what it is today without the help of my incredible team of critique partners and beta readers. Not only did all of you help shape this book in different ways, you are all treasured friends. M. G. Buehrlen, thank you for reading, rereading, and rereading again. And for the conversation that helped me realize I needed to include Logan's POV. How many hours did we spend on the phone discussing this book? I'm grateful for them all! Myra McEntire, awkward kissing scenes FTW! Asking myself *What would Myra do?* is now my new go-to for all fictional romantic situations. Thanks also for being so excited for me every step of the way. K. B. Wagers, you've been by my side almost from the beginning. Thanks for being my weapons and sparring expert, my cheerleader, and my friend. Heather Palmquist, you are not only a fabulous beta reader, you are an even more fabulous sister. I'm so glad you were part of this journey with me. Sara McClung, you rock as a beta reader. Thanks for being so excited about this book. Shannon Messenger, thanks for reading scenes even while you were neck-deep in drafting, and for being unflinchingly honest. Jodi Meadows, thanks for helping me figure out what to call the Switch. And for being a huge fan of the almost-kissing scenes. Beth Revis, thanks for encouraging me as I neared my first deadline. Even though you did almost kill me with Nutella.

Tricia Bentley, even though you didn't read *Defiance* as I was writing it, you were my first ever reader (many moons ago) and while you keep assuring me I don't need to apologize for the mess of a novel you read, I really am grateful you were interested enough to keep asking me for more. You helped motivate me to finish writing my first book. Thank you.

A heartfelt thanks to the entire team at Balzer + Bray for embracing *Defiance* and making me feel so welcome. Kristin Daly Rens, I knew from our first conversation that you were the perfect editor for me. The llama simply confirmed my hunch. Your painstaking attention to detail and your unabashed enthusiasm for Rachel and Logan challenged me to push myself to do more than I thought I could do. Thank you. Sara Sargent, you are definitely a Ninja of many things! I appreciate you keeping me on track and making my interactions with B+B so much fun.

Thank you to Alison Klapthor and Alison Donalty for my gorgeous cover. You truly captured Rachel's fierce spirit along with all the key elements of the book. I nearly licked my monitor the first time I saw the cover. Thank you also to Emilie Polster and Stefanie Hoffman for your fabulous marketing efforts, and to Caroline Sun and Olivia deLeon for being my publicity gurus. I appreciate all of you.

Thanks to my amazing Pixie sisters. You've been my cheerleaders, my readers, my source of insight, and my friends since that wonderful summer in San Francisco in 2008. I can't imagine my publishing journey without you by my side.

While I was writing *Defiance*, I went on a writer's retreat with many members of the Music City Romance Writers' chapter. I wrote eleven thousand words that weekend, and just outside my bedroom I had the soundtrack of twenty-two women singing some pretty awesome karaoke. Whip it, MCRW! (And thank you for being a constant encouragement.)

A huge thanks to the talented Tashina Falene for designing the jewelry pieces from the book and for being so excited about the story. I also want to give a shout-out to two book bloggers who have either read chapters for me or inspired me while I was drafting: Catie S. and Julie Daly. You make me want to write amazing stories. Thank you.

Finally, thank you to all of my blog readers, my Twitter followers, and my Facebook friends who got excited about this book and told a friend about it. From book bloggers to fellow writers to enthusiastic readers, you amaze me. I still have to pinch myself when I realize there are people outside of my immediate friends and family who love this book. I feel like the luckiest girl in the world.